W9-ATY-463

DEATH OF THE SOAP QUEEN

To Sue again
& so many
years
love
Peter
Jan '97

BY THE SAME AUTHOR

PLAY THINGS
AGENTS OF A FOREIGN POWER
THE GOOD FATHER

Death of the Soap Queen

PETER PRINCE

BLOOMSBURY

First published 1990

Bloomsbury Publishing Ltd, 2 Soho Square, London W1V 5DE

A CIP catalogue record for this book
is available from the British Library

ISBN 0 7475 0611 6

10 9 8 7 6 5 4 3 2 1

Typeset by Hewer Text Composition Services, Edinburgh
Printed in Great Britain by Butler and Tanner Ltd, Frome and London

'Best Actress of the Year . . . and it's Susan Strang for *The Entwistles*!'
As Susan stepped up to receive her award from the hands of a famous star, amidst the cheers of her loving friends, she must have felt herself at the very top of her world. But now, a few short years later, fame and love seem to be all behind her. Alone, exiled to a dreary Kentish seaside resort, she waits with increasing hopelessness for something to turn up and reverse the tide of misfortune.

Tom Scott appears from London, an old friend, full of good advice and sensible suggestions for restoring her career. But Susan may be too full of rage and hurt to heed him. And she has another source of guidance now in the shape of a new friend Raymond Thorne, with his gripping stories of family strife, Nazis, wicked brothers, cheated inheritances, all leading to delicious possibilities of revenge – a heady brew for the angry fantasies of an ex-soap queen.

In his previous novel, *The Good Father* (which became a Prix Italia-winning film), Peter Prince dissected the miseries and comedies of marriage and separation. Here, with equal insight, he both portrays the course of friendship, its pleasures and betrayals, and casts an accurate and entertaining spotlight on the switchback world of film and television. But his main theme is the temptation of the romantic, self-obsessed view of life. Susan Strang is not the only *prima donna* raging through this book ('. . . a monster . . . out of control. Sure the world revolves around her, crazy with rage when she finds out it doesn't'), and the story of how she and other potential monsters are drawn to the brink of total capitulation to the soap queen lurking in all of us makes a novel at once moving and funny and wise.

For Linda Romano

DEATH OF THE SOAP QUEEN

London, 1985

So long ago – eighteen years, more than half her life – and so far away from a night like this, this London glitter and blare. She had left school at the end of the winter term, had six months to kill before drama college. The college recommended that she fill in the time usefully, and put her in touch with a repertory company up north that was in need of an assistant stage manager, the last one having just made a sudden, unscheduled exit. She wrote off, was offered the job by return of post. Next day she was on her way in a daze of excitement. Her first job. The first time she would be sleeping away from home for more than a few nights. She was about to become a professional. In what she had already learned to call 'the business'. A job, achievement, success, even one day stardom itself: the trail would begin for her now, in Yorkshire, two hundred miles up the railway line.

'Awrright! Here we go . . . and the winner is . . .'

Well, it was right, she supposed, that she should have had her little balloon pricked, had had that early scraping down with reality. Except that particular form of reality had been almost too much for a hitherto cosseted Home Counties teenager to bear. A dark, sodden city sprawled across a barren moor. A cold more intense than any she had ever felt since. A threadbare company of tired hacks and inadequate juveniles hopelessly mumming the round of drawing-room comedies, trousers-down farces, panto at Christmas, and whichever Shakespeare was set for the next Eng. Lit. GCEs. All in front of asthmatic, sullen audiences whose numbers rarely rose into three figures outside the pantomime season. A scrounging management going through the last shameful penny-pinching motions before the inevitable collapse. She knew before the first day had passed that the previous ASM had been no irresponsible cuckoo, nor 'heading for a nervous breakdown' as Mr Kirkness, the theatre manager, claimed. Poor kid, she had just had a healthy instinct for self-preservation, her lightning exit had been an altogether intelligent break for freedom. 'That girl's finished in the theatre,' Mr Kirkness had threatened her. 'Finished before she ever got started.' Susan would have taken the same way out, but she was not so brave. And there was one other thing that kept her there. Almost from the beginning, in all that muddle and hopelessness, discomfort and overwork, she did at least have one true friend.

'The winner is . . . uh-oh! Just gotta . . . open this damn . . .'

How long, O Lord, how long?

They used to cry that out, as they lay shivering under the mountains of blankets they had piled on top of themselves in the twin beds, side by side. In the little room at the top of the stairs, the attic room, directly under the leaky roof of that tall, black-stained house by the railway station. How long, O Lord? How long wilt Thou continue to torture these Thy servants? How long shall our agony last? How long before You give us a break and we get pneumonia or get fired, or anything at all that will release us from this hell without the necessity of breaking our contracts, thus rendering future employment doubtful in this our chosen profession? How long?

Wendy Strong. Wendy, the sophisticated older woman. Yes, she must have been all of twenty-three. Scarlet lips and scarlet nails, flicking boredly through her copies of *Nova* and *Queen* at rehearsal, languidly drawing on one of her Du Maurier cigarettes. A husky voice, a throaty chuckle, and her every other word was a drawled and cooing 'Dahling!' Sometimes Susan received hints from other younger members of the company, hints that she understood even raw as she was, that there was something dated and, in fact, quite funny about Wendy's version of sophistication. The late Kay Kendall was her great idol and inspiration. In a period dominated by gruff, proletarian, studiedly unpretentious actors, Wendy's style stuck out like a stiletto heel. Watching from the wings every night, Susan gained a cool, mainly unflattering estimate of her friend's acting talents. It didn't matter. Wendy – the person she found Wendy to be – she came to admire and love. And never ceased to be grateful that Fate, in the scrawny shape of Mr Kirkness, had assigned her to share a room with her at the end of her first week with the company. A critical moment – she had very nearly made up her mind that whatever it cost she was going to head for the station and get back to Guildford for good. The acting career would be out of the window for ever, but there were other careers: nursing, teaching, almoner (whatever they did), probation officer . . .

'OK. *I'm getting three. Gimme a break! Any moment now . . .'*

'You'll share with Wendy Strong,' Mr Kirkness informed her. 'I'm sorry, but somebody has to.'

'Oh well, dahling,' Wendy sighed when she heard the news. 'I expect we'll manage somehow. But I warn you – I do like a little natter after lights out. So I hope, Miss Mouse, that you're not planning on any early nights. Cause it won't be allowed.'

Sex was Wendy's great theme in the endless rambling conversations that began on their first night under the same roof, and were only to end when they parted for good months later.

'Might as well talk,' Wendy encouraged her. 'Because we're too bloody frozen to sleep.'

'That's true,' Susan sighed.

'Know the best thing for a cold night, guaranteed to keep you toasty?'

'A hot-water bottle?'

'A cock.'

'. . . Really?'

'A nice big meaty cock. Purple on top, and a big pair of balls hanging down.' Wendy smacked her lips. 'Get one of those pressed against your botty, you'll sleep like a top. Works a charm. Every time.'

It was Wendy's great sadness, so she claimed, that not one of these useful articles was currently available to her.

'Nor will it be till I get out of this sodding Siberia.'

'Gosh,' Susan said, wanting to help. 'But there must be lots of chaps here – and you're very attractive, I think.'

'In this company? Not a chance. They're either homos or hideous. Or both.'

'Well, outside the theatre, then.'

'Outside the theatre?'

'Yes.'

'Don't quite follow you.'

'I mean . . . there are lots of men around the town – '

'Oh my God!' Wendy regarded her with horror. 'Dahling – you don't mean the oiks?'

'I don't know. Do I?'

'You must do. And *northern* oiks at that! Out of the question, dahling. You must see that. No,' in accents of Russian gloom, 'it's utterly hopeless. We're doomed to our lonely, loveless beds . . . Unless – you're not, by any chance, the least little bit dikey, are you, dahling?'

'Not at all,' Susan whispered.

'Fair enough. I never said a word.'

How long, O Lord?

'I'll tell yah, these envelopes don't get any easier, do they? Heh heh!'

It was that cry, shouted out against the freezing world, at one in the morning, or two in the morning, that would always make them laugh, even when they had made themselves most miserable in exploring their present discontents. And when they laughed the room, and the Palace Theatre, and the town, and all Yorkshire even, with its dreary moors and wicked winters which, as Wendy often pointed out, had done for the Brontës and would surely do for them too if they didn't find some way out soon – all of that would dissolve in their laughter and be for a little while no longer dreadful, would hardly be there at all any more, driven back, frightened off. Conquered.

And Wendy had been, as well as her night-time sharer in the cold and dark, a true friend, had looked after her, had stopped the others from using her as a handy repository for their malevolence or greed or lust, or any other dirty emotion, which, as the most junior of dog's-bodies, was a role she could have expected to have to fill. And more: when Wendy had found out that the management were not paying Susan a penny extra for the great chunks of overtime she was working, she had made a great fuss, had, astonishingly, got the rest of the company to put up a muted protest on Susan's behalf, had even involved the area Equity rep, though she was not yet in the union. In the end, the management had grudgingly given way.

'Don't mention it,' Wendy had said when Susan tried to thank her.

'But you took such a risk.'

'A risk? Dahling, I got stuffed! I won't be working for this lot again. They made that bloody clear.'

'Oh . . .' Sitting up in bed, Susan stared at her friend tragically. She began to cough then over the Du Maurier she had just been given. Wendy leaned over from her bed and clapped her briskly on the back.

'Don't worry.' Wendy's eyes gleamed. 'I shouldn't think anybody'll be working for this management again. I give 'em till Easter.'

(And it was Easter Monday that year, as it turned out, that the Palace at last went dark for good.)

'Guess what that toad Kirkness called me?'

Susan shook her head.

'Called me a "bloody shop-steward"! Me!' Wendy laughed angrily. Then thought for a moment. 'Actually I rather liked that. It gave me quite a little *frisson*, that did. I thought to myself . . . well, that's interesting.'

'You want to work for the union?' Susan asked, puzzled.

'Hardly, dahling! I mean, they're all Reds, aren't they? No – ' Wendy shook her head. 'It's just . . . well, it'd be a change, wouldn't it? Sort of like real life. And let's face it – I'm not much of a bloody actress, am I?'

'Oh, I wouldn't say that . . .'

'Can it, Strang! I know it. You know it. In fact it's not a bloody secret anywhere.' Wendy chewed her underlip and peered sadly through the blue fog that rose from their cigarettes. 'It really is a pest, though. Because I did so want to be a decent actress. And I've slogged all round this bloody country, giving it my best. You think this dump is bad? My God, the places I've been!'

Susan broke the glum silence at last.

'What else could you do?'

'Search me,' Wendy sighed. 'I mean, I know I'm pretty good at sort of shoving people around and getting them to do things my way. But where did that ever get a girl? Oh, hell!' She flung her cigarette end at the overflowing grate. 'I did so want to act.'

She collapsed backwards on to the bed, turned her face into her pillow. Silence again. Susan was sitting up, hugging herself under the mound of blankets, frowning, wishing she could think of something to help. All at once, she heard a faint giggle coming from Wendy's bed.

'I'm such a rotten actress, aren't I, dahling? How on earth did I last this long?'

Susan shook her head, smiling. She was relieved to hear her friend's laughter – but not very surprised. Wendy, she knew, would never try to add to the miseries of the night by indulging in a prolonged fit of gloom. She could be – none better – deceitful, selfish, cruel, egotistical to the world at large, but to anyone who she regarded as a fellow sufferer, within her tribe, she was profoundly loyal and kind. Knowing Wendy, in a way Susan understood for the first time her parents' stories of how people had got each other through the Blitz.

'OK! I got it now! The winner is . . .'

'Christ, what wouldn't I give for a good hard shag,' Wendy sighed, scratching herself beneath the blankets.

'Me too!' Susan piped up. She wriggled down contentedly under the covers. Not much of this talk, she knew by now, was to be taken very seriously. She was still a virgin at the time, and had no immediate plans to change her status. As for Wendy – from various hints and unguarded comments, Susan had worked out that her friend's actual experiences in these areas had been rare and disappointing. It was just ritual then, the things they said to each other in the night. Bravado. As men would bawl out rugger songs on the coach home after a game, and especially loudly after a defeat. It was like an ancient war chant that they sent back and forth lovingly to keep each other going, fighting.

How long, O Lord, how long?

'About eight inches would be very nice.'

'Ten would be even nicer.'

'Smooth as silk from the tip to the ridge, but all the rest of the way down . . .'

'Gnarled and knotty like an old oak tree,' Susan sighed sleepily.

'Two perfectly rounded spheres below.'

'One perhaps a little smaller than the other.'

'But not much smaller . . .'

The rain beat fruitlessly against the windows, the stupid wind howled around the roof, Wendy's cigarette glowed in the darkness, the ignorant cold slunk back against the far wall, far, far away. Miss Mouse sleeps beside her friend . . .

'Best Actress of the Year . . . And it's Susan Strang for The Entwistles!'

Well, blow me.

I have been listening so hard to my idol's famous, amused, laconic drawl that I don't really hear my name at first. Bill Ellis has to pound me on the back, and Molly lean right over the table to hug me before it finally gets through. I am the winner. The winner! And the first person I look at, of course, is Mark. Who hadn't even wanted us to attend this evening and had said it would be a disaster if I won. For aren't we trying so hard to change my image? Don't we want to kill off Lucy at last? Certainly we do. And he thinks it would disrupt our murder plans if I won. And – hell's bells! – I *have*. I'm sorry, sorry . . . But straight away he puts his arm round me and hugs me to him. And he is murmuring against my ear, 'Well done, sweetheart. You deserved it.' And I know he means it. He is glad for me, even though I have done the thing he told me not to do. Have won. Which must mean he loves me. Truly does.

And he lets me go then, and the others at the table are leaning towards me, clapping and laughing. Bill and Molly and John Knights and Ron Castle and Elsie and James. So pleased for me. My friends. And now I am rising from my seat, their hands are guiding me upwards, and I begin to walk towards the stage. I hope to God I look all right. My hair cut and styled by Karen Banham's man Graham this afternoon, and the demure, blue Jean Muir dress that complements my eyes so nicely. Fifty pounds for the hair cut, seven hundred for the dress. Seven hundred *pounds* . . . Oh well – we can afford it.

They are playing the theme music from the series, and on the big screen Lucy Entwistle, in that gorgeous white ball-gown, is coming down the winding marble stairs of the draughty old mansion where we were shooting for many rainy weeks last spring. In the picture the extras are staring up at Lucy, admiring her descent. It was hard that, I remember. Not tripping over that gown. And on stage waiting for me is my idol with the devilish grin and the famous what the fuck? look in his eyes. We were terribly impressed at our table when he was brought on. The rumour had gone around earlier that a big Hollywood star would be among the presenters. Even a second-rank star would have cheered us up. But they have done us proud this year. Have given us a truly big star, maybe the biggest there is at this particular time. At any rate he gets my vote. I have adored him since *Easy Rider*, and think he has only got better over the years.

'Of course – !' Bill Ellis had slapped his knee when my idol had walked on stage. 'I should have guessed! He's over here for *Terms of Endearment*, isn't he?'

We are such stargazers really, such kids. Bill Ellis is forty-five, silver haired, runs a production company that spends fifteen million a year, has a villa in Portofino. But his proudest possession, I happen to know, is a guitar pick that was actually used by Buddy Holly. And now, back at the table, he is staring delightedly at the stage where my idol is waiting for me. Thrilled to death. It has made Bill's evening. And in fact the whole room is charged with excitement. The evening has become important now, and we are fortunate people to be here.

Especially me.

And as I stumble past the tables towards my idol, hands reach out to pat me and to shake my hand. I see smiling faces everywhere I look. I see my friends' faces. Dick Banham is waving at me and mouthing, 'Well done, Sue!' He looks so pleased. Of course, it's been a good night for him. Five awards for *The Entwistles* already, including his own, Best Series. And now I make six. But I know he is pleased for me anyway. As a friend. And there are other friends here who haven't done so well tonight, but they are smiling at me too and clapping hard. Tom Scott gets up from his table to give me a hug – and he has had a miserable night. That sad little drama documentary of his about the tennis star who got multiple sclerosis was up for four awards and didn't win any of them. But he is chuckling with pleasure now, pleasure for me. 'Good for you, Sue!' he cries in my ear. 'Terrific!'

Thank you, dear Tom. (I must remember to tell you when I get the chance that it's an honour even to be nominated for an award. Though not as much as to win one, of course.) And I keep moving on, past one familiar face after another. It seems as though everyone I have ever known is lining my way. It is like a grand review of friendship. Friend after friend: all these I have loved. Grace Barker jumps up and gives me a kiss. So happy she looks too, even though she missed out on Best Supporting Actress earlier, one of *The Entwistles*' few failures. Poor Gracie. Dear Gracie. Thank you. And I am going up the steps now, straight as an arrow into the arms of my idol.

'Way to go, Susan,' he murmurs as we clinch. (Of course we have never met before, it is incredibly kind of him to remember my name for as much as twenty seconds.)

'Thank you, Jack,' I say, utterly calm. The best bit of acting I have done in months – in fact, almost the only bit I have done in months, thanks to Mark.

He lets me go, and hands me the ugly little statue, and then moves discreetly to one side giving me my moment all alone in the light. Of course, in reality he takes the light with him when he moves, but I am allowed my illusion. And surely that applause, that *cheering* I hear must be for me alone. It is my moment after all, and these are my friends out there. My dear friends.

I can't see very much. The TV lights are blinding me. But I feel the affection surging towards me. And all at once it hits me like a bolt, the real reason why, on and off all through this long, hot, noisy evening, I have been thinking of Wendy Strong. Who I have not really thought of for so long, not for years perhaps. I had been trying – it comes back to me – to remember how I got to where I am now, and it seemed to me, looking back, that I had travelled all the way on a golden road of friendship. And I had tried to walk back along that road – to do honour, as they deserved, to all those people who had helped me and cared for me over the years. And are the main reason why I am here tonight, why I am standing on this stage, a few feet from my idol, hearing my friends cheer my luck. But the journey went on and on, much further than I had imagined when I started out. I thought five years back would be sufficient, but then I remembered friends beyond that, and then friends even further away, and in the end I had not stopped until I reached Wendy Strong. And since I couldn't honour each and every one of those who had befriended me, I decided to stay with Wendy. Who deserves my thanks as much as any of them, probably more than most. For without her I wouldn't even have gone the first few yards along this road.

And one other reason why she is precious to me. Because she is the one I have lost, I think the only one of my true friends whom I have let go, let disappear from my life. Though I did try, tried my best to stay in touch. At the end of that Yorkshire season, Wendy headed for a new job in the Manchester area, I went home to Surrey. Within a week I had written off to the address she had given me. There was no reply. I wrote again two weeks later. No reply. This time I waited for a month. Her letter came back to me, the envelope marked, 'Not known as this address'.

Much later I wondered if this had been Wendy's last word of advice to me, a last offering of reality to Miss Mouse. Certainly it was a foretaste of many other relationships I was to know in the course of my working life. When the production ends, those connections are likely to end, and the warmer the apparent friendship often the sharper will be the cut off. Thanks to Wendy I became almost immune early on to this phenomenon of the life I had chosen. Though the first time it happened it had hurt.

And *this* is why I have been remembering her, I see now. Because I want to tell her that it hurt when she cut me off. That it still hurts, even though I never think of her. And to tell her too that she was wrong. That the lesson she tried to teach me at the end was too cynical and unkind. The world in which she did so much to help me first find my feet is not as cruel as she feared. This world too is full of love and loyalty and unshakeable friendship. All this *can* be found, even though we seem to live so lightly in it. I have the proof in front of me now, out in that bright roaring loving dazzle. I don't care so much about the prize – this is what I want to show you. That we can be trusted. That you should have trusted me. You were wrong. You spoiled things for us, Wendy. Wherever you are.

Silly bitch.

I remembered you tonight because I can't forgive you for misleading me. Was that a friendly thing to do?

The applause is dying away at last. I grip my statue tightly. I glance towards Jack and he nods and indicates the microphone. I must say something. Mark said – this afternoon, when we were dressing in Dick and Karen's flat – he begged me that, should the worst happen and I won tonight, I wouldn't make some soppy actress's acceptance speech.

'In fact – ' He was frowning thoughtfully as he fiddled with the buttons on his ruffled shirt front. 'Maybe we could even turn it to our advantage. We could get the message across to all those people. That we are *serious* now.'

I went to help him. He stuck his chin out and upwards as I finished his buttons and then straightened his collar and black tie. The skin of his lower face was dark, he needed another shave. On the other hand, I like him stubbly like this, particularly in evening dress. I kissed his cheek.

'How would I do that?' I asked.

'By saying something serious. Instead of a lot of waffle.'

'Serious like what?'

'Like . . . well, you could attack government censorship of the arts, or something.' He looked at me in perplexity. 'That's the sort of thing those people think is serious, don't they? Or – ' He laughed suddenly. 'You could call for greater spending on quality TV drama. That'd certainly make 'em sit up. Coming from the star of *The Entwistles*!'

Fair enough. But now I am up here, I can't be bothered with all that. Afterwards I'll say I forgot what he told me. Now – it is my moment. And if I want to make a soppy actress's speech, I'll do just that.

'I just want to say thank you – '

Oh, Wendy, my one lost friend. I wish so much you were here to see how far Miss Mouse has come. I wish you were here just anyway, sod you.

'Thank you to *all* my friends. Wherever they may be . . . And thanks especially to Wendy.'

To *who*? I can almost hear my friends out there muttering to each other.

Oh, well . . .

Such luck.

Winter

1

He was the last one off. The train was moving again as his feet touched the platform, and he had to walk forward a few steps to slam the carriage door. He saw her then, waiting near the ticket barrier, and he waved and hurried along the platform.

'I was half asleep,' he called as he came up. 'Sorry.'

'Never mind.'

'Where would I have gone on to?'

'Herne Bay. Aren't you glad you got off?'

She laughed hard at her own joke. It wasn't that funny, he thought. Herne Bay, this place – same difference in his opinion. But perhaps it was some local joke he wouldn't be aware of. And it was certainly good to hear her laughing. Could have been worse, he told himself, could have been much worse.

'How are you, Susie?'

'I'm fine.'

'You *look* fine.'

'Well . . . I am!'

'Give us a hug then.'

He reached out and pulled her to him. After a couple of seconds, she stepped back, breaking his grip on her.

'It's very nice to see you, Tom,' she said formally. Then she laughed again, 'Ha ha!'

Ha ha? 'And it's terrific to see you,' he nodded, trying to adjust to her strange merriment. He supposed it was out of pleasure at seeing him, which was sweet of her, of course. And probably out of nervousness too, which was understandable. 'Bloody cold though, isn't it?' He dipped his chin into the collar of his overcoat.

'It's always cold in Swayncliff,' she smiled.

'I remember. I can't stay long, by the way,' he added, as they walked past the unattended ticket barrier towards the booking hall.

She nodded and pointed. 'Well, if you go down that tunnel, it'll bring you on to the up platform. I believe there's a train back to London in ten minutes.'

'Now, come on!' he protested. 'That's not fair. I really have to be back in town this evening. It's something I can't get out of.'

He looked at her reproachfully.

'Don't be lousy, Sue. I'm doing my best.'

She shook her head in amazement. 'A joke, a joke . . . Good Lord, Tom, it was only a joke.'

'Oh, I see,' he said doubtfully. 'Is that what it was?'

'Of course. Come on.' She touched his arm for a moment. 'I know you're doing your best. I appreciate it.'

'My mistake. Let's start again. OK?'

They stood in the station forecourt. Across the way was a large billboard and on it, as if repetition would quell all doubts, were five identical weather-beaten posters, each proclaiming: 'SWAYNCLIFF – Gateway to the Kentish Riviera.' Below this a bronzed young couple in skimpy swimwear relaxed beneath palm trees beside a strip of Mediterranean blue.

'Shall we take a taxi?' Tom asked, pointing. The driver appeared to be fast asleep behind the wheel. 'I'll just go wake that bugger up.'

She stopped him. 'Let's walk. Unless,' she grinned at him rather coldly, 'you've forgotten how. Big Timer! . . . A joke!' she cried again, seeing his mouth turn down. 'God, Tom, you never used to be so stuffy.'

'Another joke?'

'Right.'

He nodded. 'Let's start again.'

They looked at each other warily for a moment, and then both at once turned and began to walk away from the forecourt, down Station Approach. They went along briskly for a while, not speaking. Tom hummed a few bars of a familiar tune, then stopped, embarrassed, when he realised it was the national anthem. He glanced at her walking steadily beside him. Her face was cool and expressionless. He supposed it was an improvement on all that unnerving mirth.

'So how are you, Susie?'

'You asked me that. I said I was fine.'

'I know.' He hesitated. 'But – you know – one thing and another, I wondered – '

She stared at him so coldly that he was abruptly silent.

'You said,' she stated, after a moment, 'you promised on the phone you weren't going to mention those letters. That letter. You said that.'

'Did I say anything about a letter?'

'Then what are you talking about?'

'I don't know,' he said weakly. He rallied slightly then. 'Look, all I meant is – you look fine, and you say you're fine, and I'm really glad you're fine and – '. How, he wondered grimly even as he spoke, was he ever going to find an end to this sentence? It was beyond him to suggest once more that they start again. Oh hell, he thought, with rising irritation, if she was going to be bloody difficult all the time then she could just get lost. Really. Who needed it? He trudged along in moody silence beside her.

'How is everybody?' she asked.

He took a few moments to collect himself.

'Everybody?'

'Mm. You know. Bill and Molly. Tina. Dick Banham . . . John Knights? Hugh Perkins . . .?' Her voice trailed away.

'I haven't actually run into any of that lot for quite a while . . . No, of course!' he cried, brightening. 'I tell a lie. I had lunch with Dick just after Christmas.'

'Great. How is he?'

'Oh, you know. Horrific. He's incredibly employable at the moment.'

'Yes?'

'More offers than he can handle. According to him. Really rubbed my nose in it.'

She glanced at him shrewdly. Then she smiled. 'Weird about him and Jean Ricketts, isn't it?'

'I give it three months.'

'Surely not?'

'At most. Oh, definitely,' he nodded. 'That's from the horse's mouth. Dick's furious with her. Let me tell you what young Jeannie's been up to lately. F'rinstance . . .'

It was just like old times, Tom thought, with much relief. They gossiped and laughed together in the old light, malicious, harmless way. It was not, in fact, a way of passing time that Tom much indulged in nowadays. He was too busy, for one thing. But he was happy to do it now, because it seemed to dispel that edginess and tension in Susie that had threatened to mess up their reunion before it had hardly got started. She was all right now though, very relaxed. And, he told himself again, it could have been so much worse. He was really getting off lightly.

For the truth was he had been dreading today. Duty had called, but there had been a moment this morning – at Victoria, as he was about to pay for his return ticket – when he was ready to tell duty to get stuffed. But he was glad he hadn't now. It was true. One did have a duty. If an old friend went off course a little bit, one ought to have a shot at setting them right again. One time. If this got to be a habit with Susie, he would have to let her go on unaided, of course. Regretfully – but firmly. In Tom's world, and in Tom's opinion, there were too many people lately taking the luxury of going a little bit nuts, and it didn't do to have one's life cluttered up with casualties.

But Susie, here, now, was clearly no casualty. As he chatted away, dredging up other memories of encounters he'd had with people she had known once, he watched her with stealthy care. It was still a *good* face, he thought. Strong, mobile features. Fine bones. A beautiful face really; but she could settle into mere prettiness, if preferred. She could probably descend to downright homely, in fact – director's choice. Pushing forty now, but could play ten years younger. Or much older, whatever. She was thinner than he remembered and paler; but then it was January, everybody was pale in January – except Dick Banham, who had not long returned from five weeks' filming in the Caribbean. Fair hair, cropped short and feathery. Clear, ice-blue eyes – there were dark circles under those eyes, Tom noticed. That was not so good. That spoke of sleepless nights, secret worries. But on the other hand, he cheered himself, here she was, smiling and responding so easily, as if she hadn't a care in the world. And listening. Always a good listener, Susie. At one point, when he was telling her the story of Hugh Perkins's attempts to learn to ride a horse for a part – the joke was that he didn't get the part, just multiple bruising and a sore behind – she clutched his arm, gurgling with laughter like a schoolgirl. The story was a year old by now, but it seemed she hadn't heard it.

'Oh, that's funny! Oh, I'm glad you've come down to see me, Tom. You've cheered me up.'

'Well, what are friends for?'

So was he glad now. Glad he had come down, even to this sad town, on such a dreary day. It was clear to him now that his old pal just needed a bit of fun and company, a few laughs, to get her out of whatever black fit she'd been in. It was what he had hoped – and all, frankly, that he was prepared to offer. Which was not selfishness, he told himself, but wisdom. In the past few years, so successful for him, Tom Scott had learned the value of limiting and focusing his expenditure of energy. The world was a pretty big place after all, and if he – one small character in a cast of billions – wanted to make an impact on it (which indeed he hungered to so intensely it sometimes disturbed him), then he had to pick his targets carefully and assess precisely how much effort he could allow himself to spend on each one. For Sue Strang right now he could offer four and a half hours of friendship, sympathy, and old times' sake on a dark winter's day. Not counting journey time.

He was simply being realistic. They were not kids any more, with all the time in the world to lavish on each other.

And anyway it was a sight more than someone like Dick Banham was offering. His fellow director had acted so concerned too when they had met in Charlotte Street for lunch. 'I'm really worried about her, Tom. Poor old Suze. When you think how she used to be. It's *pitiful.*' Et cetera. But who had made the bloody boring journey down to this awful place to throw a lifeline to an old mate in distress? Banham? Not likely!

Thus comforted, Tom let his friend lead him through the streets of Swayncliff. To avoid the jostle of Saturday shoppers in the High Street, she took him through a puzzle of alleys and back lanes, lined with mouldering tenements, which opened finally on to a wide, straight road, with small terraced houses on either side, a third of them with bed and breakfast cards in their front windows.

'Does any of this seem familiar?' she asked.

'Not really. I was only ever down here a couple of times, you know. Maybe three or four.'

And those times, he remembered, he had spent almost entirely inside Susie's apartment. Hers and Mark's. With all the other people. Depressing times in retrospect. Druggy times, headache in the morning times after a night on the floor, foul dry mouth and 'Where the hell am I?' times. A period he was quite happy to forget. Days when he had had almost no hope for himself and his future. Nights when – he remembered this with a slight pricking of conscience – the only person who would ever listen at serious, hours and hours' length to his troubles and worries (his whining, might as well face it) was Susie Strang.

'Does this road ever end?' he asked after a while.

He was feeling the pace now. Though he had resented her joke about not taking taxis, the truth was he hardly ever did any real walking nowadays. Lifting weights in the gym, which he did whenever he could squeeze it in, was no substitute. He enjoyed a general sense of well being, kept in shape, belly roll more or less under control, could do fifteen press ups and not really sweat. But the legs were out of practice, that was a fact.

'Susie,' he panted at last, 'I don't remember your part of town was so far from the station.'

'It isn't. I took you this way specially. Just wait a little while. You'll see.'

He waited, and he walked. The long road petered out at last. They turned a bend. Tom found himself trudging along what appeared to be a country lane. There were fields and trees. Hedges. From the other side of one of these a cow eyed him sadly. Tom was near despair. He had no idea where she was taking him, was not sure what county he was in any more. He opened his mouth to object. He was down here to offer advice and sympathy, tons of it if necessary. He was definitely not here to go on nature rambles.

'Look!' she cried. 'Isn't that fine?'

They were standing on the brow of a slight hill. Immediately before them was a field covered with thin grass. Beyond the field were two stripes of grey. The darker stripe was the sea, the lighter the sky. There was for Tom an unnerving blandness about this prospect. The field, the two grey stripes, nothing else.

'I think it's the most dramatic view in Swayncliff,' Susan said with a sigh of pleasure.

'It's very nice,' he said, trying to sound impressed. 'Where are we?'

'You should see it at night. There's just blackness all around you. Like outer space.'

She stood staring ahead. The field, the stripes. He tried to imagine it through her eyes.

'At night it feels like you could step off the edge of the world,' she said, 'and just disappear.'

He couldn't see it. Not at all. It must be, he thought, that it was very different at –

He turned and looked at her sharply. 'You come out here at night? All on your own?'

'Oh no,' she said, still staring towards the sea. 'With a friend.'

He nodded, relieved to hear it. Relieved particularly to hear that she had at least one person she could call a friend down here. For a moment he watched her. The cold breeze lifting off the sea was ruffling her short fringe and making tears start in the corners of her eyes. She blinked them away. He turned from her and looked around him. Though the air was clear enough where they stood, a thin mist began not far away and he had to strain to see through it.

'We're miles from town,' he pointed out.

She seemed surprised to hear him speak. She stared at him, and then looked to where he was pointing.

'We're less than a mile,' she said. 'And it's all downhill. You're not sorry we came this way, are you?'

What could he say? She had evidently thought to give him pleasure, to show him something that had importance for her. He shook his head.

'You see,' she explained, as they turned away from the grey stripes and set off towards the distant, mist-shrouded Esplanade, 'I've had a change of heart about Swayncliff. I've decided it's not much use to be down here and spend all my time complaining about it. So I've made a point of looking around for interesting things about the place. You'd be surprised at how many there are.'

He would be surprised. Nevertheless, this sounded like positive thinking to Tom, which was good news, of course. On the other hand, he could see an even better alternative.

'Why not just stop living here?'

'Oh, I couldn't do that,' she said immediately.

'I don't see why. I never understood why you chose to come here in the first place.'

'Well, I didn't exactly. It was Mark's idea. Don't you remember? A seaside getaway for us. For the whole gang. Everybody thought it was a good idea at the time.'

'A good idea to get a place by the sea. But *Swayncliff*! We all thought you meant Dorset, Devon . . . Norfolk.'

'But it's so near London. And the rent was cheap. Still is, thank God.'

Which reminded him. He ought to find out how hard up she was. And if he could do anything to help. And if she'd mind him trying. He was good for fifty quid, he supposed . . . Oh hell, he was good for a hundred, if it came to that.

'All right,' Tom conceded. 'But that was then and this is now. And you're not married to Mark any more,' he added. 'Which is a blessing, in my opinion.'

'In fact, you're wrong,' she said in a light though careful tone. 'We are still married.'

'You know what I mean, Susie.' He frowned at her. 'How long is it since he bunked off?'

'Is it a year?'

'You know it's a lot longer than that,' he said sternly.

After a moment she said, 'I think you should take a few deep breaths, Tom. The air's very healthy up here. And you look quite pale.'

'It's January,' Tom grunted. 'Of course I'm pale.' Nevertheless, he turned his face towards the sea and filled his lungs. It made him dizzy at first. They walked on for a while in silence. With relief Tom watched the buildings along the Esplanade grow clearer through the mist.

'What's Mark doing now?' she asked suddenly.

He glanced at her. 'You don't know?'

She shook her head. 'He doesn't write.'

'Well . . . I only hear things.' He shrugged. 'I believe he's still in California.' He looked at her again. 'You knew he went out there?'

'I knew he went to America.' A pause. 'What's he up to, do you know?'

'Trying to be a producer last thing I heard.' Tom laughed shortly. 'Well, why not? He wasn't much good as an actor. Or a writer. Nobody would let him direct. I guess he can call himself a producer and who's going to bother to argue? I expect he's got a couple of scripts in his pocket, probably sets up meetings, takes lunches, you know . . .' Tom's voiced tailed away. He was aware he was hitting at someone who was not here, could not defend himself, was forever down on his luck, and so on. But then he still happened to be very angry with Mark Gould.

'I wonder what he lives on,' Susan said.

Women, Tom wanted to say. But he held his peace, though he had no doubt it was true. She was looking so wistful as she walked along, her head bowed slightly as if in submission . . . To what? Fate? Bad luck? It made Tom so sad to see her like this. Susie. So bright. And kind. Talented too in a small, clear way. What a waste.

'You can't still be worrying about Mark,' he burst out.

'Well, you know, I did love him,' she said, smiling more to herself than to him.

'How could you love *Mark*? I never could understand it. None of us could.'

'All the same . . . I did.'

He could hardly bear to think about that sly bastard, that ambitious little con man, who had wriggled his way into their gang of friends and had (Dick Banham's phrase) 'picked off our finest flower'. Flower was ridiculous, of course, sentimental, all wrong for Susie, who had her own toughness and could be, Tom remembered well, as scrappy, prickly, bitchy and hard mouthed as anybody when she wanted. Still, she had been special, a special person, no doubt of it, and she had been picked off all right. Like a sniper's victim.

'You must remember it isn't Mark's fault really, the way he is.' Her eyes as she spoke gleamed with a sort of calm fanaticism. 'He's always been so unfortunate. Since he was a little boy.'

Ho hum. 'OK. Fair enough. But, look, Mark is history. There's no earthly reason why you have to stay on here now.'

'But I don't want to leave. I'm perfectly happy here.'

'I don't believe it,' he said after a moment.

She looked at him, surprised. 'Why do you say that?'

'Because why would you write those letters,' he challenged her, 'if you're so perfectly happy?'

She turned away from him angrily.

'You promised – '

'All right, but – '

'I *told* you – I wrote to you – I just went potty for a bit. Just for a bit – '

'And the reason you went potty,' he cried, sensing victory, seeing he had backed her into a corner, 'is because you're stuck down here, in this bloody awful place, nothing to do all day, nothing to think about . . .'

She stopped walking. Looked at him. Smiled slightly – a rather pitying smile Tom noticed with annoyance.

'You're quite wrong,' she said. 'I've got lots to think about, as it happens.'

'Such as?'

She shrugged mysteriously.

'Oh, come on, Sue!'

She inclined her head to one side and watched him teasingly. Staring back at her, he felt his irritation increase to a point – and then break and dwindle away. There was something so silly about her at this moment, a grown woman playing little girl games. He thought longingly of the train back to London, but a glance at his watch showed it was still nearly three hours away. He sighed and looked around him. Across the road, the concrete sea wall masked the water. Nothing worth looking at over there. His gaze travelled on, returned to where they stood. He looked up and above Susie's smiling face. All at once, for the first time since the station, he recognised something in Swayncliff. They were standing outside the tall, turn of the century building that contained her flat. Tom looked up at it grimly. There were other places in his life that were like this. A room in Earls Court, another in Battersea, before that an eighth share in a squat in Camden Town. Places where he had wasted time, been miserable, felt impotent, been young. He had never revisited those other places. Why the hell he had to come all the long way to look at this one was for the moment unclear to him.

Friendship, he reminded himself. Duty. A helping hand to Susie. Just once.

'Are we going upstairs?' he asked morosely.

'Not yet.' She slipped her arm in his and started to walk him away from her building. 'I'm taking you out to lunch.'

'Oh God!' he sighed, and then had to smile in hasty apology. 'I'm sorry. But it's all hamburgers and chips round here, isn't it? And my stomach won't take the grease any more – '

'It is *not* all hamburgers and chips!' Then she smiled forgivingly. 'I am in fact taking you to the Imperial Hotel.'

'I see.'

'Swayncliff's finest,' she nodded. 'Did you know H. G. Wells wrote a chapter of *The Shape of Things to Come* there?'

He shook his head.

'Well, he did. It's on a plaque outside. Also the Empress Eugenie of France stayed there.' She laughed and squeezed his arm. 'For one night!' Through her coat, and through her dress, he could feel the shape of her breast. 'I told you – Swayncliff's full of surprises, if you look for them. Why – !' She closed her eyes and then opened them very wide, as if brimming over with furious glee. 'We even have our own murderer down here, you know! At least, we used to.'

'What?'

But she only laughed again and wouldn't tell him what she meant. He watched her uneasily as they crossed the road. Once again there was that hectic merriment in her that had unsettled him when they had first met today. He remembered suddenly that at their lunch Dick Banham had suggested he looked out for a possible drinking problem if he went to visit Susie.

'Come on, Dick! This is *Sue Strang*.'

'She's an actress. That's how it often gets to them,' Dick had nodded with a sage air that Tom had found quite dislikeable. 'All alone. Time passing. Looks fading. Nobody wants them. In the wee small hours – as they gaze upon the wreckage of their lives – the old vodka martini is often their only friend.'

'Rubbish!'

Was it rubbish? Whatever was up with Susie, she clearly wasn't drunk right now. He would not have a chance to see what she did in the small hours, but he planned to watch her carefully during lunch. As a friend, he owed her that.

2

'You look anxious,' Susan said.

'Absolutely not. Looking forward to it.'

But Tom's voice lacked conviction. The Monarch Dining Room at the Imperial Hotel was much as he had feared it would be. A dozen tables, each covered with red-checked paper. Views of the Cinque Ports around the walls. A stuffed sea bass, unnaturally large, hung over the entrance in a glass case. Its single visible eye surveyed the room in a grief-stricken fashion. Only one other table was occupied, at the far end of the room from where they sat. Two business types were over there, now murmuring conspiratorially into each other's ears, now bursting into loud brays of laughter. An elderly, accident-prone waitress shuttled between the two tables and the swing doors that led to the kitchen. The faint, stale aroma of a century and more of breakfasts, lunches, dinners hung over the Monarch Room. The temperature was held at a steady fifty degrees. Tom kept his coat on.

'I can remember when your entire diet consisted of chips,' Susan smiled. 'Chips and Mars bars, wasn't it?'

'Was it?'

He had ordered the plaice. And, with misgivings, the grapefruit juice to start with. The waitress had promised it was fresh. He had his doubts. He had had to lend her his pen to get the order filled out, because hers didn't work.

'Of course,' Susan said idly, 'you've come a long way since then.'

'Now, Susie . . .'

'Rich and famous!'

'Famous is bullshit,' Tom said belligerently. 'And you know it. As for rich – last place I worked, do you know how much they paid me? Lousy fifteen thousand, that's all. Three months' work.'

'Oh, poor Tom! Lousy fifteen thousand. Poor dear!'

'All *right*. But in fact it's peanuts compared to what they're paying some directors. I could tell you – '

But before he could start naming names, an obsequious man in a crumpled lounge suit arrived at his elbow and asked what they cared to drink with their meal. After a shocked glance at the wine list, Tom sighed and asked for the house white. And then waited watchfully as Susan considered her choice.

'Mineral water, please.'

So much for Banham, Tom thought with relief. And then remembered: of course – they're crafty, alcoholics, and it's the secret drinking that is the real killer. But looking at Susie now it was hard to believe such a thing of her. She seemed so fresh, in such good shape. Apart from the pallor, and the darkness under her eyes . . . It was difficult, really difficult – and then he hardly liked to be playing the spy.

The obsequious man departed. The elderly waitress wavered into view and deposited a glass of juice on the edge of Tom's place mat. He sipped it suspiciously.

'I knew it!' he cried, his voice high with indignation. 'It's *not* fresh!' He looked round for the waitress, but she had beaten a fast retreat. 'Fresh out of a can is what they always mean.' He banged the juice glass down on the table, slopping some of its contents over the rim. 'It's too bad, it really is!'

After a moment, she leaned across the table. Her eyes, as they met his, were cold and steady.

'You are my guest, Tom Scott,' she stated. 'And you are behaving like a spoiled little prince.'

All at once, ten and more years seemed to drop away and they were back where they had been long ago. She was older than he – just a couple of years but it had seemed a crucial gap when they were younger. She had been almost like a big sister to him then: indulgent, fond, but also, once in a while, very stern if he seemed to be getting out of line. And he had been nothing then, nothing at all, while Susie had already made her start in the business and for him had all that prestige, that glamour. He was all hope and promise and wind in those days.

'Well, it is the Monarch Dining Room after all,' he responded lamely at last.

To his relief, she relaxed, chuckled, leaned back in her chair.

'I'm sorry,' he said, feeling it sincerely. 'I'm being rude. I don't mean to be . . . Look, here's my plaice!' he cried as the plate landed in the vicinity of his mat. He seized his knife and fork. 'Yum yum!' he mumbled, mouth full of fish. 'Good God, this is delicious!'

She shook her head, laughing. 'Enough! You're forgiven.'

The meal moved along comfortably after that. They talked about Tom most of the time, about his problems. They were nice problems on the whole. Whether he should turn himself into a limited company for tax purposes. Whether he and Louise should move out of their little house in Shepherd's Bush to one in Holland Park, a bigger place they had their eyes on, quite grand in fact. Which of two television plays he should direct next. There was not much to choose between them. Both were well written, both would be done on film, both were sensitive, accurate, small-scale pieces . . .

'But that's what you're good at,' she said, watching him.

'Well, I've had the practice, haven't I? That's about all I've ever done. But – ' He frowned.

'What?'

'Oh, I don't know . . . I'm just sort of tired of all this slice of life stuff. I want to do something – *big*. And vulgar . . . I want to have a thousand extras . . . big stars . . . I want to do a Western! Well, not really, but you know what I mean. Something *gaudy*!'

'You want to stretch yourself,' she encouraged him. 'That's good.'

'Well, maybe it is,' he nodded. 'In the meantime, I've got a sensitive study of Vietnamese exiles in Leeds for Yorkshire. And a wistful examination of autumn love at the BBC. So which should I do?'

Throughout, Susan listened to him intently and, in the way she had, put in questions at just the right moment, or nodded helpfully and gave encouraging murmurs to help him through a complicated or lengthy bit of exposition. And as he talked, Tom felt his confidence flowing back. By the end of dessert – apple tart and cream, not at all bad – he had achieved a proper sense of proportion once more. He knew who he was again – he remembered, though not with pleasure, how far she had fallen. As they waited for their coffee, still chatting on about his life and prospects, he was once again inwardly reviewing the themes of duty and guidance. The duty he owed to her as an old friend, down on her luck; the guidance he could offer and from which, if she would only listen to it, she could profit so much.

'Susie,' he began, after the arrival of the coffee had caused a break in his monologue, 'where do you think you go from here?'

She seemed not to understand what he meant.

'Well . . . are you really going to stay down here for ever?'

'I don't see it does much harm.'

'Well, *I* do.'

'Who does it harm?'

'You. And your career. Yes,' he insisted. 'How can you possibly get work when you're miles and miles away from anything that's happening?'

She stirred her coffee slowly.

'I don't think it has anything to do with that,' she said. Then, 'Anyway. You're wrong. As it happens there are several interesting things in the air for me right now – '

'Come off it, Susie.'

She met his gaze for a moment. And then looked away. He watched her profile. It seemed all hard edges at this moment. Her mouth was set in a mutinous line.

'Oh, all right. There's damn all in the air. But it's got nothing to do with living in Swayncliff. Plenty of actors live outside London, and they get work.'

'So?' He kept watching her. Feeling her resistance to his questions, he was beginning to get annoyed with her all over again. 'What do you think it's got to do with? In your case?'

'Oh . . .' Her eyes stayed away from his. 'I think it's sort of been arranged, you see.'

'What?'

'I haven't had a job in nine months. Haven't had a decent job in . . .' She shrugged. 'I can't remember exactly. Couple of years at least.'

'And you think it's been *arranged*?'

'In a way.'

'Like a conspiracy?'

'I didn't call it – '

'Like a *blacklist*?' He was in the full flood of derision by now. 'Oh, come on, Susie!' he whooped, as if he could break through her nonsense by sheer lung power. At the far end of the room, the business types looked up and stared across at them. Tom didn't notice. 'That's so ridiculous!' he bellowed. 'A blacklist! Come on. This isn't Hollywood. We're all human beings here. And you're well known, well respected, and – '

'Out of work,' she chuckled tensely. She sat, not looking at him, pulling at a fold in the paper table cover. He stared at her disappointedly. Then he sighed and settled lower in his seat.

'All right, why do you think you're on this . . . what do I call it if it's not a blacklist?'

'Call it that if you like.'

'Thanks. So why are you on it?'

Again she shrugged, careless and bitter. 'Who knows? Something I said. Something I didn't say. Somebody I offended.'

Now, as he looked at her, he felt almost a sense of grief. It was all much more ordinary than he had feared. Yet that somehow made it the more sad. An everyday case of rampant paranoia. He bumped into such people all the time in his world. Until now though, none of them had been worth a damn in the first place, in his opinion.

'Oh, Susie . . .' he mourned.

She shook her head impatiently. 'It doesn't matter,' she said with conviction. 'I'm not much bothered by all that now. Careers, jobs – what does it matter really? Christ, there are more important things!'

'I just can't believe you mean that,' he said.

She stared at him, insulted. 'Why can't you?'

'Because of what you wrote to me. I don't mean – ' He held up his hand as she started to protest. 'I don't mean *those* letters. I mean the first one you wrote. Asking me for a job.'

'Well . . .' She was embarrassed for a moment. 'I just did that. That's all. Forget it.'

'But how could you do it?' His voice was hushed now, as if the matter was too shocking to risk having it overheard. 'To write to a director like that!'

'I was trying to get a job. What's wrong with that? I'd have thought you'd have approved.'

'But,' he searched for words to express his distaste, 'only beginners write to directors. Or people who *can't* get jobs.'

'Exactly. Me!'

'No! I mean people who are no good at all write to directors. And the rule is – my rule is – never employ anybody who writes to you for a job. If they need one that badly then they don't deserve it. That's the rule. Oh, and Susie,' Tom shook his head, 'you sent me a photograph. *You* sent *me* a photograph!'

'Stop it, Tom.'

'I can't. Look at you. You're an established actor. You're my old friend . . . You sent me a *photograph*! I couldn't believe it.'

'It was just a stupid idea. I just – '

'You sent one to Dick Banham too.'

She gazed at him, shocked. He felt suddenly ashamed. He bowed his head. 'Well, naturally we talked about it,' he mumbled. 'Dick was quite upset.'

'Was he?' She laughed briefly. She looked across the room. The businessmen had gone by now. The ancient waitress was laying out a fresh red cover on the table they'd been using. Susan raised her hand and waved. She said, not looking at Tom, 'I think I want to get out of here.' The waitress didn't see her.

'No, don't turn me off,' he said. 'It doesn't matter really. We're old friends. We understand. We try to. As long as you don't start writing like that to anyone else.' He studied her. Then, apprehensively, 'You haven't written to anyone else, have you?'

She shrugged. Then nodded. 'Lots.' She listened to him groan, and then, in a careless, angry voice, 'Oh, well, that's that. I'll never work again . . . Oh, what does it matter?' she snapped as he tried to object. 'Prancing around in front of people, showing off. That's what Mark used to call it. And he was right. And I'm sick of it. No,' she cried, when again he tried to speak. 'I really am. I've had enough. Let me tell you about my last job. I told my agent I'd do anything, and the silly cow took me literally. Got me two weeks filling in with a touring company in Sevenoaks. Ghastly play – I couldn't understand a word of it. I couldn't even understand the title. Nineteen-year-old director – next thing to an idiot. The rest of the cast *were* idiots, certifiable. There we all were, mucking about, crawling round the stage, grunting and yelling – even for Sevenoaks it was a disgrace. The audience slow handclapped us one night. I felt like joining in. And I knew – ' She ripped off a strip from the table cover in her anger. 'I *knew* that I was miles better than everybody else. And I'd disgraced myself by appearing with them. In this shit. And for what? For the sake of having a bloody job!'

After a moment, Tom stirred.

'Yes,' he said, 'I gather that was the impression you left behind you.'

'What?'

'I said – I heard that was the message you were giving out. That you were miles better than everybody else. Daresay you were right, of course.'

She stared at him. 'What did you hear?'

'Oh – things. You know how these things get around . . .'

She began speaking very fast.

'I did my job. I did the best I could. I was right there every night, every cue, word perfect . . . grunt perfect . . . the only one.'

'I believe you,' Tom nodded. Then, 'It was backstage that the trouble was. As I heard it.'

'Where did you hear it?'

'I don't know . . . a party or something. It doesn't matter really.

It's just a bit unfortunate that something like that should get around. At this point in your career.'

She sank back in her chair.

'And you say there isn't a blacklist!'

'There *isn't*. Look, all I know is – I was with some people and they were discussing casting for something that's coming up. Nothing to do with me, I just happened to be there. And somebody mentioned you. And somebody else said – just casually, "Better not. I hear she's still trouble." That's all.'

As he watched her – she looked mortified, crushed – Tom didn't feel so good suddenly. The fact was it had been nothing more than a few chance words overheard at a party. From nobody very important. He hadn't needed to wallop her with it, like he had.

'Now, Sue, don't worry. It doesn't matter much – '

She looked up. He saw a flash of anger in her eyes.

' "Still trouble",' she repeated. 'What does that mean?'

'Oh . . .' Tom shifted uncomfortably in his seat. 'Well, you know . . . There was that time when you were being a bit difficult, Susie, you remember . . .' He shifted again as she stared at him unblinkingly. 'When you were being very hoity-toity about the parts you were offered. Everything was beneath you . . . Upset a few people at the time, I expect you know that. Of course, *we* all knew it was only Mark speaking through you, but . . . Oh, listen,' he urged, reaching out to take her hand. But she moved it before he could. 'It was just some guy saying something at a party, that's all – '

'And what did you say?'

'Pardon?'

'When he said I was still trouble. What did you say, Tom?'

'I . . . I didn't . . .' He floundered miserably for a moment. 'I told you . . . It was nothing to do with me. Now, *look*,' he said, seeing the bitterness settle in her face. 'It doesn't mean much. And nobody's out to get you. It's not Hollywood after all.'

'You keep saying that. Since neither of us has ever been there, how would we know?'

They sat in silence for a few moments, neither looking at the other.

'This is horrible,' she said then, rising to her feet. 'I'm getting out.'

'I'll pay,' he said, getting up too.

'No, you won't.'

'I will. I must.'

She stared at him. She looked angry and helpless, almost distraught.

'Oh, do what you want,' she snapped. And walked away from the table, leaving him gazing after her, and then fumbling for his wallet and his gold credit card.

When he came outside, she was backed against the hotel's side wall, eyes closed, breathing deeply. He waited near her, watching unhappily. He cursed himself for the way he had behaved to her over lunch. Send for Scott in an emergency. Watch him wade in. When the smoke clears, nobody's left standing.

'It was so stuffy in there,' she sighed at last. 'I'm glad to be out.'

'I'm really sorry.' He came closer to her. 'I meant to be helpful, and I said it all wrong.'

'Doesn't matter.'

'Don't *say* that.'

'But it's true. I wish you'd believe me. It doesn't matter about work, all that. Why should it?'

'Because it's what you do. It's what you do well. And there's no problem, Susie, not really. Just come back to London. You can stay at our place till you've found somewhere.' He was going, he knew, far beyond the limits of assistance he had set for himself. But it was what he wanted at this moment. He just couldn't bear to see her looking so lost. 'Louise will be really pleased,' he promised, more confidently than he felt, for in fact his wife had not been all that understanding even about his need to come down here today. 'We'll have fun. You'll see people. You'll soon be back in the swing of things, you'll . . . Ah,' he sighed, for she was shaking her head, 'why won't you let me help you?'

After a moment, she came to him and touched his arm. He looked up. She was watching him steadily and fondly.

'Have you got to go back now?'

He looked at his watch.

'Not for a bit.'

'Good.' She held on to his arm. 'Come to my place. I want to tell you things. I don't want you to worry about me any more.'

They began walking slowly, arm in arm, along the Esplanade towards her building. Like a devoted old couple, Tom thought, strolling along after lunch, before the nap. The tang of the sea was in his nostrils. Gulls wheeled and cried overhead. Sunlight poured through a gap in the clouds and glinted off the grey-green water.

He thought of London, of racketing streets, dirt, noise, too many people. It made him exhausted even to think of it – and he had to start back there in an hour. Perhaps she was right. Who in their right mind would choose to live in that chaos? The city wasn't for him any more. It had changed – or he had changed. It was too tough. If it wasn't for the work, he would get straight out of it. But that was it. That was what kept them all sane, hopeful, alive. The work.

'I may work again,' she said, without much conviction. 'If I got something really good I would, you know that. But it's not vital to me any more. And I don't think it's such an outrage that I'm not working. I've learned, you see,' she looked up at him keenly, as if testing his readiness to understand her, 'that there are a lot more important tragedies in the world than me being out of work. In fact, that isn't a tragedy at all. That's just nothing.'

'Well,' he sighed. 'All right. There are famines in Africa and wars in – '

'No. You don't have to go so far.' She gestured with her free hand to the few other strollers along the Esplanade. 'Terrible things are happening to people all the time. If you asked any of those people, you'd find out – oh, awful things are happening, Tom. We just don't know.'

It sounded to Tom like one of those calming, comforting, empty philosophies he had used to stitch together to help himself through his own hard times. But he felt he had used the big stick enough today, so he said only, 'But, Susie, we don't know. That's the fact. So it can't affect us.'

'But what if we did?' she asked urgently. 'Look. What if something terrible happened to Louise. Don't you think your problems – if you had any problems – don't you think they'd matter a lot less?'

'Of course they would. They wouldn't matter at all.'

'That's all I'm saying.'

'But then these people . . .' It was Tom's turn to wave at the passers-by. As if they were stage props, he thought, scenery for their argument. 'I don't know these people. So I don't know whether their problems would matter much to me. But Louise, well – well, I love Louise, don't I? So her problems would matter.'

She seemed to be pondering his reply with great care. He felt a little embarrassed to be carrying on like this, as if they were two fifth years having a grand ethical debate. But evidently she was taking it very seriously. And all at once it struck him that – in her eyes – they were not just having a debate. This was about something.

About someone. He didn't know who, what . . . He realised he didn't know what was going on.

'Yes,' she said then. 'I see that. It makes a difference. Of course it does.'

He waited to be told what they were really discussing. But she was smiling at him now. And, 'Here-we-are-again!' she said in pier show cadence.

He looked around. They were indeed once more at the doorway to her building. And again he looked up uneasily at the windows to her flat. Third floor, on the left. Couldn't forget it, unfortunately.

'Come upstairs,' she said. And when he hesitated, 'I'll make you some coffee. You didn't drink much at lunch.'

'Well . . . it was awful.'

'So it was.' She grinned, took his hand, led him through the swing doors. 'I'll do better.'

On her landing, as she searched in her pocket for the keys, he looked up the stairs towards the fourth floor.

'Does that crazy old lady still live up there?'

'Sssh . . . Yes, she does.'

'What was her name?'

'Mrs Jane Baklova.'

'Is she still bananas?'

'She's been fairly quiet lately.'

'She used to sort of leap out from the darkness whenever I came out of your place.' Tom shuddered at the memory. 'Like the angel of death . . . Didn't Mark call her that once?'

'Yes, he did,' she said sadly as she opened the door. 'To her face.'

While Susie went into the kitchen to make coffee, Tom wandered around the living room. Nothing much had changed, he saw. It was, as ever, bloody cold. Without thinking, he went to the electric fire and with the toe of his shoe pressed down on both switches. Still working, he thought, watching the bars begin to glow, after all these years. He turned away, saw the sofa. Same old sofa, scene of many noisy romps. Same cover, much patched, but clean, though there were several faint, ineradicable stains on it. He could almost pinpoint the particular stupid stunt or accident that had caused each one. It occurred to him again, seeing that so little had changed in the flat, to wonder about the state of Susie's finances. What was she living on? Social security, he guessed. But what else? Savings? He doubted if she had much left over from her good years. Mark would have seen to that. He had to get up the nerve to speak to her about it. How much did a new sofa cost? The one Louise had ordered from Heal's last month had cost over two thousand quid. But they should be much more reasonable down here. And there was nothing wrong with secondhand if the item was in fundamentally sound condition. It would be nice to go bargain hunting with Susie one day, he thought. Some other weekend.

She came back into the room then, smiling, carrying a tray, and settled it on the carpet near the fire. Automatically she reached out and switched off one of the bars. Tom squatted down opposite her and watched her pour the coffee.

'Sue,' he began carefully, 'when you were talking outside . . . Has something bad happened to somebody you know? Somebody you care for?'

He tried to see her face, but it was bowed over the coffee cups.

'Sugar?' she asked. 'I can't remember.'

'No, I've given up.'

She handed him his cup. He stared at her as he took it.

'There *is* somebody,' he guessed.

She nodded. She stirred her coffee, then looked up directly at him.

'It's a man I've got friendly with. Just in the past few months.'

Aha! Yes. A *man*. Watching her, Tom saw her eyes were lively now, full of excitement. Yes, indeed. On this visit he had seen her – mysterious, fond, angry, various emotions, but always as if she was expending them on secondary targets. Now at last, he guessed, they were coming to the main event.

'*Yes*,' he said. 'Yes, this man . . .' Without being aware of it, he was smiling at her now. He was so pleased to see her come alive at last. 'What's happened to him? What's the great tragedy?'

She set down her cup on the tray and stared at the single glowing bar.

'It's pretty bad,' she said.

Leukaemia. All at once he knew what it was. It was his own personal private terror. His smile faded in an instant. The poor bastard had leukaemia. He saw it all now. Susie. The poor bastard. They had met. Become friendly. Got involved. Passionate. A future. A reason for going on. And then one day . . . one dark day . . . It was horrible, senseless, cruel. It was the stuff of a thousand bad plays and movies too – Dick Banham-type efforts, he had them categorised mentally – but that didn't make it any less ghastly when it happened, like now, in real life.

'Go on,' said Tom. 'Tell me.'

'He's been disinherited,' she said in a low, appalled tone.

Her voice died away. They sat in silence. Gradually he became aware of sounds, the life of the room carrying on without them. A clock ticking somewhere. The sound of footsteps above, from the realm of craziness upstairs. The sea sighed beyond the windows. A speck of fluff drifted against the single red bar, and the fire spat as it consumed it, making Tom start at the sound.

'Oh,' he said then. He felt considerably disappointed. 'Well . . . that's a shame.'

'A shame!' She stared at him. 'It's *wicked*. It's – ' She shook her head, not able to find the word bad enough to describe it.

But it's not leukaemia, he wanted to point out, though he knew already it was his own fault if he was disappointed. He had fixed on the disease – she had not tempted him to think in that way. And certainly there were many other tragedies in the world than his own particular dread. Such as suicide, for instance, or incest, famine, massacre, or catching AIDS, or being murdered, or getting –

Disinherited.

'It's wicked,' she repeated, turning away from him.

'Well, of course . . . But I don't really know the circumstances, do I? I mean,' he added, when she seemed likely not to speak, 'you haven't given me a lot to work on, have you?'

She turned towards him again and seemed to study him. As if considering his fitness, he thought. Checking him to see if he was worthy to hear her story. Which was so very important. Oh, come off it, Sue, he thought, suddenly feeling sour. I've heard a few actors' stories in my time and never lost much sleep over them.

'Shall I tell you?' she wondered out loud.

'Sure. Why not?' He smiled agreeably. 'Aren't I your pal?'

'I don't want you to miss your train.'

That was something he took seriously. He thought for a moment.

'I know – I'll book a taxi, then there won't be any problem.'

It was soon done. He hung up the phone, and accepted another cup of her good coffee. Settled himself comfortably on the carpet, facing her, his back resting against the edge of the sofa, one side of him at least warmed by the fire.

'It began about three months ago,' she started. 'Three or four. This man came to see me. A reporter from the *Argus*.'

'The – ?'

'The local rag. He wanted to interview me.' She looked up, smiling. 'If you can believe that.'

'Go on, Susie,' he said gently.

'Well, I thought it was pretty strange. In fact, I thought at first it might be a joke. A wind up. But he turned out to be perfectly serious. He's a great fan of *The Entwistles*, you see . . . Don't you remember, Tom?' she said then sadly. 'I was Lucy Entwistle: "Wild, passionate, fate-driven Lucy. Storm-tossed child of a powerful, death-haunted, nineteenth-century Yorkshire clan. A character to rival Scarlett O'Hara, Lorna Doone . . ." At least, that's what the publicity said.'

'Oh *that* thing,' Tom got it at last. 'That was one of Banham's, wasn't it? Had about a million episodes?'

'Just twelve.'

'Right. Right . . .' He stared at her then. 'But that was – '

'I know,' she nodded. 'Years ago. Who'd have thought anybody would have remembered it? Or me? But there he was. Terribly pleased to meet me. Very excited to find me living in Swayncliff. Embarrassed that it had taken his paper over three years to discover that I was. All very flattering . . . Although, of course – ' Her mouth turned down at the corners in a grimace that was half humorous, half pained. 'The next time I met him, he hadn't a clue who I was . . .'

Tom sipped his coffee. He had just now suddenly remembered that years ago – before Mark, before Louise, practically in the pre-history of their group – he and Susie had been lovers. Though that was overstating it. They hadn't lived together, had hardly even been a couple, the whole thing had been over and done with in a few weeks. It was something that had happened after parties, several parties. She had taken him home with her – because she was lonely, he had supposed. Himself, he had felt . . . honoured. That was the word.

He remembered best the apartment she had taken him to those nights. At the time he was living in the Camden Town squat, a grim filthy place. What pleasure it had been to sleep in and then to wake up in Susie's room. How tidy and orderly and cosy it had been. He used to get such an impression of sweetness and goodness in her room. On her mantelpiece she had a photo of her parents, and also one of herself, a solemn ten year old on a pony. All standard Esher, Surrey stuff, he supposed, but such a relief after his usual surroundings. Over the mantelpiece she had stuck up a famous dramatic poster of Ché Guevara. Well, it was all that long time ago, and even by that period the poster, then decorating half the squats and student dormitories and bedsits in London, had become more of a piece of homely kitsch than a revolutionary symbol.

As he lay in Susie's bed, between Susie's clean sheets, gazing up at Ché in the early morning light, Tom had always felt especially pure and cosy.

3

Well! After all that – the bastard – not the faintest *idea* . . .

She let the ripple of anger rise freely in her at first – and then, ruefully, contained herself. It was only a hazard of the profession, she reminded herself, being forgotten. You could be in a wildly popular series – *The Entwistles*, for instance – and there'd be minor mob scenes at Sainsbury's when you went shopping. And then three weeks after it had ended – nothing, nobody knew you, couldn't get arrested. So this was really nothing new. Embarrassing though. She wished she hadn't spoken her greeting so loudly.

She had left the women's changing room and had been walking across the lobby to the Leisure Centre's main exit. As she approached, she could hear the patter of rain against the glass doors and her spirits, always high after an exercise class, dropped a couple of notches. She hadn't brought an umbrella tonight, and some of Swayncliff's expert vandals had recently sheared off the roof of the bus shelter, so if, as was likely, she had to wait more than a minute or two for the bus she was going to get soaking wet.

There was a man standing at the doors looking out at the car park. Medium height, reddish hair, fortyish, standing in three-quarters profile to her. There was something familiar about him, but she couldn't place it at first. He was wearing a navy-blue track suit, a towel draped round his neck, white trainers. If he's going out like that, she thought, he's going to get wet through too.

Then she got closer to him and she remembered. She felt a stir of pleasure. When she had lived in London she had always loved to run into somebody she knew just by chance, out of the blue. In Swayncliff it practically never happened, and so when it did it seemed that much more important. It seemed miraculous almost.

'Why, hello!' she beamed. 'Fancy meeting you here.'

The man she had accosted turned and stared at her. For a moment, she could see, there was not a glimmer of recognition in his eyes. Oh wonderful, she thought, mortified; I must have made a really huge impression here.

'Hi,' she said in a much quieter voice. 'I'm Susan Strang.' The man continued to stare at her as if she had dropped into the lobby the moment before from a distant planet. 'Don't you remember? You came to talk to me a couple of weeks ago. Or was it three?' She wouldn't mind so much, except that he had behaved so admiringly towards her on their first meeting. But there you go, she thought grimly, out of sight, out of mind.

And why not? she told herself then. What else did she expect? This man was more or less a stranger really. She had been forgotten by much better, much older friends than him, she certainly had . . . And then, what did that matter either?

The light of recognition at last flickered in his eyes.

'Oh, God! I'm so sorry. I was miles away. Miss Strang!'

'It's quite all right. I expect you talk to lots of people every day in your job.'

She heard a rather plaintive note in her voice, which didn't please her. She must push on, get past this awkward moment. He certainly did look very apologetic. She could hardly stay angry with him when he looked like that. What was his name now? Thorne. Yes. Something Thorne. Miss Strang and Mr Thorne. A Victorian couple, it sounded like. It was rather a Victorian situation now, the pair of them bobbing and smiling uneasily at each other.

'I must thank you, Mr Thorne, for the very nice story you wrote about me.'

'Oh . . .' He shook his head. 'I'm just sorry it was so short. I thought they'd give me more than three paras, but – '

'It was fine,' she promised him. 'Really.'

They stood side by side, looking out at the darkness of the car park. Flurries of rain spattered against the glass; then, as they continued to stand there in silence, it started to fall in a regular drum beat.

'Rotten night,' he commented.

'Do you think it might pass over soon?'

'Might do.'

'Well, do you want to wait it out in the bar? I'd like to buy you a drink. To thank you for your story.'

He glanced sideways at her. He seemed flattered, and tempted. But then he shook his head. 'I'd better not. My wife'll be waiting for me.'

He's married. It was an automatic thought, didn't mean anything.

'I was only thinking of, say, ten minutes.'

'All the same . . .'

She was rather touched by this evidence of attachment to his partner, though it seemed to cast her in the role of temptress, *femme fatale*. Which she certainly had no desire to play. Anyway it left her with no excuse now not to face the weather. Drinking alone was something she had so far resisted. When you start doing that, she had told herself many times, you'll know you're down for good.

Smile then, and no regrets and no hanging about. She squared her shoulders.

'Right, then. Off to the bus for me.'

'Ah . . .' He looked across at her again. 'Aren't you driving?'

'Haven't got a car.'

'Oh well, in that case . . .' He tugged at the ends of the towel around his neck. 'Um – if you could use a lift . . .'

She watched him. He was really having trouble getting the invitation out. He must be quite a shy man, she decided. It made her wonder how he could do his job. But perhaps it was only with her that he was so bashful. That was sweet of him if it were so.

'Won't it be out of your way?'

'Not really.'

'Lead on, then!'

Stooping and ducking, they pushed through the swing doors and ran out into the pouring rain.

As she settled into the passenger seat of his car, she shook the rain drops from her hair, laughing.

'Really coming down now!'

He nodded, didn't speak; he was puffing, badly out of breath.

'I think it's set in for a bit,' she said.

He took in a few more deep breaths, and then drew the towel from around his neck. He was about to touch it to his wet hair, when he hesitated, then offered it to her. She dabbed at her neck and hair, and then passed the towel quickly across her face. It smelled freshly laundered and was crisply dry apart from where the rain drops had moistened it. She handed it back. He used it, and then tucked it away in the panel compartment beside him. She looked around appreciatively as he started the engine.

'Nice big car.'

'Yes.' He switched on the lights.

'What is it? It's like a boat.'

'It's an Oldsmobile 88.'

'Must be expensive to run.'

'Well, we get a petrol allowance from the paper, you see.'

He pushed up the gear lever, and the car moved in a slow and stately fashion towards the exit. She felt herself rocking ever so gently against the smooth upholstery. She giggled suddenly, and he glanced at her.

'Sorry. I felt for a moment like I was in a pimp's car . . . That's terrible,' she said earnestly, after a moment. 'It's a lovely car. Really.'

He didn't reply, and she watched him worriedly as they turned out of the car park on to Chaucer Road. I've offended him, she thought. My big mouth. She wouldn't blame him if he stopped this weird, enormous vehicle right now and threw her out.

But he kept driving. Soon they were sailing along Chaucer Road, and in a while she relaxed. The rain hissed down, the great wipers moved ponderously back and forth across the windscreen, the heater filled the car with an even warmth. They went past the bus stop. There was a line of people standing there, huddled unprotected in the storm. She recognised a couple of women from her class. Poor sods, she thought contentedly.

She glanced at him again. In the orange light of the street lamps the metal zip on his track suit gleamed dully. She stared at it for a moment.

'I didn't know you went to the Leisure Centre,' she said.

'Oh yes,' he nodded, after a moment. 'I work out on the Nautilus quite a lot.'

'That's strange. You didn't mention it when we had our talk. And I went on and on about the Centre.'

'Did you?'

'Don't you remember? I was trying to think of reasons why I liked living in Swayncliff . . . In fact, you said how I loved the Centre in your article.'

He turned out of Chaucer Road into the High Street. He nodded thoughtfully.

'That's right. I did . . . Yeah, I joined the Centre quite a time ago. I don't know why I didn't tell you.'

'Oh, it's not important.'

She glanced out of her side window. They were passing the Radio Rentals showroom. A dozen TV sets flickered away in the window, unwatched. Next to the showroom was the Swayncliff and Thanet Building Society. Three hundred and ten pounds of her money were held in there. My entire fortune, she thought, with a stir of panic. Apart from their car, the High Street was empty.

'And I was doing all the talking, of course.'

She felt she was acting too much like an interrogator. But she was still curious.

'I don't think I've seen you there before.'

'Well, you probably wouldn't have remembered if you had,' he pointed out. 'Though I don't think I'd have forgotten you.'

It was that note of unreserved admiration that she remembered so pleasantly from the interview. Nevertheless, before she could stop herself, she said, 'You forgot me tonight.'

He turned quickly to her, as if alarmed. She was disgusted with herself. Again that note of complaint in her voice, that mean whine. And he deserved so much more, her admirer, her only remaining fan . . . *No*. Stop that. You will not get maudlin tonight, Strang. She smiled warmly at him to show it was all right, she was only joking. Relieved, he shook his head.

'I don't know what came over me tonight. I had something on my mind, you see.'

'Really, I was joking.'

At the roundabout, he took the road that led to the coast.

'Sure it isn't out of your way?'

'Hardly at all,' he said.

She nestled deeper into her seat. The exhilaration she had gained from the exercise class had settled into a cosy glow in all her limbs. She felt a yawn coming up, and stifled it. The rain was slackening now. He switched the wipers to intermittent action.

'I was thinking about you the other day,' she said.

'About *me*?'

'Mm. When I read about that poor girl at the petrol station.'

'You've started to read the papers, have you?'

So he did remember some things she had said at the interview. It had happened when he was fiddling with his tape machine, reversing the cassette. She had asked him if this was his speciality, interviews, and he had smiled and told her that there were only three reporters on the *Argus*, no opportunity for any of them to be specialists, they all did pretty much whatever came along. He had leaned back in his chair, glanced at the machine to make sure the spools were turning again. 'It's sort of dull on the whole,' he had said. 'But once in a while something interesting comes along.' He nodded at her. 'Like today.'

'You must have had more interesting jobs than this,' she had smiled.

'Not really.'

'Go on!'

'Well . . .' He considered. 'The Sweet Shop Murder – that was pretty interesting. People from the nationals came down for that one. And from TV.'

She had shaken her head. 'I'm sorry – what sweet shop murder?' He was looking at her, surprised. 'I don't read the papers much,' she'd explained.

'Couple of months ago. Over on Merrick Street. This fellow came into the shop carrying a shotgun. Took about fifty pounds from the till – all they had. And then blasted away at the woman behind the counter.' He nodded. 'She died, eventually.'

'God! Merrick Street! Did they catch him?'

'Not yet.'

'God . . .' She'd stared at the machine. The little spools turned steadily on. Merrick Street was only a couple of hundred yards away. It was incredible that she had heard nothing about this. Once in a while it was brought home to her how much of a cocoon she was living in. She had shivered slightly – on her own behalf. And then she'd felt ashamed. It was not her who was at the centre of this drama. There was a poor, dead woman. There was a brute with a gun in his hands. Still on the loose. It was all horrible. She had said the first thing that came into her head.

'Can you imagine killing somebody for fifty pounds?'

She had laughed unhappily and shaken her head to show how much the idea shocked her. But then she found him looking at her in a strange way, not returning her smile, studying her. She had already got used to a steady flow of admiration from this man. It rattled her, and made her suddenly uneasy to be regarded so coolly by him.

'Have I said something wrong?'

'No. Not at all.'

'Then why are you – ?' Her face cleared suddenly. 'Oh, I *see*.' She'd nodded. Now her laugh was one of embarrassment. 'That's terrible, isn't it? Terrible of me. Of course – if he had taken a thousand pounds, if he'd taken ten thousand, it wouldn't have made any difference, would it?' Again she had shaken her head. 'How could you possibly set a price on a human life? How could I say such a thing? You must think I'm a . . .' She didn't know what to call herself.

'Absolutely not. I know just what you mean.' He had been about to proceed with the interview when she'd spoken up again.

'Please don't put that in your story.'

'What's that?'

‘That I was so . . . careless. About that poor woman.’

‘Course I won’t. You’ve got nothing to worry about.’

She’d thought for a moment. Perhaps she was overdoing it. She probably was. It had only been a casual, throw-away comment after all. Anybody could have said it.

(Nevertheless, when she’d finally read the story in the newspaper she’d felt anxious until she’d reassured herself that he’d been as good as his word and had not exposed her moment of foolishness.)

Now she smiled at him through the car’s gloom. ‘Actually, I was looking for your story about me. And I saw this thing about the petrol station.’ She faced front again. The wipers swept across the glass, stopped, waited, swept across again. ‘It’s the same man, isn’t it?’

‘Looks like it.’

‘It must be. How much did he get this time?’

‘Less than a hundred.’

She would not repeat the error she had made at the interview, though when she had read the account in the *Argus* it was again the gap between the horror of the crime and the murderer’s paltry gains that had most struck her. But it had occurred to her since that the real gain for him might not have been the cash.

‘He must hate women,’ she said.

He glanced at her. ‘Why do you say that?’

‘That’s who he kills.’

The wipers driving back and forth. The car slowing to take a bend in the road. So dark, it was hard to see immediately ahead. But out of her side window, towards the sea, the sky seemed lighter. They were headed that way.

‘I should think he kills them so they won’t be able to identify him. If it had been a man working at the petrol station he’d probably have got the same treatment.’

‘Maybe,’ she sighed after a while. ‘I suppose so . . . Are you working on that story too?’

He shook his head. ‘Somebody else has got it.’

They rose over the crest of a hill, the last hill before the coast. In front of them sea and sky appeared as if welded together in uniform blackness, except for the stars and where below them a few other points of light glimmered from ships standing out in the Channel. It was as if there were stars on the ground as well as in the sky. The moon was cloud hidden. Only the blackness and the widely separated pinpoints of light.

The car was slowing down.

‘I just want to stop here for a moment,’ he said.

He pulled on the hand brake, and switched the headlights off. No longer held back by the high beams, the darkness poured towards them. She leaned forward in her seat and stared through the windscreen intently.

'It's as if it never ends, isn't it,' she heard him say. 'Like outer space.'

And then a moment later, 'As if you could step off the edge of the world. And never be seen again.'

She heard a yearning in his voice and felt herself, without knowing why, responding. The darkness seemed so friendly to her, like a kind uncle – closer, like a father, with outstretched arms . . . as if she was a child again standing on a high and scarey wall, but it was all right, she could hurl herself across the void into those loving arms and not get hurt at all.

I would like that so much, she thought, to throw myself into those strong arms.

Did I think that? she thought, a moment later. But that isn't what I want. Surely it isn't. No matter how bad things have been, I have never wished for that before.

She turned to look at the man beside her. She could hardly see him, only the outline of a profile. Had he put such thoughts into her mind? she wondered. Or had his words searched out and discovered thoughts that were already there, that she had never been able to face before? She considered the question almost dispassionately.

'How have you been?' he said then suddenly, his tone surprising her, it was so conversational.

'Oh . . .'

All at once, it came to her that she was sitting in a stationary car, a mile from anywhere, in darkest night, beside a stranger. Practically a stranger. She remembered his first name suddenly. Raymond. That made her feel a little better.

'I've been OK.'

'Has that right part come along?'

'Sorry?'

'You said at the interview you've been waiting for the right part to come along. That's why we haven't seen you on our screens lately.'

'Ah. Yes . . . No, it hasn't come along yet.'

She thought about bringing up this wife of his, waiting at home for his return. Better move on, don't you think? Raymond? But then she thought, relax, what is the problem, for heaven's sake? It was an odd place to have a friendly conversation, practically on the edge of a cliff, but it was nice to have one at all in Swayncliff; and the fact was, she reminded herself, beggars can't be choosers. And he was a nice man, as far as she could tell, and respectful, and could be trusted not to harass her in any way . . .

'There are some interesting things in the air for me though,' she added.

'Really? That's great.' Then, almost fiercely, 'But you won't take anything unless it's absolutely right for you.'

It sounded like an order almost. She was silent for a time. Then she said quietly, 'You know, actors can't always choose exactly what they do. Somebody has to offer it to them first.'

'But they can choose what not to do.'

'Well, that's true.'

'And that's what you'll do. No rubbish for you.'

She laughed uncertainly. 'Oh, I don't know . . . Look, I've been in some pretty dreadful things in my time.' She had decided it was time to disabuse this fan of hers. However flattering to her, it was unfair to let him go on with these unrealistic notions. 'You know, some people even thought *The Entwistles* wasn't so hot.'

'Then they're crazy.'

'"Romantic tosh" I've heard it called.'

'What?' He swung round to face her.

'Soap opera.'

'*Soap* – who called it that?'

She shrank back, feeling without hardly seeing the force of his gaze. Oh Christ, she thought, what's going on?

'My husband said it actually . . . Well, he's my ex-husband. Sort of.'

He stared at her for several moments, then faced front again.

'I can't agree with him,' he said in a muffled voice.

She watched him, the shadow of his profile, and then she too turned in her seat to look out of the glass. The vision of night and eternity had lost all its appeal for her. She wished they would move on now. She really did. Oh, please start that damn engine, she begged silently.

But he was speaking again.

'*The Entwistles* was about everything that matters in life,' he said. 'Everything that really matters.'

Oh? Is that what you think? Right. She felt along the side of the door next to her. Where did they keep the damn handle on this huge space-ship?

'Well,' she breathed, 'it's nice of you to say so, of course . . .' *Where was the fucking handle?*

He ignored her. 'It was about love and fate and family and death – '

She heard a horribly strained note in his voice and in the same moment felt a trickle of real fear drift up the back of her neck. Oh, Jesus – she saw it all now. The rabid fan, the idol victim: she had heard those stories. Grace Barker, who had played Laura Kershaw, daughter of a rival clan which feuded constantly with the Entwistles, used to get threatening letters regularly. Terrible, menacing letters. 'I am coming for you, Laura, soon . . . very soon. Prepare to meet my phallic glory . . . prepare to meet my shining knife!' They were traced eventually to an old man living in Woodford, Essex. His daughter used to pop the letters in the post for him, not knowing what they contained. Old, bedridden, incontinent – it was a joke really, phallic glory and all. Even now she had an urge to giggle at the memory. But it might not have been a joke, and in any case it had given Grace a few bad weeks.

'I really ought to be getting home now,' she managed to say.

Her voice, she knew, was thin and wobbly, an invitation to mischief . . . But, dammit, she thought with a rush of courage, he's not going to find it so easy, he's going to get his scars too. She had taken a self-defence course once back in London. She tried to recall what she needed to know now. The vulnerable points: eyes, throat, groin. Hard to reach his groin when he's sitting like that. So eyes, throat . . .

Oh shit, she thought next, her courage ebbing as fast as it had come. O God, please help me . . . O God, oh shit –

'Of course,' he said gently. 'It's time to go.'

She looked at him, almost in disbelief. He had turned on the engine and the lights, they were heading away now, swinging back from the dark void, following the road as it ran beside the cliffs. Already she could see the lamps along the sea front, a dim half circle of light all around the bay.

She leaned back in her seat, relaxed, closed her eyes for a moment. Now her fright was passing, she felt ashamed at having panicked so easily. And ashamed too of her suspicions of this perfectly nice man beside her. Who had been kind enough to give her a lift home on a rainy night. When you have one fan left in the world, she thought grimly, the least you can do is not accuse him – mentally, all right, but that was bad enough – of being about to rape or butcher you . . . But it was the darkness that had scared her mostly. And now the lights of town were all around her, and she was safe, and anyway had never been in danger at all.

She glanced across at him. Raymond. Raymond Thorne. Ray for short, she supposed. Suddenly to her he looked very young, and – she peered at him carefully – he looked very hurt too. Was it me? she wondered, confused. Did I speak my suspicions out loud back there, any of them? Surely not. But maybe I upset him in some way, just thinking them. His face was screwed up as if he was on the edge of tears and was fighting them back. He took one hand off the steering wheel and passed it over his eyes. When his hand was gone, she saw a trace of moisture on his bony cheek.

Now what? In her life, in her world, she was not unused to the spectacle of men weeping. And she thought that on the whole, theoretically, she approved of it. In that it showed sensitivity, absence of the macho spirit, all of that. But right now what she mostly felt was a creeping embarrassment. She didn't know this man. Basically didn't know him from Adam. He had no right to cry openly in her presence, no right to intrude in this way.

But then she told herself crossly to stop it. Stop being so tight, indifferent, so English. The man was hurting. Evidently. There was trouble here. That was enough.

'Are you OK?' she asked cautiously.

After a moment, he spoke in a muffled voice, 'I'm sorry. Been a bit on edge lately.'

They were so close to her home now. What a pity they had not made it home a minute or two earlier. Then she stifled the thought. Here was a nice, shy, kind man who had shown her a great deal of welcome attention. She could afford to give a little in return.

'Is something wrong?' she asked. 'Do you want to talk about it?'

The car slowed down, pulled in at the curb. She glanced out of the window. Her building, right enough. He had delivered her to her door, safe and sound and dry. The yucca tree, the stained couch, and the two-barred fire waited for her upstairs. OK, she thought. He looks dreadful, but he doesn't want to talk about it. Perfectly understandable. Two strangers, friendly strangers. That was all they were, and no need to make anything more of it. On the whole, she was glad. She found the door handle, started to pull on it.

'Well, thanks so much for the lift.' She smiled tentatively, though he still wasn't looking at her. 'And I hope you're feeling better quite – '

'Nothing's exactly wrong. My father died at the weekend. That's all.'

The first thing she felt was a warm rush of relief. She had been expecting the worst, she realised. Some sad, sordid drama, something intimate probably about this wife of his which she, as a stranger, had no right to hear. But this – this was so normal. And understandable. The father had died – and the son was mourning. It was normal, decent, creditable. She let go of the door handle and moved instinctively towards him.

'I'm so sorry,' she murmured.

He did not look at her.

'It wasn't as if it was a surprise. He had a heart attack last spring, so we were more or less expecting the next one. But now it's happened . . .' He shook his head. 'I dunno. It's brought up all these feelings in me.'

'How old was he?'

'Seventy-three.'

'Well . . .'

'Yes,' he nodded. 'I know. He lived out his time, had a fairly good innings, all that. It's all quite normal, I know it is. But, still . . .'

His head drooped forward, he was staring at the centre ring of the steering wheel. She had an urge to put her arm round his shoulders, but couldn't do it, not quite. She must do something for him though. There was not much time, but she felt she could help him, if only a little. She was equipped for it, she reminded herself. Empathy, understanding, responsiveness – they had all been part of her professional training.

No, but it was more than that. She could help him because – because she was his friend. She really felt that. Something had happened. It was just the beginning, but they were not strangers any more. The ride they had shared, even those few strange minutes on top of the cliff, most of all what he had just confided to her had changed things fundamentally. They'd made contact. It made her feel very good to think that.

'Were you close to him?' she asked, suppressing a smile of contentment. Friends.

'Close?' he repeated vaguely. He was silent for a moment. And then, to her surprise, he laughed suddenly, a short, unhappy laugh.

'What?'

'Oh, I was thinking . . .' He looked round at her. 'If you'd asked me that ten years ago – five years even . . .'

'Yes?'

'I'd probably have said I hated him.'

This, she thought, in the silence that followed, is not going to be so easy. Still, she would like to help if she could – and also, she admitted to herself, his announcement had definitely added to her interest. There was a story here, and she had always loved to hear a new story. Like anyone else would, she told herself immediately. It was only human nature. She hesitated, then said, 'Look, do you want to come up to my place? Have a cup of coffee? Talk it over?'

Immediately he shook his head. No, she remembered, wifey was waiting. She had a sudden mental image of wifey – a Flopsy Bunny in a red-checked apron, waiting by the front door with a rolling pin. And then was puzzled by the contempt she felt for this unknown woman.

'I don't want to be indoors,' he said quietly. He turned to her. 'But I wouldn't mind taking a walk with you. I'd be grateful for that.'

'A walk?'

'Just along the front.'

She couldn't resist saying, 'Won't your wife be worrying about you?'

He smiled faintly. 'I was only thinking of, say, ten minutes.' He looked at the windscreen. 'It's not raining at all.'

He seemed, in his shy way, to be almost begging her.

'Of course,' she said, 'I'd be happy to walk with you.'

4

They had been walking for five minutes before a word was said. They had come from the eastern edge of the Esplanade, that point just outside Susan's building where the lamps that stood at regular intervals began to be entwined with strings of light bulbs that shone red, yellow and green during the season. 'The Illuminations' the tourist brochures called them. They were turned off in mid-September every year, not to be switched on again until the second week of June. When the first half-dozen of these lamps had been passed by, the sea-front business district began: Chiari's Ice Cream Parlour, Dallas Hamburgers, Glitterland, Krazy Golf, the Neptune Café (Soft Drinks, Chips, Cream Teas). They were all shut now, some for the night, most for the winter, a couple perhaps for ever for the holiday season had been particularly bad that year.

'I've got you out here, and now I don't know what to say,' he sighed at last.

'You don't have to say anything really.'

'No, but I'd like to talk. I ought to talk.' His tone was baffled, almost angry. 'Trouble is – it doesn't make much sense, even to me.'

Silence again. Except for them, the Esplanade was deserted. Above, the damp air made yellow indefinite haloes around the lamps. The light these cast was weak, illuminating only a circle a few feet in diameter at the base of each lamp standard. All the rest lay in darkness.

'What did you quarrel about? You and your father?'

'Politics,' he said.

She had been expecting almost anything but this.

'We quarrelled about politics, that's the truth.' He ducked his head, embarrassed. 'It's probably hard to imagine, I know – but I was pretty radical once. In fact, you might say I was a revolutionary.'

There was something very boyish about his manner. He was so thin and solemn and awkward. And she was open to that sort of adolescent appeal, she knew. Mark had had it by the spadeful. She saw that he was frowning now, assuming an air of great seriousness. So sweet and grave. Like a wise child.

'You were?'

'Oh, yes. Really committed.' He was silent for a moment. Then he nodded. 'At school I became a Marxist. A kid called Lefferts got me interested. Jewish kid . . . Not that it matters, he just happened to be one. I was grateful to him. All of a sudden I could understand things. I could understand the whole world now.' His laugh was like a sneer. 'And I thought – give me a couple of years, I could tear it all down with my bare hands! No problem.'

Whoah, she thought, slow down. This – indeed this was not what she'd expected.

'I'm sorry. I don't quite understand. What's this to do with your father?'

'My father was a fascist.'

Now what did that mean? Couple of Tory posters in the window at election time? She frowned. She hated this kind of imprecision and inflation. Bad actors were usually bad in just that way.

'No.' He had seen her frown. 'I mean – he was a real fascist. As far as an Englishman could be one. Back in the thirties he'd marched with Mosley. At least,' Raymond said, 'he wrote for Mosley.' He lowered his head and muttered, 'You see, my father was John Blackstone.'

On their right, the Anchor Pub, Breezytime Bingo, the Winter Gardens, Madame Melissa – Fortunes Told, the latter closed for two seasons now, though the board still hung in place. Susan had had her palm read there once. Madame Melissa had stunk mellowly of Guinness. All the signs were excellent, she'd said.

Raymond laughed suddenly. 'Doesn't mean a thing to you. Does it?'

'Well . . .'

'I forget. You'd have to be in your sixties, probably your seventies, for it to mean much. And even then – who'd remember my father now?'

'I know quite a bit about Mosley though,' she offered, wanting to encourage him. 'I was in a TV play once. Long ago. A drama-doc. Mosley was the main character. I just had a tiny part . . .'

Leonard Cope had played Oswald Mosley. She remembered him stalking around the rehearsal room in Acton, muttering to himself, giving stiff-armed salutes in corners. Once he had confided to her that he was longing to start work on the scenes of Mosley's mass meetings. He saw himself high on a rostrum, alone, picked out by a single powerful spotlight, two or three hundred extras hanging on his every move. A roll of drums, the arena comes to attention, the Leader speaks . . . But in the end the production had been unable to afford these extravaganzas and had had to use news footage of the pre-war rallies of British Fascists instead. Leonard's disappointment had been intense.

'Well, my father was pretty close to Mosley. He wrote for their papers, *Action*, *Blackshirt*. He got to be assistant editor of *Blackshirt*, and he couldn't have been more than twenty-two, twenty-three at the time. And he was damn good at it.' She could not miss the note of pride in the son's voice. 'He was famous then. Notorious anyway. He was the only fascist writer the Left feared at all. They used to call him the "Viper", and he certainly sank his fangs in.'

Raymond fell silent, brooded for a while. When he spoke again his voice was controlled and terse. 'When I discovered what he'd been – I was seventeen, still at school – I wanted to find out all about it. It's not hard. They've got this newspaper library at Colindale, up in north London. I sat in that bloody room all one day. Read everything he wrote. And it was . . .' He paused. 'Disgusting. Cruel. Vicious.' Then he shrugged. 'And brilliant too. There's no other word. My father had a gift.'

He stopped walking and stood at the railings, looking out at the dim, shifting shape of the sea. She stood beside and a little behind him. After a while she touched his elbow. He turned round. The lamplight gave his skin, stretched tightly across the prominent bone structure of his face, an almost translucent quality. His fine eyes, with their large, light pupils, shone in the vague yellow glow. Montgomery Clift, she thought. On the tip of her tongue since she'd first met him. That's who he reminded her of. Not nearly as beautiful, of course; but it was there in the strangely luminous eyes, the tentative smile, the manner that was a mixture of assertion and hesitancy . . .

(Late nights, early mornings, crouched on her sofa, watching old movies. Dead film stars. With Mark beside her. 'The quickest way out of Swayncliff,' he used to say.)

'Tell me more,' she murmured.

He smiled slightly, a shy Clift smile. 'More about the Viper?'

He faced the sea again. 'They put him in prison during the war. A danger to the safety of the realm. Lies, of course. My dad and his friends wanted nothing so much as to fight for the safety of the realm. Camp Peel, Isle of Man. That's where he was for four years. Like Alcatraz.'

Raymond turned away from the railings and began to walk again at a fast pace. She had to make long strides to catch him up. As she did, he slowed down for her.

'After you read what he wrote . . .?'

'Oh, I went home and yelled at him. It was quite a scene. There's me in my corner, all righteous, shouting my head off. There was my dad – just sitting there, taking it – my father . . .' He stopped. Thought for a moment. 'I guess he always knew he'd have to explain himself to me one day. In his own time. But I found out before he was ready.' He looked at her. 'He'd left it too late, you see.'

'How did you find out?'

'My brother told me.'

'Brother?'

'Yuh. I got an older brother. Phillip. He told me. Just to see how I'd take it.' Raymond smiled. 'You'd have to know Phil to understand that . . . So there we were. Me and my dad. I told him I was going to have to change my name – the shame being so great, you see. And I did it. I've been Thorne ever since – my mother's maiden name. I told him too I wasn't going to live under his roof any more, my actual words.' He smiled again. 'And that was no idle threat either. Since I was off to medical school in a couple of months – '

'Medical school?'

'Yeah, I studied medicine for a while. That was my first love. But I had a bust up with a couple of the profs. Through jealousy mostly. On their part. So I switched to a fine arts course.'

'I'm sorry,' she said after a moment. 'I interrupted you.'

'Nothing much else to tell,' he sighed. 'Except my dad certainly looked like a squashed-up old viper when I'd finished with him.'

In silence they turned at the end of the Esplanade and began to retrace their steps. She wanted him to tell more, had many questions, but judged it best not to try and force him, to let it come out as he wished.

'I didn't see him for years,' Raymond went on at last. 'Just once when Mum died. And I didn't speak to him even then. I should have done. It was the right time. Mum hated it that we had quarrelled and there she was, dead. But – ' He shrugged. 'Just didn't happen.'

'Did you ever make it up?'

'In the end,' he nodded. 'Couple of years ago, bit more maybe. It was my wife's doing really.'

'How?'

'She just said, over and over, it was daft, it was about nothing that made sense any more. And she was right. Dad had left all that stuff behind him forty years ago. And I – ' He smiled sideways at her. 'I wasn't much of a revolutionary by then. Never had been really. Just . . . full of shit. So what did it matter? Course it didn't. One morning I got in the car and went up to Canterbury, to his house . . .'

'And?'

'He was glad to see me. We had a long talk. I stayed the night. We've been pretty good friends ever since. Were good friends,' he changed it to sadly.

They had reached the business district again, the clock tower was just ahead. Then Glitterland, Dallas Hamburgers . . .

'Look, excuse me – ' she began. Then was unsure how to go on. She tried again. 'Look, this is all about politics.'

'You asked what me and my father quarrelled about,' he pointed out.

'I know I did. But, look . . . I used to go to this sort of group once. Sort of psychotherapy group – mostly for interest's sake,' she added quickly, seeing him glance at her. 'And I thought it might help my work. Though I was feeling a bit sad at the time too. But what I mean is: I think if they'd been listening to you – all this political stuff – they would have said you were hiding something behind it.'

'I'm sorry,' he said after a moment. 'Don't follow you. Hiding what?'

'Well, I don't know, do I?' She was beginning to feel a little desperate. Also that she was being bloody inquisitive. 'I mean, how did you *feel* about your father?'

'Oh . . . well, he was my father, you see.'

'But did you like him? When you knew him again, did you like him as a person?'

'Oh, yes,' Raymond said vaguely. 'He was quite likeable.'

Highly disappointing, she thought. But it was clear it was all she was going to get from him tonight.

'Well, I'm glad you made it up with him.'

'Yes, it was a good thing.' He looked at her warmly. 'Thanks for letting me go on about it.'

What are friends for? she was about to say. Then remembered that he might not know yet that that was what they had become. So she said instead, 'It must be a difficult time for you now.'

'Lot of running around,' he agreed. 'Death certificate. Undertakers. Funeral.'

'When is it?'

'Friday morning.'

'In Canterbury?'

'No. Here. Dad moved down to Coveney a year ago.'

Coveney, she knew, was a small village two miles east of Swaycliff. 'Are you having to do everything yourself?'

'Well, Kate's been terrific – '

'Kate?'

'My wife – she's done a lot. But I've had to do most of it, it's only right.'

'Can't your brother help?'

'Phil's not around.'

'Where is he?'

'In Atlanta, I think.'

She looked at him, surprised.

'My brother flies for an airline. Heathrow-Atlanta. Or Heathrow–Calcutta. He alternates. I spoke to him on the phone last night. He can't get away just now. He reckons he can make it for the funeral – '

'Well, I should hope so!'

'But only just. So that leaves me and Kate.'

They stopped walking. They were outside her building. He looked across the street. 'Well . . . here we are.'

'Yes.' She felt strangely cut off. She wanted to know more. She was sure there was more to know. Characters had been introduced and yet hardly explored at all. This wife, who had a name now at least, and was so wise and helpful. This brother whose feet hardly ever seemed to touch firm ground. The father. If this was on TV she would have to wait a week to find out what happened next. In this case she might never know more than she did now.

Still there was nothing to be done about it. He seemed to have cheered up a bit, and she thought she had been of some help there, and was glad of it. She smiled at him.

'Thanks for driving me home.'

'Thanks for walking with me.'

'Perhaps we'll run into each other again. At the Centre?'

'Maybe.'

He didn't sound very interested in the possibility.

'I hope it'll be all right on Friday. And up to then.'

He nodded. 'It'll be all right . . . Dad was ready to go, I think he was. He'd had enough.' He looked away from her. 'The only thing that's not so good – well, Mum's dead. Now Dad. It's the end of the story, right? It's all over.'

She wanted to say: not so long as you remember them. But it

seemed suddenly too easy, too glib. He was right. It had been so with her own parents. A story had ended, no avoiding it. She held out her hand, and he took it. Though they might not see each other again, it didn't seem false at all to hold his hand tightly for a long moment.

'Good night,' she said.

'I'll wait till I see your lights come on.'

She smiled. 'Oh, I always feel safe in Swayncliff.' Then all at once she thought: dead woman in the sweet shop, dead woman at the petrol station. 'Do you remember which flat it is?'

'Third floor. On the left.'

She thought about him, his sadness and his story, all the way up the dark stone staircase. Opening the door, she made haste to switch on the lights to signal to him that he could leave. After a moment, standing near but not at the window, she heard a car start up and then drive away. He had waited for her.

She felt hungry then and went into the kitchen and served herself a bowl of cornflakes and milk. Eating at the living-room table, she still thought of Raymond Thorne. And then it occurred to her that for quite a long time she had actually been absorbed by a situation, a story, that was not her own. She felt so good about that, and felt great gratitude towards him. She wondered if it was a good sign, a sign that she would get better one day soon, be happier, that life and luck were going to change for her.

Then she realised that she was once more back to thinking about herself. Back in the trenches – and after all she had only escaped from them for a pitifully short time. How long had she spent with him this evening? An hour? Ninety minutes at most. Ninety minutes away from her own damn self. Pitiful.

She was all set, she knew it, for a lengthy session of berating herself, and then of berating herself still further for taking so much time on her own problems – when there was a sudden pounding on her front door. Three or four heavy blows. From where she sat, she could see the door knob quiver as it was shaken and turned from the other side. Then came a hoarse, ragged voice, shouting. Mostly incomprehensible, but a few key words could be made out. 'Whore!' she heard. 'Bitch!' And, 'You wait, you little tart!'

Oh shit, thought Susan, here we go again.

She got up and crossed swiftly to the front door and threw it open. Even so, she was too late to confront the culprit. She stepped out on to the dark landing. She heard a faint scuffling noise from up above.

'Now that's enough!' she called out. Then, 'Mrs Baklova?'
Silence.

'You're not to do that any more,' Susan called. 'Do you hear me?'

There was the sound of a door closing, very quietly. Silly old bitch, she thought. Poor old bitch. Then, almost as the door closed upstairs, she heard another one opening down below. The light came on in the landing downstairs. Susan went to the banister rail.

'Sorry, Miss Chalmers,' she called down.

The old lady, frail, stooped, beautiful, wrapped in a lavender dressing gown, peered up at her.

'Is that silly old woman up to her tricks again?' asked Miss Chalmers.

'I'm afraid so.'

'It's too bad of her.'

'Oh, well . . . she's been quiet for ages. Mustn't complain.'

Susan smiled at her downstairs neighbour and started to withdraw into her own flat.

'Oh,' said Miss Chalmers, 'I've got a letter for you, dear.'

'For me?'

'Just wait a moment.'

Miss Chalmers hobbled back into her flat. Susan came downstairs to the front door.

'There, you see,' said the old lady, showing her the envelope. 'They've put Flat 2C on it, instead of 3C.'

'Thanks.' Susan took the envelope. On the back flap was Dick Banham's name and address. He had replied! Weeks late, the old sod, but still he had written. She smiled happily at Miss Chalmers. 'Good job they didn't put Flat 4C!'

'Wretched old woman!' Miss Chalmers shuddered theatrically. She could have been an actress, Susan often thought. She must have had the looks, and she certainly had the style. But she had been a teacher in a private school for girls, in fact.

'Well, good night Miss Chalmers.'

'Good night dear.'

Susan paused for a moment at her own front door. She stared upwards through the gloom towards Mrs Jane Baklova's landing.

I'm not going to end up like you, she thought. Daft old bat.

As she cleared away the bowl and spoon from the dining table, it occurred to her that she was not all that keen on ending up like Miss Esmé Chalmers either. Though always sweet and presentable in public, the other old lady spent most of the day and half the night talking to herself. If she listened for it, in her own flat. Susan could usually hear Miss Chalmers murmuring away down there, as constant as the sea.

I've got to get out of here soon, Susan thought. She settled down near the electric fire and slit open the envelope. (Good old Dick, he'd come through for her after all.) I've got to get out because I am not going to dwindle away here and waste my life.

I am not going to do it for very much longer anyway, she corrected herself then. I'm not old and I'm not helpless and I do still have my wits about me. I'm sure I do. I'm sure one day I'm going to wake up from this dream and I'm going to get out of here. No question about it. Because I am a survivor.

★

To: Dick Banham
47 Drake Mansions
Lyla Road
London SW18

Nov 4th

Dear Dick,

Thanks for your letter. Don't worry about it taking so long to reply. As a matter of fact I'd forgotten I'd written to you, so no offence was taken!

I'm pleased to hear everything is going so well for you. Your new project sounds most exciting. West Indies! Lucky you. Jeannie Ricketts, I've always thought, is a most unusual person. You both deserve each other. Are wedding bells on the horizon? Or am I being premature? Old-fashioned?

Dick, there was one part of your letter I didn't quite understand. The bit where you write 'Honestly, Sue, I haven't got anything I could seriously offer you right now, or in the near future, so perhaps this isn't quite the right time for us to meet.' I'm embarrassed to think, Dick, that *you'd* think that the reason I wrote to you was in hopes of a job. I can't really think how you got that idea. I thought I told you quite clearly in my letter that things were, in fact, in that respect going rather well for me. Without wishing to boast.

You probably got the wrong impression because I sent you that stupid photograph. Really – I feel a bit silly explaining it – I just did that as a sort of friendly gesture. A souvenir or something.

I think what I'm saying is – it seems a pity that I can't write to an old friend, who happens to be a director, without that old friend jumping to all the wrong conclusions.

Sorry if that sounds a bit cold. The truth is that I am more and more aware that things like jobs, careers, et cetera, all that sort of thing that seems so important up in London, don't amount to very much when viewed in perspective. A good friend of mine down here has just lost his father. When I see his sadness, and how dignified he is in his mourning,

I get a true sense of what is important in life and what isn't. And frankly, Dick, getting a job in some play or film or other, even one directed by your own good self, is just not that totally crucial.

So I'm sorry we're not going to be seeing each other soon. And I'm even sorrier that I wrote you a letter that could be interpreted so incorrectly.

Love to Jeannie.
Be well,
Susie

P.S. I note you refer to Swayncliff as 'the sticks' in your letter. I suppose we are a bit off the map down here. Isn't it funny though? When I lived in London we all used to think that your new address was more or less where 'the sticks' began!

5

He was waiting in the same place, in the lobby beside the glass doors. When she saw him, the moment she left the changing room, she realised how much she'd been hoping he'd be there. She had been worrying about him, on and off, during the week. Last Friday, the day of his father's funeral, he'd been on her mind all day.

But keep it light, she told herself as she crossed the lobby, keep it casual. Though he had opened up to her so much last time, under the stress of his father's death, she had no right to assume that he would ever want to be so frank with her again. They hardly knew each other really. They were just a couple of fellow Leisure Centre members bumping into each other by chance for the second week running. So keep it merry.

'We've got to stop meeting each other like this!' she smiled as she came up to him. Which didn't sound merry, she realised instantly, but facetious. Worse, somewhat pathetic. Her smile grew brittle and anxious.

He ducked his head – a shy mannerism that by now was so familiar to her – and returned her smile.

'It's not a coincidence this time,' he admitted. 'After the Nautilus, I looked in at the dance studio and saw you were there. So I thought I'd wait around. Felt a bit stupid about saying no to a drink last time. Maybe we could have one now?'

'Are you sure your wife won't be worrying about you? You must have got home pretty late last week.'

He shook his head. 'I told Kate if I saw you we might have a drink. She was very interested to hear about you. Very keen on *The Entwistles* too, you see.'

Susan felt strangely disconcerted to hear that. She had no idea why. She was quite clear that she had no designs on this man, nice as he'd been to her. But the idea that the wife had in a way given permission for their meeting made her feel rather rebellious.

He was waiting for her answer.

'Of course. Sure. I'll have a drink.'

'Great. I can run you home afterwards.'

'Oh, well . . .'

He looked at her, his eyes were suddenly troubled. 'Listen,' he started. He hesitated, then made a rush at it: 'Listen, if you don't want me around, you just have to say so. I'm very easy to brush off.' Again the embarrassed duck of the head. 'It's just I was grateful to you for letting me talk – you know – like I did last week. I just wanted to show my appreciation.'

'Let's have a drink,' she said.

The Metropolitan Bar was a popular feature at the Centre. The bar itself was tucked away behind a wall of vegetation. The main space, carpeted throughout, was filled with sofas and armchairs, modernistic in style, arranged in groups, each group circling a low-level glass and steel table. No fire burned in the brick fireplace, the room was warmed by underfloor heating. But there was a pleasing arrangement of brass objects in and around the grate: poker, toasting fork, tongs and a coal bucket, fire screen, all polished and shining. The dusky orange walls were lined with sideboards, writing desks, a set of china displayed on a Welsh dresser, pine bookshelves that contained real books. Landscapes and seascapes by local artists hung at intervals along the walls, a price tag fixed discreetly in the corner of each frame. None of them cost over fifty pounds. Ceramic bowls and urns were placed at several points, containing an assortment of indoor plants, including one of a variety Susan had in her own living room. When they'd first met, Raymond had asked about it and she'd had to confess she couldn't remember what it was called. She pointed it out as they settled with their drinks at a table beside the curtained french windows.

'It's *Philodendron hastatum*,' he told her. 'I went and looked it up after I interviewed you.'

She stared at him, pleased and surprised. 'That was resourceful!'

'Oh, I don't like to be in the dark about anything.' He raised his glass. 'Cheers.'

He sipped at his drink, then settled it on the low table. She held on to her glass and watched him.

'So . . . how did it go? I'm dying to know.' She had not struck the right note. She added more carefully, 'Was it all right, the funeral?'

'Oh, yes,' he nodded. 'It was fine. There weren't many people there. We didn't expect many. We don't have a lot of relatives left, and Dad wasn't much good at making friends. But there were enough there, it wasn't awkward. Kate fixed a terrific spread at the house, and people seemed to think we'd done everything just about right.' He grinned. 'And I was relieved.'

'Relieved?'

'Yup. I had an idea some of Dad's old comrades would turn up. Fire a salute over his grave or whatever they do. But they didn't show. I suppose there aren't many of them left by now.'

She finished her drink. It was her round now but looking at the glass that he had replaced on the table she saw that it was still half full. He was looking around the room as if he was quite a stranger to the place. He was so thin, the lines of his face sharp, deep hollows under the bones. That wife of his might be a marvel at cooking up funeral feasts, but she was no good at putting flesh on her husband . . . And that was a prehistoric thought, she realised guiltily. He could perfectly well take responsibility for his own diet. A nice thick steak would do him a lot of good, plenty of potatoes, gravy . . .

'Well, I'm glad,' she said hastily, 'that it went off well.'

'Oh, yes . . .'

There was something in his voice that made her stare curiously at him. He noticed her gaze, smiled reluctantly.

'There was one rather weird thing that happened.'

'Weird?'

'Sort of,' Raymond nodded. 'Sort of strange . . . You see, we went over to Dad's before the service to check everything was all right. The food and everything. Give the place a last quick hoover . . .'

'And?'

'And when we drove up outside the house, we saw the front door was open. Well, we knew nobody was staying there – '

'Burglars?'

'That's what we thought.'

'I've heard they read the obituaries. On the look out for deserted houses.'

'But it wasn't burglars.'

He lifted his glass and drained it. Looked across at her placidly.

'Like another one?'

'Not now!' She was half laughing in her impatience. 'I want to know what happened next. Who was it? . . . I know!' she cried. 'Your brother?'

'Not exactly.'

'Raymond! Tell me.'

It was the first time she had called him that. They looked at each other. Raymond was the first to look away.

'OK . . . There we were. Open door. Kate was all for going right in and seeing what was up. I thought we should get the police.' Raymond smiled. 'Kate's like that. I'm always the cautious one . . . In the end, we went inside. But cautiously. Soon as we got past the door, I shouted, "Anybody there?" To give 'em time to get away, you know? I'm no hero. But right away back came this voice, "Hello! Who is that?" Very cheery voice. I'd never heard it before. It was coming from my father's study, at the back of the house. Which he always kept locked. And when we went a bit further along the hall, we saw the study door was open.'

'Burglars,' breathed Susan, watching him intently.

'I said it wasn't burglars.' His tone was unexpectedly impatient, almost as if he thought he was speaking to a fool. She looked at him, more surprised than offended. He didn't notice. He was deep in his story.

'I looked inside. There were a couple of guys in the study. One in his forties, say, the other younger. Both very nicely dressed. The older guy is at Dad's bookshelves. He's on a little ladder. He's taking down each book, saying something to the fellow next to him, who writes it down in a notebook every time. Well, they stopped as soon as they saw us. And they smile at us, easy as can be. "Hello!" the older guy says. "Who the hell are you?" I say. "And what are you doing in my father's study?" . . . Sure you won't have another drink?'

'Who were they? What were they doing?'

'Would you believe they were appraisers? From an auction room up in London. My brother had sent them to value Dad's collection. Well, I'm going to have another drink,' Raymond said, standing up. 'Same again for you?'

She nodded automatically. Then she recollected herself. She reached for her bag.

'Let me pay.'

He shook his head. 'My treat.'

She was left to sit there, full of questions not yet answered. She looked across the room. A woman from her exercise class was talking intently to a skinny male companion. They were leaning towards each other close, heads almost touching. They were like conspirators, she thought – or guilty lovers – the rest of the world held unregarded beyond their ardent concentration on each other. She wondered if the man was her husband. Probably not. Married people didn't carry on so fervently with one another, not in her experience. Except when Mark and I –

No. Don't need to think of that.

That couple across the room, anyway – that was a love affair, for sure. And then she thought: if they'd looked across here a minute ago they'd have seen her and Raymond apparently wrapped up in each other's regard, talking like lovers themselves. It was so easy to jump to the wrong conclusions, fatally easy. Which notion brought up thoughts of bloody Dick Banham. Though that wasn't really fair. He hadn't jumped to any wrong conclusions. Of course she'd been after a job when she'd written to him. And – she forced herself to admit this – it wasn't his fault if he didn't have one to give her. All the same, he hadn't needed to make her feel so small when he turned her down, didn't have to rub her nose in it. It made her so angry, just thinking about it. So *angry* –

'It's a nice room this, isn't it?' said Raymond as he set their fresh drinks on the table. 'Almost like being in somebody's living room.'

'So it is.' She dismissed Banham from mind, dismissed the couple across the room. Turned with pleasure back to Raymond and his adventures. 'What do you mean "appraisers"? What were they appraising?'

He nodded. 'Those two blokes. Yes . . . You see my father made his living buying and selling books. Some antiques too, but mostly books. That was the trade part of it. But he also collected on his own account. You know, in a small way. First editions and so on. Manuscripts. Autographs. He'd been doing that since the thirties.'

'And your brother sent these people to appraise this collection?'

Raymond nodded again. 'I suppose it would have to be valued at some time or other. And as we're the only two heirs – far as I know – I guess one of us had to arrange it.'

'But on the day of the funeral! That's ghoulish.'

'Oh, I don't think Phil intended that. He just didn't think. He gave these guys the keys and told them what he wanted, and they just happened to pick that particular morning to do the job. Just a coincidence. They were very embarrassed when we explained about the funeral. They wanted to leave right away. But we said – no, now you're here, might as well carry on. Kate made us all a cup of tea. They finished before long. They were out before the first guests showed up. So it all turned out all right.' Raymond wetted his lips from his glass. 'It was just a bit strange, that's all.'

'It was very thoughtless of your brother,' she said sternly.

'Ah, well . . . Phillip.' He shrugged.

There was something that she was quite curious about now. But wasn't certain if it was in good taste to put the question.

She sipped her drink. She looked around. The woman from her class and her skinny companion had gone. Just disappeared, and she hadn't noticed.

Oh, well, she thought, I *am* curious.

'This collection, is it – I mean, if it's going to be sold up in London, does that mean it might be quite valuable?'

Raymond considered the question. He shook his head slowly.

'Hard to say. I never thought about it much. I mean, I always knew it was there. Dad was very careful about keeping his study locked. There were bars at the windows too, and a burglar alarm just for that room. But probably the stuff he had was mainly of sentimental value.'

She could see that. An old man's treasure trove, a lifetime's hoarding, trinkets and souvenirs precious only to himself.

'On the other hand,' Raymond said thoughtfully, 'these auctioneer fellows seemed quite impressed. The older guy told me that in his opinion Dad had bought early and bought well. And they were very interested in the manuscripts too. Dad had a lot of political stuff from before the war.'

'What political stuff?'

'Fascist stuff,' said Raymond shortly. 'Anyway they didn't want to give any figures – well, I didn't like to ask them, of course, considering what day it was. But, as I say, they seemed impressed.'

'So you might be rich!' she cried happily. Then, 'I'm sorry. That was crass.'

He chuckled. 'Shouldn't think I'll be rich. Also it's got to be split two ways, me and my brother. But there should be a few hundred coming to me, maybe a couple of thousand.' He chuckled again. 'So I might be able to get the roof fixed this year after all.'

They were the only people in the room now. Distantly the beat of dance music from the exercise rooms could be heard, and the squeak of rubber soles from the squash courts up above. Raymond glanced at his watch. He'd be wanting to go soon, she thought, to get back to Kate.

'I can't get over what your brother did, though.'

'I told you – ' He seemed rather bored with the subject. 'He wouldn't have known these blokes would arrive on the day of the funeral.'

'But not to tell you he was doing it at all . . . He didn't tell you, did he?'

Raymond smiled and shook his head. 'Complete surprise.'

'Well, I think it's extraordinary. Did he apologise to you?'

'Hasn't yet.'

'You didn't talk about it at the funeral?'

'He wasn't at the funeral.'

'What?' She stared at him in dismay.

'Couldn't make it. He was half-way across the Atlantic when Dad was buried. On the way to Atlanta. Some other pilot got sick, so he agreed to take over.'

'Well, that's incredible!' she fumed at length. It had taken her several seconds to find the words and she felt they were very far from adequate. 'You mean he had time to fix up having your father's collection valued, but he couldn't make it to the funeral? His own *father*?'

'That's my big brother,' Raymond shrugged.

'He sounds dreadful!'

'Oh, well . . .'

'No, I mean it. That's the most disgusting thing I've ever heard. How do you stand him?'

He looked past her into the empty room. 'I've got used to Phillip,' he said.

She started to protest. About this awful, unfeeling, world-travelling brother, about Raymond's lack of fire in condemning him – when she saw he was about to speak again.

'Things have never been that easy between us,' Raymond said quietly. 'I've learned to get along with him – more or less – but for a long time things weren't so good.'

At that moment a crowd of young men in shorts, sweaty and excited from the volleyball court, came rollicking into the room. She heard Raymond now through a din of braying laughs, insults, shouted orders for drinks.

'I guess it all started back home,' he said.

'Back home?'

He grinned. 'That slipped out. I guess I mean: back in Australia.'

'That's it!' She sat up straight. 'Your accent. I couldn't place it. Australia!'

He grinned again, sheepishly. 'Still shows, does it?'

'Now and then.'

'I don't know why. I left the place when I was fourteen, never been back.'

Some of the new arrivals now moved to occupy a group of armchairs near theirs, and began to heckle each other and those friends still beside the bar. Susan grimaced at the young men, then turned back to Raymond. 'Your brother? Things weren't good between you?'

His eyes seemed hooded now, and she could not read them. 'They weren't. I'll tell you what,' he said quietly – aggravatingly quietly, she had to strain to hear him against the surrounding racket, 'there was a time, when we were kids, when I – '

'When you hated him.'

He looked up. Stared at her for a moment. 'Why did you say that?'

Because I know how you think. I can read you now, and I'm getting better and better at it.

It could not be said, of course. It would scare him off, she was sure, if he suspected that.

'Isn't that what you were going to say?' She smiled at him reassuringly. 'I just thought it might be.'

He watched her for a moment, and then lowered his head. 'Not exactly. I was going to say: there was a time when the thing I most wanted to do with Phillip . . .'

'Yes?'

'Was kill him.'

A great shout of laughter rose from the nearby mob. Raymond reached for his glass and drained it in one swallow. He leaned towards her politely then.

'It's getting a bit noisy,' he said. 'Shall we get out of here?'

6

He was eight years old when he decided his brother needed killing; his brother was just eleven.

(They were in the car now, heading for Susan's home. Left out of the Leisure Centre car park, down Chaucer Road, on to the High Street. She was leaning against her door, turned to him, watching him, listening.)

That was in 1954. The summer of '54, just after Christmas. They – father, mother, little Raymond – were living in a small town called Baccara Bay, on the Victoria coast, just within commuting distance of Melbourne. Looking back, it had probably been a pretty deadly place, Raymond thought. A Down-Under Swayncliff. But to a child it had seemed like paradise. They lived near the beach and near a park; there were wide lawns to play on, empty roads to race tricycles on, there was sunshine, fresh air. Australia was the place then that people went out to 'for the children's sake'. John Blackstone, of course, after the war, had other reasons for wanting to leave a Mother Country that had treated him so badly. But whatever circumstances had brought his parents to their exile, Raymond always saw it as a piece of fantastic luck to have been able to spend his earliest years in Baccara Bay. Really, until that summer, it was a paradise without a serpent.

It was John Blackstone's second marriage. He had married Raymond's mother towards the end of the war, about eight months after his release from Camp Peel. A year later the couple sailed for Australia. Back in England, along with a discarded first wife, the father had left behind a three-year-old boy, his son and Raymond's half-brother. Of the existence of this brother, a whole world away, Raymond was always kept aware. As an only child – which effectively he was – he would complain sometimes about his solitary state. He wanted brothers, sisters; all his friends seemed to live in the midst of teeming families, and he didn't want to be different. (Much later he learned that his mother was unable to bear more children.) His father would try to cheer him up when he got into these moods, pointing out that in the paradise of Baccara Bay he had very many friends and playmates, reminding him always that he did indeed have a brother all of his own, even though he was twelve thousand miles away.

('I don't understand. I thought your father was in prison all through the war.'

'He was, practically.'

'Then how did he manage, how was your brother – ? If he was three when the war ended . . .?'

'They let the prisoners have visitors, of course.' Raymond sounded a bit impatient at the interruption. 'Conjugal visits, sort of.'

'Ah. I see . . .')

A photograph of Phillip was obtained from England.

'I remember that photo,' Raymond said. 'Black and white in a blood-red frame, little gold horseshoes all round it.'

It used to stand on the mantelpiece of his bedroom in the house on Summerdale Street, placed so that he could see it as he lay in bed. First thing he saw in the morning, last thing before he slept. At around four and five years old he used to rain kisses on it every night and morning. When his father put him to bed, Raymond would instruct him too to kiss the photograph. And he felt no jealousy, bitterness or rivalry whatsoever as he watched his father's lips touch his brother's image. He had no bad feelings connected to his brother at all, they were all warm and yearning.

His brother. In his imagination Phillip was the constant companion of all his adventures. What a pal he was! The evidence of the photograph was not all that encouraging. It showed a slight, thin-faced boy, standing under a tree, wearing an English prep-school outfit of grey flannel jacket and long grey shorts. The tree cast shadows over Phillip's face, and it was not easy to make out his features exactly. But Raymond's imagination got to work and – lo, there his brother was, just as he wanted him to be. A merry, open-faced boy, handsome in a tough way. Tall for his age and, though slim and gracefully formed, possessed of an unexpected strength, so that he was able to crush and destroy any of Raymond's actual playmates that he happened to be feuding with.

'You wait! I'll get my big brother on to you.'

'Yeah? Where is he, then?'

'Don't worry. He's coming. And he'll bash you, you'll see!'

He did come. Raymond's prayers were answered at last. His big brother came all the way from England to spend his Christmas holidays with his father and half-brother. He came for three long weeks. But, as it turned out, he didn't bash anybody in Baccara Bay, except Raymond.

'I remember the first words we spoke to each other,' Raymond Thorne smiled. 'The day we met. When it all began.'

(The car was parked on the side of the road, on the last hill before the coast, at that spot where one could look out and see no separation between sky and sea, or between the lights of passing ships and the cold stars above. He had stopped there without suggesting it beforehand, as if it had been prearranged between them. There was no break in his story. He carried on in the same calm, faintly amused, almost dreamy voice, and she listened to him, hardly stirring. The moon was low and almost full, and lit the car's interior with a silver light. She had forgotten that for a moment she had been badly frightened last time they had sat parked here.)

His parents went out to the airport to fetch Phillip home. Raymond wanted to go with them, but they said no. It was the last day of the school term and they didn't want him to miss it. He was told that his brother would probably be in bed sleeping when he got home from school. It used to take an extraordinarily long time from England to Australia then, even by plane. It used to take days. Phillip would probably be tired out when he arrived.

When Raymond came home, sure enough Phillip was upstairs. The father had bought a camp bed and had put it in Raymond's room. It thrilled Raymond to think of sharing a room with his own brother. He was told to leave Phillip alone till he was ready to get up. But after a while he couldn't hold back any longer. When his parents weren't looking, he crept upstairs. He looked in at his bedroom. Right enough, there was a shape under the sheet on the camp bed and a bit of dark hair on the pillow. Raymond was so happy to see this. It was true, then. It wasn't, for once, just a story he'd made up. His brother was really here!

He couldn't see Phillip's face. The sheet was drawn up nearly over his head. So Raymond crept closer. Still he couldn't see much. So he reached out and pulled the sheet down a few inches. And –

Oh Christ.

'What?' she breathed.

'There were these *eyes* looking at me. He hadn't been asleep. I hadn't woken him up, I'd swear to that. These eyes staring at me, and the strangest expression in them. Well, it was hatred, I worked that out later. But at that moment, I had no idea, I was just sort of confused and excited. I was ready to wet myself, I was so excited.

'So I looked at him and I said – sort of ridiculous, I suppose – I said, "Are you my brother?"

'He took a moment before answering. And these eyes were just drilling into me. Very dark, they were. It must have been a trick of the light, Phil's got eyes like mine. Sort of light grey. But when I looked into them the first time it was as if his pupils were black ice . . . And then he said, very clear, very clipped – you know, very English – he said, "Mind your own beeswax." '

Raymond Thorne chuckled and stroked the steering wheel.

'Mind your own beeswax!' he repeated. 'Well, I wasn't sure what he meant exactly, but I got the drift. So I pushed off downstairs and hung around for a while, thinking things over, and then I had my tea. During it, Phillip showed up. He's in these pyjamas, heavy gear, blue striped, tied up with a cord.

' "Oh, Phillip," my mother says, "couldn't you sleep?"

"Yes, I was sleeping," my brother says, "but Raymond woke me up. And afterwards I couldn't get back to sleep."

'Well, that was me in the shit. My parents yelled at me in this half-volume, Phillip's-first-day type of way. And in the middle of it, my brother pipes up, "Oh, I'm sure Raymond didn't mean it. It was just an accident." And I saw the look my mum and dad gave each other. What a nice boy, they were thinking.'

After Phillip had had some tea, it was suggested that Raymond take him out to show him the beach. Phillip went up to change and came back wearing a dark-blue Aertex shirt and a pair of long grey flannel shorts, just like those he was wearing in the photograph. The two boys set off into the sunshine. As they rounded the first corner and were out of sight of the house, Phillip challenged Raymond to a race. Raymond was a head shorter than his brother, but he intended to do his best. For the honour of Australia. 'One-two-three-go!' his brother chanted, smiling. Just as Raymond was getting into his stride, Phillip – running easily beside him – stuck out a foot sideways. Raymond went sprawling on to the pavement, cutting his knees and elbows badly. He limped back in tears to the house.

'He tripped me, he tripped me!' he bawled.

Phillip arrived then, wearing an air of startled innocence.

'We were just running along,' he explained, 'and he suddenly fell over.' There was such a flavour of honesty about his voice and manner that Raymond would have believed in his innocence absolutely if he hadn't been there when the incident happened. 'Is he all right?' Phillip added, casting a concerned glance at his brother.

This performance enraged Raymond. He launched himself into a tantrum. In a while his parents had had enough. He was sent up to his bedroom. Lying there, he could hear talk and laughter from below. His parents' voices. Phillip's clear English tones. Raymond fumed in his exile. The unfairness of it all. He caught sight of the precious photograph of Phillip on the mantelpiece. He felt like getting up and hurling it at the wall. Instead, he stuck his tongue out at it.

During the night, he woke up. He could hear – what he had never heard in his room before – the sound of another breathing in sleep. He listened to it, half resentfully, but half in pleasure too for it was what he had dearly wanted for so long. Then a strange, disturbing feeling crept over him. It was if he could tell that his brother was not asleep after all, but was lying there, watching him. Even in the darkness. Watching him out of black, unblinking eyes.

Raymond took a long time to get back to sleep after that, and was still tired when he woke in the morning. Phillip seemed well refreshed, however. After breakfast the two boys set out together. Once out of sight of the house, Phillip administered the first of many beatings he was to give Raymond during his three-week stay.

'He was very good at it,' Raymond Thorne acknowledged now, almost proudly. 'I don't know whether he learned it at his school, or he just had an instinct for it, but he knew exactly where to hit. Where it hurt a lot and where it would be least likely to raise any bruises. He never touched my face, for instance. It was always low down or round the back. Very good at kidney punches, Phillip was. Or rabbit chops on the neck. And this went on day after day, you see, three or four times a day. He never got tired of it. Never said much while he was doing it. Just bang, bang, bang. And this look of . . . *satisfaction* in his eyes. He only ever had two expressions when he looked at me. Satisfaction when he was beating me up. Hatred the rest of the time.'

'But didn't you tell your parents what was happening?'

'You bet. I told 'em every time at first. But he was incredibly clever, old Phil. He could come on all innocent better than I'd ever seen. And afterwards he'd bash me up a bit more for being a sneak. Old English custom, you understand.' Raymond chuckled softly. 'Also he took care that it should never happen in front of anyone else. Nobody ever saw him doing it. Yes, he was brilliant, my brother. And he was very popular. Nobody could think bad things about Phil.'

'Popular?'

'With the other kids.'

Raymond was silent for a time. When he spoke again his voice sounded almost wistful. 'See – in many ways he *was* the brother I always wanted. He was quite friendly – to everybody but me. And he was a very daring kid, which did a lot for him, of course . . . Look, I admired him myself, most of the time. Even though I'd still be hurting like hell from the last bashing he'd given me.'

He looked at Susan and smiled at her.

'I don't understand. How could your parents not know what was going on?'

'Well, I told you – he was very clever.'

He leaned forward and turned the key in the ignition, shifted into gear. The car rolled down the far side of the hill, and then turned away from the coast on to the stretch of road that led back to the town.

'My mother got a bit suspicious half-way through his stay. When I kept on saying how Raymond was hitting me. Also, in spite of how careful he was, a couple of bruises started to show on me. Dad wouldn't believe anything was wrong. Probably didn't want to. His two fine lads, it was only horseplay, all that. But Mum started to think – well, no smoke maybe without fire. So she went out and collared a few of the neighbourhood kids and asked them if they'd ever seen Phillip bullying me. And of course they hadn't. Even if they had seen anything, they probably wouldn't have told, for he was such a favourite by now. All they knew was that Phillip was this really terrific bloke.' Raymond chuckled. 'One kid – Malcolm Hope, one of my best friends – he piped up: "Can't Ray go back to England, Mrs Blackstone? And Phil stay here?"'

He glanced merrily at Susan.

'That's horrible,' she said seriously.

'Ah, come on. Children are like that. Treacherous. Mal didn't mean anything really.' He shrugged. 'So Mum goes back to Dad: "Raymond's making it all up," she tells him. In good faith, you understand. So they tell me off for being a liar and having bad thoughts about my brother. And Phillip catches me a couple of extra whacks afterwards. Sneaking again, you know?'

'How could you stand it?'

'What could I do?'

'Something! I'd have done *something*.'

He smiled thoughtfully. 'I did once get an idea, one evening, just at bedtime. Phillip was out in the backyard, all alone. I was watching him from the bathroom window. And I suddenly thought – I could so easily drop a brick on his head right now.'

'Yes! You should have done it.'

He stared at her. Then turned back to the road, shaking his head. 'I wouldn't do anything like that. Not my style. Not then, not now.'

She brooded for a moment. 'You said – back at the Centre – there was a time you wanted to kill him. Wasn't that it?'

'Only for a moment. When I looked down at him, the top of his head. I thought how easy it would be. Like smashing an egg. And my troubles would be over.' He breathed deeply. 'But I wasn't serious, of course. As soon as I thought it, I was shocked at myself. Really. Look,' he said, 'I knew he was going back in the end. I just had to wait out the three weeks. It'd hardly be fair to kill my own brother, just cause I couldn't stand him for a few weeks.'

After a moment, he added, 'Also, I didn't happen to have a brick with me at the time.'

He smiled to show he was joking. He pulled the car carefully in at the curb. She looked out, almost surprised to see her own building. Turned back to him.

'Do you want go for a walk again?'

He shook his head. 'It's getting late. I'd better get back. My wife . . .'

'But – ' She was definitely disappointed. Also somewhat irritated at the way his wife kept appearing and disappearing, almost to suit his convenience. 'I want to know what happened.'

'You've heard it. After three weeks he went back home. Peace returned to Baccara Bay.'

'Did he ever come back?'

After a moment, he nodded.

'Three years later. Another Christmas. I wasn't too worried about it. I figured: forgive, forget. What happened before was when we were just young kids. Now we were all of eleven and fourteen. It was bound to be different.'

'Was it?'

'First time we were out of the house together – once round the corner – bang! he caught me one right over the kidneys. Phil was back. Nothing had changed.' He held up his hand before she could say anything. 'Actually, it wasn't so bad this time. I was much faster on my feet for one thing, almost as fast as him, and if I got a head start I could usually get away from him. Also I had a bunch of real close friends by now, three or four other boys, real good mates, and we always hung around together. So he had a job catching me alone. He knocked me around three or four times a week, average. First visit it was three or four times a day. Definite improvement.

Another thing,' he added, 'my mother was a lot more suspicious of him this time. Well, I was her son after all – and he wasn't. She used to say – after he'd gone this time – that Phillip had a dark angel. I wasn't sure what she meant by that exactly, but it sounded about right. And when my dad suggested Phil come out the following Christmas, she put her foot down. She wasn't going to have him.

'So that was the last time he came out to Australia. I didn't see him again till we came to England. I was fourteen then. I went over to his mother's house in Streatham, not long after we got to London. A visit to my big seventeen-year-old brother, you know. Two young gents. Dad thought it'd be a nice idea.'

'What happened?'

'What do you think? He bashed me up, of course. But I got away from him after a few minutes. I do remember as I went out the front door and down the drive I called out over my shoulder, "Thanks for a lovely time, Phillip!"' He grinned at Susan. 'Very well brought up, you see.'

She shook her head. 'Poor little boy,' she said.

He watched her curiously. 'I wasn't that little by then. I was almost as big as him.'

'I was thinking of the first time he came out. You must have been devastated.'

'Only because I expected so much of him,' he pointed out. 'So it was my fault really if I was disappointed.'

'*How* was it your fault?' she snapped. 'The bastard!'

He still watched her. He seemed puzzled.

'Why are you so angry?'

'I don't know . . .'

She was angry. Until he had spoken the word, she had not realised how much. It was like a noose round her neck, tightening and choking her. She breathed in and out deeply, trying to free herself of its grip.

'I'll tell you why,' she said at last. 'I've started to believe there are just two kinds of people in the world. The takers and those who get taken. People who hurt, people who get hurt. And I'm sick of it. And angry about it. And I think it's time the people on the bottom started hitting back.'

She was quite surprised to have delivered herself of that. Raymond too seemed taken aback. He waited for several moments after she had finished speaking. Then shook his head. 'Well, I would have,' he said then, laughing. 'I definitely would have hit back. Only I couldn't even reach him when I was eight! He was a lot taller than – '

'Oh, stop it,' she said curtly. 'Stop laughing. I don't know why you're laughing all the time. It's a horrible, sad story. It makes me sick.' She shook her head again. 'I would never get over something like that.'

He was quiet for a moment. Then, not looking at her, he said, 'I'll tell you what I remember was the saddest thing of all, that first visit. The day he went back, we went to the airport to see him off. I went along too. I wanted so much to see the bugger off, to make sure he got on the plane. And then I saw the look on his face just before he went through the gate. In a way I don't think he'd really accepted he would have to go, that he'd really be sent back.' Now Raymond turned urgently to her. 'Don't you see why he hated me? His dad had this other little boy now. And I was sitting pretty out there in Baccara Bay. And he – what was he? Just a cast off. No wonder he took it out on me. What was he supposed to do? Forgive me for something like that?'

He turned away again, reached out to touch the wheel.

'I always remember how Phil looked at the airport. And since then I've been able to make allowances for him. He's always been a bit strange with me, but . . . we get along now.'

'He doesn't hit you any more?'

He grinned, shook his head. 'Hardly. We don't see much of each other anyway. He's got a place out in Portugal, on the Algarve. It's pretty nice. He spends most of his time out there. When he's not flying. And when we meet we're friendly. Distant – but friendly.'

She was no longer fuming on his behalf. What he had just said had not made her think much more kindly of this violent, appalling brother of his. But Raymond had given her a reason for his own lack of animosity. She didn't agree with it entirely – if the seeds of violence lay with the father's desertion, why did it have to be the young brother that got punished? – but it made Raymond seem less weak, less of an unresisting victim.

She would have dropped that brick though, she knew she would.

She leaned towards him and touched his arm.

'You're a nice man,' she said.

'Oh – '

'Yes, you are. I would have said: he's just evil, and left it at that.'

'Phil's not evil.'

'Well, he's got a dark angel, then.'

'Not that either. Not really.'

'At least you must admit he's pretty high-handed. This thing about your father's books,' she reminded him. 'And the auctioneers. That's awful!'

'Yup.' Raymond smiled ruefully. 'He went a bit far there, didn't he? I'll have to say something to him about that.' He yawned suddenly. Smothered it. Then, in a rather weary, offhand voice, 'We're supposed to show up together at Dad's solicitors next week. I'll talk to him then.'

'Why the solicitors?'

'Legal stuff.' Raymond yawned again. 'Reading the will. All that.'

'Well, tell him from me,' she said, 'if he lays a finger on you, he'll have me to deal with!'

At last they were able to laugh together.

'Families!' said Susan, shaking his head.

'You said it!' Raymond agreed with a comical sigh.

He didn't say this time that he would wait for her lights to go on. But she guessed he would. Just as an experiment, she hung around inside her flat for nearly a full five minutes before she turned on the light. She was rewarded then by hearing the sound of his car moving away. Then she felt disgusted with herself, and wondered what she was trying to prove. The problem is, she thought, as she paced her living-room floor, that people like Raymond Thorne were so good natured, so accepting – so weak, she almost added, but that really wasn't fair – that it was a temptation always to find out exactly how much they would stand. Just for the interest of it.

Still she shouldn't have given way to temptation, she knew. It was only cruelty by another name. And after what she had heard tonight she hated the thought that – even to the smallest degree – she had joined the company of those who practised it.

The names of that company ran through her head for some time after Raymond Thorne had driven away, starting with that evil brother of his, and not ending till they had included some of her dearest and oldest friends.

★

To: Tom Scott
17 Mayberry Avenue
London W2

Nov 12th

Dear old Tom,

Congratulations on the award! I sat up to watch the fun, crossing my fingers and toes for you all night, and behold! there you were at last, bowing and smiling, and making your nice little speech. How I clapped for you! Bravo! Great.

So how are you, and what are you doing? Apart from very well, obviously. I'm a bit parched for news of the old gang. Dick Banham's been writing to me faithfully, but he never seems to get much news into his letters. By the way – what about him and Jean Ricketts? How it all goes round and round, doesn't it?

Things are going pretty well for me down here. Sometimes it's a bit quiet but on the whole I like it that way. I get offered quite a lot of work, but nothing that's really tempted me so far. I really want something rather tasty for my next, I've decided. Is that a hint to you? Well, why not? You're not likely to jump to the wrong conclusions, are you? And I've decided there's nothing shameful about asking for something. Not when you've got something good to offer in return, and I know I've got that.

So I'm going to go the whole hog and enclose a recent photo of myself. Not begging, Tom, really – just enquiring.

Enough. I really just wanted to send my congratulations, and say I'm thinking of you with much affection. Also pride, if you don't mind. I'm one of those who can truly say 'I knew him when'. Remember how depressed you used to get? You thought you'd never ever get higher than second assistant. But it all turned out OK, didn't it? I used to tell you it would, do you remember? And I was right. You got your break and you took advantage of it. It's all any of us can ask for. To have a chance.

Sorry. I get into a rambling fit every now and then. Old age do you reckon? Really I just wanted to say – well done to an old mate!

WELL DONE

Write soon.

Come and see me if you want.

love,

Susie (Strang)

P.S. How could I forget!! Very much love to Louise too!!!

7

In Swayncliff in the off season, which is most of the year, I.G. Zofahr's Rainbow supermarket on Merrick Street is the only shop that stays open after seven p.m. There is nowhere else to go, in an emergency, after dark. So perhaps it was not such a coincidence that, one evening in early December, as she straightened up from searching through the frozen food display, she should have spotted Raymond Thorne standing at the far end of the aisle, frowning as he inspected the prices on the tinned fruit labels. Nevertheless, she was startled. It was almost a month since she had last seen him. No sign of him at all, complete vanishing act. And then, suddenly, there he was.

Her first instinct was to back away, to get to the check out and slip out of the store unnoticed. Then she was puzzled that she had thought such a thing. It was nice to run into somebody she knew, just coincidentally, out shopping. It should have been nice – it was rare enough. His shyness must be catching, she smiled to herself. She was over the shock of seeing him now.

She was probably blaming him unconsciously because she hadn't seen him for weeks. As if he had stayed away from her on purpose. Well, that was certainly ridiculous. She was not going to be ruled by fantasies.

And anyway, she had to go to where he was standing to get a tin of peas to accompany the frozen cod and parsley sauce that she had chosen. She set off up the aisle.

'Hello,' she said quietly. And then, very casually, 'Fancy meeting you here.'

Like hers, his first reaction was surprise. And then she thought his eyes lit up with real pleasure. The light was gone in a moment though. He frowned slightly.

'Oh – hello.' And then, as if explanations were required, 'I'm doing some shopping, you see.'

'I thought it might be that,' she risked teasing him, very gently.

Close up she saw that he was looking very pale. The hollows

under his cheekbones were deep caverns. The skin, drawn so tightly across his face, was chalk-white. Sickly. It might have something to do with the harsh, glaring lighting in the Rainbow. On the other hand, it occurred to her that he might have been taken ill recently. And that was why she had seen nothing of him. As she watched, he seemed to shiver once or twice.

He had turned towards the towers of tinned fruit beside him.

'The prices here seem pretty high,' he said.

'Oh, well, the Rainbow . . . It's a little penalty you have to pay if you leave the shopping till too late.'

He nodded. After a moment, when he seemed to have nothing more he wanted to say to her, she turned away to the nearby stacks of canned vegetables. She hesitated, then selected a small tin of peas at twenty-three pence.

'You prefer those to the frozen ones?' Raymond enquired in a serious tone.

'I do. Also they're cheaper.'

'They'd have been cheaper still if you'd waited till tomorrow and gone to Sainsbury's.'

'True. On the other hand I wouldn't have had them to eat tonight.'

She couldn't help thinking that he had sounded extremely priggish just then. Also that it was entirely her own affair how much she spent on a tin of bloody peas.

'You could have saved a bit too if you'd waited.'

'Well, we ran out suddenly,' he explained.

She inspected the contents of his wire basket. A large box of household matches. A tin of brown shoe polish. A can of peach slices in syrup. It was not clear to her exactly what he could have run out of that needed replacing so urgently.

She looked again into his face. So pale. And . . . she could not remember if his expression had always been so sad. She remembered him as often quiet and diffident – and then full of emotion, sorrow, the night he had told her of his father's death. But this fixed quality of sadness? He looked as if he had been sad for ever.

'Have you stopped going to the Leisure Centre?' she asked him suddenly. Then quickly, so as not to give herself time for second thoughts, 'Only, you see, I've looked for you every time I've gone.'

He turned away and picked a tin of button mushrooms from the shelf and transferred it to his basket.

'No, I haven't been going,' he said quietly. 'I've been rather busy lately.'

'I see.'

She stared down at the two items in her own basket.

'Well, I think that's me finished.'

'Yes, me too,' he said.

He followed her to the check-out counter. Her bill came to one pound twenty-five pence. Uncertainly, she waited for him to pay for his purchases. Two pounds seventy. Each clutching a plastic bag with a faint rainbow pattern on it, they stepped out on to Merrick Street. She recognised his car, parked just across the street. The huge, potent, absurd shape. It was nice to see it, a familiar sight in spite of the weeks that had passed since she'd seen it last, or ridden in it. She wondered if he would offer her a lift. She supposed he would. But really, she thought, there was no need for them to go through all the performance of getting into the car at this end and then out of it at the other. Her home was only a few hundred yards away. And her carrier bag wasn't at all heavy. It would be perfectly all right if he just offered to walk her home.

He ducked his head in the shy way she well remembered.

'Well, goodbye,' he said, and smiled a smile that did not nearly reach his unhappy eyes. 'Nice to see you again.' He was silent for a moment, thinking. Then he looked away. 'I might be going back to the Centre soon, I don't know.' He shrugged. 'Maybe we'll run into each other.'

She watched him cross the road and start to unlock his car door. Her surprise was so complete, it almost made her laugh out loud. Though she was far from being amused. What a nerve! This was the man who would wait out in the street until he was sure that she was safe inside her flat. Would wait nearly a full five minutes if necessary – she had tested him. Would, she had assumed, have waited half an hour, more, if she'd chosen to experiment that long. Anger soon followed the surprise. She didn't, she conceded, have the right to expect a lift. Fair enough. But just to brush her off like that . . . That was sheer rudeness. That was crazy, considering the things that had passed between them. She marched across the road. He had not yet got into his car.

'Look – what's going on?'

He turned to her. Looked at her sadly, questioningly.

'I mean – ' She struggled to make her point. 'You tell me all these stories – and then I don't see you for weeks – and then I see you – and now you're going off, just like that, I don't understand . . .'

He was watching her. And she was floundering. What was she trying to get at? she wondered helplessly.

'All this *stuff*?' she cried. 'You tell me all this stuff. Your father – your mother – your bloody awful brother and . . . and I've been worried about you,' she added in a muffled voice. 'And you look awful. You look sick. You shouldn't be out.'

Silence followed. Now she only felt confused and embarrassed. Her anger had dribbled away – she had no right to be angry. That was suddenly perfectly clear. She didn't know him, she really didn't know him at all.

She had just made a fool of herself, that was all.

'You've been worrying about me?' he said in a wondering voice.

She shrugged, felt suddenly weary. 'I suppose so. I wondered where you'd got to.'

She was remembering now that one afternoon, the week before last, she had tried to get in touch with him. It was on a day when she had done nothing much between getting up and three o'clock in the afternoon except wander vaguely from room to room or else sit curled up on her sofa, watching the Australian soap opera she followed, and after that just watching the rain spatter against the windows, letting her mind drift aimlessly round and round. A day, in fact, like all her other days. She had found herself thinking particularly about Raymond that afternoon and the urge had come to her to speak to him. She had got out the telephone book to look up his name and number, but then the thought that she might get his wife instead made her feel for some reason shy and unwilling. Then she had the idea of ringing him at the office, so she had found the number of the *Argus* and had dialled it. But before anybody answered, she had hung up the phone. It was pointless, she saw. For what had she to say to him except a series of inappropriate questions? Where are you? Where have you been hiding? Why have you deserted me?

What had she to say to him now?

He was standing holding the car door half open. The light was on inside, lighting up his features from below. His pale, drawn, sickly features.

'I was going to follow you in the car,' he said quietly.

'What?'

'To make sure you got home safe. I was going to follow you.'

She stared at him.

'Why don't you just walk home with me? I'd like you to.'

He shrugged and looked away from her. Puzzled, she watched him, the angular profile, the lips downturned, his whole expression so troubled, sad. And something else. What was it? Embarrassment, she thought. Yes, he looked secretive, and shy, he looked to be hiding something . . .

All at once, she thought she understood. Ah yes, if that was the case, if that was what was holding him back, yes . . . It made things rather difficult, no question. But it was not something she should blame him for. Or be angry about. It was flattering more than anything. And, yes, it made it reasonable that he should have stayed away from her. She felt a flutter of excitement rising inside her. My God, she thought, so long since I felt *that* . . . It was tricky, of course. No question. As he was married. Kate. The ever present. But she felt it could be handled. One way or another – if that was what the problem was.

'I feel I'm not in a fit state to be with you,' he muttered.

'Now what does that mean?'

She spoke firmly but, on purpose, not unkindly. She was determined to force it out of him. It was best that it was out in the open. Where they could deal with it.

'I didn't want to walk with you . . .' he started slowly.

Of course not. If it was true, if he was getting – felt himself to be – attracted to her, as a woman.

Now why phrase it that way? Like a romantic novel? She felt like giggling. She felt very excited. She'd better listen to him. Don't worry, she wanted to say to him. We can handle it. I can handle it. One way or another.

'I didn't want to see you – ' he stopped again and sighed heavily, 'because every time I do, I seem to dump a whole load of my troubles on you.'

Breathe easy, Kate, she thought sadly, no need for you to worry about a thing.

Well, serve her right. She shouldn't make these big assumptions. So it was not *that* that was bothering him. It was more complicated, less flattering. She was still interested, but the excitement died away within her.

'I've been thinking,' he said. 'We never talk about you. And that's ridiculous!' He shook his head, angry at himself. 'Here you have this exciting life . . . I don't know . . . famous friends, I expect. All sorts of stuff going on, great stories I dare say. And yet, what do we ever talk about but *me*. Me and my problems. All the time. I was sick of it,' he sighed. 'And I didn't want to do it any more.'

She watched him carefully, shrewdly. Now she thought she could see another possible reason for his reticence tonight. And this one, she had to admit, made much more sense.

'Is there something new you want to tell me?'

He shook his head again. 'Nothing I want to tell you.'

'But something's happened,' she said quietly.

It was obvious. From the first moment she'd seen him inside the store, she'd known it really. Something had happened. Something to make him very sad indeed. It was absurd to pretend she didn't know this man. In fact, he was quite transparent to her. He couldn't keep things hidden even when he tried.

'Something's happened,' he muttered at last. 'But – '

'You don't want to tell me.'

'Please!' he begged her. 'Just let me follow you in the car. For my peace of mind.'

She smiled. He was so endearing really.

'Why don't you just walk me home?'

'I told you – '

'We won't talk about you. We won't talk about me either, if we don't want. We'll find . . . other topics.'

He hesitated. Then looked down at his hand, still gripping the door handle.

'Why don't we take the car?'

'No, let's walk,' she said.

She remembered that, in their other times together, he had always needed a firm push from her to get him started. Then he was fine usually. Then he would talk freely. But it would not be so easy now to get him going, for they had sworn off talking about each other. It was cold, cold December. Merrick Street ran all the way, uninterrupted, down to the front, and the wind that was gusting off the sea was strong and cutting. She thought about slipping her arm into his for the warmth. And to encourage him. But then thought better of it.

'Those Zofahrs always interest me,' she tried after a while.

'Sorry?'

'Mr Zofahr. Mrs Zofahr. The little Zofahrs. They own the supermarket.'

'Oh, yes.'

'Yes. I always wonder,' she carried on valiantly, 'how on earth they found their way to Swayncliff. I don't think there's another Indian family for miles . . . Or are they Pakistani? I can never tell.' She was sounding completely mindless, she knew it. So she shut up, hoping he'd start to talk.

Silence. Nothing doing. Nobody home.

'Do you think they picked out Swayncliff on the map with a pin?'

'I think all these Indian and Pakistani shops are owned by a few wealthy families,' Raymond said. 'And they assign each one to various relatives as they come over to England.'

'Well, I should think our Zofahrs must be pretty unfavourite relatives. I mean – to get Swayncliff. Perhaps he's the black sheep of the family,' she smiled.

'Perhaps he likes the sea.'

Well, perhaps he did. Thank you and good night. Nothing more to be got from the Zofahrs, that was plain. A few more yards in silence.

'There's the sweet shop.'

He glanced at her, puzzled. She nodded at the shop they were passing. A dark blind covered its windows. On it was written in genteel white script: THE BON-BON. Sweets, Tobaccos, Ices.

'Where that poor girl was killed.'

He nodded. 'Right. So it is.'

They came to a stop. Raymond stood staring at the blind. They were not far from a street lamp, and she had a clear sight of his face.

'I wonder why he chose this particular shop.'

He shrugged. 'It's isolated. No other shops near by. If she cried for help, she likely wouldn't be heard.'

'What about passers by? Other shoppers?'

'He went in at closing time, after dark. There's nobody much about then.'

He seemed ready to move on. But she still lingered.

'Perhaps you could write about it,' she said. He stared at her. 'Yes,' she nodded. 'It might be just the thing. To make you known. To get you out of the *Argus*. Articles. A series. Perhaps a book.'

'A book about what?'

'About this. *You* know . . . The fifty-pound murderer. The Sweet Shop Killer. Garage Killer. The town in the grip of fear. Will he strike again? What are the police doing? Is he crazy? How crazy is he?'

She noticed that he was looking at her strangely.

'What's wrong with that?'

'Didn't you hear?' He watched her a moment more, then nodded. 'They caught him.'

'They did?'

'A week ago.'

She swallowed. She felt unexpectedly a great surge of relief. 'Who is he?'

'Some kid. Seventeen, eighteen. Lived up in South London. He used to go on day trips. He didn't just come here, it turns out. He killed in . . . Reading, Norwich, up in the Midlands someplace. Anywhere he could get to and back again the same day. The papers called him the AwayDay Killer. Didn't you hear about it?'

'No. I didn't.' She looked again at the sweet shop's front. The feeling of relief had given way to something less innocent. Curiosity. Worse, a sort of sickly fascination. 'Seventeen. My God! Where on earth did he get hold of a gun?'

Raymond smiled at that. 'Oh, that's not a problem nowadays,' he said softly. He looked up the street towards the sea. 'Apparently, it was something he used to do to fill in the time on weekends. Know what he said when the police caught up with him?'

She shook her head.

'He said, "Well, I'm not interested in football, you see."' Raymond chuckled briefly. Then his face settled again into stern, unhappy lines. 'So there you are. Poor bloody Swayncliff doesn't even have its own murderer any more.'

She looked up at him. 'What is it?' she said. 'What's happened to you?'

He made a quick, irritable gesture.

'I told you – '

'I can't walk with you and know something's wrong and not know what it is . . . Please, Raymond.'

'I don't have to tell you everything,' he muttered.

'You've told me everything else. Haven't you?' she demanded when he wouldn't reply.

'You're making me wish I hadn't.'

'Well, too bad!' she snapped. 'Because you have.'

She was being – she knew it – incredibly nosy. Yet right was on her side, she was sure of it. You don't fill somebody up with stories, get them involved and then yank down the curtain whenever it suited you.

Then she felt ashamed to have thought of the matter in this way. He was, after all, a real live person – not just some instrument for her entertainment. She was heartless, a heartless voyeur. She bowed her head.

'I'm sorry. Of course you don't have to tell me.'

They stood in the silent, freezing street. Raymond sighed and put his hand to his bony forehead, drew it across his eyes. All at once she guessed he was about to tell her what she had begged him to. The idea alarmed her now. It was clear to her suddenly that she didn't want to know. She had been, she realised, in a position where Raymond and his stories were the most interesting things in her life. Knowing that it probably wasn't him or his stories that were so wonderful, but that her life – her life . . . She shook her head. It had been an awful state to be in. She didn't want to return to it. Four weeks ought to have given her the chance to escape.

'I'll tell you,' he said quietly, 'if you really want to know.'

She had a memory then, clear like sunlight, of the old days, when she had lived in London, and every day had seemed exciting and bright, full of promise, full of work. And every evening, if she wasn't working, she used to go out with the gang. They were all young, all in the business, all on the way up then – or at least kidding themselves they were on the way up, and nobody could tell who in reality was going to rise and who would fall, so they were all equal. Many nights they would go to the theatre together to check up on the work of their friends, or of their enemies. She remembered settling into her seat, her friends all around her. The murmur of the audience dying away. A moment's silence, darkness. And then the stage lights coming up so slowly, tantalisingly . . . An instant before, she had been willing her friends to do their best. Or, if they were 'enemies' up there on stage, to do their worst. That seemed so malicious to her now, but it had all been a game then, nothing serious, like a playground: gossip and hugs, kicks and punches, and up with him and down with her. But as the lights came up and the show began she only really ever had one desire – to be absorbed, to be allowed to forget herself, to be taken in. To be enchanted, if that was possible.

'Yes,' she said faintly. 'Tell me. I want to know.'

She hardly noticed that he had placed his hand under her elbow. She hardly wondered that Raymond – so shy, so bashful, always so retiring – was handling her now with practised assurance as he walked her away from the shop, scene of the crime, towards the sea, to where she lived. His voice was murmurous and low, seductively so, beneath the higher registers of the wind that streamed towards them. She had to lean against him so that she could hear all that he was saying. She felt his heart beating against her arm – and sometimes she could feel the involuntary shudders that jarred his frame every now and then.

Oh, what's wrong with him? And how can I help? I'd give anything to help, she thought.

'Do you remember I told you last time that my brother and I had an appointment with Dad's solicitor?'

'Yes.'

'Remember I told you that one of the things we had to do was hear Dad's will read?'

Yes.

And do you remember –

Oh, yes. I remember.

Tell me, she willed him.

Enchant me again, if it is possible . . .

★

To: Tom Scott
17 Mayberry Avenue
London W2

December 21st

Dear Tom,

Some time ago I sent you a letter. With it I enclosed a photograph of myself. As you obviously have no use for it, and as it's not all that cheap to have new prints made, do you think you could let me have it back soon? Thanks.

Yours
Susan Strang

PS. i.e. the photo.

To: Tom Scott
17 Mayberry Avenue
London W2

Fuck you Tom. I think you're despicable. You're so fucking busy aren't you. Such a hot little shit. Far too busy to waste time on a dreary out of work actor, right?

Well listen to me. I don't feel the loser here. I think YOU are the loser. I really and truly don't give a damn personally if you don't reply to my letters. I'm just appalled by your disgusting and fantastic arrogance. The world is full of arrogant twisted greedy people who take and take and take and I'm so terribly fucking glad I'm not one of them and very sorry that somebody I used to care about is. Arrogant twisted greedy.

Fuck you

Fuck you fuck you

You're not even a big shit Tom. I know about much bigger shits than you now. You all need stepping on – if I could bear to step on shit

To: Tom Scott
17 Mayberry Avenue
London W2

December 22nd

Dear Tom

Yesterday I posted a couple of letters to you. I wish you would disregard the first one – it's written on the same kind of notepaper as this. The other one – the one written on toilet paper – that was a bad joke. I wish you would just flush it away and forget about it.

I had a bit of a brain storm yesterday. Nothing serious. Just went a bit potty for a while. I've been feeling a bit down lately. One thing and another. And I was somewhat hurt that you hadn't replied to a letter I wrote you about six weeks ago. It probably wasn't your fault. For all I know you've probably been away filming or something.

So please forget about yesterday's nuttiness. I'm very ashamed and it won't happen again. Please don't tell anyone else.

I expect Christmas will be past by the time you get this. Merry Christmas anyway, Tom. Happy New Year. Why not? I wish everybody the same. I'm sure they all deserve it.

Yours
sorry again
Susie

8

'So the bad brother copped the lot?'

'Everything. It's all gone to bloody Phillip.'

She was still, he saw, caught up in her tale, her eyes bright with passion and outrage. Tom watched these symptoms with great interest, as he had watched them all through her story. Experienced as he was, he could still be impressed at the ability actors had to be involved in the stories their bodies and lips were revealing.

'Can you imagine the scene?' she breathed. 'Poor Raymond had to sit in that solicitor's office . . . in that bloody little room, right next to his brother, and listen to that will. And every word, every clause, like a dagger . . .'

'Awful.'

Tom was never quite certain whether actors really did feel so completely involved. Sometimes he thought that, for professional ends, they were just awfully good at faking it. So much the better if they happened to have some decent material to work on. But it was the fact of performance, not the reason for it, which seemed to mobilise their talent. The question was: were these the sort of people who would believe anything? Basically rather silly people. Or were they – for the joy of being involved, for the gift of being allowed to perform – prepared to do almost anything to make themselves believers? He had never quite worked it out.

But this, he reminded himself, was not the occasion for speculation on the question. For this was not fiction he was hearing. This had happened.

He wanted to think this. At the same time he had a stray, distracting image to contend with. Something that had happened to him a score of times. Two hot-eyed young amateurs, desperate to get into the business – 'Hi, I'm the producer, he's the writer' – cornering him in a pub or a restaurant, waving their half-dozen pages of treatment at him. 'There's this happens, and then this happens, and it's set in Morocco, incredibly cheap, and then this guy kills the other guy and it turns out he's his brother, this other guy – or possibly his son, we're keeping our options open . . . and there's this third guy who's really an agent of the Czech secret police. John Hurt would be wonderful, wouldn't he? Or Robert de Niro – why not?'

Thank you. Thank you so much. It sounds great. Really terrific. But I'm just so terribly busy at the moment. And for the rest of the year, yes. And for the next five years, as it happens. So thanks. So sorry. Goodbye.

And now, he just wanted to ask: all this stuff – Nazis and wills and beatings and child sadists – are you sure it's kosher, Sue?

But of course he couldn't. In the face of her passion, her conviction, he just couldn't say it.

'Awful,' he repeated gravely. 'He must have been very fed-up, your friend.'

'Fed-up! He was *devastated*.' She plucked distractedly at the side of her face. 'Can't you see it? It was as if his father had cursed him from beyond the grave!'

'Yes . . .' There was a wild, melodramatic note to her voice now. Tom felt a pressing need to lower the temperature here. 'Well, they sound a pretty unsavoury family, don't they? Apart from your friend, of course.' She was staring fixedly at the fire. He was not certain she was hearing him. 'Which one of them was the Mosleyite, by the way? I didn't quite gather that.'

'The father, of course.'

'Ah. Right.'

'It's quite simple.'

'Sure . . . And your friend quarrelled with his dad over that.'

'But that was ages ago. And it was all cleared up. They were *friends* by the end. It was all forgiven, forgotten . . .'

'Well, evidently not.'

Before, he had hoped that once she had told her story, it would relieve and relax her. But he saw that she still seemed tense and burdened. He leaned a little towards her.

'How does he feel about it now?'

'Raymond? He feels terrible. Wouldn't you?'

'I suppose. But . . . how long ago did he hear the will?'

'A month. Five weeks. So what? It's not the sort of thing that goes away, is it? Of course he's still suffering. He doesn't talk about it much. But I can tell.'

They were silent, both now staring at the fire. At last Tom sighed.

'I don't know, Susie. Doesn't seem much one can do about it, really. All I know is, when something rotten happens – a really ghastly flop, or something – all you can do is just sort of step over it. And keep on walking.'

'That's your advice, is it?'

The note of sarcasm was faint but unmistakable. It irritated Tom to hear it. 'Well, what else can he do? He knows now his father didn't forgive him. That's hard – but he'll have to live with it, won't he?'

She didn't answer. Her silence irritated him still more. Then he checked himself. It would do no good to fight with Susie, it was not what he was here for. He was here to help, and he hadn't done much of that so far. And there was not much time left. He set his mind wandering over the details she had given him. It occurred to him there was one area she hadn't touched on.

'What did you say his father was? Shopkeeper?'

'He sold antiques, books.'

'Ah, right. So I guess he didn't leave an amazing amount of money.'

She was silent.

'I mean,' said Tom, 'I know it's the rejection that hurts most, of course, but all the same . . .'

She was still silent. He watched her carefully.

'How much did he leave, Susie?'

She got to her feet. 'Just a moment.' He watched her walk from the room. He was struck suddenly by how gracefully she moved, the long back and the long legs, the loose springing walk. Our Susie, he thought proudly, she can still make an exit. Then she was gone, and he looked back at the fire. Poor sod, poor Raymond. He could feel for him. For the first time, he really could. It wasn't a story, it was real life. And in real life . . . well, in his own family there had been nothing so dramatic, of course. Just an edge of dislike always there between himself and his father. Coldness. Well, they had been strangers really. It would have been good to have settled all that before his father's death. He regretted they hadn't. Perhaps his father had wished for it too. He had given no sign. Nor had Tom. A death-bed reconciliation. There had been time for it. His father had spent six weeks on his death bed.

Ah – Tom's nose wrinkled unconsciously in disgust – it would have been awful. Like a scene from an American soap, false and indecent. Better the old English way, he supposed. Silence and missed opportunities to the bitter end.

'There you are.'

She had come back into the room, unnoticed by him. He looked up, confused, his thoughts still half with his father. She was thrusting a newspaper at him.

'Page two.'

'What's this?' He turned the paper the right way up, peered at it in the dim light.

'The local paper. Raymond's paper.'

Tom nodded, checked the date under the masthead. It was several days old. 'Page two, you said?' He turned to the page. The main headline. '"Disappointing attendance at St Saviour's Bazaar,"' he read out.

'Underneath!'

'Ah. OK . . .' He turned the page a little towards the glowing bar. '"Coveney Man Leaves Fortune."' He looked up.

'Go on,' she commanded.

'"Excitement is growing among London and international dealers and collectors over the forthcoming sale by auction of a collection of rare books and manuscripts. The collection is from the estate of Mr John Blackstone, who lived at 11 Ashburnham Lane, Coveney, until his death last October. One dealer, when asked what he thought the collection might fetch, gave what he called a conservative estimate of around one million – " Jesus Christ!' Tom cried out.

He stared up at her. She nodded sombrely. He looked down again at the paper in his lap, shaking his head. 'Jesus Christ,' he said again.

'Yes.'

'That makes a difference,' he said in the same hushed tones.

'Does it?' She was crouching before him now, looking intently into his face. 'I don't know. Does it make a difference?'

He looked up into her eyes. They seemed to be searching him, as if she would claw out his real belief.

'I mean – ' She shook her head. 'Of course it's the rejection that's most important, I know that, but – '

'Sure, but . . .' his gaze drifted down to the paper again, 'a million quid, that's serious money!'

'Yes.'

He looked up. 'He – Raymond – he must have known?'

'No.'

'He didn't have any idea his father was worth this much?'

'He knew about the collection, of course, but he thought it would be worth, at most, ten thousand maybe. Not – '

'One million pounds,' Tom intoned. It gave him a certain satisfaction to say the words.

'Of course,' she said, 'he could only have expected to get half of that. There was always the brother.'

'Even so . . . Half a million. Bit more probably. That's still pretty serious.'

He looked down again at the news story. Coveney man leaves fortune. All the big buyers were expected. Not just from England. The Continent, the Far East, America. Even the legendary H.P. Krause of Manhattan was expected, if not in person, then certainly represented. Everyone expected at the auction, to be held on . . . Tom stared at the date given in the paper, and then held his watch against the fire's dim light.

'The fourth. That's today!'

'You can see why it's on my mind.'

'God, yes.'

Coveney man leaves fortune. To be held on the fourth. One million quid.

'How can books be worth that much?' he wondered out loud.

'It's possible.' He looked at her. She nodded firmly. 'I remember I had a part in something once. I was a nice, poor girl who'd married into this incredibly wealthy family. One of the scenes was set at a rare book auction. And the prices the stuff was fetching were unbelievable!'

'But that was fiction, Susie. You can't rely on that. You can never tell if the sodding writer bothered to check the facts. It's been the bane of my life that kind of thing.' But even as he spoke he was answering his own question. For he remembered a year ago watching a story on the nine o'clock news. About an auction that had taken place that day at Sotheby's. He remembered it well because the sums of money mentioned had seemed so incredible to him. One item had been a set of volumes of nineteenth-century bird paintings. The price: two million two-five-oh.

'Yes,' he said quietly. 'I think you're right. It's possible.'

Half a million quid. Five hundred thousand pounds . . . Jesus Christ.

'Poor fellow,' Tom sighed, taking the paper from his lap, settling it on the floor beside him. 'I suppose he could have used the money?'

She stared at the fire. 'It would have changed his life,' she said. 'He could have stopped grinding away at that rotten little job, and have had a chance to do something important. I know he's capable of it. He's such a talented man, Tom.'

'Yes? At what?'

She looked at him suspiciously. He hadn't intended his question to sound sceptical. He smiled to show his innocence. She looked away again.

'Oh, at so many things,' she murmured. 'Raymond can talk . . . well, just about anything. He knows about art . . . and medicine . . . politics . . .' She stopped for a moment, as if marshalling the evidence. Then, 'Do you know that when he was seven years old he passed his grade six piano exam?'

'Is that good?'

'It's incredible. It means he was practically a prodigy.'

'Is that what he'd have wanted to do? If he had the money. Music?'

'Perhaps. Or perhaps something else. He's always had a secret longing to travel and write books about it. He could have done that with five hundred thousand. Or he could have taken up his painting again. Or gone back to the law – '

'Law? Didn't you say he studied medicine?'

'Law was after art college. Which was after medical school. And they were all before journalism . . .' Her voice trailed away. As she stared at the fire, she looked suddenly rather exhausted. 'He really is so talented, Tom. And the money would have given him the chance to show it.' She glanced at him again. 'You must believe me,' she murmured.

'I do,' Tom assured her. 'Of course I do.'

'And there are other things,' her voice was firm now, rid of its temporary uncertainty. 'He and his wife, Kate . . .' Susan smiled fondly. 'They're the sort of people who don't believe you should bring children into the world unless you can give them the best. You know: the best schools, a grand piano if they're musical, a pony if that's what they want, all that sort of thing. And Raymond wants so much to be a father.'

'Dammit,' said Tom, suddenly angry at the unfairness of it all. He thought for a moment. 'Why doesn't he see a lawyer? Maybe he could challenge the will.'

'He's done that. He's talked to a lawyer. I persuaded him to.' She shook her head. 'The will's quite legal. Signed. Witnessed. Sound in body and mind . . . As far as anyone can prove,' she added darkly.

Tom decided to ignore that comment. 'Then maybe he could talk to this brother.'

'Phillip!'

'Right. I mean he – Phillip – he must see it's unfair. He must – '

He stopped for she was shaking her head again. 'He's done that too?'

'He didn't want to. I had to persuade him again. For Kate's sake. For the children they want to have. He went up to London. Phillip was passing through. He's going to live permanently in Portugal. He's retiring from the airline. He can afford to!' She laughed softly, bitterly. 'I gather it was quite a scene when they met.'

'Nothing doing?'

'Not a penny. Phillip told him he didn't feel he ought to go against his father's clear wishes. Except that he was prepared in the circumstances to pick up the whole cost of the funeral. Which he hadn't gone to . . . Raymond declined the offer. His pride, you know.'

They sat in melancholy silence, watching the fire. Outside, the evening was advancing rapidly. Inside, beyond the glow of the electric fire, the room was filling with shadows.

'It's too bad,' Tom sighed at last. 'It's a rotten shame.' He looked up then. 'But you know, what I said before still goes. With something like this you can't do anything much but hold your nose, step over it – and keep on going.'

She did not respond.

'I mean,' he urged, 'he's no worse off than he was before. Is he? Still got his home, got his job, his health. It's not as if he'd come down with – leukaemia. Or something. It's just a bit of lousy bad luck. So I say, leave it there, stinking on the ground. And keep going on.'

'And that's all?' she murmured.

'Well . . . what else is there?'

'Justice,' she said.

'What?'

She said another word then. He could not quite hear it – or rather, just barely hearing it, he could not believe she had said it.

'What did you say?'

She had moved slightly away from him, withdrawing her face from the fire's glow. He peered into the gloom, trying, failing to make out her expression.

'You said "justice", didn't you?'

She came a little nearer, into the circle of light. Her eyes were calm and contemplative.

'Do you think it's just – what's happened to Raymond?'

He shrugged, said reasonably, 'It's an unjust world, Susie.'

'Yes, isn't it?'

She withdrew again into the shadows.

'What else did you say?' he asked then.

She was silent.

'Did you say "punishment"?'

Tom smiled. 'I think you did . . . Who are you going to punish, Susie? The father's dead. It's too late for him.'

Still she was silent.

'The brother – it's hardly his fault, is it?'

Her hands came into the circle of light. As he watched, they passed slowly along her thighs, smoothing down the wrinkles in her skirt. He heard her clear her throat softly.

'I mean,' said Tom, 'he's a bugger for hanging on to all the loot, I guess, but – '

'I'll tell you something interesting,' she said, in a conversational tone. 'That will was written not long before the father died. And it turns out Phillip was staying with him at just that time. The first time in years he'd been down to stay with his father.'

Tom found he had to swallow before he could speak again.

'Meaning what?'

'Oh, nothing much,' she said dreamily. 'I just worked it out from some things Raymond said. He hadn't even seen the connection . . . Poor man,' she added after a moment.

'What connection?'

She didn't speak. Tom decided it was time – past time – to inject a note of reality here. 'I don't think you should mess around with ideas like that.'

Silence.

'Are you listening to me?'

She shifted back into the firelight. Smiled at him politely.

'I'm not sure what you're talking about.'

'I'm talking about . . .' Tom shook his head, confused. 'Didn't you just say something about "punishment"?' He watched her innocent eyes. 'I'm almost sure you did.'

'Oh,' she sighed, 'it was just an abstract sort of a thought.'

'Well, I wouldn't think thoughts like that, if I were you. And I wouldn't make . . . allegations about people. Unless you've got some proof. That's dangerous.'

Silence. Tom wondered if the comic approach would work better.

'What are you going to do to this brother anyway? Bombs in the post? Strychnine in the coffee? Creep up behind him on a dark night and club him to the ground?'

Nothing. So much for comedy. He reached out and took her hand.

'Hey, Susie! Be serious. I mean – it's clearly all very unfortunate what's happened, whatever's happened, but – that sort of thing . . . no, you have to leave that to fate. Or the hands of God.' Tom chuckled tensely. 'Remember. Time wounds all heels.'

But did he believe that? He tried quickly to think of any examples to show her, and himself, the truth of the quip. It wasn't easy. Dick Banham? Not noticeably wounded by time. Anyway, Dick wasn't a heel, not really, not seriously. Who else? Mark Gould? A certified, one hundred proof heel, and definitely his life at last report was not an enviable one. But the wounds Mark had collected over the years had been as nothing to the wounds he'd handed out. He had the proof of that before him now.

Susan withdrew her hand.

'I really don't know what you're talking about.'

'Oh, in that case,' he said, annoyed, 'I'd better shut up then, hadn't I?'

The next thing he said was, 'There's my taxi.' At the sound of the front-door buzzer he had got to his feet fast, and he was unable to keep the note of relief from his voice. He felt ashamed of himself then.

'Ah, Susie, I don't want to leave you like this.'

'Then stay,' she said, still watching the fire.

'I can't,' he said immediately. And then, only half fibbing, 'I wish I could.'

She stood up and looked around her. 'So dark in here,' she murmured. She went over to the switch on the wall and turned on the lights. The bulb in the overhead lamp shone dimly but still the sudden increase of light made him screw up his eyes. She looked across at him, and then burst out laughing. 'You look terrified!' she teased him.

He smiled back reluctantly. 'Well, how would *you* feel? If I'd said things like you've been saying.'

'But you have.' She came to him and touched his shoulder, smiled at him. 'I remember. I was with you when that play you did, Play for Today . . . ages ago . . . with the mongol child – '

'Oh, God!' he groaned. '*Born in Chains*!'

'Right. And the reviews weren't so good. And I remember the things you said you were going to do to the critics . . . Murder was the least of it!'

'But I was just blowing off steam.'

'Well, exactly.'

'Is that all it is?' He watched her hopefully. 'Just blowing off steam?'

She shrugged, smiling at him still. He put his arm around her neck and gave it a playfully homicidal squeeze.

'Why didn't you say so, you bugger!'

She laughed and broke away from his grip. The doorbell rang again, much longer than before.

'Go on,' she said. 'You'll miss the taxi.'

'You're coming with me, aren't you?'

She shook her head. 'Don't think so.' She looked vaguely round the room. 'Raymond's coming over later. I want to tidy up.' She opened the front door for him. 'I wish you could stay. I'd really like you to meet him.'

'I wish you'd come to the station.' He went past her, on to the landing. 'Come on, Suze,' he urged. 'Taxi's on me. Both ways. It'll take you twenty minutes, there and back.'

'Well . . '

Whatever she might have said was cut off then by a high piercing shriek from up above. Tom jumped as if he'd been stung. 'Bloody hell!' Susan swore. She stepped out on to the landing and peered up the stone staircase. No one could be seen. 'Now stop that, Mrs Baklova!' she called into the silence. 'That's *enough*!' The moments passed. 'You know Miss Chalmers isn't well. You mustn't be doing that.'

'I'm going up to talk to her,' said Tom firmly. 'This is outrageous!' But the doorbell rang for a third time, and he stopped irresolute at the foot of the stairs.

'Come on,' said Susan disgustedly. 'I'm not staying here. I'll go to the station with you.'

She went back into the flat to fetch her coat. Tom still stared up at the dark landing on the fourth floor.

'You're a witch,' he murmured, probably not loudly enough to be heard. 'Old lady, you're a witch.'

Nothing stirred in the gloom above, no sound, nothing.

What a house this is, Tom thought. What a zoo!

9

At the station she broke away from him, leaving him to pay off the taxi. When he followed her into the building, he found her near the bookstall, a copy of the local paper in her hands. She was searching through it, scanning the columns of print, frowning.

'I don't understand it,' she said as he came up.

'Nothing?'

She began again at the front page and, as he watched, went through the entire paper once more. When she had finished, she shook her head. She looked very puzzled.

'Well,' he soothed her, 'there you are. I guess it wasn't such a big event after all. What probably happened,' he said, as they walked towards the ticket barrier, 'is that they spread these stories – million quid, all that – just to get the dealers interested. But there was nothing in it after all.'

There was nobody guarding the barrier. He looked for his return ticket anyway. Found it in the inside pocket of his coat.

'But you'd think there'd be *something*,' she protested. 'After all, it's of local interest.'

They walked on to the platform. A small cluster of travellers waited near the barrier. Tom and Susan turned away from them and began to walk towards the platform's far end. The taxi had made good time, and the train was not due for several minutes.

'Listen: no news is good news,' Tom said. 'The less those books went for, the less your friend has lost. Maybe they only fetched a couple of hundred thousand,' he encouraged her. 'In which case – divide by two – he's only out a hundred thou. And that . . . Well, it's quite a lot,' he admitted. 'But it's not a fortune. Not these days. And in comparison it's – '

'I know what it is,' she said. 'This is probably an early edition.' She screwed up the paper and tossed it into a rubbish bin. 'The news hadn't come in when that was printed.' The anxious note had quite gone from her voice. She nodded confidently. 'Anyway, Raymond will explain everything when I see him.'

They had come to the end of the platform. Tom peered over the rim, and then looked up to where the rails ran away from the station into the night. For a little way they were lit by lamps, but then either the line curved off round a bend, or there were no more lamps for he could see nothing but darkness out there. He turned back to Susan. They smiled at each other quickly, and then Tom looked away.

'Can I say something?'

'Of course you can,' she laughed.

'Well . . . look . . . I think it's great to blow off steam, et cetera, once in a while. But I do think it's a shame it's somebody else's troubles you're blowing off steam about.'

She looked at him with apparent interest, but did not speak.

'I mean,' he said firmly, watching her now, 'I think it's high time you put yourself first for once. Old number one, right? You see,' he reached out and squeezed her hand, 'it's always your way, isn't it? To put somebody else's problems first. And you lose a lot of energy like that, Susie. Energy you *need*. For yourself.'

'I did put my own problems first,' she remarked. 'I wrote you some letters about my problems. But you didn't seem to like that.'

'All right,' he said, after a moment. 'I didn't like it. But maybe you were right to do it. And it worked, didn't it? I came down here, didn't I? To talk about your problems. And what do I find?' Tom was aware of something hectoring in his tone, but it was too late to hold back now. 'I find you don't really want to talk about your troubles. You want to talk about someone else's. And it's your way, Susie,' he insisted. 'It was just the same with Mark. You got sucked into all his silly dramas. And you lost *energy*. You lost ground. It cost you, Susie.'

Before this, she had been listening to him with an almost placid air. But now she looked up sharply.

'What do you mean?' And when he didn't answer, 'This is nothing to do with how I was with Mark. Nothing like that.'

'Well, I'm sure – I hope – *he's* nothing like Mark.'

'Nothing at all. Why – ' She laughed angrily. She began to walk away from the platform's end. He caught her up. 'Why Mark never let up. I couldn't have got away from his problems if I'd tried. Morning, noon and night, that's all we ever talked about. Raymond – he's totally different. If you knew!' She laughed again, but with a certain tenderness this time. 'I have to drag everything out of Raymond. It's like getting information from the enemy.'

'All the same,' Tom persisted. 'However it happens, it ends up in the same old pattern. You get involved with some guy, and all at once his troubles are your troubles – and where are you?'

She stopped walking, stared at him.

'But I'm not involved with Raymond.'

He turned to look at her.

'I was *married* to Mark. I was in love with him. For a while. Raymond's just a friend. A good friend I see sometimes. That's all.'

'Well . . .' Tom hesitated. 'Surely you're – '

'Surely I'm what?'

'Well . . .'

'Sleeping with him?' She shook her head, amazed. 'Why would you think that? I told you – he's married.'

'Well, sure you did, but . . . I just naturally assumed – '

'Well, don't! He's very close to his wife. Loves her very much. I can tell. And I think that's great. She sounds like a really good person. It makes me happy to think about them.'

Incredible. It had never occurred to him that Susie and this fellow weren't lovers. He felt crass, shallow, metropolitan – a metropolitan busybody, shoving people into bed with one another, and on no better authority than his own too quick assumptions. He had just been so sure of it – from the moment he'd seen the light of excitement and devotion in her eyes when she'd spoken Raymond's name.

All at once, as they stood in silence on the dark platform, Tom found himself questioning the whole basis of his mission down here. For it was true he had come to her like that, a missionary from the great greedy world. What he had wanted for Susie was to put her back on the track of chasing single mindedly her career, her success, her ambition. To be, in fact, as much like himself and all the people he spent time with as possible. And he saw now that he might have missed all along the true self she had been nurturing, perhaps for years without anyone else knowing, and that had come at last to fruition down here, in this lonely backwater.

He glanced at her quickly and humbly. Could it be that her particular virtue, her true self, might be one of self sacrifice and caring? Not old number one after all. She was no good at serving that any more. But the explanation might be – not that she was messed up, but that her real vocation, her destiny, lay elsewhere. It wasn't a fashionable vocation any more, not for a woman – or perhaps it had become so again, he didn't know, he'd lost track of these things. All he knew was, at this moment, he was uncertain whether her way, her virtue, was any less worthy than the one he'd been trying so hard to peddle to her.

He felt too a stab of loneliness. He felt that she had slipped away from him, and that they never would meet again with the illusion that they both still stood on the same ground. How many more times would this happen? he wondered. How many other old friends would he find striking off on to different paths from his? How many times had it happened already, and he'd been too busy and self centred to notice? Who would be left to him by the end?

'I'm sorry,' he said at last. 'I believe I may have got it all wrong.'

She smiled at him serenely. 'You're forgiven.'

He thought he could hear the mutter of the train approaching and was half glad of it. He wanted to go now – but not to leave her.

'Why don't you come and stay with us soon?' he asked suddenly.

'Oh – '

'Come on. Just for a week. I'm not saying you should leave this place. Maybe you're right, maybe you're best off down here. But it might help to get away for a bit. Chance to look back on things. It just might help. And I'd like it,' he added quietly, 'I really would.'

He thought she was going to refuse him instantly. But instead she stood thinking, head bowed.

'I don't know,' she said, looking at him at last. 'Perhaps I will. Sometimes . . .' A small furrow of doubt appeared on her brow. 'Sometimes I'm not sure what's going on with me down here. Perhaps a week away would help.'

'Ah, wonderful!'

He was so delighted that he reached out and pulled her to him. He pressed his face against her cheek and neck. Her skin smelled sweet and childish. He breathed in and closed his eyes. When he opened them, he saw beyond the dark outline of her head the lights of the train rounding the bend down the line. He stood away from her, still holding on to her shoulders.

'Oh, that's great!' he cried, above the squeal of brakes. 'That's fine.'

He let her go then. She nodded, smiling, pleased by his enthusiasm.

'We'll arrange it then. I'll write to you. No, I'll phone. We'll do it soon, yes?'

'OK,' she grinned.

'Week after next. No, can't manage that.' He frowned. 'How about the week after the week after – '

She shrugged, still grinning. 'Any time,' she said. 'I'm always free.'

'Right. Pencil it in. I'll be in touch next week to confirm.'

'You'd better get in,' she advised.

He climbed into an empty carriage, pulled the window down and took her hand. He felt so pleased. This morbid feeling he'd had that they never would meet again as friends was quite gone. So much for Fate, Doom, Destiny and all other storybook characters. 'We're going to have such a great time,' he laughed. 'Louise'll be so pleased. Just the three of us. We'll go out. Have fun. And I won't lecture you again. Nothing about . . . work . . . or Raymond. We'll just have fun!'

Along the train, doors were being slammed. A little way to their rear, the guard was stretching his legs, glancing at his watch.

'There's just one thing I want to say about work,' Tom said awkwardly.

On the platform, she laughed up at him.

'Well, but I do. It's important. It's this. I know – well, I guess you feel I haven't done much for you. I mean, I haven't *used* you. And not just me. People like Dick Banham too . . . And it must seem that we don't care, we're being callous. But the truth is – ' Tom took a deep breath, 'it's bloody hard to direct an old friend, it really is. And complicated. You sort of know too much – though you don't know enough – if you know what I mean . . .'

He was beginning to lose it. She laid a hand on his arm as it rested on the window rim.

'You're not to worry about that,' she said.

'But I feel bad about it. Look – ' He took another deep breath. This was a little gift he'd brought all the way down from London to offer her. He felt somewhat foolish offering it at this point – but then he would blame himself afterwards if he didn't. 'Look, there's a little tiny part in this thing I may be doing soon at the Beeb. I mean it's nothing. Three lines and a sneeze. It's yours if you want it. Just to get you started again.'

'No,' she said firmly. 'I don't want it.'

The whistle was blown. The guard climbed back into his compartment.

'You're not angry I offered it?'

'Of course not. It was sweet.'

Moving, the train jerked her hand from his.

'Oh, Susie . . .'

'Goodbye, dear. I'm glad you came down.'

'Week after the week after next. Don't forget. And Susie – '

'What?' She was walking down the platform to keep pace with him.

'Don't be thinking all those things any more.'

'What things?'

'Well, things like – '

She had stopped walking. She stood there, waving after him. He leaned out of the carriage window.

'You know what things,' he shouted. 'Like justice.'

And punishment.

But he was so far from her now that he didn't bother to say the word. He stood at the window watching her. A figure all alone, waving. Then the train rounded a curve and he could see her no more.

10

And Station Approach leads into Market Street, and from there five minutes' steady walking takes you into the High Street. You will know it is the High Street because it is totally deserted, not a soul about, not a sound – after all it is past seven o'clock in the evening – except the traffic lights clicking on and off.

You choose not to take the coast road. You make a couple of zigzags after Wells' Walk, and you are in Merrick Street in no time. One thing that can certainly be said in the town's favour – and there are others, don't try to be funny – is that it's certainly a handy size for getting around. Merrick Street already, then – and there, in the distance, are the lights of the Rainbow supermarket to tell the world that there *is* life in Swayncliff after nightfall. It is not, as everyone likes to make out, just dead. Dead. There are living people here after dark. I.G. Zofahr is here, for instance, in his shop, with his family, keeping watch. And I am here, for instance. I am living here.

Call this living?

Yes, I do. I certainly do. Today, I know I am living. For I have friends who will come miles and miles just to see me and make me smile and put me to rights just when I happen to be in danger, the least little bit of danger, of going too close to the edge. To where the earth stops and there is no more land, or sea, or sky, only the void. That is living, to have friends like this, to do this for me, to grab me and hold me back from the edge . . . Anyway, I have one friend who has done this for me, thank God for that.

Infirm of purpose. Give me the daggers!

Whoa! What? What was that? Whoa . . .

That was enough to make you stand, stock still, open-mouthed, half-way down Merrick Street, still three hundred yards from the Rainbow. Where I.G. Zofahr is living, and keeping watch, as far as anyone knows.

Infirm of purpose –
Oh shut up!

It was all bloody Kate's fault, of course. Her and her jokes. And the spirit of Christmas too. Christmas that would have passed, not counting ten minutes smiling and chatting on the stairs with Miss Esmé Chalmers (and even she was being picked up later in the day by somebody, some niece or cousin, and taken off to a house full of Xmas cheer and Xmas people) that would have been passed by her –

Alone. Solitary. Sod all.

If Raymond hadn't come round. As arranged. It was all arranged, so there was no sense of panic in her as the day drew near. She had her Christmas planned. Just like a normal person. She knew exactly what was going to happen. Except that she had half an idea – and certainly a hope – that this time, as a Christmas surprise, he would break with custom and bring Kate along too. She would so much like to meet her. And though she understood perfectly well Raymond's need to keep his friends – well, herself anyway – separate from his home life, still she had a hope that on this special day he would break his rule. For surely Kate must have some degree of curiosity about her. She certainly did about Kate.

But he did not bring her.

'Are you *sure* she doesn't mind you seeing me?' she had asked him the last time they met.

'Why should she mind?' Raymond had asked blankly.

'Well, no, I don't mean that exactly. There's no reason why she should, of course, but . . . it just seems a bit strange, that's all.'

'Strange?'

'Strange. I mean, I hear about her, and we send each other messages and hellos and all that – through you – but I've never set eyes on her. Sometimes I think she doesn't exist.'

'What?'

'Well . . .' She shrugged. She smiled at him too, to show that she wasn't exactly serious. 'She's just so invisible. She's like a ghost or something. What have you done with her, Raymond? I suspect foul play!' she laughed giddily.

He had watched her until her smile had turned awkward and was beginning to fade. Then he had stood up.

'Oh look, I'm sorry,' she started, feeling quite foolish now. 'It was just a joke, really.'

'No, I understand,' he nodded. 'You've never seen her, have you? Never heard her voice. No wonder you're suspicious.'

'I'm not *suspicious*, exactly.'

But he wasn't looking at her. 'Here,' he said, 'I think I can help.' He made his way across her living room and picked up the phone from the floor. Dialled a number and listened. And then he held the phone out to her. She took a few steps towards him. Then she came closer and she could hear a woman's voice issuing from the ear piece, a pleasant, even voice.

'Hello?'

Raymond pushed the phone towards her again, inviting her to take it. But she shook her head, and made a backward step.

'Hello?' came the woman's voice again, naturally sounding a little irritated now. 'Who's there?'

Again Susan shook her head, declining the phone. Raymond put his head slightly on one side and watched her. The ear piece came to life once more.

'Oh, sod off,' said the woman, bored now rather than irritated, 'you stupid person.' There was a click, then the hum of the dialling tone. Gently Raymond replaced the phone on its stand.

'There you see.' He smiled at her. 'That was Kate.'

Now it was too late, she felt it was quite stupid of her not have taken the phone. In fact, the whole incident struck her as rather silly.

'Why didn't you talk to her?' she asked him.

'Why didn't you?'

She shrugged. 'I don't know.' She thought for a moment. 'One of us should have, though. It's horrible for a woman alone, getting a call like that. I know what it's like.'

Raymond nodded seriously. 'Didn't think of that,' he said. Then, 'It's all right. I'll tell her what happened when I get home.'

'She'll think I'm such a fool.'

'I'll leave you out of it, if you like.' Carefully he replaced the telephone on the floor. 'Not to worry,' he smiled, straightening up. 'She's pretty fearless is Kate. She doesn't scare easy.'

So that was more or less all right. And at least she'd had it proved to her that there really was a Kate, and she had heard her – a nice, steady, clear voice, sounding younger than she had expected – and she, Kate, was hard to scare, apparently, which was a fine way to be. And she had many other excellent qualities, no doubt, though Raymond did not often introduce her into their conversation, was not all that forthcoming about her in detail, but forthcoming enough at least for Susan to know that Kate also had a wonderful sense of humour. For wasn't it she, in those tense, awful days just after the news about the plundered inheritance, about the terrible wrong that had been done to Raymond, wasn't it Kate who had cut through that fog of bitterness and sorrow and fury with one single swift riposte?

'The bastard ought to be shot!'

Good joke. A1. By Kate. As told to Susan by Raymond on Christmas Day. Bloody good joke. They had laughed and laughed.

And done their best – it was Christmas after all – to keep the joke going.

Well, what if . . .? And what if . . .? Is he in London? No. Atlanta? Calcutta? No. He's left the airline. Doesn't need the money now, of course. Is a filthy millionaire now, you see, rolling around in the heaped up piles of loot . . . Well, come on, Raymond, don't be dull – *Where is he?*

Portugal.

Portugal?

Yes. Don't you remember? I told you he had a house there, on the Algarve. He's spending the winter there. Working out how he's going to spend the dough.

I see . . . So. Portugal. How to get there? Come on, Raymond, keep the joke going. How do we . . .? Well, a plane of course.

No.

No good. Airport security. You could never get a gun on a plane with all those devices they've got. No, no, too risky. Spend the next ten years in jail? For a joke?

Fair enough. Even a joke needs to stay in some touch with reality to keep going, to stay funny, and airport security was a real complication, the detector gates, the X-rays, the frisking, bit of a problem definitely. The joke had to rest there for a while, outside the detector gates. Susan had served turkey breasts. Raymond had had to decline his helping. He'd already eaten turkey today – with Kate – and his appetite was never large.

So she ate, and he drank a little wine, and she drank considerably more, and every now and then their eyes would meet across the table, and they'd burst out laughing again, both in the same moment, at the memory of Kate's bit of fun.

Kate. She had only lately discovered how protective Raymond was of his wife. That time he had phoned Kate so that she could listen to her voice had continued to trouble her. She wished that either Raymond or herself had spoken. She wondered how he could have put his wife through that. But then, a couple of days ago, wanting to change an arrangement she had made with him, and not having his home number, she had rung the *Argus* office again. This time she stayed on the phone, pleased to think that at last she had a proper reason to talk to him. As soon as the *Argus* receptionist answered the phone, Susan recognised the voice. She recognised now too certain background sounds she had not been able to identify when she had been listening to 'Kate'. She heard the whirr and click of electric typewriters, phones ringing, the busy hum of a newspaper office.

'Hello?' the receptionist said again. 'Can I help you?'

Susan collected herself. 'Yes. Sorry. Can I speak to Raymond Thorne?'

'I'm sorry, Mr Thorne doesn't work here any more.'

'I beg your pardon?'

A chatty, slightly malicious tone entered the receptionist's voice. 'He was only with us for a few weeks. Just for a trial period, to see if he would work out. And, well, he didn't, you see.'

Susan sat in silence, staring at the phone dial.

'Hello?' said the receptionist. 'Would you like to talk to anyone else?'

'No, I wouldn't,' said Susan softly, 'and you had absolutely no right to tell me that.'

She hung up then. She was relieved at least to find that her worries about Kate and her reaction to the anonymous phone call were groundless. She was somewhat hurt that a trick like this had been played on her, even though it was with the best of intentions. If Raymond still didn't feel ready to have her meet his wife, then she could understand and accept it. There was no need for these complicated games. She decided that she would talk to him about it when they next met. But that next time she had somehow forgotten to bring it up. And forgotten the next time too. And, in fact, she had still not yet got around to it.

She was hanging back, she supposed, mainly because she would have to tell him that she also knew that he had lost his job. She felt unwilling to do that. He had the right to tell her about it in his own way, his own time. Which had not yet come round obviously . . .

Infirm of purpose.

Just shut up!

Infirm of porpoise.

She chuckled. Infirm . . . From? What the hell was it from? Shakespeare, of course, but which . . .? Of course! How could she even hesitate! Fool, idiot, illiterate.

The Scottish Play.

Yes, of course. Lady Macbeth. The very thing for her. The sort of part Mark had had in mind when – you had to laugh – he had decided to take over the direction of her career.

'But I've got all these offers, Mark. And really, you know, we could use the money. And I like to work, you know that . . .'

Say no.

We are not wasting our time on trash any more.

We are going to be a great actress.

Please don't argue, Susie. We are going to surprise the world.

Well, that sounds like fun, so – say no to Johnny Richards and six months' work in a farce he was bringing into the Savoy Theatre, a script that when she read it had made her laugh till she ached. And had turned out to be a huge hit, of course. West End. Broadway. Everywhere. But, sorry, Johnny, we're much too good for you. And having got her breath back from turning down the West End, it was no to Mike Conroy and his *Woman Police Constable* series at Granada. Well, all right – the money was terrific, but the scripts weren't so hot, and fair enough – turn him down, why not? Except she wished that her refusal had been a lot less abrupt and, basically, unpleasant than it had been. Mike deserved at least a nice letter from her, for he had been a help to her back when she was getting started. He deserved better than just no. Relayed via her agent. But as Mark pointed out – they've got to get the message that they simply can't offer you such work any more. Do they send scripts like this to Peggy Ashcroft? he'd demanded. Or Glenda Jackson? Claire Bloom? Judi Dench?

Well, I don't know – I've seen Glenda in some pretty naff stuff. And as for Judi –

Do they?

But, honey, be reasonable –

Do they?

I suppose not.

Then they shall not send them to us. And the only way to convince them is – hit 'em on the head. Just cut 'em off. Curt, final, just shoot 'em down.

Oh . . . well, all right. And while we're at it: no to Jim Hayes, Roger Plant, Tony McNee, Alison Babbage . . . Alison, who was a tough lady, rang up and called her names. And then started calling Mark names, which was just not necessary. 'Tin-pot Svengali' was the mildest of them.

'Are you insane, woman? This is a terrific part I'm offering you.'

'I'm sorry, Alison. It's just not the way I see my career developing.'

'What career? When was the last time you worked? . . . You can't remember, can you? Listen, you silly bitch – are you going to tell that idiot husband of yours to lay off, or am I?'

'Now, look, Alison. It's clear you just don't understand – '

'I understand you've said no to every decent part you've been offered this year. And you say no a couple more times and that's it. Forget it. They only give you so much rope. After that, it's bye-bye Little Miss Maniac. Down the drain for you.'

Right. Thanks so much, Alison. Good to talk to you. And onwards and upwards and . . . oh, real regrets for this one –

Say no to the personal appearance tour in the United States that spring.

Yes, that was one she had been really sorry to lose. *The Entwistles* was showing on the PBS network over there, and was a great success. Fan mail came in. From New York and Denver and Boston and Seattle. Someone sent her a clipping from the *New York Post*. In one Manhattan store they were introducing a spring line of dresses and accessories to be known as 'The Lucy Entwistle Look'. Wasn't that touching? Wasn't that . . .

Fantastic!

The tour would include tea at the White House. The First Lady apparently was a besotted fan of the show. And the President too was said to like it pretty much.

We can't say no to this, Mark.

Mark, it's the bloody *White House*!

I already have said no. I phoned the producer yesterday and turned him down. On your behalf.

Ah, that was harsh, that was . . . not fair. Not fair. Susan stopped walking for a moment to catch her breath, to gulp in air. Bastard. Stupid, officious bastard – to do that to her. Without even telling her . . . So Grace Barker had gone instead. The Americans, so she had heard, were taken aback at first to be getting the second team like this, but they had swallowed their disappointment and had made Grace very welcome and – and hadn't she had a great time? And hadn't it been so useful for her? And wasn't she – Tom had mentioned it casually this very afternoon – over there right now, doing a film? Oh, probably nothing wonderful, but so useful to have connections over there, and the money was amazing, and oh: sun, sun, sun . . .

We are going to turn our back on Lucy Entwistle, Mark had said.

Although when Dick had offered her the part it had been she who had been doubtful about accepting it. It was such a change from the muted, cerebral roles she mostly played. But they were very broke then. It was the time Mark was writing scripts on spec.

'We'll just do it,' he'd said. 'Get it over with and get out with a pile of money. Just think of the money, that's all.'

So she had done it. And to her surprise had liked doing it. And had liked it even more when the series was shown and all of a sudden she found herself recognised in the street, to find that people were made happy and excited just to see her walking by. To see *her*! God, she didn't like to think how pleased it made her to be famous for that short time when *The Entwistles* was running.

But of course: 'You weren't famous,' Mark had explained to her patiently. 'You were notorious. You were flavour of the month, in an up-market soap opera. Flavour of the minute. Like a Yorkie bar.'

Oh, I see.

'And now it's over, thank God,' Mark had added – and indeed people by now had stopped running after her and phoning her up and making a fuss over her when she went out. 'And now we can turn to the real thing.'

The real thing. Oh, good.

She had reached the Rainbow. She pressed her face at the window, locating herself between the Spar Spaghetti Rings offer and a notice advertising last week's St Saviour's Bazaar. She could see Mrs Zofahr sitting at the cash register. One of her children – Susan thought there were three or four – was playing near her. About five years old or six, this child, Susan guessed. She frowned as she watched the pair. Surely the child was up much too late. It was nearly eight. What time did five year olds go to bed? she wondered.

Well, how would she know? Never having had any children of her own. Only the abortion.

We've got so much to do. We've got no room for kids. We are reaching for the stars, Susie, and a child would only drag us back down to earth.

So out it must go.

You know I'm only thinking of what's good for us. For you. At this time. One day – who knows? – perhaps . . .

But give him this: he had driven her to and from the clinic. And had been a perfect sweetheart, both going and coming back.

Oh, hell – she hadn't put up much of an argument, so she couldn't complain. She'd gone along with the abortion. He hadn't forced her, she'd agreed. She'd listened to him. We've got to make sacrifices, he'd said. Nothing stupendous is ever achieved without sacrifice.

So she had sacrificed.

Listen to me, he had said, holding her as she had cried and cried like a disappointed child because she could not go on the US tour, *listen*: in a year, maybe two we are going over there – the Lincoln Center, off-Broadway, the Kennedy Center – we are going there as Cleopatra, and as Juliet, and as Portia, and as Lady Macbeth. Do you want to ruin it all by having them think of bloody Lucy Entwistle the moment you step on stage? Do you?

And later, when at last she had accepted, submitted, bowed to his persuasions, she had said sniffily, 'I'm too old to play Juliet.' And he had stroked her hair and said 'Rubbish', and told her about Mrs Patrick Campbell playing Juliet at fifty, and her with only one leg. And then he had jumped up and mimicked Mrs Pat and her limp for her, his back to the window, the awful white Swayncliff light turning him into a monstrous, capering shadow before her.

> Come, night! come, Romeo! come, thou day in night!
> For thou wilt lie upon the wings of night,
> Whiter than new snow on a raven's back.
> Come, gentle night; come, loving, black-brow'd night,
> Give me my Romeo . . .

And she had laughed and clapped and had been so entranced by his performance. For Mark had one fan as devoted as himself, and that was her. She thought he had a streak of genius and could never understand why nobody else ever saw it. Why nobody else ever saw anything much in him. It dismayed her sometimes to think that love or obsession, whatever it was, might have so corrupted her judgment that she could not see him right. But at moments like this, as he worked just for her, as Mrs Pat flowered before her – outrageous, like a nightmare, but staunch and valiant too, queenly, plunging on – she had no doubt that she was right about him, everyone else was wrong.

Go, get thee hence, for I will not.
What's here? a cup, clos'd in my true love's hand?
Poison, I see, hath been his timeless end.
O churl! drunk all, and left no friendly drop
To help me after? I will kiss thy lips;
Haply some poison yet doth hang on them,
To make me die with a restorative.

His mouth a fraction from her own.

Thy lips are warm!

And it seemed contemptible finally that she should make such a fuss over some petty deprivation – six weeks of American adulation, tea at the White House, glory, glory all the way – when Mark had to bear such burdens of anonymity, lack of appreciation. So she cheered up entirely, and when he'd finished performing – a good twenty minute show, plus encore – they went to bed and she was so pleased with him she scarcely thought any more of what she had lost. So happy in his arms. We were happy. Why did nobody else appreciate him? The white light fading, darkness over them as they lay together. It had been a lovely show he had put on for her. It mattered not at all that he had got it wrong, that it was Bernhardt that had lost a leg, not Mrs Campbell. That was the sort of nit-picking complaint that their friends – well, her friends – would have levelled at him. What Mark called the typical mediocrity's concern for minor detail. Thank God they were free of those so-called friends now. That they had stopped coming down to see them. Had stopped even calling them. (Had Mark told them to stop?) Thank God there was just the two of them now, in their own world, in which everything made –

A kind of sense.

Mrs Zofahr, turning suddenly from the cash register, caught sight of her at the window. She stared at Susan alertly for a moment, and then relaxed and smiled. Susan, surprised, waved back. Christ, she recognised me. After – what? – five years? six years? buying stuff from her shop, she finally knows who I am. Now she felt she could not pass by the Rainbow without going in. Also she remembered that Raymond Thorne was due at her place later, and it would be nice to get something in for him. He had a sweet tooth. Very sweet tooth. She had never seen him much interested in regular food, but he was often stuffing sweets into his mouth, and never said no when she offered him chocolate digestives or cake with icing. In fact, he had cleared her out of digestives last time. Here was a chance to replenish supplies – and to take this friendly moment with Mrs Zofahr a little further. No saying where it might lead to. In no time (Susan's mind skidded ahead as she pushed the swing doors open) she would be known as a regular, a cherished customer, and then, the months racing by – God, why didn't they ever? – treated as one of the family, Auntie Sue to the little Zofahrs, our kind, English lady friend to the grown-up Zofahrs. I would have been so good in that Indian thing that was on TV a few years back. Geraldine James had scored a great triumph there. Well, good luck to her, but I could have done it too. I could have done it awfully well. If the bastards had only given me a chance. But, as far as I know, I was not even considered. Who had I offended in that set up?

However, I'd said no long before to the whole world, so can't complain.

Mrs Zofahr did not seem to notice her entrance. She must have thought it was someone else at the window after all. Susan dropped the smile from her face, and took a wire basket from the pile and started up the first aisle. Now, think ahead: something tempting for Raymond – although, the way he was, a bowl of granulated sugar would probably do as well as anything. Mark, in contrast, had a taste for the piquant and sour. He liked sucking lemons and limes. Also he was proud of his flat stomach, so sugar was out, brown or white no matter, and also butter, white bread, fat meat, potatoes, except the very new kind which he loved. She didn't know if Raymond had a flat stomach. He was certainly very skinny, but there was something slack and unhealthy about him; under those shabby clothes he always wore there might well be a few ripples of flab. He ought to go back to the Nautilus, tone himself up. She hadn't seen him at the gym since . . . Couldn't remember. Couldn't remember the last time she'd been there. Life had closed in a bit lately. But on the other hand – she grinned to herself – had opened up too in certain unexpected ways. Definitely had.

But now, enough, she should stop comparing Mark and Raymond. So very different. Mark had been her husband, loved one, her – tin-pot Svengali? Not at all, her friend and guide. And Raymond was . . .

Uh – no. I'll think about that later. What Raymond and I have become. Are on the verge of becoming. Later. When I see him. Maybe it'll all blow away before my eyes, the fresh breeze Tom brought down here – dear old Tom – clearing out all that musky, unreal stuff that has been clogging the air lately. And we'll laugh together, Raymond and I, to think that we ever, the two of us, ever, for one moment, contemplated . . .

Such a thing.

All Kate's fault – her and her stupid jokes.

Lord God, thought Susan blankly, it can't be true, what we've been up to.

Can it?

Now Mark – the past, full of pain, but safe now – Mark, my friend and guide, who guided me all the way. Into the deep swamp, damn him . . . No. No more blaming. If I chose to trot along obediently behind him, then I chose to do it, nobody else. And agreed with him all the way.

Except I thought we said no too many times. Just one little job along the way wouldn't have hurt. Would have kept hold of a friend or two, a couple of contacts. Would have got me out of Swayncliff for a week or two. But we always said no.

Ah, but that didn't describe the situation exactly. We wanted to say yes – to the right people. We very much wanted to say yes to the Royal Shakespeare Company, for instance. And the National Theatre, for instance. We would have said yes like a shot to either of those – if only they had answered our letters.

Well, be fair, they did. The first ones. They wrote very nice letters back. Yes, they knew her work, and they were interested, but the problem was . . .

'I really don't think we ought to specify the parts I should have, Mark. Not on first approaching them, anyway.'

But he had scoffed at that. 'Do you think we're going up to Stratford to waste our time playing Cleopatra's handmaiden? Or hanging round the South Bank with a couple of lines in some rotten revival?'

'Well, it wouldn't be wasting our time. We'd get to know the set up, the people, we'd get to be – '

'One of the gang? No, thanks! You see, Susie . . .' He stroked her hair thoughtfully, as he told her this. 'You have an amazing instinct for settling into the crowd, don't you, love? And I've got to protect you from that.' He let go of her, and wandered over to the window. 'No,' he said, 'we'll wait them out. They want you, no question. They'll crack before we do.'

'Christ, I hate this view,' he said after a moment.

He turned to her then, and stared at her. He seemed for a moment unhappy at what he saw, and it made her stomach lurch to see him looking like that at her. My God, if he gives up on me too, where am I then? But then he smiled. He shook his head. 'No, we're going in as stars, as conquerors, or else . . .'

We're not going in at all. Which, of course, was what happened. The letters from the RSC and the National in reply to theirs got crisper, shorter, then impatient, then irritated, then – frankly – quite insulting. And then stopped. Mark could never get to see any of the directors at either company. Secretaries were the closest he got. On the phone. And they weren't at all encouraging. Susan begged him to be reasonable.

'Look, they're right to be cautious. I haven't done much theatre lately. If I could just go in and start small . . .'

Susan small. He shook his head. 'We're not small. We are not *small*.'

'Then let me try and get something in the provinces. I'll play Lady Macbeth in Sheffield. Or anywhere. Then, when I've shown what I can do – '

No, no, no, no.

'Please, Susie, trust me. We are not going to fucking Sheffield. We are going straight to the top.'

So he paced up and down. And he thought and made plans and calculated and called anybody who could help, and then anybody who would talk to him. And she'd watched him, fascinated, as the weeks passed, then months, a year went by, and still he wouldn't give up. This was more entrancing to her than anything else, to watch him perform, to watch him carry the whole burden of pretence on his shoulders. That he knew what he was doing, that he was doing the best for her. That it would all turn out right in the end. Between hanging around in a rehearsal room in Acton or wherever, and the chance to watch this great endeavour, this stellar performance, there was no comparison. She could not feel cheated.

We've just got to hang on, and hang on, and . . .

They spent so much time together, whole days, many days, reading through play scripts. To 'hone her skills', he explained, to keep her sharp. So that she would always be ready for that moment, that magical phone call that would set everything right, and waft them out of this bizarre backwater to the warmth and fame and glory that waited for them only sixty miles up the railway line. Mark believed in magic, she came to realise. Growing up in south London, not so long after the war, he had learned about life in the stalls of the Eros, Catford, the Lewisham Odeon, the Brixton ABC. It had all made much more sense to him than his other life with his immigrant parents, who had hardly twenty words of English between them, and were still stunned with grief at the horror that had befallen the rest of the family not long before, in countries the little boy knew nothing about, and which were certainly never shown or spoken of in the cinemas where he spent the rest, the important part of his life. Mark truly believed in the MGM version. And thought that stars were born just by wishing it. And that trapdoors would open to carry away all opposition. And that every ending would be happy. And that one day that bloody phone that sat there squat and silent on the floor of the living room would ring and on the other end would be not some two-bit producer with a dodgy series to peddle, but the awaited one, the magician from on high, abracadabra, and all their troubles would be over.

In the meantime, they honed their skills. She was St Joan. She was Nora. She was Viola, Millamont, Portia, Blanche Dubois, Hedda Gabler, the Duchess of Malfi . . . of course Lady Macbeth. Susan's head was spinning. She was dazzled and consumed, performing these parts, day after day, in the living room, no other actor in *history* had had such a succession of roles. And she was damn good too, even Mark was impressed. Sometimes he would jump up from the sofa on which they sat, side by side, reading – he'd jump up and stride up and down and cry out, his voice trembling with longing, 'Oh, God, when it happens – when it *happens* – ah, Susie, we're going to *kill* them!'

Ah, Mark, I'm sorry, so sorry . . .

In the back of the biscuit shelf, Susan made a fine discovery. Among the ranks of McVitie's and Cadbury's, she found squashed away in the rear a couple of packets of biscuits from West Germany that even she, no connoisseur, knew to be the very best, state of the art. They looked like they'd been on the Zofahrs' shelves a long time, however. She couldn't find a 'Best Before' label. But she only hesitated a moment before dropping both packets into her basket. It was true that Raymond probably wouldn't care what quality biscuit he was offered as long as it was sweet. But it mattered to her and she was doing the offering. Be extravagant in little things was her motto. It made up for having to be pinched and mean in everything else.

God though, she could hardly afford to be extravagant even in the smallest matters for very much longer. She thought of how much she had left in her savings and she felt suddenly faint. Thirty-seven years on this earth and she had accumulated – why, people spent what she had in the building society on dinner for four up in London. It was grotesque. Something had to happen. She was incredibly poor – and meanwhile there were people in this world who had so much, and still they cheated and schemed to get their hands on more, still more money that was not theirs, that they had gained by treachery, deceit, lies . . .

No. Stop that.

Tom. Tom Scott. It was important just now to think of him. She had had an idea, several times during the afternoon, that Tom was on the point of offering her money. Well, of course, that would have been embarrassing, and not possible for her to accept . . . Bullshit. She would have taken it like a shot. And that would have been another step down. Mooching off friends. How could she have faced him again? But then she was mooching off the state as it was, and that wasn't all that much better, was it? Mark would never sign on. Too proud. Oh, always that. He was nothing. In the world's eyes the completest of nobodies. Yet he had his pride, and only the best could ever be good enough for him.

And *she* was the best for a while, as long as he believed in her. Best in the world. Surely this was what had held her prisoner for so long. And why – though she knew perfectly well his advice was disastrous, she was throwing away her career – she had never put a stop to him. (Though every morning she had woken up swearing to herself that she would tell him today to lay off, let her alone, she'd accept the next bloody job that was offered to her, no matter what . . . But she never did.)

People like Alison Babbage, they thought they understood what it was all about. That old man/woman thing. A slave to the cockocracy – had Alison really called her that? She thought she had. But it was not so simple. It was that sometimes Susan had an insight into the way Mark thought of her, what he hoped for her. And she saw, in those moments when she looked through his eyes, saw herself as a clear and shining light, a jewel held aloft above the murk and muddle of the world. Herself. A true star, blazing forth, a beacon in heaven that all could worship, Mark could worship . . .

Of course, it was preposterous. It didn't happen any more. It belonged to the age of Garbo . . . and Jenny Lind, Sarah Bernhardt, the Duse . . . And all she was was Susie Strang, Susan small, ex-Guildford Grammar School for Girls, ex-Central School of Drama, working actress, steady trouper, many varied roles, good old Susie, made a bit of a splash as Lucy Entwistle, didn't she win a prize for that one? but since then –

Oh, to be thought of in that way. To be that shining jewel, if only in one person's eyes. Nothing could compare with that. Nothing. Yes, he was manipulating her, using her. He wanted to put her on to a pedestal – but perhaps not even as much as she wanted to step on to it. And when his desires coincided so closely with her fantasies, who could say which of them was most to blame, who was most using the other?

11

At the check-out, she showed her purchases to Mrs Zofahr, who shook her head doubtfully.

'I don't know how long those biscuits been there, you know. They might be stale.'

'It's all right,' Susan said. 'I'll risk it.'

'They are good biscuits. They ought to sell. But the people here . . .' Mrs Zofahr gestured dispiritedly at Swayncliff beyond the windows.

'I *know.*'

Inflamed with sisterly feelings, Susan tried to look directly into Mrs Zofahr's eyes. But the woman now, having rung up her purchases, was not looking at her, was holding out her hand for the money, and at the same time calling sharply in her own language to her little girl who had just knocked over a small tower of cat-food tins in a far aisle. Susan paid up in silence, and then thought she needed a carrier bag and tried to pay for that. But Mrs Zofahr, handing her the bag, shook her head again.

'No, no.' Still not looking at Susan, she frowned at the probably stale biscuits.

'Oh. Thanks.'

The other woman nodded, and then relapsed into silence and stillness, into a posture too indifferent to be called sullen. Susan took her bag and pushed her way out of the swing doors, on to the street again. A couple of hundred yards to go. She remembered walking this stretch of pavement with Raymond that time, ages ago, when he had told her about the will, about Phillip's treachery . . . Well, it was only last month, she realised. But so much had happened since then, it seemed like an age. Like now, they had walked along this street, in the dark, past the Bon-Bon sweet shop, scene of the horrible crime, the mystery killer who still stalked the streets . . . No, that wasn't right. That had been cleared up. Raymond had told her about that. Some kid, some devilish kid. What had Raymond said about it?

'So you see,' he'd said, 'poor bloody Swayncliff doesn't even have its own murderer any more.'

And was not going to get another one. For sure.

Infirm of purpose.

Stop that.

So it turned out that the nearest she would ever get to Lady Macbeth was still the school production, when she was twelve years old, and in kilt and grey beard had played a thane, one of the crowd of retainers at the Scottish court. All the other male parts had been taken by girls too, except the title role, for which an actor had been drafted in from the boys' grammar school. A raven-haired hero – Rupert? Robert? – he had caused great excitement, especially in costume: a bear-skin robe draped over a short dark tunic, which displayed his fine muscular legs and, in moments of high drama, also the brief black underpants supplied with the costume. Snobbishly, as the rest of the cast thought, Rupert/Robert had confined his attentions almost entirely to his acting partner, Sylvia James, the school's star thespian. Once Susan, rounding a corner in a dark corridor backstage, had seen two forms standing against the wall, pressed close to each other, undulating together in a fast, rhythmic motion. She heard loud breathing, gasps. She had not been noticed. Out of curiosity, she lingered, keeping herself in the shadows. The grey beard was tickling her nose and she wanted to sneeze, but held it back. After a few moments she heard a louder gasp and a faint cry. The figures separated then abruptly. And then came Macbeth's voice, clear, irritated, disdainful. 'Oh, Christ,' he said, 'I've shot into these vile black pants.' And Lady Macbeth, in a disgruntled voice, said, 'All over my hand, you mean. Honestly, you are a beast!' And Susan, though not really knowing what was happening, couldn't help laughing at that. In a moment, Sylvia James was standing before her, looking down at her furiously, calling her a little pig, and a disgrace to the House, and giving her two demerit marks before she swept away up the corridor. And Rupert/Robert, as he went past her, had winked at her kindly. 'Silly bitch,' he'd murmured, and Susan knew he didn't mean her. And that was her clearest memory of the Scottish play, and the reason why – to Mark's irritation – she couldn't help often chuckling whenever they were honing her skills on that particular piece.

I used to chuckle a lot, she thought. I used to laugh and giggle and fall about. Even when things were so desperate with Mark, I kept my sense of humour, more or less. But not any more, it seems. When I laugh it isn't really laughing any more, at least it doesn't make me feel good. And my jokes . . . there's something sinister about them now. And I'm not even sure if they are jokes at all. This joke that Raymond and I have been sharing for the past few weeks, for instance. I think we know it is a joke, though Raymond's sense of humour seems pretty weak, and mine – well, that's it: where has it gone to nowadays? Is it up to appreciating any more what might be called the Scottish joke? Raymond as a skinny, uncertain version of Macbeth. Myself as his awesome wacky lady – well, at least my skills are honed on it. And in the role of Duncan – ah, infirm of purpose!

Oh Christ, he'd said, I've shot into these vile black pants!

And Susan, now remembering it, laughed out loud, as she had used to do. A laugh that wasn't crooked, sinister, or complicated. Cleansing laughter, normal, that threatened no harm to anyone. Oh, where is my beautiful Macbeth now? she thought longingly. She felt a sudden flush of desire, acutely localised, so that she stopped walking and leaned over slightly as if she had been stabbed down there. My God, she thought, with a tingle of amazed delight, I feel horny as hell. And then was amazed that she was amazed – a grown woman, after all, and when was the last time . . .? Her mind roamed back across the glacial months – why, not since Mark . . . No. Wrong! There had been a party up in London, a couple of weeks after he had left her, and she gone up to it in a spirit of great defiance, packing a couple of condoms, and determined to have a good time. The hell with Mark, the hell with husbands, hell with everything. And she had picked up somebody, some actor, and gone home with him – who was it? Try as she might, she could not picture his face, or any other part of him. It had been a disaster, of course. 'It's quite difficult,' she could remember him – whoever it was – saying this in a clear, resentful voice, 'it is, in fact, *very* difficult making love to somebody who is crying all the time.' And so it must have been, poor man, though technically he had just about managed it in the end. And since then – nothing at all. Zero.

How long, O Lord, how long?

Now where did that come from? Where the hell – ?

How long, O Lord, how very –

Oh, Christ.

Of course.

Wendy. Wendy Strong. That town. That other bloody town. And the Palace Theatre. And the wind howling off the moors. And I am seventeen years old . . . Look, I have come full circle, it seems. I started off in a freezing backwater, and here I am, it looks like I am ending up in one too.

My Wendy. My long lost friend, sharer of the darkness and cold. Who I never think of, but is always there somehow.

'How long, O Lord?'

'About eight inches would be very nice.'

'Ten would be even nicer . . .'

Dear ally against the hostile world. Who made me laugh and kept me sane when I was seventeen, when I was Miss Mouse. Long before I was Miss Maniac. And who hurt me so much when she abandoned me . . .

Well, stop hurting for a little while, she told herself caustically. And remember your friend with gratitude. And use her. Use her. For nothing is lost as long as it's remembered.

Then I could laugh, laugh with my friend, and all the shadows in my life were driven away. I could do it then? Why can't I now? Why can't I – thus – raise my eyes and stare without flinching at the night and the cold stars and – holding on to my friend's hand . . . How long, O Lord, how long?

It works. See! I feel much better.

Laughter the best medicine.

Hopefully, Susan peered up at the moonless Swayncliff night, and laughed. And then, feeling herself indeed so much stronger, happier (watch me, Wendy!), she laughed again. The night was icy, as icy almost as in that other town, over twenty years ago – but never mind! She had the cure to hand. Again, bolder and louder and merrier than before, she laughed. You can't get me! she mocked the frigid sky.

'You sound like you're having a good time,' came a voice, faintly accusing, at her side.

She winced and looked round almost fearfully. She saw his car parked at the curb near by. He must have been sitting there, waiting, as she had come chortling up the street. She looked at him unwillingly. In the matter of friends, she thought sadly, I have come down a long way in twenty years. 'Raymond,' she said faintly. Then, 'I'm late. I'm sorry. I stopped to do some shopping.' She held out the plastic Rainbow carrier, as if she needed to prove her story to him. In the same moment she saw that he was carrying a bag just like hers, bearing the same faint rainbow design. 'Snap!' she almost said, to give them a laugh. But she no longer felt very humorous, all that laughter seemed far behind her suddenly, driven away in the moment of his appearance at her side – so she said nothing.

He shrugged. 'Doesn't matter.' He watched her for a moment. 'Nice to see you looking happy.' On his bony face, a smile struggled to be born. It made him seem almost sadder than usual. 'Want to share the joke?'

She shook her head. 'It's nothing. You wouldn't get it.'

'Oh.' The effort to smile collapsed. 'All right.'

They stood looking at each other. There was something reserved and almost hostile in their stares. After a moment, she shifted her gaze awkwardly away from his and found herself looking at the plastic bag that dangled from his right hand. The carrier was not full, not bulging, but seemed very heavy as it hung motionless in his grip.

'Look,' he said then, 'if you're not in the mood for me right now . . . I understand. I'll be off.'

It was as if an escape route had opened for her, a gleam of light at the end of darkness. Not in the mood? I am not at all in the mood for you, she thought, my skinny, unfortunate friend. She was examining him now, staring at his features in the lamplight. As if she had raised a rock and was looking in distant distaste at the creature that scuttled away from under it. Had she ever thought this man was – almost – handsome? (Montgomery Clift, for God's sake!) She felt a stab of true dislike as she looked into the weak, unhappy eyes. Christ, how do I know you? How has it happened? How can I get away . . .? But then she thought in a sudden panic: ah, no, he *is* my friend. I can't let him go. Anything is better than what was before. Alone, so alone. And then another voice within her, calmer and as if from a higher place, said: nonsense! – wasn't Tom Scott down here with you only this afternoon, all afternoon, well into the evening? You certainly have other friends than this sad disastrous man. At least one other friend.

Who isn't here, the first voice capped the other. Who isn't here now. And Raymond is always here. Which is all that can matter to a desperate woman.

And then – sign of health, sign of precious sanity, the two voices blended together, harmonised, calmed her down. But you are no longer desperate, this single voice told her. Tom helped. My good sense helped. The laughter helped. And I can put things into perspective now. I can certainly put this poor Raymond into perspective.

And it was best to do it now, when she was feeling so much

stronger than usual, than she had been for months maybe. Thanks to Tom. And when she could – she had just proved it – laugh. Laugh innocently. Have a joke. A laugh with Raymond would be a very good thing. Not at him – *with* him. An important distinction. The essence of all good comedy. And it was a comedy they were enacting, that was clear. That had to be made clear to him. Whimsical comedy, a flight of fantasy . . . not some sort of ghoulish melodrama. Even if they had got their wires somewhat crossed along the way. They could both now do with a good laugh. And a general putting of things into perspective. A sorting out of what was fact from what was fancy. And an agreement to put a stop to certain silly jokes that had gone on for far too long and were in danger of taking on a weird life all of their own.

('I've got it! Oh, yes, I have. Of course. Of course!'

'Yes?' He had watched her eagerly. Already she could see, though she hardly had time to enjoy it much in her excitement, that his eyes were glistening with admiration for her. For she was good at this game, she was definitely far superior to him. She had the imagination for it, and the will to crack the problems as they came up. Where he saw always obstacles, her brain was already feeling out solutions, preparing to move on.

'Oh, yes!'

'Yes, what?'

'OK . . . no planes. Boat and train!'

'Ah . . .'

'They don't search you on a boat,' she had grinned exultantly. 'Nor on a train, I'm sure.'

'But you can't get a train all the way to Portugal.'

'Why not? I'm sure you can. Let's see – get a boat right here. And then – what? – through Paris? I don't know. Across France anyway. Through Spain, and then – you could certainly get to wherever – Lisbon, is it? – by train, I bet you can.'

'Then what? He's a hundred miles from Lisbon.'

'I don't know. Buses, trains . . . it must be possible. And as long as we keep away from planes, there'd be no problem. Oh, can't you see it?' Watching him from the sofa, she had hugged her knees against her chest. 'Overland all the way. Oh, wonderful!' *She* could see it. Like a ghost moving across the map of Europe, silent, unobserved, unstoppable. What a game! What inspiration. What admiration – almost adoring – in Raymond's eyes.

The admiration. The thing I crave above everything. It was in Mark's eyes when I held him dazzled with my skill. And in the eyes of the crowd, for those few weeks when I was Lucy Entwistle, whenever I deigned to pass amongst them, in the street, in a shop, on a bus, as if I was an ordinary mortal and not a queen. It is what I desire. It fills me and hurts me, more than love, more than sex. It is the best thing in the world. And I lost it. Both times before – with Mark, with the crowd – I lost it, they got tired of me, I wasn't good enough to hold them. But I have found it again – and dare not lose it now. I can't stop, I must dazzle him, run harder, faster, never stop. I cannot step down from the throne a third time, dare not . . .)

He was watching her now, in the cold street, but not with admiration, with alarm in his eyes. Poor man, she thought suddenly, poor friend. I have been using him without mercy. And, look – he's scared now. He's terrified I'll say the word that will send him away. 'If you're not in the mood for me . . .' But it would be weak to do that, she understood – and she felt strong. No, the sorting out had to be done. And now was the time. The separation of fact from fantasy. For both their sakes. And since she was so much the stronger, it was up to her to take the lead.

She held out her hand to him, and smiled.

'Of course I'm in the mood for you. In fact, I've just bought you some special biscuits. You're going to love them.'

He moved his hand awkwardly towards hers. But it was the one that held the Rainbow shopping bag so he could not cleanly grip her outstretched fingers. He smiled, embarrassed, at his clumsiness. She was staring at the bag as it swung heavily with the weight of what it contained. She had known all along really what that burden must be – he had said he would bring the thing over 'one of these days' to show her. She had to get acquainted with it sooner or later, after all.

Oh shit, she thought grimly. I have come to my senses only just in time. Thanks be to Tom. And to Wendy. Thanks be, especially and above all, to London, to where I will be escaping in a little while, in just a week or two, away from this mad place, this awful man. My awful self.

Her smile dropped away, she withdrew her hand.

'Come inside,' she said, and turned her back on him and pushed open the swing doors into her building. She didn't bother to look round to see if he was following. She knew he would follow her. He would follow her anywhere. Up into the clear light of sanity, which she had just glimpsed on her journey home, which now she could almost touch. Or down like devils into the pit. Wherever the queen should choose to go.

Dining

12

Louise, after a week of dithering, settled finally on the roast duckling with Bigarade sauce.

'It came to me in a dream. It's a brilliant idea. It'll taste great, not too hard to make, it's just the thing. Watercress soup to start with, then duck, then – '

'Profiteroles?' urged Tom hopefully.

'Ice cream. Just right for Mrs Bee. It'll remind her of home – but it'll be different too. I shall make it myself.'

Louise leaned heavily against the kitchen counter to study the recipe book. She was only four months gone and showed few signs of her pregnancy. But already she was carrying herself differently, moving around slowly and deliberately, taking every opportunity to rest her body.

'We'll need two ducks, I think,' she said thoughtfully. 'Listen – "Though ducklings have more fat than chicken, there is less flesh on their bones, so you should allow at least twelve ounces dressed per person,"' She looked up. 'Maybe we should get three ducks – you know what a pig Dick can be when he's eating out.'

'Then we'll get three, no problem. But you know,' Tom warned, 'we don't want to be too obviously extravagant. It's not the expense,' he insisted. 'Sod the expense. All I mean is – we don't want it to look too much like a triumphal banquet. We've got to think of Dick's feelings.'

They looked at each other seriously, and then in the same moment both burst out laughing. In truth – they were both thinking – they had a lot to feel triumphant about, they were a fortunate pair. So many good things had happened to them in the past few weeks, it was hard now much of the time to decently hold in their joy. The baby was the crowning glory, of course. So long put off – they had been together for nearly ten years, and had argued long and often about having children and had dreaded having children – and now it had happened, a semi-accident really, and it seemed they had waited cleverly for just the right time in their lives. Almost any time before this, Tom was sure, the news that he was about to be a father would have left him winded, demoralised, full of fear. But in fact the moment Louise had told him – which was the moment he had stepped into the house, still the old house then, on returning from that strange expedition he had made to the seaside (When was that? Before? – no just after Christmas, ages ago) – he had been filled with new energy and purpose. The very next day he had rung up the estate agent who was handling the house in Holland Park over whose purchase they had been dickering uncertainly for weeks and told the man he was ready to pay the asking price, no more haggling. On condition that the sale was completed and the present occupiers out within six weeks. And because everything these days was going right for him, it was done exactly as he had wished. A week ago he and Louise had moved without a backward glance across the line, the motorway ramp and the giant roundabout, which separated Shepherd's Bush from Holland Park. Now they had living on one side of them a high official from the Kuwaiti Embassy. On the other side was an orchestra conductor of international renown – this week Royal Festival Hall, next week Dallas, next month Tokyo. And Tom at last had a house in which he could feel proud to serve up roast duckling with Bigarade sauce to an important new business connection. He could also find room to include on the same night certain old acquaintances whose fortunes, at the present time, were not quite matching his own.

'If you feel bad about having Dick to dinner,' Louise said, 'you should put him off. Invite him for another night. We'll serve spaghetti and look sad. That'd cheer him up.'

'Well, I could hardly do that,' Tom argued. 'After all, Dick and Jeannie were asked first.'

'Then you should have given the Bee another date.'

Tom shook his head. 'Impossible. She has to go to Paris tomorrow and sew up *De Gaulle*. And by the time she gets back I'll be far too busy. No,' he sighed cheerfully, 'this is the only possible night. Dick'll just have to bite his knuckles and be a big boy.'

'I wonder if we should have four ducks . . .'

If the baby had provided the greatest motive for securing the dream house, it was Mrs Bee – 'Please call me Gwendoline' – who had turned out, completely out of the blue, to be the means of paying for it. Before her sudden and almost miraculous arrival on the scene, Tom had faced up to the fact that he was going to have to go irretrievably into debt to buy Holland Park.

'We'll never finish paying for it in our whole lives,' he had told

Louise, though – this was the strange magic the baby already spread before it – he did not feel so bad when he said it. He felt almost excited at the huge burden he was about to assume. But then a couple of days later – one phone call from his agent, one thirty-minute meeting with Gwendoline Bee – it turned out he would even be spared having to carry most of that burden. He came home from the meeting and, in a low voice, almost a whisper, told Louise the size of the fee he had been offered. She had to sit down when she heard it, she felt suddenly faint.

'Is it the baby?' Tom had asked anxiously, helping her into the chair.

'No, soppy – it's the money!' she cried. And then let out a whoop of joy, like a war cry, and put her arms up and hugged him to her.

Though afterwards, when she had absorbed the news, Louise did ask him quietly if this, the project with Mrs Bee, was really the sort of thing he wanted to do.

'I mean, it's a bit of a change of pace for you, isn't it? And what you're so good at is – '

'I know,' he nodded. He paced around the little living room (they were still in Shepherd's Bush then), hardly conscious that his feet were touching the carpet. He felt as if he was a good six inches off the ground, as if he was skimming over the surfaces of life where once he had just trudged along like everyone else. So much was happening – the baby, the move, Mrs Bee, he loved his wife now more than ever . . . 'I know what I'm good at. Sensitive, accurate, touching, small – bugger that lot. I've had enough. Enough of playing safe.' He stopped pacing for a moment, felt himself hovering splendidly in place. 'I was telling somebody the other day – now who was it?' He frowned. Tried to remember. Genuinely could not. 'Well, anyway, I was telling them that what I really want to do is something huge, mythical . . . a Western! Well – ' He turned, effortlessly wheeling in air, and beamed at his wife, 'This isn't a Western, OK, but near enough. Damn near! And I'm hungry for it. So thank God for Mrs Bee!' And he put his head back and, as Louise clapped and laughed with delight, improvised a chant for the day, for the future, for all their wonderful good luck:

> Oh, Mrs Bee
> Is paying me
> A socking great fee . . .
> And I'm so hap-pee!

Mrs Gwendoline Bee had arrived in town from California, or some said from New York, just nine months before. On arrival she had taken a suite in the Hyde Park Hotel, opened an office off Charlotte Street, and had announced to the press that she was here 'to make things hum'. Specifically to arrange a marriage between British creative talent and American organisational energy. 'We are going to take the best writers, the best directors, the best actors,' she had told the first press conference (thinly attended, for few had heard of Mrs Bee yet), 'and we are going to give them pots of money, projects they can get their teeth into, and – best of all – a good old-fashioned American kick in the ass!'

Dutiful, rather tired smiles had followed this announcement. Like all Britons, the reporters had been hearing this sort of inspirational stuff for the past ten years, not least from their own Prime Minister. Also for them, as for most Europeans, in the same period clarion calls from across the Atlantic had lost much of their previous power to impress. Mrs Bee had studied her sparse and tepid audience thoughtfully for a minute or so and then had risen from her chair and terminated the conference. The shrewdest of women, she guessed, without knowing exactly how, that she had hit a false or a dated note, and she needed time to investigate the phenomenon. Moreover, lack of enthusiasm, as those who were going to work for her soon found out, was something Gwen Bee just could not tolerate. Very soon BeeHive, her new production company, announced its first project: *Coward!* (subsequently changed to *Noel!*), a four-part mini-series based on the career of the celebrated author and entertainer, starring Denis (now Sir Denis) Haxton in the title role, with Isobel Pane as Gertrude Lawrence. John Gardner – fresh from his latest Oscar triumph – had agreed to direct; the script would be written by another veteran award-winner Mark Mannersby. *Coward!/Noel!* was pre-sold around the world within a few weeks of its announcement and, as a follow-up BeeHive press release triumphantly pointed out, the project was in profit before a word of the script had been written. This press release also initiated a feature that was to become very familiar to the growing band of Bee-watchers, being decorated round the margins by cartoon representations of Mrs Bee's large and handsome person, from whose mouths speech bubbles rose, each containing some perky, positive, ginger-up BeeSlogan like: 'Awllrright!' or 'Why the h--- NOT?' or 'We Can Stand the Pace – Can You?'

The same week as this release appeared, two more BeeHive projects were announced: *Montgomery* with David Lee Knight directing, script by Tom Watson, Ivan Ross playing the General, the Yugoslav army playing the Desert Rats; and *Fab Four – the Rise and Fall of the Beatles*, Roland Remarque directing, Angus Mott, a fine new Merseyside talent, writing, and a search to be launched in Liverpool directly to find the youngsters who would play the four principals.

Mrs Bee's second press conference was crowded to the walls and those attending showed all the interest and enthusiasm she could wish for. She was asked at one point how she managed to attract such eminent names to her projects. 'I pay them the goddam earth, that's how,' smiled Mrs Bee, with a direct honesty that many there found refreshing and endearing. Another reporter asked if the talent search for the Fab Four wasn't basically a gimmick. 'Of course, it's a gimmick,' Mrs Bee said, sounding surprised. 'So what? And don't forget,' she added, her voice dropping to a deeper register, 'it will also offer four currently unemployed kids the chance of their young lives.' A youthful reporter then tried to tease her on this point, dressing up, in the guise of a question, an elaborate joke about TV stardom as a solution to long-term unemployment in the northern cities. Mrs Bee cut him off before he had half finished. 'Don't get smart with me, young man,' she rasped, showing there that glint of steel that was to become as much associated with the Bee-style as her amiability, her directness and her huge energy.

Other questioners tried to clear up certain mysteries surrounding Mrs Bee's personal life. It was rumoured that the never-seen Mr Bee was a lawyer, also that he was the real power, or at least the financial muscle behind BeeHive. Mrs Bee was quite ready to talk on the subject, though in the end not wholly forthcoming.

'My husband is a very dear, very clever man whose work keeps him in Manhattan. We are in touch by phone just about every day. He is descended from an important family in the States, the Bees of South Carolina. You might know,' she told her bemused audience, 'or maybe not, that it was General Barnard Bee who on the field of Bull Run gave the famous General Jackson his nickname. "*There* stands Jackson like a stone wall!" ' cried Mrs Bee, throwing out her right hand and pointing with such dramatic authority that her whole audience turned to stare at the grey velour drapes that covered the windows of the conference-room. ' "Rally behind the Virginians!" The next moment,' she added sadly, 'General Bee fell, mortally wounded. Are there any more questions?' (A search of the Manhattan phone book did turn up a firm of lawyers called Hart, Higson, Somerset and Bee. But all attempts to reach Mr Bee proved abortive. 'Not available for comment,' was the only answer ever given.)

Two more projects were announced at this conference as being under active consideration: *De Gaulle*, and *Vivien Leigh – Her Life and Loves*. Mrs Bee's preference was always decidedly for the factual, and above all the biographical. It was rumoured that on her arrival in London she had sat up one night and made a list of eminent men and women of the twentieth century, and that her whole production programme consisted of working her way methodically down this list. Good as her word, she was indeed prepared to spend very large sums to bring her projects to the screen. Her creative employees had no complaints in that direction. The only area where Mrs Bee was inclined to be stingy was in the amount of controversial material she would permit in a BeeHive production. 'We are in the business of affirmation,' she was fond of saying. 'We're not here to dig up dirt on people – but to celebrate them. That's what my audience wants.'

Another peculiarity of Mrs Bee's was that she would not allow any criticism of her own country, its inhabitants, actions, or policies in any of her projects. 'I can't help it,' she'd explain, drawing a line firmly through the offending words. 'I'm paying for this thing, and I happen to be a patriot. Also my audience won't stand for it, believe me.' In fact, given BeeHive's worldwide sales, the non-American viewing audience for Bee-products was probably much larger than the American. Nevertheless, the United States constituted the single, largest share of the total, and in terms of income contributed far more than any other country. So here, as in other instances, there turned out to be a hard, rational instinct at work behind Mrs Bee's whims and foibles. As one of her press-release cartoon bubbles summed it up, 'We Really Know What We're Doing – and We're Really Doing Great!'

Coming somewhat late to the scene, Gwendoline Bee had had to accept early on the fact that quite a few people had got in ahead of her in the biographical stakes, that many of the more dramatisable figures of the century – Churchill, Kennedy, Gandhi, Mrs Gandhi, others – had been, or were in the process of being 'done'. To keep up her productive momentum eventually she would have to spread her net wider in history. This did not dishearten her. She was personally favourable towards the sort of 'colour' and 'dash' that a historical subject might be expected to offer. She was not afraid of spending the kind of money a costume drama demanded. And there was the benefit too that, everybody concerned in the story being long dead, controversial detail could be included, could even be encouraged in the interests of a livelier show. Mrs Bee then put her best energies into this new strand of BeeHive endeavour. In the long term, she cherished a project – 'It'll cost zillions,' she confided to her senior executives, 'but I'm not scared' – for a multi-episode series dramatising the life of the first Napoleon, from the Corsican boyhood through to the final exile on St Helena. Feeling a particular affinity for the subject, she saw this project as in many ways the culmination of her career, and perhaps for that reason she was in no special hurry to get to it. In the meantime she would practise her skills on certain other, lesser conquerors and world stirrers. It was to discuss one of these projects that Tom Scott had found himself unexpectedly summoned one morning to an audience at the Hyde Park Hotel.

'I woke up yesterday,' Mrs Bee told him as they took coffee and brioches on her balcony, 'and it just popped into my mind. Genghis Khan! Know anything about him?'

'Not much I'm afraid,' Tom confessed, sitting on the edge of his chair. He saw Jack Palance, he saw Charlton Heston . . . no, that was wrong, that was *El Cid* –

'Well, nor do I,' said Mrs Bee, flashing her famous, honest smile. 'But I saw a cloud of dust on the horizon, I heard the drum beat of horses' hooves, I saw a vast, empty steppe – Hungary would do very well there, incidentally – and I saw a million savage warriors streaming past me westward to conquest!'

'A million?' breathed Tom, faint with excitement.

'Well, they will look like a million, I guarantee that. Azure-blue skies, a blazing, burning sun, a world trembling under the scourge of Mongol domination. Rape, pillage, torture, a mountain of skulls . . .' Mrs Bee sipped her coffee. Her bright golden hair shone in the light of the watery orb that gleamed fitfully over the trees of Hyde Park. 'What do you say, Tom? Six-part TV series for the US and Europe – but you can cut it as a feature for the rest of the world. Are you with me?'

Mrs Bee by now was a figure of considerable importance in the entertainment world. Indeed, her fame had spread much wider than that. There were numerous admiring articles and profiles devoted to her in the press. Only very occasionally was heard a discordant note. Thus it came as a surprise when, in the course of an otherwise flattering profile in the *Observer*, one unnamed source was quoted as calling her 'an aggressive defender of the status quo before yesterday, an unashamed propagandist for American cultural and political values, a dynamic purveyor of mediocre pap and pabulum under the guise of quality production values'. In general, the cruel words were dismissed as being precisely an example of that negativism, pettiness and typical British whining and envy that Mrs Bee, by her presence and her activities, seemed to have a mission to suppress. In any case, as more than one fair-minded observer pointed out, there were quite enough home-grown purveyors of mediocre pap, et cetera; there was no need to pick on a woman who, while she might possess her natural share of human failings, had set radically new standards in rewarding her employees, the shock waves of which policy were still radiating through the industry, so that it was already customary to talk of 'pre-Bee' and 'post-Bee' scales of pay. Very many, both of those who were privileged to work with her, and of that multitude who were still hoping to, were ready to say with Tom Scott, 'Thank God for Mrs Bee!' and to bless the day that had brought her to these shores.

It was then with much excitement and some anxiety that Tom hurried to answer the emphatic ringing at his front door on this evening late in March. He opened the door to welcome his distinguished and formidable guest.

'There you are, you treacherous bastard!' a slurred and angry voice greeted him.

'Oh, hello Dick,' Tom said, with falling enthusiasm.

Banham stumbled past him into the hallway. Tom peered out into the gloom. He thought he saw a movement in the street.

'That you, Jeannie?' he called.

'It's me. Just locking the car.' After a moment Jean Ricketts came in through the gate. 'Hello, Tom.' She kissed him on the mouth. 'Are we late? It's *his* fault.'

'Right on time.' They went inside the house, and Tom shut the front door. He helped Jeannie off with her coat. 'Look, is he drunk?" he asked anxiously.

'Pretty much,' she nodded. 'He has been practically ever since.'

'Since what?'

'Since he heard about your new job.' She laughed gaily. She was looking very pretty tonight. 'I've never seen him so miserable.'

They made their way along the hall and down a short flight of stairs and into the basement kitchen, where they found Dick trying unsuccessfully to neck with Louise.

'Get off her, you oaf,' ordered Jeannie. She placed both hands on her husband's shoulders and pushed him into a chair. 'Now you just sit there.'

'Want a drink,' Dick announced. Tom and Louise exchanged glances. Tom shook his head.

'Oh, give him one,' Jeannie sighed. 'Just half a glass. And that's *all* till dinner,' she instructed her husband, 'or you're going home now.'

Dick, without protest, accepted a glass one-third filled with white wine. Tom sat down opposite him, and smiled awkwardly across the kitchen table. Dick peered at him.

'You little snot,' he breathed.

'Now, Dick – '

'You know,' cried Banham, waving a hand at Tom, 'you know, I always used to admire this fellow.'

'All right, Dick – '

'While others were out there selling their souls for a bigger budget, there he was, pottering away at those glum little films of his. *Nice* little films,' Dick nodded. '*I* liked 'em. Others might be saying, "Christ, this is tedious, must be a Tom Scott film." But I was always a fan.'

'Shut up, Dick,' Jeannie said automatically. She was over by the stove, scooping a taste of Louise's duck sauce onto her forefinger. 'Mmm,' she murmured appreciatively.

'They had a kind of jewel-like consistency, Tom's films,' Dick reminisced. 'If ever I saw something about a ten-year-old orphan on a kidney machine, or about a love affair in a terminal disease clinic, I never had to look at the credits. I knew it would be my old pal Tom Scott, soldiering on, doing what he knows best . . . But now!' Dick shuddered. 'All of a sudden – what do I find?'

'Where's the great lady?' Jeannie asked. 'Isn't she late?'

'No.' Louise glanced at the wall clock. 'We said eight for eight-thirty. She's got ten minutes. She's pretty punctual usually, isn't she?' she asked her husband.

'Famous for it,' Tom nodded.

'I find,' persisted Dick, 'that my old pal – for whom I had so much respect, whose integrity was a byword, and so on and so forth – has gone off and done the dirty on all of us who trusted him and looked up to him. Has sold out. For a mess of pottage . . . Genghis Khan!' jeered Dick, with furious hostility.

'Rubbish!' snapped Tom.

'Shut up, Dick!' chorused the women.

'Do you deny that you have signed to make such a project?'

'You know I have. So what?' Tom shook his head irritably. 'All right,' he sighed then. 'Now, if you've finished – '

'I'm serious, you silly bugger!' Dick snapped. And looking up, Tom was discomfited to find that the whoozy, drunken look in Dick's eyes had been replaced by an expression serious indeed, and almost compassionate. 'I really do respect your work. Even if I didn't like a film of yours, at least I always thought I understood what you were trying to do. But Genghis Khan? For Christ's sake, Tom!'

'Oh, crap,' said Tom uneasily.

'Yes, crap,' Jeannie nodded. 'You tell him, Tom.'

'Well, what do you think you're doing?' Dick asked, with a show of reasonableness. 'Go on, tell us. Just explain.'

Of a sudden, Tom found that three pairs of eyes were studying him with interest. He shifted in his seat.

'Say you're doing it for the money,' Dick cut in before he could get started, 'and fair enough. I can understand that.'

'I *am* doing it for the money.'

'That's all you need to say.'

'But not just for the money.'

'Here we go!' Dick sighed.

'I am *trying*,' Tom gritted, 'to move away from realism and miniaturism and all that, which I've been doing for years – '

'Which you're so good at.'

' – which I'm so good at – and so fed up to the teeth with – and I'm moving into an area of myth . . . and grandeur . . . and large gestures and – '

'Listen to him!' chuckled Dick.

' – and without sacrificing quality. And care . . . and all the rest of it that you think I'm so hot at.'

'Impossible.'

'You think it's impossible to do good work on a large scale? What about John Ford? Hawkes? . . . Abel Gance? Coppola, if you like?'

Dick shook his head patiently. 'I'm not saying it's impossible for everybody. I'm saying it's impossible for *you*.'

There was a silence, broken finally by an exasperated and apologetic sigh from Jeannie. Tom shrugged moodily.

'Well, we'll have to see, won't we?'

'Uh-huh,' Dick nodded. 'How's the script?'

Tom hesitated. 'Colourful,' he said at last.

'I'll bet!' Dick chuckled.

There had been major problems already with the script. From the brief vivid sketch that Mrs Bee had given him at their first interview,

Tom had understood the story of Genghis Khan would culminate in a gaudy, no-expense-spared depiction of the Golden Horde's sack of the city of Rome. Mrs Bee had waxed lyrical in her effort to inspire him with the possibilities offered by such a climax, creating for him such sights and sounds as the great temples and churches of Rome being overthrown, the Colosseum in flames, blood and death on the Appian Way, the Emperor shut up in an iron cage, the Vestal Virgins consumed by barbarian lust, the Pope led forth at the end of a halter to do penance on his knees before the Conqueror. The whole of Christendom shattered by the fearful news. The Holy City, the city that was to stand until Christ should come again in all His glory, now raped, dismembered, fallen.

All this seemed perfectly all right to Tom, even though he was aware as he listened that in her enthusiasm Mrs Bee was certainly mixing up historical epochs. But he felt the confusions here were trivial, and even as she was speaking his quick director's mind was coming up with the solutions – for Vestal Virgins read nuns, and so on. What was much more disturbing was to find when he began a period of independent research, as was his custom with every project, that the whole scene as described by Mrs Bee was a nonsense and untrue from start to finish; that, though some of his lieutenants had made war in Georgia, and perhaps had reached the Ukraine, the Khan himself never in his life once penetrated Europe. Had never been within a thousand miles of Rome. It was clear that Mrs Bee had got him mixed up with some other conqueror, Attila or Alaric. Quite understandable. But it meant that one of the best scenes in the drama was out, and he didn't relish having to explain that to Mrs Bee. She had been very keen on that scene.

The difficulty was made worse by the arrival of a first-draft script, on whose cover Mrs Bee had written, 'I think this is very promising. Like especially pages 63 to 71.' It was more of a treatment than a script, a scene by scene narrative with a very few lines of dialogue. To his dismay, Tom discovered that this draft included, between pages 63 and 71, a riotous orgy of plunder and rapine in a city that could only have been Rome.

'Well, now hang on,' said Dermot O'Connor, the writer, when Tom finally tracked him down by telephone. 'I don't actually ever *say* it's Rome.'

'What do you mean?' Tom demanded. 'You call it "the Eternal City". It's got a forum. It's got seven hills. Where else could it be?'

Silence at the other end.

'Come on, Dermot, I've got to *film* this. Come clean. It's Rome, isn't it?'

In the end, O'Connor confessed. He knew perfectly well that any scene set in Rome would be historically out of the question. But he had been too scared to point it out.

'I couldn't tell that awful woman,' he quavered down the telephone line. 'She's set her heart on bloody Rome. She's obsessed by the damn place. I just thought I could . . . sort of fudge it.'

It was Tom then who had to break the news to Mrs Bee. In contrast to O'Connor's terrified imaginings, she did not scream or rage. She accepted immediately that history could not be falsified to such an extent. With a flexibility and a lack of pointless repining that Tom had to admire, she asked him straightaway to come up with an alternative site, for she felt the principle was right, a city somewhere had to be sacked. It would make a fine scene, and her audience would be expecting it. It was a shame that the new city would necessarily carry so much less symbolic weight than Rome. But there it was. She did not directly blame Tom. In fact, she mostly seemed cross at herself for getting her facts so mixed up. Nevertheless, from that time on Tom felt she was never as friendly to him as she had been. There was a certain reserve between them now. It was a striking fact, he thought, that he could detect no particular anger on Mrs Bee's part towards the writer who had encouraged her in her delusion. She seemed more amused than anything at O'Connor's timid duplicity. Thinking it over, Tom decided it was because O'Connor in his foolish way had tried to keep from Mrs Bee what she would not want to hear. Whereas he, Tom, had clearly not been seen to be trying to spare her. Tom did his best to comfort himself by thinking that it was at least good preparation for the job he was about to do. Messengers of evil tidings were likely to get short shrift at a barbarian khan's court too, were likely to get their heads handed to them on a platter if they were out of luck.

In the end Tom had proposed Samarkand as a replacement for Rome. The city's name had a certain lustre, he argued, certainly more than any of the other candidates – Bukhara, Herat, Merv. When the Golden Horde burst into Samarkand in October 1221, seventy thousand of the city's inhabitants had been killed: surely enough, Tom hoped, to slake his employer's thirst for a blood-drenched climax. Mrs Bee heard his arguments and accepted them. Samarkand it would be. O'Connor was given his instructions.

Still Tom felt an undercurrent of disappointment over the transaction, specifically disappointment on Mrs Bee's part with him.

Sometimes at the end of a production meeting, he would find her looking at him in a certain way. Then she would shake her head, and murmur in ironic, unforgiving tones, 'Samarkand!' And Tom knew precisely what she intended to convey in those three exotic syllables. That he had failed in some essential, central way, he had missed the point. That though he might be technically right in small things, he was not a man who could be trusted to comprehend the big picture, to grasp the larger truth that lay behind a cloud of petty errors and confusions. Since this was something that Tom, at his worst moments, suspected of himself, the accusation wrapped up in that word troubled him every time Mrs Bee pronounced it.

'The script will be fine,' Tom told Dick firmly. 'Wants work, of course, but it's all there. Lots of action . . . excitement . . . and yet it goes beyond the obvious images and public faces.'

'To the private Genghis?' Dick suggested.

'If you like.' Tom studied his colleague across the table with much dislike. 'Look, I know perfectly well why you're carrying on like this.'

'Why's that, Tommy?'

'Because you think you ought to be directing this one. Don't you?'

Over by the stove the women, who had been chatting quietly, turned and watched the two men. Dick examined the palm of his right hand, picked at it thoughtfully.

'Well, if we're talking about logic,' he said, 'it would, of course, make much more sense.'

'Why?'

'Because that's what I do. I am a *physical* director,' declared Dick, with much force. 'I love all that stuff. I love action, big scenes, lots of people. I know you think it's all very crude,' he said, fixing Tom with a hostile stare. 'But it's what I'm about. I just never had the money to do it properly. Peanuts – that's all they ever give me. And then something like this comes along, with all the money in the world to spend on it . . . What is the budget?'

Tom told him. Dick swore softly.

'Do you know what can be done with that sort of money?' he sighed. 'Do you know what *I* could do with that much dough? And who do they give it to?'

'Me!' snapped Tom.

'Right. Isn't it fucking tragic?'

There was a tense silence. Then Dick seemed to sink down in his seat. He shrugged wearily.

'What do I care?' he sighed. 'I don't care. Anyway – ' he looked spitefully across the table, 'I wouldn't feel too pleased with myself if I were you. I know exactly how you got picked for the job.' Dick nodded smugly. 'It was just your turn, that's all. It's like how she chooses her projects. Apparently she's got a list of directors – we're all on it – and she's just working her way down it, one after another. Nothing more complicated than that.'

'In that case,' said Tom, 'clearly I'm above you in the list. And since it can't be alphabetical, it must mean – she thinks I'm better.'

The two directors stared angrily at each other. Dick's short, burly frame was hunched forward, and his thick arms moved restlessly on the table top. The women held their breath. Tom, keeping his eye all the time on the other man, inched his chair backwards, putting himself a little further out of Dick's reach. There was no trace of drunkenness in the latter now. His eyes as he stared at Tom were clear and bright, sharp with menace. On the wall behind Dick, the kitchen clock ticked away the seconds, unnaturally loud.

But then, suddenly, Dick put his head back and laughed. 'All right!' he chuckled. 'All right. Clearly that's what it means.'

Tom sighed and closed his eyes for a moment. The women relaxed. Dick laughed again.

'Wonder what Mrs Bee will be offering when she gets to my name. A little blind girl and her lost seeing-eye dog, I'll bet.'

'I shouldn't wonder,' Tom smiled.

'Actually,' said Dick thoughtfully, 'I think I could make something of that. I always fancied trying a tear jerker. Did you ever see *Old Yaller*?'

Jeannie came over the table, frowning. 'Honestly, you two!' she protested.

Dick looked up at her innocently. 'Us two what?'

'Going at each other like that.'

'Nonsense. I'm just a bit worried about Tommy here. He understands. Right, Tom?'

'You're jealous as sin!' Jeannie said.

'Bullshit!'

'Don't bullshit me.' Jeannie gave her husband a smart crack on the shoulder. 'I think it's disgusting. Actors are never like this.'

'Bull – ' Dick yelped as she punched him again.

'We're not. We're always pleased when we hear somebody else has got a good job . . . And for heaven's sake,' she punished her husband further, 'what kind of guests are we? We've been here fifteen minutes. We've not said a word about this lovely house. About the baby . . .'

At last Dick did look ashamed. 'You're right. I'm a hound . . . You know I really wish you all the best in the world, don't you, Tom?'

'Sure, Dick.'

'Don't be sarky. I'm serious.'

'OK. You wish me the best in the world.'

'I do. And I'm going to shut up about this bloody Bee woman from now on. OK?'

'OK.'

'Except for one thing,' said Dick, after a pause. Jeannie made throttling gestures at his throat. Tom smiled wearily.

'What's that, Dick?'

'She's going to eat you up.'

'What?'

'And spit you out. Trust me.'

Tom raised his arms in the air. 'How the hell would you know?' he demanded. 'You've never even met her, have you?'

Dick shook his head. 'I've just got a feeling about her, that's all.'

From the floor above came a brief, firm trill on the front-door bell. Dick smiled wolfishly.

'And now,' he said, 'I'm going to know for sure.'

13

Often in the weeks that followed, Tom thought that if he ever got to heaven, a place where with any luck every wish would be granted, or at least one, he would ask for a replay of that evening when Mrs Bee had been the honoured guest, the Banhams in homely support, the poor relations as it were, and himself and Louise playing the genial hosts. For he was sure that he had missed something. Something had happened that evening, evidently something profound, for life was never to be the same again, never to be so happy, carefree, so magical again. So something must have happened – but either he had not noticed it, or he had immediately forgotten the incident as soon as it had occurred. His mind was a blank.

What happened? What happened? Really, it had gone very smoothly – as Louise pointed out, tired but happy, when the evening was over and she was watching him wash the dishes.

'Mrs Bee – Gwendoline – is much less of a dragon than I thought she'd be.'

'Yes, she was sweet tonight,' Tom agreed.

Already he was feeling doubtful and perplexed, and was rummaging through his memories of the evening to find the cause of his unease. Gwendoline Bee had been a perfect guest, no question. Jeannie had been fine, of course, all her actress's charm working at full power. And Dick had behaved very well too – amazingly so, considering the state he'd arrived in and the scene he'd caused in the kitchen immediately before the distinguished visitor's arrival. Tom had been so stirred up, and made so apprehensive by Dick's outburst that he'd gone upstairs to answer the front door fearing the worst, half-expecting indeed a dragon to burst over the threshold, breathing fire and ruin.

But Mrs Bee had been entirely demure and friendly from the start. Tom had helped her out of her white fur, and ushered her into the drawing room. A wide, high-ceilinged space, hard to heat, but both radiators were on and the gas coalfire burned cosily in the grate. At one end of the room the table was set for five.

The wine glasses sparkled, as did the silver, there were good linen napkins on the spotless tablecloth, the chairs all matched, it looked a picture. Tom felt proud to view it, proud to know it was his. The others joined them. Mrs Bee greeted Louise most graciously, handed her then a tissue-wrapped parcel. Louise, surprised and pleased, carefully unfolded the paper, taking care not to tear it. Inside, was a baby's shawl, exquisite, Irish lace. Louise was overwhelmed. Tom too, presumably, for the next thing he said, after giving thanks for Mrs Bee's present, was pretty silly.

'These are the Banhams.' He indicated his friends. 'They didn't even bring us a bottle of wine.'

Yes, that was silly, Tom thought, in the early hours of the following morning, as he swirled his rubber-gloved hands in the soapy water. That was downright idiotic, and graceless. And inappropriate. For whoever brought bottles of wine to a fairly formal dinner party at their age, at their stage in life? Dumb, silly remark. Maybe malicious too; it had certainly sounded that way. Must have sounded that way to Mrs Bee, who could not have been expected to know that it was only a mild example of the sort of casual spite and winding up that was the small change of conversation in his and Dick's circle. When they were on their own, Tom reminded himself as soon as he'd said the stupid thing – when they were in private. And Mrs Bee's presence made the occasion all very public. He had definitely said the wrong thing.

Could that have been the moment then, the moment he searched for, when everything had started to unravel?

Anyway, Dick had handled it extremely well. Had smiled enigmatically at Tom's lapse. And put out his hand to Mrs Bee, and spoken quietly, warmly, 'Hello. I'm Dick Banham.' And Mrs Bee too showed no inclination to dwell on Tom's foolishness – both of them seemed to prefer to overlook it, as if it was a little boy's bad joke. She took Banham's hand.

'I've been so looking forward to meeting you,' she said. 'I know your work, of course.'

To which statement, Tom feared, had it been addressed to him, he would have returned some feeble, self-deprecating remark – at least he would have done so in the anxious condition he was in at the start of the evening. Or just have stood there hopefully, mouth hanging open, longing for Mrs Bee to throw in a few words of praise. Now why, thought Tom, as he finished washing the last of the dinner plates and started on the dessert bowls, hadn't Dick done any such thing? Dick was a notorious fisher after compliments.

A dedicated reviewer of his own good reviews – few as they were, Tom smirked briefly, as he worked away at the sink. Dick *framed* his good reviews, for God's sake. He might have been expected to make a little bit of a fool of himself at this moment. But no – he only smiled his enigmatic smile and, turning slightly, brought forward his partner.

'My wife, Jean Ricketts,' said Dick with fond pride. 'The actress.'

'An actress?' said Mrs Bee, a note of surprise and delight in her voice – assumed, Tom knew perfectly well, for he had told Mrs Bee days before who her fellow guests were going to be. Mrs Bee, still holding Jeannie's hand, took a half-step backward and regarded her with great appreciation. 'My!' she sighed. 'My – but you're a pretty one!'

And Jeannie, who Tom had always figured as a hard case, quite a cynic, instead of breaking into mocking laughter, blushed and simpered like a young girl. Well, she was only twenty-five, twenty-six, Tom remembered, watching her. It was understandable, and charming really. The whole atmosphere was charming. They made a fine circle – Jeannie glowing after being complimented so warmly, Dick implicitly complimented too for having had the good taste to marry her, Louise holding the beautiful shawl to her breast, Mrs Bee the open-handed bringer of all these compliments and gifts. A fine, warm little circle. Tom felt strangely outside it.

'So – why don't we eat?' he said finally, his voice sounding unpleasantly harsh in his ears.

Louise, sitting now at the kitchen table, yawned loudly. Tom glanced back at her.

'Go to bed,' he advised.

She shook her head. 'Can't. Still wide awake.'

'Sounds like it!'

'I am, though. Sort of.' Louise smiled sleepily. 'Wasn't it a nice evening? I did enjoy myself.'

The washing-up water had turned purple from the dessert bowls. Louise had put her best effort into the pudding. The duck had been a great success - Mrs Bee had come back for a third helping – but then she'd been confident about the duck, she'd made the dish before, knew what she was doing. Ice cream was a new departure and she had spent an anxious few hours that afternoon stirring together the milk and sugar and eggs, then cooling the mixture, folding in the cream and the fruit, half-freezing it, stirring again to get rid of the flakes of ice that had formed, then freezing it all the way until the mixture was stone hard. At the last possible moment she had turned it out of its mould and decorated it round the edges with orange glacé slices. It sat there on its dish on the kitchen table, a large bluey-purple shape, tricked out with slivers of orange.

'Don't you think it looks a bit abnormal?' she whispered to her husband, who had come downstairs to carry the dessert plate up for her.

'Looks great,' Tom assured her, inspecting the colourful mass, sounding more confident than he felt. He gripped the plate and started for the stairs with it, Louise following, looking troubled. A burst of laughter came from the drawing room just before Tom went in. It was cut off by his entrance. The guests' eyes focused on the object he was carrying. A slight satiric smile appeared at the corners of Dick's mouth. Only Tom could see it, he was sure, but it was like a rocket flare of danger. Oh Christ, he mourned, we've made a balls' up. The occasion teetered on the brink of disaster. A joke. Poor Louise. A public humiliation, for this was bound to get out, Dick had a mouth like a leaky drain. The great purple thing sat there in front of him, like an absurd bomb about to blow up in his face.

But then Mrs Bee rose to the occasion.

'Blueberry ice cream, I don't believe it!' she cried. 'Is it? Why that's wonderful.' And she clapped her hands in delight. Thus cued, the other two guests gave murmurs of appreciation. Thankfully, Tom carried his burden to the table and set it down.

'My very most favourite!' Mrs Bee enthused. 'How did you know?'

'It's a bit of an experiment,' Louise confessed. 'Just thought I'd try it.'

'Well, I couldn't be happier you did. The one thing I've missed over here,' Mrs Bee declared, looking round the table, nodding firmly, 'is some decent ice cream. And I just adore the stuff. Back home, I can't get enough of it, it's a sin!'

'Well done, Lulu,' Dick smiled, reaching over and patting Louise's arm as she sat down. Tom felt very good now. The ice cream no longer looked to him like a dangerous mauve device, or a madman's creation in silly putty. It was all changed by the alchemy of Mrs Bee's favour into a delightful, fun-looking dessert, perfectly suited to the honoured guest's particular taste. Well done, Louise. Well done, Mrs Bee.

Well done all of them, in fact. Looking approvingly, proudly round his table, Tom was struck again by how well, for instance, Dick was handling himself. He had been almost certain that Banham would have made at least a bit of a fool of himself in Mrs Bee's presence. Nervousness, truculence, an ambition to prove that he was not overawed by the company, residual traces of drunkenness, all might have been expected to colour Dick's behaviour this evening. But not a bit of it. He was being just splendid. He was treating Mrs Bee in a manner that, while far from deferential, was properly respectful and attentive. But not heavy either: Dick was displaying a grave but delightful wit, a drollness, that had Mrs Bee often chuckling appreciatively – and which much surprised Tom who hitherto had associated his old friend with a much broader, in fact an oaf-like sense of humour.

It occurred to him that he had never before seen Dick dealing with what might be called serious people. Employers, present or prospective. People of stature and power, people Dick needed to impress. Well, he was extremely good at it, that was clear, and Tom thought he wouldn't be at all surprised if, somewhere down the road, this evening and Dick's well-conducted performance during it should lead to some useful business being done between him and Mrs Bee. Which was perfectly fine by Tom and he was happy for the other director. He would be no dog in the manger. He had his Genghis Khan. Dick was welcome to his . . . little girl and the seeing-eye dog. Old Yaller.

And it further occurred to Tom, as he considered the mound of ice cream before him and wondered in which direction to cut it, that he really had very little first-hand experience of how other directors operated, when they were out there, doing the job, or getting the job, doing the serious work. He only ever met them – and they him – in the intervals of rest, when they were off duty, at parties, screenings, in pubs, waving to each other across crowded restaurants.

Why, they were like the old knights of the Round Table, Tom mused fancifully – he had drunk quite a lot during dinner, more than anyone else, but then he was enduring all the strains of being the host – yes, like Arthur's companions they were. For they would set off on their separate quests, he and his colleagues, after the Holy Grail – a masterpiece, or just a decent piece of work, or finally anything intelligible that could be brought in within the budget – whatever the scale of ambition or the freaks of chance. And most of them would come back more or less alive, and get together and yell and complain and laugh and boast, like knights in the banqueting hall. That was what it had been about between him and Dick, down in the kitchen, before Mrs Bee arrived. One should not be misled by the apparent fury and dislike that was revealed in such encounters – though it was easy to be misled, Tom found it easy. But after all, it was nothing more than a pair of knights, home from the wars, relieving the tension after all the horrors and dangers they had been through by rousting and buffeting each other.

And what horrors there were really on those quests. Tom saw, as in a vision, a score of separate figures, draped in heavy anoraks (armour, he wanted to call it), each standing on his wind-stormed hillside, each having to contend all alone against an ocean of troubles – inadequate writers, miserly producers, inept actors, prima donna cameramen, mutinous crews, the fading of the light. Tom's eyes misted over with love and pity as he thought of all the cruelties and indignities suffered by his fellows since the beginning of things. Great names brought low by the snarling pack of envious inferiors. Von Sternberg raped by MGM. Orson Welles – a career-long crucifixion. James Ivory forced to apologise publicly to Raquel Welch – Raquel Welch! – on his own set. Right back to D.W. Griffiths, dying alone, broke, discarded, in a cheap hotel. And so many others of lesser name, but no less in their suffering and endurance in the face of insult, incompetence, treachery. The tomb of the Unknown Director.

What more epic existence could there be than the one that he and Dick Banham shared? Why, next to their's, Genghis's story was mere random bloodletting and futile agitation. He picked up the long, spatula-shaped knife that had been set there to carve the ice cream. The blade gleamed in his hand. In a kind of homage, he turned it to where Dick was sitting.

'Serve Mrs Bee first, Tom,' Louise murmured alertly from the other end of the table.

Surprised at first to hear her speak, he gathered himself quickly. 'Of course,' he said irritably. 'I don't need telling.' Then he remembered where he was, and who might be listening. Dick smiled cheerfully at his own wife. Tom turned to Mrs Bee.

'I hope we can tempt you to a nice big helping?' he smiled. Damn, he thought, I'm fawning. Too obsequious by at least half. Watch Dick, learn from Dick. Amazingly, he seems to have the knack.

'You certainly can!' Mrs Bee grinned. She patted herself on her firm, round midriff. 'Watch out, tummy. We're taking no hostages tonight!'

Tom bent over the purple shape. It was beginning slightly to melt away, dribbles of liquid ice cream were seeping out from under the mass, like blood from a great sore. Laying the edge of the blade upon the rounded surface, he made his first incision. At that moment the telephone out in the hall began to ring.

'Yes, a nice, nice evening,' Louise sighed, resting her elbows on the kitchen table, balancing her chin in her hands. 'Everything went so well. Even the ice cream . . . And you know, Tom, I think you're quite wrong about Mrs Bee. I think she really likes you.'

'Never said she didn't.'

'But you've been worried, haven't you? And I really don't think you need to. After dinner she was laughing away at what you were saying. She seemed to take a lot of interest in you.'

'She took a lot of interest in Dick too.'

'Oh, well . . . I expect she was being polite.'

'Uh-huh.'

'You're not jealous, are you?' Louise smiled at her husband's back as he stooped over the sink. She saw him shake his head firmly.

'Not at all. Happy for him. Just a bit surprised they got on so well.'

'Oh, Dick's got a lot of charm, when he cares to use it.'

'First I've heard of it,' Tom grunted. He was down to the coffee spoons. Soon they would go upstairs, go to bed, after what – even Tom had to admit – had been a more than satisfactory evening. Apart from these lingering feelings that something – *something* – had gone . . . not wrong exactly, but somehow awry.

'The only thing that was a bit sad,' Louise mused, 'was poor old Susie.'

Tom said nothing.

'I do think you could have talked to her.'

'I was cutting up the bloody ice cream!'

Louise raised her eyebrows. 'OK,' she said pacifically. 'OK.' And then, 'I didn't mean the first time actually . . . I meant the second.'

The first time – Tom holding the knife, the blade an inch into the ice cream, the phone ringing and ringing. He had looked up at Louise, imploring her.

'I'll get it,' she nodded, heaving herself up from the table, making for the door with her new, heavy-woman gait. Tom went back to work, cutting off a generous slice, scooping it on to a bowl. He handed it down the table to Mrs Bee.

'Not too much, I hope?' he smiled at the guest of honour. The phone had stopped ringing. He could hear Louise talking out in the hall.

'Are you kidding?' Mrs Bee chuckled. 'Watch me. I'll be back for more!'

Fascinated, the others watched as with fast, efficient movements she began transferring the ice cream from the bowl to her mouth. Tom, with an effort, tore his gaze away.

'How about you, Jeannie?'

'Oh . . . not quite as much for me, love.'

Louise appeared in the doorway. She was looking slightly anxious.

'For you, Tom.'

Tom frowned.

'It's Susie,' Louise added, dropping her voice, as if speaking of something a little awkward, embarrassing.

'Oh, hell,' Tom grunted.

He stood there, irresolute, holding his knife. The others looked up at him. Mrs Bee, for a moment, stopped mining for ice cream. There was a little smear of the stuff, Tom noticed, at one corner of her full, red mouth.

'She rang yesterday,' Louise said uncertainly. 'I forgot to tell you. I said you'd be in this evening . . . She sounds a bit upset.'

Tom looked down at the mass before him. It was melting quite rapidly now, a blue-purple lake was spreading out inexorably from beneath it. If he left it much longer, he'd have to use a spoon to serve up the helpings.

'Ask her to ring back in twenty minutes,' he said, with sudden decision. 'Or half an hour. Please,' he urged when Louise hesitated.

She nodded reluctantly and left the room. Again they could hear her talking in the hall. Tom looked round at his guests – to find they were all watching him. Mrs Bee, in particular, seemed to be eyeing him with curiosity. So he spoke directly to her.

'It's an actress. She's in a bit of trouble. Out of work. Lonely . . . I know she'll want to talk to me for ages.'

'Oh, God!' sighed Mrs Bee. 'Don't tell me. Poor you!'

She went back to her dessert. Dick glanced at Tom, who had begun again to carve out a portion for Jeannie.

'Is that Susie Strang?' Dick asked quietly.

Tom nodded.

'Is she still on at you?'

Tom nodded again. Then, wanting to be fair, 'Well, not exactly on at me – '

'Didn't you go down and see her?'

'Yup. Few weeks ago.' Or was it months, he wondered. He really wasn't sure.

'How was she?'

'Oh, you know . . . OK. Not too bad. Bit miserable.' He thought for a moment, trying hard to remember that day. 'She seems to have got herself mixed up with a rather strange bloke down there – '

At that point, Mrs Bee, who did not seem to have noticed that Tom and Dick were talking, swallowed and sighed once more. 'Out-of-work actors! I have had 'em up to here!' she declared in tones of great disgust. 'They are the worst pests in the world.' She looked round the table as if seeking support for her views, and Tom found himself, almost involuntarily, nodding in sympathy. 'I have had actors calling me,' Mrs Bee carried on, 'from all over. They call me from hospital. They call me from prison. From the nut house. From *Thailand* . . . They always get through. They're just a plague. Want, want, want. It's unbelievable!'

Mrs Bee picked up her spoon and struck again into her ice cream. The others sat in silence. Tom handed a heaped bowl to Jeannie. Dick glanced down the table at Tom and gave him a slow wink. Mrs Bee looked up at that moment. Tom wondered if she'd caught Dick's somewhat disrespectful grimace. He was surprised and quite sorry to find that he was rather hoping she had.

But it seemed not. At least she didn't look at Dick, angrily or otherwise, but put out her hand and, with a charming and apologetic smile, laid it on the arm of Dick's pretty wife.

'No offence, dear,' she said. 'I'm not talking about every actor, of course. Just the pests.'

'Oh, I quite agree with you,' Jeannie said brightly. 'I would never nag anybody for work, myself. I just couldn't do it.'

For a moment, as Tom watched with amusement, Dick and Jeannie's eyes met. Jeannie coloured slightly then, and looked away. Dick moved in his seat, looked down the table and smiled easily.

'After all, Gwendoline,' he said. (Gwendoline! thought Tom, chagrined.) 'It doesn't take much to make them happy. They just want to talk to someone usually, that's all.'

'Then let 'em pay for a therapist. Like the rest of us.'

Which, thought Tom, was telling Dick. Serve him right for being so sanctimonious. And hypocritical. Dick was notorious for the short shrift he gave importunate actors. Well, look at what he had done for Susie, for instance. Absolutely nothing. Whereas he, Tom . . . He wondered suddenly where Louise had got to. She'd stopped talking out in the hall long ago. The faint sound of the toilet flushing from the floor above answered his question.

Dick was still smiling, apparently untroubled by the abruptness of Mrs Bee's reply.

'I don't know,' he sighed. 'I always think it must be pretty much hell being an actor. Unless you're very well established. What's the statistic? Eighty-five per cent out of work at any one time?' Dick shook his head. 'That's a tough one to deal with.'

'Who held a gun at their heads and told them to be actors?' Mrs Bee demanded. 'They can't take unemployment, they should have been accountants.'

Tom kept his head down and concentrated on dividing up portions of ice cream for Dick and Louise. He found himself seriously unsettled at the pleasure he was deriving from hearing Dick being put down so forcefully. His eyes on the purple mound before him, he heard Dick chuckle light-heartedly. Poor fool, Tom thought with guilty amusement.

'You're a hard case, Gwendoline,' Dick said.

'I have to be,' Mrs Bee retorted. 'In this business there's no room for charity. I'm surprised you haven't found that out yet, Mr Banham.'

Looking up, Tom expected to find Mrs Bee frowning severely at the culprit, and he had half a mind to step in and – without, of course, excusing his colleague's softness and general lack of realism – saying a few words in mitigation of Dick's behaviour. But to his surprise, he found that Mrs Bee was smiling at Dick, almost tenderly. Almost in a motherly way. And Dick seemed to be enjoying her fond regard greatly, grinning back at her in an impish fashion, just this side of insolence. Tom didn't at all know what to make of this. Confused, he passed Dick's helping of ice cream up the table.

'Ready for a second?' he asked Mrs Bee uncertainly.

The tender look faded from her gaze as it shifted from Dick to the remains of the ice-cream mound. Her red lips came together and parted again in a predatory smack.

'You bet!'

Her bowl was passed down the table. Before it reached Tom, Louise came back into the room. Glancing at her, Tom thought she looked rather pale.

'Are you OK?' he asked anxiously.

The others turned to watch her. She tried to smile at them, but didn't manage it quite. She touched her stomach.

'Felt a bit funny for a moment, bit sick. No, it's all right,' she said, as the others murmured their concern. 'I'm fine now.'

'You sit down and take it easy, dear,' Mrs Bee ordered, pulling Louise's chair out from the table. Louise obeyed. Mrs Bee smiled at her. 'You've got a great big husband who can run around and do things for you.' She glanced at Tom in a less than friendly way. Then turned back to Louise. 'Just take it easy now, you hear?'

'Have some ice cream,' Tom advised his wife. He had decided, had forced himself not to be offended by the look Mrs Bee had cast at him. 'It'll settle you.'

Louise, glanced at the ice cream. She seemed on the brink of shuddering, but controlled herself. She shook her head. 'Not just now.'

Tom began to cut off a second helping for Mrs Bee, as large as the first.

'Oh . . .' Louise remembered. 'Susie. She said she'd ring back in half an hour.'

'The pest? Tell her you're out is my advice,' Mrs Bee grunted, stretching to take the bowl as it came along the table towards her. 'In fact, tell her you're out permanently. It's the only way to deal with those people.'

Louise. who had heard nothing, of course, of the earlier exchange, turned and looked at Mrs Bee in surprise. 'Why, we couldn't do that. Susie's our friend.'

She looked across at Tom for confirmation. Mrs Bee too raised her eyes from her sweet to inspect his reaction. For a moment Tom was tempted to deny his wife's claim. And then was shocked to think he had ever thought such a thing.

'Well, I don't think it would sound too convincing . . .' He smiled at Mrs Bee. 'Me on the phone, saying I'm out!'

Nobody seemed too impressed by that. Mrs Bee made a small, uncomplimentary face, and then dug into her dessert again. Dick smiled to himself, another rather satirical smile. And Louise – just looked sick.

'Are you sure you feel OK?' Tom said now, in the kitchen, in the early hours. The job was done. The huge array of dishes stood stacked on the draining board. He had run the hot tap and wiped the sink. He took off the rubber gloves and hung them on a hook. Now he came and stood beside his wife and stroked her hair.

'I feel fine, really.'

'You looked so pale for a while.'

'I just felt queasy, just for a moment. I think it may have been the duck. It was so rich.'

'Could have been,' Tom nodded. 'Maybe the whole thing was too much for you.'

'Oh, God,' she protested. 'It shouldn't have been. I'm only in my fourth month.'

'All the same . . . no more big occasions, eh? Unless somebody else is doing the work.'

'Suits me.' She looked up at him then. 'But I didn't spoil things tonight, did I?'

'Not at all. You were great.'

'So were you.' She tugged at the sleeve of his shirt. 'I'd forgotten what an old charmer you can be. After dinner . . .'

'Put old Dick in the shade, did I?'

'I'll say!'

After dinner . . . After dinner, groaning at the amount of food inside them, they had shifted across to the easy chairs around the fire. Tom had settled his wife in the easiest chair of all and had insisted on dealing with the coffee by himself. He was rewarded by an approving smile from Mrs Bee. By the time he returned with the coffee things, Louise was looking better and, relieved to see this, and generally encouraged by the success of the evening so far, Tom had found it easy to relax and concentrate on making the rest of it go smoothly and happily. At last he hit upon the right note to strike with Mrs Bee. A sort of deferential teasing was what she clearly enjoyed in her off-duty hours, and Tom proved himself so nimble at dispensing this that he soon had the lady quite under his spell, 'eating out of my hand', as he said to himself, watching her stretch and bask under the treatment. It was a fact that from the moment he found the right formula poor old Dick seemed to fade very much into the background. Quite outclassed. Tom tried to be generous, and to bring the other back into the conversation. But Dick, though he smiled cheerfully and nodded whenever Tom spoke directly to him, scarcely seized his opportunities. In the end, Tom got rather irritated with him, which must have been why at one moment he worked into his monologue a little story at Dick's expense, an account of a minor but pretty ridiculous foul up that had happened on his last production. The others laughed very heartily, nobody harder than Mrs Bee. For a moment, Tom felt panicky, seeing how quickly the favourite of half an hour ago had become a figure of fun, a chump. To ward off bad luck and retribution, he immediately began on another story in which he himself was something of the victim. Everybody laughed at this story too, and he felt comfortable again.

When the phone rang the second time, they were drinking armagnac and the atmosphere had grown quieter and more mellow. Except that Jeannie kept getting caught up in giggling fits and had difficulty suppressing them. Then she had succumbed to a bout of hiccoughs. In the end, apologising, she had left the room to get herself a glass of water.

'I think that girl's had about enough to drink,' Mrs Bee observed crisply to Dick when Jeannie was almost out of the room. 'She's been putting it away all evening. I've been watching her.'

Tom smiled at his own wife who sat there next to him, quiet and entirely sober. Dick seemed about to make an equally crisp reply to Mrs Bee. 'Mind your own damn business,' Tom had fantasies of hearing him say. But in the end, he only shrugged and, keeping his head down, murmured, 'She'll be all right.' Tom yawned comfortably. It was late enough in the evening, so he knew a yawn wouldn't look impolite. And at the same time it might help nudge the guests into thinking about leaving. He smiled across the hearth at Mrs Bee.

'A little more coffee, Gwendoline?' he asked. 'Or brandy?'

The phone rang before she could reply. Tom and Louise exchanged rueful glances.

'Susie.'

'I know.' Tom prepared to heave himself out of his comfortable chair.

'The pest?' Mrs Bee put in. She shook her head. 'Don't answer it.'

Tom hesitated. Louise looked at him, startled.

Abruptly the ringing was cut off. A moment – and then they heard Jeannie's voice out in the hall. A spluttering giggle, and then in a high-pitched, breathy, accented tone, 'Harro! Wang Ho's Chinese Take-away heah!'

Nobody in the living room laughed.

'For Christ's sake,' Dick muttered.

Listening, they heard nothing for a moment from the hall. And then Jeannie's voice again, serious, without the giggle.

'Oh . . . sorry. Right . . . yes, he is. Hang on a moment, would you?'

They heard the phone being set down carefully on the hall table. Jeannie appeared in the doorway, looking chastened. She looked across at Tom and nodded. Again he began to rise.

'Might as well say good night now, Tom,' Mrs Bee spoke up. She smiled sternly at him. 'This is all we're going to see of you.'

The moments passed . . . Tom sank back into his armchair. He looked directly at Jeannie.

'Could you tell her it's not convenient just now?'

'Tom!'

Shocked, Louise gripped the arms of her chair and started to push herself up. Tom put his hand out fast, and held her shoulder and pushed her down again. He kept his eyes on Jeannie.

'Tell her I'll be in touch as soon as I can. Maybe tomorrow.'

Now he turned and looked at Louise. They stared at each other. In the end she looked away. Tom looked back at Jeannie.

'Give her our love,' he said.

After a moment, Jeannie nodded and left the doorway. They heard her pick up the phone. Louise glanced at her husband again. Then shook her head and turned to stare at the fire.

'Good for you, Tom!' Mrs Bee crowed. 'That's telling her.'

Tom nodded in acknowledgment. He was amazed at what he had done. He felt shaken, out of breath, he felt he had taken a stand. He looked suddenly, defiantly at Dick – who held up his hands in mock surrender.

'Did I say anything?' Dick smiled.

'Tom did the right thing,' Mrs Bee said loudly. 'It's pest control, that's all it is.'

'Absolutely. Keep 'em down!' Dick yawned and then gazed comfortably at the fire. 'Although it has occurred to me,' he mused aloud, 'that they have their uses, people like Susie. Kind of handy having 'em on the scene. Or rather,' he chuckled, 'not on the scene exactly . . . Off in a corner somewhere.'

'Stop it, Dick,' said Louise in a troubled voice. She seemed to be trying to hear what was going on out in the hall.

Tom deliberately was trying not to hear. He stared at Dick. 'What the hell are you talking about?'

'Oh, I don't know . . .' Dick said in the same easy-going voice. 'But isn't it so? Makes us feel better for not being them. Sort of "there but for the grace of God". That sort of thing. Adds spice to life, don't you think?'

Mrs Bee broke the silence that followed Dick's remarks.

'What stuff!' she cried wrathfully. 'What utter nonsense.'

Dick looked across at her and smiled. 'Ah, Gwendoline . . .' He shook his head in frank admiration.

'I don't know *what* you're talking about.'

'I believe you.' Dick put his hands behind his head and then turned slightly and winked at Tom.

'For Christ's sake,' Tom rasped. He still felt out of breath. 'I'm going to ring her tomorrow. I'm – '

'Hang on.' Dick held up one hand. 'I feel some poetry coming on.'

He sat frowning at the ceiling as Tom stared at him. Jeannie came back into the room. Louise watched her she took her seat.

'Is it all right?'

'Oh, sure,' Jeannie nodded. She was looking quite subdued now. 'Yes, she's fine. She thanks you for your love – '

'Got it!' Dick cried triumphantly. He closed his eyes. 'Ta-tum-tee-tum-tee-tum . . .' he prepared himself. And then in a clear, melodious voice, much different from his usual growl:

'Pity would be no more
If we did not make somebody Poor.
And mercy no more could be
If all were as happy as we.'

He beamed around him. 'William Blake. Learned that in school, twenty years ago. Not bad, eh? . . . Of course, it's not quite applicable here – '

'I told you,' Tom said in a low, heated tone. 'I'm going to call her – '

'Well, that's what I said,' Dick nodded. 'Not quite applicable.'

Mrs Bee was gathering herself together in her seat. 'It's getting late,' she announced. 'When somebody starts quoting poetry, I know it's time to go.'

Dick and Tom joined in urging her to stay. Tom, though he felt the evening had gone on long enough, did not want it to end on such a note, on Dick making such a bloody fool of himself. And Dick seemed quite contrite.

'I promise. No more poems.'

But Mrs Bee had made up her mind. She was ready to go. Dick volunteered to give her a lift back to her hotel, but she declined the offer. She liked to go under her own steam, she'd take a cab. Tom thought that was probably the best solution. The taxi would take ten minutes at least to arrive, which would give just enough time to wind up the evening in decent style. He went out into the hall to telephone the mini-cab company.

As he left the room, Jeannie spoke up.

'It was so strange,' she said, 'talking to Sue Strang. You know – '

she glanced at Louise, 'I worked with her once. On a *Tales of the Unexpected*. I don't think she'd remember me, though.' They could hear Tom dialling out in the hall. Jeannie sighed. 'I wish I hadn't said that stupid Chinese restaurant thing.'

'We all wish that,' Dick said.

Louise put out her hand and touched Jeannie's arm comfortingly. She was about to say something, when another voice cut in.

'Did you say, "Sue Strang"?'

They all looked round at Mrs Bee in surprise. She was leaning forward in her chair, looking intently at Jeannie.

'Yes,' the younger woman said, faltering slightly under Mrs Bee's gaze. 'Susan Strang . . . Sue . . . Do you know her?'

Mrs Bee relaxed then, leaned back in her chair. She shook her head very slowly. Dick was watching her with interest.

'You probably know her from television,' Louise suggested. 'She was quite famous for a while. *The Entwistles*, do you remember that series? A few years ago . . . Why,' she smiled across at Dick, 'I forgot. You directed that, didn't you?'

Dick acknowledged the fact with a slight bow. Mrs Bee nodded thoughtfully. 'Maybe it was that,' she murmured.

'Although,' Louise glanced again at Dick, 'I don't know if they saw it in America . . .'

'They certainly did,' Dick said. 'On PBS. We went down well. Very well.'

'So,' Louise nodded, 'that must have been it.'

'And she's out of work now?' Mrs Bee asked.

Again they glanced at her.

'Pretty well permanently,' Dick confirmed. 'She's been having quite a hard time of it of late.'

Tom returned before anything more could be said. 'They're pretty busy,' he announced. 'Should be here in twenty-five minutes. Which, I think, is just enough time for another little nip of brandy.'

The suggestion was well received. Mrs Bee was the first to hold out her glass. She drank her brandy in thoughtful silence, and the others, following her lead, were also very quiet. But then she seemed to shake herself, and remember her duties as a guest. When the doorbell rang at last, thirty minutes later, to announce her taxi, she was chatting away as animatedly as when she had first come into the house, hours before.

Tom felt the weight of all those hours as at last he undressed for bed. And the weight of that other thing too, a sense of deepening depression, a sharp contrast to the euphoria he had felt when the front door had closed at last on his guests. Then he had been sure that the evening had been a success. He felt it no longer. Something was not right . . . but he could not put his finger on what it was. Most of all he wanted to sleep now, long hours of sleep. Maybe in the morning he could sort out what the mystery was. He crawled into bed and burrowed his head into the pillow. 'G'night,' he murmured. He hoped he wouldn't dream. He just wanted to lie in blackness for a dozen hours.

'I want to say one thing.'

'Oh, no.'

'One thing,' Louise insisted. She waited for a moment. He opened his eyes. She was lying on her back, staring at the ceiling. She didn't look at him when he spoke. 'About Susie.'

Tom sighed. He rolled over on his side, away from her.

'It was a shitty thing to do, Tom.'

A pause. He opened his eyes again.

'Agreed,' he sighed at last. 'It was a shitty thing.'

He rolled back towards her. She turned her head on her pillow and looked at him. They smiled at each other sadly.

'Do you know what she wanted?' Louise asked. She hesitated. Then, 'I don't know, when I spoke to her she sounded so . . . hurt.'

Tom knew very well why Susie might have sounded hurt. But the fact was he had never told Louise that he had invited his old friend up to stay with them so many weeks ago. He could not altogether explain to himself why he had never got in touch with her since. Not once. He had excuses: as soon as he'd got back from Swayncliff, he'd been plunged into all the distractions of his newly eventful life. The baby. The house move. The new job. These served to make his behaviour understandable to himself, most of the time. But he knew they would not survive a close hard look. The truth was the new life had not turned them into hermits. They had gone out of their way in this period to seek out their friends, to share their happiness, to see their joy reflected in the faces of others. All except Susie. Deep down, Tom had a good idea what he was up to. He knew that Susie represented bad luck to him. Bad luck, disappointment, failure. And as much as he was happy – more than happy – joyous nowadays, so he feared now a change in his fortunes. He felt he could not, would not come down from this high and glorious pinnacle he had reached. And, primitively, he feared bad luck might be catching. It was hard on Susie, but with so much to lose, Tom was prepared to do anything

– cross his fingers, not walk under ladders, search out black cats – anything to hang on to his luck. He was certainly prepared, just for a little while longer, to disappoint an old, dear friend.

But he would not like to talk about it, not even to Louise. 'I don't know why she would be hurt,' he lied. 'Except I suppose she's lonely.'

'Then we must do something about it.'

'I keep telling everybody,' Tom protested, 'that I'm going to call her up tomorrow. Today.' He struggled up into a sitting position. 'Or maybe I'll write to her, what do you think?'

'No, you'll call,' Louise directed in a voice both firm and sleepy. 'And why don't we invite her up here for a bit?' she added. 'Just for a few days. I'm sure she'd like that.'

He stared at her. 'Well, you've changed,' he said.

'What do you mean?'

'Don't you remember? You didn't even want me to go down and see her.'

'I know I didn't,' she said at last. 'It was wrong of me.'

She was quiet then, for so long he thought she might have drifted off. He leaned over and looked down at her. Her eyes were open, she smiled at him. Then said sadly, 'I hated what Dick said. That we all enjoy Susie being in trouble.'

'Dick made a fool of himself tonight. Anyway,' Tom said, 'Susie's not in trouble, not really.'

He rubbed his eyes. He tasted suddenly a foul wash of acid in his mouth. Ah God, he prayed, please don't let the damn duck get to me too. I have got to stay healthy. I've got a million things to do tomorrow, next week, next month. For the survival of my house . . .

'I was showing off for that bloody Bee woman,' he said suddenly. 'I know she suspects I'm a bit soft. I wanted to prove to her what a hard nose I can be. That's why I shafted Susie.'

'I know. And that's why I didn't go and talk to her the second time too.' She was silent for a few moments. Then said, not looking at him, 'We're not bad people, are we, Tom?'

'Sssh.' He leaned over and stroked her hair. 'We're not bad people. It'll be all right. I'll call her . . .' He grinned suddenly. 'I'd better call her. Otherwise she might send me one of those letters.'

'God, yes!' said Louise, awed. She had been with Tom that morning when the slip of toilet paper had fallen from the envelope, covered with angular, deep-scored, crazy writing. She could see the funny side to the incident now, but at the time it had been distressing. 'Yes, don't want that again.'

'Poor Susie,' Tom sighed comfortably.

'Lucky us.'

They cuddled for a moment. Then Louise moved away and turned her face upon the pillow. 'Right. I'll shut up now.' She closed her eyes.

Tom, however, still sat up in bed, frowning into space. He was trying to see something, some shape that was just ahead of him. Dick's satirical smirk. Jeannie's nervous giggling. Mrs Bee, sometimes caustic, sometimes purring. The ice cream all empurpled and veined like a sheep's heart. The evening. He felt a sense of dread overwhelming him, and to stop it he spoke out abruptly.

'I wish she hadn't said that when she was leaving.'

'What?' Louise murmured. 'What did you say?'

'Mrs Bee, she said to me . . .'

Tom peered at the shape in front of him. If he could only see it right, he would not be afraid. A minute passed, then another, as he tried to make out what it was, its dimensions, the size of the threat. He did not know he had been silent for so long when he spoke again.

'Samarkand,' he said. 'On the doorstep Mrs Bee said "Samarkand" to me.'

There was no response, and when he looked down he saw that she was sleeping.

In the night, they both woke up together. Downstairs the phone was ringing. They had no idea when it had begun. It went on and on. They rolled confusedly towards each other. 'It's Susie,' Louise muttered. 'It must be.' 'Damn her,' Tom groaned. 'She's persecuting us.' On and on, like a madman's lament, or the crying of a tortured child, 'You've got to answer it, Tom.' 'I will not. She's got no right. It isn't fair . . .' Louise was already asleep again. Tom listened to the distant peals a few seconds longer and then was asleep himself.

Sometime later, Tom woke up again. It was still dark outside. He listened for the phone, but there was nothing to hear. It could not have been that which had woken him. The bedside light was on. He could not remember whether he had turned it off before he slept. The space beside him was empty. He got out of bed and went downstairs.

He found Louise in the kitchen, sitting at the table, crouched over it, holding herself tight. He went up to her, and put his hand on her forehead. The fringe of her hair was damp under his touch. She looked up at him, her face screwed up in pain.

'Oh, Tom, oh, Tom . . .'

'What is it?'

'I don't know. I'm scared . . . I feel so bad.'

Daydreaming

14

South of Tours the morning sun, which had been struggling to shine since Paris, broke free from the clouds at last. The train had been travelling for many miles through a sodden landscape, under an overcast sky. Now the gleam of light, dazzling at her window, woke her from her reverie. She peered through the glass. They were running beside a river that was bordered with a fringe of tall, wispy trees. In places the river had broken its banks so that the trees stood half-drowned in the black flood. Beyond stretched enormous damp fields. She had been thinking how strange it was, and depressing, to have come so far, to know that she was in a foreign land, and yet to feel the same tired sense of familiarity wherever she looked. Dark fields, dark skies, and the small, mist-shrouded towns slipping by at intervals – if it were not for the ultra-modern design and decor of the train, and the way it had of sliding noiselessly into and out of the stations they stopped at along the route, she might as well be taking a winter journey in her own country. But now, under the sun, the river gleamed, the woods reflected the light in half a dozen astonishing shades of green, and the huge fields steamed fatly in the heat. *France*, she thought suddenly, with joy. France in the springtime.

She wanted to break through the glass that separated her from the picture of France out there, and seize hold of it all, and hug it to her: woods, fields, the black shining river, the April light – hold it to her close, breathe it all in.

She had crossed by ferry from Swayncliff harbour, and by evening she was in Paris. She had spent the night in a hotel near the Gare d'Austerlitz. This morning she had caught the Sud-Express: Paris-Orleans-Tours-Poitiers-onwards. It had all gone like clockwork.

Raymond had made a great fuss when she told him she would be stopping the night in Paris. He could not understand it. He thought she was being pig-headed. It didn't bother her. She wanted the night in Paris, 'to sleep in a real bed one last time', she'd said. And no matter how many times he had waved timetables in her face, and demonstrated how unnecessary it was, she would not change her mind.

(The flat was filled with timetables then, the living-room carpet littered with them, timetables and maps and brochures and phrase books, all underlined and with notations, little arrows pointing this way and that, cryptic signs of which only she and Raymond knew the import. And then, in a swoop, the night before her departure, they were all gone, burned in the kitchen sink and the ashes washed down the drain.)

'I need a base,' she had kept telling him. 'I need to start from somewhere.'

'This is your base. Start from *here*. Look – ' She was shaking her head. He spread out the timetable before her. 'Don't you *see*? You take the night ferry, you're in Paris at six-oh-five in the morning – '

'Feeling like hell.'

' – you take a taxi to Austerlitz – or get on the Metro, plenty of time – you catch the Sud-Express, nine-forty, it couldn't be easier!'

'No.'

Raymond thought it was only with a view to her comfort that she resisted him. It wasn't so – though she had felt like telling him that even if it had been, she was perfectly within her rights. It was she who was committed to perform, to go out there, to do it. She – certainly not him (the idea was a joke) – who would make real the thing that if not for her would remain only a web of words and wishes and double dares: insubstantial, floating, something to tease and excite each other with. Charades, nothing more.

For this was the magic time when what was not real became – only because of her – solid, of consequence, fact. And dammit: if in the course of that process she required something, even something out of the ordinary, a little indulgence to help her through – then she was entitled to have it. People – people who didn't know – made jokes about performers' demands, the items, say, that rock stars inserted in their contracts. There must be a crate of brandy, ten dozen roses, a hundredweight of Smarties and a baby elephant in their dressing room before the show. Big joke. They had to go out on that stage and, in her opinion, whatever it took to get them there was exactly what had to be provided. No less.

She waited till after Poitiers before she left her seat and went to find the dining car. Poitiers had looked a handsome town – a river, a gorge above the river, clustering white houses with identical red roofs, stately old buildings set high on a hill. She had thought idly that it would be nice to step off the train, spend the day wandering around. Catch the Sud-Express again tomorrow. Then she had a vision of how Raymond would look if he could read her mind at that moment, and she couldn't help chuckling. After all the fuss over the Paris stopover. How sure he had been that it was only a whim on her part, the old prima donna surfacing. But in truth she had never been particularly demanding in her professional life, never had a reputation (except when Mark was handling her career) of being 'difficult'. If it had been only an indulgence to stay the night in Paris, she would have let it go. But as she saw it, it was pure necessity. For she could see no way of drawing a straight line from Swayncliff to where she had promised to go and to what she had promised to do there.

'I can't make that jump,' she had explained, begging him to understand. 'I can't do *that* . . .' She had held her hands up wide apart, like an angler measuring a prize. 'I think I might be able to do *that*.' Now she moved her hands closer together, brought them down once, then moved them to one side, brought them down again. Two steps, she was trying to show him, not one. Swayncliff to Paris, where she would be . . . nothing specific, settling into the character, gathering herself, accustoming herself to the release from home. And then the second step – Paris to her goal, where she would be . . . the new person, if she had got it right. The woman coming from a town that was not her own, going to a place she had never been to and would never revisit. The woman who was capable of . . . well, who knew what she was capable of, this woman? She was newborn. Always before her was an image she had fastened on to early and pushed towards as steadily as she could – a thing of anonymity, unweighed, uncalculated, a speck on the map of Europe, moving fast and unerringly across it, so that this combination of speed and direction and seeming insignificance might carry her eight hundred miles and more across the continent without a soul noticing, as if she travelled under a cloak of invisibility, or was like a missile: too fast for the naked eye to catch, only the damage it did giving, too late, a clue to its existence.

Well, that was the idea. But the woman who rose out of a familiar bed, in a familiar flat, in a town where she felt weighted with the knowledge of its every street and building, every brick and stone almost, every seagull – that woman could never do it. She must start her true journey from Paris. Only in that was there a hope of success.

But Raymond couldn't see it. Raymond still thought it was only a whim. Which, she thought, as she settled down comfortably, anonymously, in the dining car, among the other passengers, with a steak and a salad and a glass of wine before her, was just too bad for Raymond. It was her show. It was going to happen as she wished. She had the power.

After Bordeaux, they ran for many miles through pine woods, long straight lines of tall trees, commercial plantations. The scene soon became monotonous. She found herself yawning, wondering what to do with herself. She had not thought to bring a book with her, or pick up any magazines in Paris. The idea that she would need distraction on this particular trip had not once occurred to her. She stared at the seat back in front of her. It carried a notice on a small plastic card. Good – it would spin out a few minutes. 'Vous êtes à lière classe dans un wagon fumeurs,' she read. And nodded cheerfully. Yes, she had insisted on first class, first class all the way. It had provoked another outburst from Raymond. Second class, he had sworn, was perfectly adequate. On French trains, certainly, though he had to admit he couldn't speak for the Spanish ones. She wouldn't listen to him in any case. If she was going to have to travel overland a thousand miles almost, two thousand with the return trip, then she was damned if she was going to do it in anything less than first-class style.

And there would have to be, of course, a first-class outfit to go with the first-class travel. New dress, new shoes, new underwear, the complete course of treatment at Charisma beauty salon on Swayncliff High Street the day before she left . . .

'Well, it's up to you, of course – '

'You're going to have to pay for all of it, Raymond.'

'Christ!'

Christ indeed. But, as she had argued, what man would confidently open his door to a woman who came to him looking like a sinister frump? If I'm tarted up a bit, she had explained patiently, I've got that much more power, more *weapons*, don't you see? Some sun-lamp treatments too would be a help. There couldn't be many of these for in the end they only had about two weeks, sixteen days exactly, to get ready. But a few visits to the solarium at the Leisure Centre served at least to take away her winter pallor. Raymond paid. And for the course of massages that restored some suppleness to her limbs, that toned up her slack muscles . . . It is *not* an extravagance, Raymond. It's a necessity. Please don't let's spoil the ship for a ha'porth of –

It was strange though how the terms of the contract between them had emerged, bit by bit, and as a sort of counterpoint to the major theme of their dealing. Which was of justice, of course, and retribution. And the rising up of the insulted and injured. Yes, and the first-class ticket, the new outfits, the solarium . . . Deep down, she knew she was following a sure professional instinct. If there is cheapness about the peripherals of a production – costume, make up, scenery – sure as sunrise, that cheapness would show up in the performance. Raymond was not a professional and could not understand it. She was, and would take the responsibility. She did not intend this production to be botched through Raymond's miserliness. She also did not intend to pay a penny of her own money to obtain what was necessary. Again, she knew she was responding to professional standards. If she had to pay to be allowed to perform then she would be in the position of a mere enthusiastic amateur. From amateurs came amateur results. If Raymond wanted nothing more than that, then he had no business to be dealing with her. Since he was, he had to accept the conditions that came attached. Which were: no pay, no play.

One day she had mused aloud, 'I think a fur coat wouldn't be a bad idea. For the total effect.'

Raymond had paled. 'I – ' he began to stammer, 'I – can't – '

She had let him twist and turn for a little while, as a punishment for all the irritating penny pinching she'd had to endure from him. And then she laughed.

'Relax, Raymond, I've already got it. It's my mother's old coat. It still looks rather swish.'

Outside her window the rows of pines marched on, rank after rank. Nothing had changed out there, nothing to do but read on. 'Vous pouvez par une simple mouvement du corps avancer l'assise de votre siège en position repos.' She'd already discovered that, though it hadn't been 'une simple mouvement' particularly; she'd had to tug and rock the seat hard to get it to move back. '2 WCs sont à votre disposition du côté du wagon fumeurs.' Well, that was an idea. She stood up and stretched gratefully. Then picked up her carry-all from the seat and went to find the door with the tiny silhouette of a woman on it, a few steps back from where she had been sitting. Inside the cubicle, she used the toilet and then, balancing herself at the sink, pressed down a button on the floor with one foot to make the tap water flow. She splashed her face and dried herself on a paper towel. She looked at herself critically in the mirror. Mirror, mirror on the wall – her hair was a mess.

She opened her carry-all to get at her comb. Damn, she couldn't find it. She rummaged around inside the bag. It was down there somewhere, on the bottom, but all this other junk was in the way. She balanced the bag on the low-level toilet cistern and began to unpack it carefully. First, she took out her passport. She couldn't resist glancing at the photograph on the third page. Unlike everyone else she knew, she liked her passport photo. It had been taken four years ago, she had worn her hair longer then, and slightly waved. It made her features look much softer, less severe – maybe she should go back to that style. Maybe she would after this trip. But what she liked most was the lively glint in her eyes. She looked happy in the photo, confident, going places. She would have taken bets that things would work out well for the young woman with that bright steady gaze.

And have lost.

She frowned. Well, she would see if that was so true. The game wasn't over. Nobody had won or lost permanently yet, and there were often nasty surprises in store for those who felt most confident in their success. Oh, yes. She closed her passport firmly, turned it round in her hands. It was this, this navy-blue square of cardboard with the green pages in between, that had bothered Raymond most, and had made him argue so strongly against her staying in Paris. For they had gone to such lengths after all to camouflage her journey in advance.

'We won't buy the ticket here,' he'd said. 'I'll go up to Canterbury and get it.'

'Is that necessary?'

'I think so. And I'll need a false name for you. Yes,' he nodded in the face of her sceptical grin. 'It's a sleeping-car ticket, they'll want a name.'

He asked her to choose a name she'd feel confident with.

'Raymond! It's only for forty-eight hours. Any name'll do . . . How about "Harriet Scroggins"?' she giggled.

He'd asked her to be serious, but she found that hard. Her next suggestion was 'Lucy Entwistle'. He had looked at her grimly, in disappointment, then had walked across her living room to stand staring out of the window at the Esplanade, the mist beyond. Watching him, his long thin back and legs, his ugly clothes, she felt a twinge of pity. He was trying so hard, poor man. At the same time she found herself wondering what the hell he was doing in her apartment, how she could have ever let him in.

'If it's all a joke to you . . .' he'd sighed, his back to her. He shrugged. Why bother? he meant.

She'd come to him then and said she was sorry. She promised to think hard. But it was very difficult. Every name she came up with seemed either facetiously over-simple – Jane Dunn, Joan Dunn, Joan Smith, Jane Brown – or incredibly unlikely. Nothing seemed to fit her. She could not imagine herself passing under any of those names. Lavinia Prendergast? Edwina Huntingford? Not a chance.

She was practically on the brink of giving up and saying it might as well be Harriet Scroggins, she could think of nothing better – when exactly the right name popped into her mind.

'Wendy Strong.'

'Wendy . . .?'

He turned it over, examined it, and seemed to approve. She was sure it was right. Perhaps because the names – Strang, Strong – sounded so close. They had a sisterly ring. And she didn't think that the real Wendy, her old friend and protector – wherever she was – would mind her borrowing her name for a short season. Anyway, she would never know about it.

He looked at her closely. 'It's not the name of anyone real, is it?'

'Well,' she'd half-lied, 'I suppose *somebody* might be called that. It's sort of common – '

'But not too much,' he'd nodded. 'Wendy Strong. Yeah, that sounds OK. Think you can live with it?'

'For forty-eight hours? Course I can.'

So, according to her ticket, she was Wendy Strong. But her passport, of course, was in her own name. There was nothing to worry about as long as she kept moving. Passports, they knew, weren't checked seriously at European frontiers any more. But if she went to a hotel in France –

'They'll take your passport. They'll keep it overnight, write down the details, send them to the police. The police put 'em into a computer – '

'I bet they don't. There are millions of tourists in France every night. It would be impossible . . . And anyway, even if they do, so what?'

'But then they can *trace* you!'

'Only as far as Paris. And why would they do that anyway unless something goes wrong. And nothing is going to go wrong.'

He was obsessed with her blasted passport. He'd taken it in his hands, stared at it miserably.

'It's just paper,' she'd scoffed. 'Paper and cardboard.'

'It's real,' he had said bleakly. 'It matters. It matters to *them*.'

Obsessed. 'If it's such a big deal,' she'd said, when he would not let the passport question drop, 'why don't you buy me a false one? We'll put Wendy Strong's name on it, how's that?' He had stared at her then, with sudden intensity. It made her uneasy to be looked at like that. She guessed that he didn't understand what she was suggesting. And even though she had meant it as a joke really, she did not like him to think that she'd put up a completely foolish notion. 'You can do it,' she assured him. 'I've heard you can buy them – '

'What the fuck do you know about that?' he had snapped and he had turned away from her contemptuously. 'You don't know anything,' he muttered. She was left floundering, amazed at his sudden assault. And then became angry. And would have told him off. Might have ordered him from the apartment – she wasn't going to be talked to like that. Cursed at like that. In her own home. Definitely not by *him*.

But he had quickly turned back to her and, with a ghost of the apologetic, charming smile she remembered from when she'd first met him, had shaken his head and said he was sorry, he didn't know what had come over him. 'I'm nervous, I suppose.' He had handed her passport back to her. 'I'm sorry. I'm making a fuss about nothing. Won't mention it again.'

For a while, she had wondered at the reason behind his sudden rage. It wasn't nervousness she had seen in his eyes, she was sure. More like – deep scorn. And yet when she went over her words there seemed nothing that should have precipitated such an outburst. In the end, she concluded that Raymond must be experiencing towards her the same irritated, hostile feelings she knew she was having about him. They saw too much of each other, they were prisoners inside the cell of their plan. He would be glad to see the back of her, she guessed. She was certainly glad now to have got rid of him.

At least he had kept his word and never mentioned the passport again. She had never changed her mind that it was the least of the possible hazards that faced her in the days ahead. Nevertheless, at the hotel last night, she had felt a stir of unease as she'd pushed it over the counter. The dark young man who served her – North African, she guessed, or Italian, rather than French – studied her passport photograph with interest before placing it in a drawer. Maybe she should have kept moving, never stopped, a speck drifting across the map of Europe . . .

She put the passport now on the cistern surface to one side of her bag. Well, she had got it back, no problem, it had all gone perfectly smoothly. The dark young man hadn't even kept it overnight; he'd given it to her when she came into the hotel lobby later that night after her meal in a near-by brasserie. There was no sense in worrying about it now. Whatever he'd done with any details he'd taken down, it was all water under the bridge. The thing to worry about now, the only thing to worry about was –

Where the hell had her comb got to?

This other blasted thing was the major obstacle in her search. This flat, square container riding at the top of her bag, this heavy brute. They had wondered and worried for so long what she was going to carry the . . . thing in. (It was how she saw it. The 'thing'. Or rather, when she thought of it, it was just as a blip streaking across her mind. Might as well translate that blip as the 'thing'. Or as 'it'. Might as well. No matter. Keep moving. Don't think.) Now this thing, or *it*: what to keep it in? Couldn't just have it rattling around free in her carry-all. And a paper bag might tear. And a plastic bag – well, perhaps, but they could do better surely. And in the end Raymond had come to the flat one night with just the right item. Which she had recognised immediately. It was the little black leather-like case that had held his miniature tape recorder, the instrument that had lain between them like the recording angel during their first meeting. The interview. They had laughed together briefly, remembering that occasion. Strange beginning. It certainly was, and look where they were now . . . and look how perfectly the thing fits in. Bulk it round with a bit of tissue paper – and it's like a bug in a rug. Snug. Isn't it just? And anybody looking into your bag –

Who's going to look, Raymond?

Well, they might, I don't know – but *if* they do, all they're going to see is –

A tape recorder. Or a radio. Some little Japanese music box that any traveller might take with her on a long journey. Perfect. Ideal. Well done, Raymond. It was so convincing that since the start of the trip she'd had another name for the thing to add to her list. She thought of it mostly now as 'the radio'.

Of course she could say the real word if she wanted. She could say it out loud if she wanted, this very moment . . . But why bother? She had other things to do. The radio was definitely in the way. She gripped it, lifted it out of the bag – bloody heavy brute – and placed it on the cistern on top of the passport.

Now at last she could reach her comb. Feeling more relaxed, for she never liked handling the radio, even in its case, she turned to the mirror and dragged the comb through her hair. She studied herself critically in the little mirror. Better. Much better. In fact, she could not deny she was looking quite passable. There seemed to be a lightness about her features, they were more intense, defined, younger. She turned her head from side to side.

She looked happy. That was it! She looked just like she felt. Such happiness to be here, on this train, first class, tearing across a foreign country, miles behind her, miles ahead. Bracing herself as the carriage swayed beneath her, she watched the mirror with great interest. So that was what she looked like when she was happy.

Not bad.

A slight sound at the door made her turn round swiftly. She saw the knob turn. A moment more, and then there came a discreet knock. It occurred to her that she must have been in here – regarding her lovely face, she grinned, feasting her eyes – for ages. And some poor person in need had been out there, waiting patiently. Oh, well, she couldn't blame herself too much. It made up for all the months of slinking past mirrors, not wanting, hardly daring to look in them. Still enough was enough. She took a last friendly look at her reflection. She winked at herself. You'll do, she thought. Then she gathered up her bag and unlocked the door.

Outside, a woman, middle aged, gentle looking, was waiting. She smiled at Susan as the door opened.

'Pardon, madame,' Susan murmured, holding the door open for her.

'Mais pas de tout . . .'

The gentle-looking woman passed into the cubicle and closed the door behind her. Susan went back to her seat. She felt very refreshed. The thought of coffee or a cup of tea appealed to her. She looked at her watch – two-thirty. She wondered if the man with the canteen trolley would be making another run soon through the train. She decided to give it quarter of an hour and then go and look for him. The sun was no longer falling so strongly on her window and she pulled back the curtain a little further and looked out. She was pleased to see that the pine woods had given out at last. They were in a more rolling country now, and the trees were mostly deciduous. They were in full leaf. Down here the spring was well advanced. Back home they would call this summer. She realised suddenly, joyously that she was truly in the south now. She had come through to another climate, another zone. And everything bad was far away and receding further with every mile. That was something. Something to sing about:

Pack up all my care and woe
Here I go
Singing low . . .

She beat time to the tune as it danced across her mind. Wouldn't do to sing it out loud, she smiled to herself. Not the way for a speck on the map of Europe to carry on, not at all. Better get up and look for that man and his coffee machine. Stay out of trouble. Just one more look at the south, the bright south, and she would be on her way.

The hand on her shoulder made her start. She looked up. The gentle-looking woman who had succeeded her in the lavatory was smiling down at her. She was saying something, but too quietly and too fast for Susan to make it out. She was holding something out to Susan.

'M'selle, ces sont à vous?' the woman repeated.

In her right hand were a British passport and a black, square, plastic case.

15

After hundreds of miles and a day and a half she was at the seaside again. Bayonne had been all grey apartment blocks and a wide muddy river, and they might have been anywhere in France. But the station at Biarritz, where they stopped for ten minutes, had the real resort flavour. New paint on the buildings, baskets of flowers, and the old-fashioned, well-preserved lamp standards. Not just a point for travellers to get on and off; it was bait too, a lure for tourists. Leaving Biarritz, they ran for a little while through woods and meadows, and then, glancing across at the window on the other side of the carriage she saw at last the sea, just a glimpse at first through a break in the woods. She got out of her seat and, holding her carry-all pressed tightly to her chest, as she had held it for the past many miles, she crossed over to sit by the far window. She watched intently and was rewarded every minute or so by more glimpses of silver and blue through the trees. And then they broke out of the woods and she held her breath for it was all laid out below her: a wide bay, tall cliffs, and the shining water going on and on for ever. Home again! she thought with a swell of contentment. And then had to laugh at herself. Since she was so very far from home – thank God – and there could not be a much greater contrast between the scene spread out beneath her now and the weak, sullen tide she had watched day after day after day drifting up the flat beach on the far side of Swayncliff Esplanade.

In a while, the train came to a stop again and she went back to her old seat and peered out of the window. St Jean de Luz. She wondered how near they were to the frontier. She had a map somewhere. In her bag. She could look it up . . . Oh, what the hell. They must be pretty near. Knowing exactly how far wouldn't get them there any sooner.

It was like a ghost station, this one. There were no porters about. No friends and relatives waiting. She couldn't hear the sounds of anyone getting on or off. She wondered if she was the last passenger left on the train. She was the only one left in this carriage. Her gaze went down the aisle to where that woman had been sitting, the gentle-looking woman who had returned to her what she had idiotically mislaid – had abandoned in a lavatory of all places, like an unwanted baby, for Christ's sake . . . She had to stop thinking about that for again she felt the approach of that wave of murderous self-disgust that had overwhelmed her back then, when she had looked up and seen the woman holding out her belongings.

'M'selle, ces sont à vous?'

Of course the woman hadn't looked inside the plastic case. Maybe she had checked the passport, had a look at the photo to make sure it was Susan who was its owner. That was OK. Normal. But nothing else. Not possibly. The woman had gone back to her seat. She hadn't looked round at Susan once for the rest of the journey. She had got off at Biarritz with the rest of the passengers, and hadn't looked round then. Of course, she could have gone straight to the police at Biarritz . . .

No.

Think of other things.

The train, which had been running along slowly for five or ten minutes, lurched to a sudden stop. It waited for a few moments and then eased cautiously forward again. Above her head the intercom, which had kept her company for so many miles, now sounded its prefatory two notes – ping, pong! Then the voice, attractive, growling, speaking a French that was usually too fast for her to understand in detail, though she thought she usually got the gist of what he was saying. This time she heard the names 'Hendaye' and 'Irun' repeated several times. She knew that one of these was on the French side of the border, and the other on the Spanish, so that this phase of her journey would very soon be over. She heard the announcement without concern. Frontiers held no perils for her. Safely inside her long-distance train, she would just breeze past them. That was the perfection of the plan they had worked out, she and Raymond. Up to then it had just been a game, charades, just a silly, tipsy game. It had been like that right up to that moment when, Christmas night, she had been prowling around the living-room floor, two fingers held rigid before her in imitation of a weapon, and Raymond watching from the couch, laughing and clapping at her show, and . . . she had stopped for a moment, and stood there, and then had just turned to him and whispered, 'Why, Raymond – I could do it!'

I really could.

And I know how to get there, so I can really do it.

A train, Raymond! A train all the way! Can't you see it? A magic carpet . . .

And here she was. On a train in France. Her magic carpet. Which wasn't moving right now. She looked again out of the window. Saw the sign: Hendaye. Now it came back to her. Last exit to France. At Irun, according to the timetable, they were going to have to wait for nearly an hour. She wasn't sure how she was going to spend that hour. Maybe she would get off the train and see if there was a bar on the platform. But maybe that was a bad idea. Even though she had no fears about the frontier, still it might be best to just sit quiet, drawing no attention to herself, until they were well past it. Also she wanted to hang on to her seat, and there might be a lot of new passengers getting on at Irun. She could hardly leave her carry-all to keep her seat while she went roaming. Though she wouldn't mind getting up and stretching for a bit. She would like to locate her sleeping compartment too, and see if it was open for her yet. Then she could move in and shut the door, and she'd be perfectly safe. At the moment, however, she had no idea where the sleeping cars were on this train. She had looked for them along the platform at Austerlitz, but couldn't find them.

That's it, she thought suddenly, that's why we're stopping for an hour at Irun. They'll be joining the sleeping cars on there.

So after Irun she'd go looking. And meantime – the train jerked forward, they were leaving Hendaye – she'd just sit here, and let the time pass, and concentrate on what she was doing. And be positive about it. For it had not all been shame and self-disgust the past couple of hours. She had made at least one gain. She had reality on her side now. When she'd looked up and seen her belongings in the Frenchwoman's hands, almost her first thought had been: I must stop calling that thing a 'radio'. That thing is not a radio. It is a gun.

What made it so useful a thought was that it swept away the last traces of pretence and coyness in her performance. She had arrived at something firm, a rock. Always it had been the element that had marred her work in the past, a final refusal to believe in her characters and what they were set to do. So that there had been a thin skin of irony separating herself from complete immersion in the material. A director had once told her, 'Everybody else might see it's a fiction, what you're doing, but *you* cannot, the actor must not.' She had tried hard to follow that rule, to give up the privileged position of, as it were, sharing in the joke. It had always been so difficult. For if she believed altogether in what she was doing, then what would be left of her, of that part of her that was not the actor? Even worse: what if she believed to the hilt – and then she failed? What could she fall back on then? Not irony, she would have surrendered that. I believed . . . and they didn't. They saw through me and they laughed. Horrible thought. So always she had worked in a little distance between herself and her roles. For security. And yet she knew it had cost her, and cost too some of the productions she'd been in.

'Extremely nice of you to show up and indulge us silly people,' the same director had remarked after a particularly supercilious reading.

'Well, I just can't believe in all this.'

'Who cares what you believe? Leave that to other people. All you have to know is – this is what you are, this is what you are doing. Nothing else. Surrender to it, for Christ's sake!'

For Christ's sake, she had better do it. It never was more important than now. Take a deep breath and admit it: unlikely as it was, she – Susan Strang, resident of Swayncliff, Kent, unemployed actress, nice person, thirty-seven years old, estranged wife of Mark Gould (present whereabouts unknown to me), only child of Charles and Mary Strang (deceased), et cetera, et cetera – was carrying a revolver in her carry-all bag. And three bullets. Susie Strang, no one else, was doing this.

There. Felt better, didn't it?

Count it up then. No more evasions: one real passport, one international rail ticket purchased under a false name, one real gun. That was the situation. And after all, looked at straight on, it did not seem so strange or fantastical any more. She had dazzled herself with the idea that she was this unique and spectacular entity, this remarkable speck racing across the map. But she felt suddenly certain that she was not at all unique, that the map of Europe, of the whole world, contained many similar specks, on their way, their quiet workaday way, silent, determined people like her, travelling from point A to point B, like her with a deep purpose behind their travels, like her with something in their bag, or in their pocket, or strapped to their leg, or against their shoulder which would give a terrible reality to their purpose, which could not be – though *they* might be – ignored.

I've got something in my pocket/ It belongs across my face/ I keep it very close to me/ In a most peculiar place . . .

She smiled without knowing it. This was the great boon her acceptance of reality had brought her. She no longer felt alone. She knew she was part of a brotherhood, a sisterhood. She was involved in life, she was in her time – ask not for whom the news bulletins toll, they toll for me. For me and all my brothers and sisters. Their causes were not her cause. But they shared the same high function. They were the spanners in the works. The world might roll along as ever. Evil doers might flourish as always – but in the end they too would be hurt. Yes. There would be a penalty. Hide yourself behind high walls and steel bars and armed guards as you may, and still we will find you out, my brothers and sisters and me.

Of course she anticipated no such difficulties on her own mission. No walls, bars, certainly no guards – it would be a cinch. 'You just walk up to the door,' Raymond had explained. 'It's a Sunday. It's the maid's day off. She goes down to see her family in Sagres. Every Sunday. So he'll open the door himself. And then . . .'

And then that would be that. Turn around. Get the bus back to Lagos. The other bus to Lisbon. On to the Sud-Express again. And all the way back to Paris. Like clockwork, like clockwork, not thinking, just doing, and the miles turning and turning under her, so mechanical, it couldn't go wrong . . .

The train, which for hundreds of miles had seemed a miracle of smoothness, now began to jerk and stop and start again in a routine that went on for several minutes. At last they came to a shuddering halt beside another platform. As far as she could see, there were no destination signs on this platform, but she was sure they could no longer be in Hendaye. Which meant that this must be Irun, and she was now in Spain. She looked out of the windows with interest, though there was not that much to see. On one side a high dark brick wall, on the other an empty platform, and beyond that railway sidings, an engine standing all alone. She could hear a few doors slamming further down the train, then silence. In a while, though still pleased to be across the frontier, she got tired of both views and, since the train showed no signs whatever of impending movement, boredom soon set in. She was quickly alert then, for she remembered that the last time she had felt this bored she had been betrayed into the foolish slip she had made over the passport and the – the *gun* in the lavatory. One gross slip like that was enough for this journey and clearly boredom was the great enemy and must be fought.

She yawned.

Luckily, the door at the far end of her carriage slid open then, and a man came through and started up the aisle. She watched him with interest – anything to break the tedium. He was short and stocky and his head was large for his body. He had his jacket slung over his shoulder and was whistling cheerfully as he walked. At the moment his gaze fell on her, he stopped whistling and seemed to stare at her in surprise. She smiled at him, wondering if she was seeing her first Spaniard of the trip. She thought about trying a casual 'Buenos dias' on him. Though her basic scheme was to make no significant contacts on this journey, to be as inconspicuous and anonymous as possible, yet she couldn't see that an occasional encounter could do much harm. In fact it would probably draw less attention to herself than would a policy of deliberately ignoring everyone. The vital thing was to be natural at all times. And what could be more natural than to say 'hello' to a passer-by in a stalled train? It couldn't go any further after all. 'Buenos dias' would practically exhaust her store of Spanish phrases.

At that moment the man began to speak French to her, pretty fast, so that she could not work out what he was saying. So she kept her smile on her lips and nodded at him, trying to be agreeable. And anonymous. She thought his voice sounded familiar, and then she realised that it was the attractive growl she had been listening to on the intercom since Paris. So this was the face that went with the Jean Gabin voice. Then she got more serious. If this was the same man speaking, then he must be something to do with the running of the train, he must be somebody official. She straightened herself cautiously in her seat. And when he came to the end of his speech, she asked politely, 'Pardon, Monsieur?'

The man sighed, discouraged to see that his efforts had been pointless. He took a breath and then, very slowly, and in a voice adapted to explaining things to a rather dull child, he said, 'Madame – vous devrez descendre ici.'

That she understood. She stared at him, then shook her head violently. 'Mais, non!'

'Mais, si!'

'Mais . . .' Oh, Christ. 'Mais pas de tout. Voilà . . .' She opened her bag and searched in it. 'I have a ticket . . . un billet . . . going all the way. Je vais à Lisbon . . . Lisboa . . . whatever you call it. Voilà, monsieur.' She showed him the ticket – Wendy Strong's ticket. He gave it a brief, unimpressed glance before he shook his head.

'Vous devrez descendre ici,' he repeated.

She stared up at him. She wondered for a moment if he was mad. He was certainly very mistaken. Now she too employed a voice suitable for explaining simple things to simple people.

'Monsieur, je vais à *Lisbon*. Dans *Portugal*. Je vais tout le voyage – '

He cut into her explanation. 'Sur un autre train,' he nodded. 'Le reste de votre voyage sera dans un autre train. Il arrivera dans quelques minutes sur un autre platform.' He stared down at her and then, pulling himself up to a great effort, 'Anuzzer train. Anuzzer platform. You must go . . .' He made a walking motion with two fingers of his right hand. 'Must go . . .' He stopped. Searched for the correct word. She watched him with a sort of fascinated horror. He found it. 'Immigration!' he announced proudly. 'You must go.' He stood waiting for her to get herself together and out of her seat, and when she did not – when she continued to sit motionless, no longer looking at him, staring ahead of her – he frowned. 'But you must go, madame,' he growled in a voice that permitted no more argument.

She was thinking how much she hated and despised Raymond. She would like an hour or two at least to concentrate on that thought – the bloody fool with his timetables and maps and assurances . . . and to get it so horribly wrong – imbecile, fool . . . But the man now beside her could not be ignored, nor the tone of his voice. She looked up and he nodded at her, and stepped aside a little to make room for her exit.

'Another train?' she said, hoping to the last that there had been some mistake.

'Oui, madame!' He smiled charmingly, pleased that they finally understood each other. 'Exactement!'

Her carry-all over her shoulder, the fur coat on her arm, she stepped down from the train that she had not thought to leave for another five hundred miles. The man pointed out to her the way she must go, and she walked slowly along the platform away from him. In the distance she could see the entrance to a large metal shed. The French flag was flying over it: she was still in France. She thought of Raymond, his stupidity. Stupid, inept, untrustworthy (like them all, like Mark, like that bastard Tom) . . . but her feelings now – to Raymond, to them all – amounted to no more than a dull and weary hostility. There was nobody she wished to think about now, except herself and what she was about to receive. Maybe it wouldn't be so bad, she prayed. She had gone past immigration at Calais and it had been nothing, they'd nodded her through before she'd even got her passport out of her bag. There was no reason to think things would be any more difficult down here. The whole of Europe was pretty much wide open now. Except at airports. Which was why she was trudging down this platform at the far end of France – having left a train that Raymond had promised her ran all the way across three countries and which she never would have to leave, not once . . .

But don't think about Raymond, she told herself. Think about the veil of anonymity she must draw across herself, the everyday traveller, the ordinary woman, woman in a crowd. She hoped there would be a crowd when she reached Immigration; perhaps she could slip past the officials with the rest of them. She quickened her step. She'd been sitting on the stationary train so long she feared everybody else must have gone through long ago.

She passed into the great shed. She saw a wooden gate erected at the nearer end of it. It was attached to nothing, just a gate standing in the middle of the floor, like a movie prop. The red, white and blue emblem was fastened to it, and a man in the slick uniform and kepi of a French official lounged near it. Beyond him, about thirty yards further on, she could see another similar gate, this time bearing a red, gold and white shield. She could see a few people standing down there, at the far end of the shed. Civilians, evidently her fellow passengers. Their numbers almost amounted to a crowd. It made her feel better to see them. I'll just get through this, she thought. I'll get through and maybe it won't be so bad, and anyway I was feeling bored, wasn't I? And . . . I'm certainly not bored now. She had reached the French official. He glanced at her without interest but did not, as she'd hoped, just wave her on through. He held out his hand and, after some fumbling in her carry-all, she produced her passport and gave it to him. He glanced at a couple of pages, then nodded and handed it back. Really it wasn't so bad, she reassured herself. She started to replace her passport in her bag, then thought she'd probably need it at the Spanish gate too. She stepped through the French gate – what a farce it was, she thought, her courage rapidly returning. Like a board game. Advance to Spain and collect 200 pesetas. No problem.

Five yards outside France she came to a sudden stop. She had a clear view now of the Spanish gate and of what was happening beyond it. The little crowd she had noticed before was gathered around a long table. The surface of the table was piled with luggage. On the other side of the table were officials in khaki uniforms and military caps. They were going carefully through the luggage, their hands rummaging deep into the unzipped and opened suitcases, carry-alls, handbags. Nobody was being excused from this search.

16

Her best bet, she decided, thinking about it later, would have been to turn right round and go back into France. That way might have caused problems too, explanations would have had to be made, it would have looked suspicious. Still, nothing could have been worse than to advance on this apparently alert and efficient group of customs men, carrying a bag inside which was . . . at that moment her spirit failed, almost died in her and, in spite of her good resolutions, she could not give a name to what she was carrying. But she *was* carrying it, and to keep going onwards with that knowledge – well, that would be crazy. Yet it was what she had done. One foot after the other. Like an automaton. True, for one moment she had looked back longingly into France. The officer at that gate, seeing her hesitate, had waved his hand helpfully, directing her on to Spain. And at his gesture – she must have lost all grip on her senses – she had obediently started into motion again, trudged the fifteen yards, then ten, then five – until she was standing, like a sick animal waiting to be shot, at the Spanish gate. Without looking at the guard, she handed over her passport. The only coherent thought she had as she stood there, head bowed and shoulders slumped, was: please get this over with. As quickly as possible, please. Just let it be over. Take me to the police car. Take me to prison. Just get on with it.

Nothing happened. She frowned and looked up at the guard. She held her hand out to him. Come on, she thought, give me the bloody thing, let me go on. I know it's all up. I'll make no fuss. The guard was staring at her. Oh, come on, she thought bitterly. There's nothing the matter with the passport at least. It's mine. And there's no chance – sweet dream – of being banned from entering Spain. I've never committed any crime in Spain. Never even been here before. This is my first entrance, and what a stunner it's going to be . . . The guard was still staring at her. In fact, the eyes seemed to be protruding out of his rather sallow face. And now, as she watched, he did a strange thing.

He giggled at her.

She gazed back at him, nonplussed. The only possible explanations for his behaviour that occurred to her were either that he found her passport photo hilariously funny or weird, which seemed very unfair to her, or that he was drunk. Either way she was uncertain how to deal with him. But she took comfort in the fact that his manner, though peculiar, did not seem at all hostile or accusing. He was wearing a smile now which, even under the threateningly high peak of his cap and its sharp shiny visor, could be described as seraphic. Yes, it was the look one saw on the faces of the audience at revival meetings, born again, blissed out. Maybe he was high as a kite, she thought suddenly, drugged to the eyeballs, and she felt a wild distant hope in that moment that perhaps she could bluff her way through this predicament after all. If she was dealing here with a bunch of happy, spaced-out Spaniards . . . and if she acted conciliatory and very silly herself:

'What's this? I've no idea. I think it's a radio. Somebody gave it to me on the train . . . Good heavens! Is that what is it? I never guessed . . .'

No, impossible, it would never work.

All the same, from somewhere she found a friendly and rather simple-minded smile, and from somewhere too she dredged up another Spanish phrase, holding out her hand again for the passport.

'Por favor,' she murmured.

To hear her speak seemed like passing an electric shock through the guard. He quivered to attention. He closed the passport with a stylish snap and held it out to her. And then in a voice that throbbed with emotion, 'Señora,' he said. And again, in the same voice, full of echoes, loss, yearning, devotion, 'Señora.'

She stood there, staring at him, into his passionate eyes. He was having her on, she understood suddenly, it was some kind of cruel joke. The kindly-looking woman on the train had turned her in at Biarritz and they had been waiting for her all this time. Now they were just having some fun with her before the knife went in.

She took a step back from the guard. His warm and loving eyes followed her. Then she turned and began to walk slowly towards the customs table. She looked round – mainly to see if that remarkable guard had ever really existed. He did exist. He had his hand up and was waving past her, towards his colleagues at the customs table. And he was calling something to them in a light though carrying voice. And when they looked up, he turned his waving hand into a signal, pointing at her. Then, seeing that she was watching him, he seemed to grow feeble with embarrassment. He shrank back against his gate. He was giggling again.

A fair cop, she thought sadly. They had known all along. And now she had been well and truly fingered. Well, at least she'd given them a few laughs. Perhaps they'd take a couple of days off her sentence in return. She pressed forward grimly to the table, the waiting officials, nemesis.

The officials had stopped their work, they had gathered together in a little cluster to watch her approach. The opened suitcases lay there ignored. And not only the customs men were waiting. The passengers too, alerted by the guard at the frontier gate, had turned to watch her. A buzz of excited chatter rose from them, and then as she got close it died away entirely. She trod the last few paces to the table in an immense, quivering silence.

Oh come on, for Christ's sake, she thought angrily. I'm not Ronnie Biggs. Or John Dillinger. This won't be very exciting. No shoot outs, no resisting arrests, and you'll get no tears from me, if that's what you're looking for. Bloody sadists. She came to a stop. Her gaze moved along the line of officials, trying to pick out their leader. Come on, she thought defiantly, get on with it. And might have said it aloud, except she knew that probably no one would know what she was saying. And anyway she couldn't be bothered. Come on. Here I am. Do your worst. What do I care? I only wish bloody Raymond was here to share the disaster.

An official, older than the rest, and with several more lines of decorations on his tunic, detached himself from the crowd and came round the table to her.

So now it would begin, she thought, her defiance seeping rapidly away. Discovery, handcuffs, police dogs, the prison cell . . . She held out her carry-all to the man. There. Take it. And then take me.

He waved the bag aside with an elegant, almost apologetic gesture. He held out his hand, and when, startled, she did not take it, he reached forward and seized her limp fingers. A quick, respectful pressure, and then he let her hand fall. He drew himself then to his full height – about the same as hers, though his cap gave him an advantage – and spoke in loud and earnest tones.

'Señora Strang – '

'. . . Yes?'

'Welcome to Spain!'

A strange staccato series of reports followed his words. Susan looked round fearfully. The passengers, mobbed behind her, were flapping their hands together. They were grinning idiotically at her.

Though when she looked individuals in the face, trying to work out what they were up to, their gazes dropped bashfully away from hers. She turned back to the customs table. Behind it, the other officials were also applauding loudly. She stared at the man in front of her. He bowed his head, and then gracefully gestured towards the far end of the hall, to the exit. 'Please,' he said. It was clear that he wished her to accompany him. She watched him for a moment more. She was utterly confused. At last she started walking, assisted by the polite pressure of his hand on her elbow.

Am I under arrest? she wondered wildly.

As she went past them, the passengers again started clapping, and a low cheer rose from them. She looked sideways at the official, who smiled at her in a sort of respectful complicity. At the exit he made her stop.

This is it, she thought. Joke's over.

'Please . . .' he murmured again. He was taking her fur coat from her arm. You bastard, she thought. Let it go. That's mine. That was my mother's . . . But she didn't struggle. What was the point? She was in his power. He went round behind her. Tenderly he draped the coat around her shoulders. 'It is . . . un poco . . . a little cold out there,' he explained.

Again he took her arm and they passed out of the shed and she found herself blinking in the daylight. They were walking along a platform, another platform, but this was very crowded. There were people all over the place, standing or squatting on the concrete, waiting, holding on to their baggage. As Susan and the customs official walked among them, the people at first watched them incuriously. And then, like a forest fire, excitement spread along the platform. People got to their feet, began to stand on cases to get a better view. Children were hoisted on to the shoulders of parents, women were lifted up in the arms of their men. There was the sound of running feet, as those a long way up the platform hastened to find out what was going on. As these new arrivals joined the edges of the crowd, people already there explained to them the action so far in short, excited bursts of chatter. In the heart of the crowd the voices were all merged together, an unbroken, ecstatic roar.

Looking neither to the right nor the left, the official steered Susan steadily through the mob. She kept her head down, she did not think. She did not think at all. She did not know where she was going. She did not know . . . She felt something pushed into her hand. She looked down at it. It was a small bunch of spring flowers. She looked around to see who had given it to her. She could see nothing but excited faces, mouths open. Something was shoved into her other hand. This time it was a bar of chocolate. She looked across at the face of the man who was guiding and protecting her. His eyes were calm and exalted. She drew comfort from them.

Half-way down the platform, the official stopped at an open door and indicated that she should go in ahead of him. She found herself in a long dim room, faintly lit by a neon strip. The walls were a dirty green. There was a counter at one end, with rows of bottles behind it. The three or four customers in the bar had gone to the windows to see what the uproar was out on the platform. Now they had turned to her, and were staring open-mouthed. She smiled weakly in response.

The customs official, after a few sharp exchanges with those of the platform crowd that had tried to follow them inside, now shut the door firmly on the mob. He turned then to Susan and gave her a dazzling smile of reassurance and sympathy. The man behind the bar had come out into the room. The official spoke crisply to him. The barman nodded understandingly and then, bowing to Susan, indicated that she should step into a sort of alcove set within one wall. There were a table and a couple of chairs there. She did as he asked. Meanwhile, the official was drawing shabby green curtains across the windows, blotting out the faces that were pressed against them on the other side.

Susan sat in the alcove. The barman, holding himself in an attitude of devoted attention, said something to her. She shook her head helplessly. The customs official came to their rescue.

'Something to eat?' he entreated Susan. 'Something to drink? Vino? Cerveza?'

'I'd like some coffee,' she murmured.

'Café!' The barman sprang to attention and sped across the room towards his counter. The official smiled again happily and then turned and with stern, shooing gestures ordered the other customers back to their tables. They did as they were told, though they could hardly help themselves turning to watch Susan as she sat all alone in her alcove.

The coffee – expreso, on a silver tray, with a single long-stemmed rose laid tenderly beside the cup – was brought to her. She thanked the barman, and he smiled joyfully when, in addition to her English words, she offered a 'gracias' too. The news that she had condescended to employ a Spanish word spread through the bar. The faces turned towards her were now wreathed in grateful smiles, and a couple of customers began clapping. Susan bowed her head slightly in acknowledgment. Though her heart was beating very fast, her mind was calm and clear now. It was a relief to know that she was in touch with reality, that she had not just swooned into some crazy, self-infatuated dream. For she knew now what was going on – though she was far from having absorbed its full import yet. She had been able to separate out at least one of the phrases that the people had been yelling at her as she had passed along the platform. And still she heard the echoes of it now, a low repetitive rumble, from the people outside. 'La Entwistle!' they had been shouting, were shouting still. 'La Entwistle, La Entwistle!'

Susan looked up. Immediately the barman and the customs official, who had been sitting at the nearest table to her, sprang to their feet.

'I wonder if you could tell me . . .' she said in a low voice.

'Señora?'

'How long is it till the train leaves for Lisbon?'

'Ah, señora . . .'

A long explanation followed, mostly in Spanish, sometimes in broken English. She could understand little of it. La Entwistle! came the roar from outside, like surf thundering up the beach. La Entwistle, La Entwistle, La Entwistle . . .

This is better than prison, Susan thought gleefully. She had a sudden unpleasant urge to laugh out loud at the infatuated faces before her. The next moment, however, to everyone's surprise, including hers, she began to cry helplessly.

At San Sebastian a journalist joined the train. He was a local correspondent for one of the national newspapers, and also had contacts with several major magazines. 'Serious and responsible publications,' he kept emphasising during the conference that took place in the corridor outside her sleeping compartment. 'For only intelligent readers.' His name was Julio Pidal, and he was about forty-five, small and dark, with a nervous, not unpleasant smile. He was sweating a lot and had to keep mopping his forehead with a Kleenex. She guessed he had been alerted to her presence on the train by a telephone call from Irun, and had had to move fast to get here in time. She wondered if the sleeping-car attendant had had any part in tipping him off. This person waited at a discreet distance, further down the corridor. He was called Señor Gomez. It said so on the small tag he wore over the breast pocket of his dark-blue uniform blazer. She did not know his first name, but knew that his wife's was Anna. This she had found out because, at his request, she had already written a short note to the wife. 'To Anna, I am so pleased that you like Lucy Entwistle. With best wishes, Susan Strang.' She had not minded doing this, for he had been very decent about the matter of the sleeping-car ticket. When he had first glanced at it, and had seen the awkward fact that it bore a name that was not her own, an ominous frown had appeared on his brow. But then it cleared, he had smiled understandingly. 'Of course,' he had murmured. 'Comprende, Señora Strang . . .' Evidently he believed that she was travelling under a false name in a vain attempt to shield herself from the effects of her fame.

Her fame, for God's sake.

She tried to concentrate on the man in front of her. With his winning smile and his urgent entreaties. 'I really don't know,' she sighed. 'I haven't got much to say, and I'm sorry but I don't think I want to be talking to reporters all night – '

'Exactly,' Señor Pidal interrupted her. 'And if you will just talk to me there will be no need to see anyone else. If you will just give me a . . .' he hesitated fractionally, 'an *exclusive*, yes?'

'But what's to stop anybody else getting on the train to talk to me?'

'Well, for instance – ' The reporter glanced down the corridor to the waiting steward. 'For instance, Señor Gomez might say that you were no longer here, you had got off at San Sebastian. Or Vittoria . . .' Señor Gomez bowed to indicate that this was indeed a possibility. So that's the deal, Susan thought. And Gomez was almost certainly the person who had turned her in at Irun. Still, he had done good work ever since – to thunderous applause from the crowd on the platform – she had boarded the train. He had kept away all the numerous vociferous admirers who wanted to see 'La Entwistle'. And he had permitted requests for her autograph from only a handful of particularly important people – such as the engine driver and the head chef in the kitchen galley. So if she fell in with the plot hatched by these two, she could perhaps rely on his protection for the rest of her journey. She looked thoughtfully at the eager reporter before her. He offered his most charming smile, and then what he must have thought was the clinching argument.

'After all, Señora Strang, you could not expect to come to Spain and be ignored, could you? A star of your magnitude!'

A star of her – she would become hysterical if this went on much longer. She pushed open the door to her sleeping compartment. 'You'd better come in,' she murmured.

Señor Gomez, unasked, brought them a bottle of wine and two

glasses. Susan sat on one end of the couch that later would turn into a bed. Señor Pidal sat at the other. He smiled at her, then looked round the tiny cubicle.

'Old-fashioned, isn't it?'

Susan too examined her surroundings. They were, indeed, a change from the bright contemporary style of the French trains. The lighting was dim, the prevailing colour a dull beige, the overall look reminiscent of the late 1950s. The windows were very dirty.

'I am always distressed at the thought of foreigners travelling in such a train as this.'

'Oh, no need to be.'

'Of course, we have many up-to-date trains now too. But not this one, regrettably.'

They were silent for a time. Then Señor Pidal brightened up. 'Shall we . . .?' He seized the neck of the wine bottle and poured them each a glass. He raised his glass, and Susan took up hers. 'Saluza!'

'What's that?'

'Saluza – it means "cheers!"'

'Ah – saluza then,' she smiled and drank.

Señor Pidal watched her thoughtfully over the rim of his glass. 'You know,' he said, 'I have the idea you are a little surprised by the reception you have received in Spain.'

'I'm amazed.'

'You did not know that *The Entwistles* is a great success here?'

'I didn't even know it was on.'

'Remarkable!' Señor Pidal shook his head. 'Why, it's on tonight.'

'Tonight?'

'Monday evenings. Nine o'clock. *Prima cadena* . . . that's like your BBC One.'

'And it's doing well?'

'Doing well?' The reporter laughed softly. 'It is the phenomenon of the year. The greatest television series ever shown in Spain. Above *Shogun*, *Roots*, *The Winds of War* . . . There are complaints, you know – from people who own restaurants and cinemas. They are empty on Monday nights. Completely deserted. Everybody is watching *The Entwistles*. In fact,' he chuckled, 'the people on this train cannot be considered your greatest fans. For they are travelling on a Monday night . . . of course there is the repeat on Saturday. They will watch that. But it is not quite the same. They will have nothing to talk about tomorrow morning, when everybody else is discussing the latest episode.'

'You're going to be in the same boat tomorrow, aren't you?'

'There is no problem,' said Señor Pidal complacently. 'I have a videotape machine. So I shall not be "in the same boat".'

'Well, I just didn't know,' Susan sighed, holding out her glass for a refill. Señor Pidal poured the wine. His expression had become suddenly rather reserved and gloomy.

'I am surprised,' he said, as he turned the bottle towards his own glass, 'that you would not know of the great interest in your work in this country.' He laughed again, but somewhat bitterly this time. 'Of course I know that Spain is of an importance that is sufficiently negligible, we are not perhaps one of the great markets, we can be overlooked . . .'

'Oh, I'm certain it's not that,' said Susan hastily.

'And yet you knew nothing?'

'Well . . . you know we finished working on *The Entwistles* a long time ago. Four or five years.'

'I did not know that,' said Señor Pidal gloomily. 'Five years . . . and at last it reaches Spain!'

'Yes. And I suppose they – the TV company – are mostly concerned now with their latest shows. So it wouldn't occur to them . . . Perhaps they *did* try to let me know,' Susan improvised, wanting to spare the man's feelings as much as possible. 'They'd have contacted my agent. And she – ' Her voice became sincere, hostile, 'she's completely useless. She probably just forgot to pass the information on.'

Relieved, she saw that he seemed at least a little consoled by this suggestion.

'I am surprised that an actress of your stature would employ such an incompetent agent.'

'So am I,' said Susan grimly. 'And, in fact,' she added, making up her mind on the spot, 'I'm going to fire her as soon as I get back to England.'

As if prompted, the reporter reached into his jacket and brought out a notebook, elegantly bound, and a gold ballpoint pen. 'And when will that be?' he asked. 'How long do you intend to stay in my country? And – this will be the question my readers will most want answered – what exactly are you doing here, Señora Strang?'

She could not afterwards clearly remember her answers to that or many of the other questions Señor Pidal asked her over the next half-hour. Fortunately he was the obliging type of reporter who, when she stammered and stumbled over a response, filled in for her the answers he was hoping she would give. So the big question, the matter of what she was doing here, which should have given her most trouble, resolved itself quite satisfactorily. 'La Entwistle was the soul of discretion when I sought to discover her reasons for entering Spain,' he translated to her from his notes. "A holiday," she murmurs, in that so-familiar voice. "A visit to a country where I have never been but have long wished to see." When I put it to her that her mode of entry – alone, unannounced, without press agents or bodyguards, practically incognito – was particularly stealthy, the ravishing slayer of Jason Groves smiles her enigmatic smile. "I am happiest when I am alone," she says. "It is my nature." Who would dare challenge the formidable Lucy? And yet I was emboldened to press her a little further. Would there be, I chanced, any occasions on this undoubted holiday for meeting with directors or producers, a business lunch in a secluded corner of a famed Madrid restaurant – the possibility, in fact, that she was considering offers to work at her profession in Spain? "Señor Pidal," she chides me. "Enough!" And she will say nothing more – except to allow that she is a great admirer of the Spanish cinema. "Buñuel," she murmurs, "Saures, Omutti, I adore them – Olea, Borau, Pedro Almodovar . . ." Would she then, I persist, be meeting any of these great heroes of hers? Again La Entwistle shakes her head. But I think I know now . . . and I know she knows I know –'

'Surely they won't print all this stuff,' Susan interrupted.

'Stuff?' Señor Pidal enquired stiffly.

'Well, all that stuff about directors.'

'You said that you liked Luis Buñuel.'

'Well, Buñuel . . .'

'And Omutti.'

'I saw a film of his that I liked very much. But the others, I've never heard – '

'The others are also very good,' Señor Pidal assured her.

'But I'm telling you, I'm not going to be meeting any of them.'

'And that is exactly what I have written. I have reported you faithfully. And I have provided my own comments on what you have said. They'll print all I send them,' said Julio Pidal then happily. He shook the last few drops of wine into her glass, and leaned back against the wall. 'It will be a great thing for me. My name will be on everyone's lips. It is a grand . . . *scoop*, you know. To interview any of the Entwistles would be something. But to talk to Lucy Entwistle . . . alone . . . on a train between San Sebastian and Vittoria . . .' He shook his head in amazement at his luck.

Though Señor Pidal's methods of interrogation were more florid and dramatic than she was used to, after a while she saw that the questions followed much the usual pattern of these interviews. Most of all he wanted to know about her relations with the rest of the cast, and whether they at all reflected the tempestuous emotions of the Entwistle stories. Did she, for instance, harbour a murderous hostility – not unmixed with a strange, doomed attraction – for Michael Whiting, who played Jason Groves? And then there was Grace Barker, who portrayed Laura Kershaw, as dark as Lucy Entwistle was fair, and yet very much Jason Groves's good angel as Lucy was his evil one . . . well, surely the fierce female rivalry displayed between Laura and Lucy could not have been confined to the moments of filming? And Geoffrey Peers, who played Arthur Entwistle, stern, inflexible patriarch of the clan? And Viviane Cavendish ('Jemima Stronghold') – the old maid who lived in the cottage by the river and who took the secret of the Kershaw inheritance to her watery grave? And Tim Underwood ('Ben Cragg'), the orphan boy – who *were* his real parents? – with his revolutionary dream that the manufacture of woollens might be taken out of the weaver's cottages and into a specially built factory . . . how did she really feel about Tim Underwood?

I can't remember, I can't remember. Christ, it was five years ago. It's not how I feel about Tim Underwood that escapes me – or Mike Whiting, Grace Barker, all the others. I can hardly even remember what the hell they looked like. Which would never do, of course. And somehow she fudged together some semi-sensible answers and as she did, one or two real details of the people she was telling stories about filtered back to her. Though mostly of a nature that could not be repeated.

So Michael Whiting – of course she didn't feel murderous hostility towards him. Why, Mike is a sweet, lovable man, everybody had adored him. (Though not too much, otherwise they would have had to deal with his suspicious and bad-tempered and ever-present boy friend.) And Grace Barker – we were the dearest of friends (though nobody knowing poor Gracie would ever claim that she was exactly the brightest young thing ever to come out of North Wales. When Grace had once got all her lines in the right order in a long scene, Dick Banham had called it 'the Miracle of Hebden Bridge'.) Geoffrey Peers she did allow was sometimes a little difficult to get close to (not least because the poor man was dying by inches all through the filming and in fact did expire just two weeks after the final wrap). And Viviane Cavendish?

(That affected bitch.) Well, Viviane has a very roguish sense of humour, you wouldn't guess it from the character she plays, would you?

'The direction of course is masterly,' Señor Pidal told her. 'Richard Ban-ham . . .' He pronounced the name with profound reverence. 'Can you tell me what other work he has done?' He poised his gold pen above his notebook.

'Dick? Oh God, I don't know. He's done masses of stuff. Whoever'll pay him the most, you know.' And then, seeing the uncomprehending frown that was gathering on Señor Pidal's brow, she added hastily, 'Let me just try and think about it for a moment.'

But before she had to confess that she couldn't for the moment think of another thing that Dick had done, a discreet tap on the door saved her. Señor Pidal rose to open it. Señor Gomez stood outside. There was a low, hurried conversation between the two Spaniards. Then Señor Pidal turned back to her.

'Your steward enquires whether you shall wish to dine in the restaurant car or in here.'

'Well,' Susan watched the two men, a little helplessly, 'I wouldn't mind going to the restaurant. I'm going to be cooped up in here all night. But is it possible?'

Señor Pidal turned back to the steward and shot some rapid questions at him. Señor Pidal turned again to Susan. 'Si . . . It is possible. But you must eat now. Before the regular sitting. They will hold the restaurant completely empty for you.'

'Gosh!' sighed Susan.

Señor Pidal drew himself erect. 'May I suggest that to save yourself from the embarrassment of dining alone, you will permit me to join you for dinner?' He bowed slightly from the waist. 'It would be a great honour for me.'

'It would be nice for me too,' Susan smiled, and got to her feet. Señor Pidal stood back from the door to allow her to go through. She had just passed him, when she turned back suddenly and went to retrieve her carry-all bag.

'It will be quite safe in here,' Señor Pidal said. 'The steward will lock the door after you're gone.'

'All the same . . .' said Susan, tucking the bag firmly under her arm.

The restaurant car was a cavern of white tablecloths, empty seats. The head waiter – large, portentous, deeply moved – bowed them to a table in the centre of the carriage. Reverently he handed them menus. At the far end of the car, cooks and other waiters were loitering, trying to get a view of them. Susan and Señor Pidal smiled at each other across the table.

'It is rather enjoyable,' he murmured, 'to be treated as a celebrity.'

'I suppose it must be,' she nodded.

'Of course, you are very used to it.'

'. . . Of course.'

'But for me it is a – novelty.'

'You speak such good English,' she said.

'Ah, well, I lived in New York for a while, you see. That is a fine city.'

'Yes, isn't it?'

'And I have visited London many times. Also a fine city.'

'Mm.'

'You live in London, of course.'

'No. No, I don't.'

He was surprised. His notebook appeared on the tablecloth. 'Then where is that you live?'

'I live in Swayncliff,' she said, surprised at the thought. 'It's in Kent. It's by the sea.'

'Sway . . .?'

She spelled it for him.

'Is that a fine city too?'

'It has its points,' she said after a moment. 'But I may not be living there very much longer.'

'Perhaps you are like me,' he smiled shyly. 'I can never stay in one place for very long. I have the wanderlust, you know . . . Ah!'

The head waiter had returned with a bottle of wine held tenderly in his hands.

'We didn't order that, did we?' Susan murmured.

'No matter. They will have picked it out for us. And it is bound to be good.' Señor Pidal sipped at the measure of wine that was poured out for him. 'Perfect!' he sighed. 'You will like this very much.' He nodded at the head waiter, who then poured a full glass for Susan.

'I mustn't get sloshed,' she smiled.

'Sloshed?'

'Mmm. Plastered. Drunk. Wouldn't do, would it?'

'Sloshed . . .' Señor Pidal wrote it down in his notebook. He smiled at her then. 'I am sure you would be sloshed with great dignity, all the same.'

'Don't bet on it!' she chuckled. She raised her glass. 'Well, here's to you, Julio. You don't mind me calling you Julio?'

'Please! An honour.'

'And you must call me Susan. Or Susie, if you like.'

'Oh, I don't think – '

'I insist.'

Señor Pidal flushed with pleasure. 'OK.' He lifted his glass to her now. 'Here's to you . . . Susan.'

'Will you do just one thing more for me, Julio?'

'Whatever you ask.'

'Put that bloody notebook away,' she said, smiling at him to show it was mostly a joke.

At one point during the meal – soup, fish, rack of lamb, all excellent – she mused, 'You know, Julio, I can't think why *The Entwistles* should be so popular here. It all seemed very English to me at the time. Old-fashioned English. And all that awful, cold, damp Yorkshire landscape. I would have thought Spanish people would have found it horrible.'

'But exactly not.' Julio set aside his fork, reached for his wine. 'I have a theory about this,' he said. 'You know – here in Spain, these past few years, we have been trying very hard to become a modern people. Modern Europeans. Rich, go ahead, maybe a bit shallow. That is the way the people want it – and yet they are sad too that the old ways are going. I think we look at *The Entwistles* and see a mirror of what we once were, what we still secretly believe we are. For they are – as we remember we were – a proud, passionate people, who allow no insult to pass unpunished. They suffer grandly,' he sighed, 'and their vengeance is dark and pitiless. And above all there is Lucy . . .' He smiled across the table at her, a smile that was half amused, half deadly serious. 'That imperious and beautiful animal, fiery, sensuous – she is tempted often and often she yields. And yet, however many times she falls, still she retains her dignity and, in a strange way, her chastity. She is a virgin of the soul . . . Lucy Entwistle,' Julio Pidal murmured devoutly, 'is what every Spanish woman still in her heart wishes she was. And every Spanish man – he would long to have the chance to master her. Even if, like Jason Groves, it was only to die magnificently in the very moment of conquest!'

'Heavens,' breathed Susan, overwhelmed.

Julio seemed to remember where he was. He looked down at his plate, then picked up his knife and fork again. 'At least,' he said, 'I think it is something like that.'

Susan wiped her mouth with her napkin. She hesitated for a moment, then in an embarrassed voice, 'You know, Julio, it's all guff about me being here to talk about work. It's nothing of the sort, you know.'

'Then why are you here?' Julio watched her shrewdly. 'I don't think you're on holiday?'

'Why not?'

Julio seemed puzzled. 'I don't know,' he said at last. 'I don't know why I think that.' He stared into his wine glass. 'Your ticket says you are travelling all the way to Lisbon – ' She looked up, surprised. Julio shrugged an apology for this breach of confidentiality. Then he frowned. 'Surely you are not going to travel through Spain and see nothing of my country?'

'Well . . .' she murmured after a while, 'I might get off somewhere.'

'Of course.' He smiled understandingly. 'You must protect your freedom of movement. Which is certainly why your ticket bears a name that is not your own. But if you're not here to discuss work, and you're not here on holiday . . .'

'Perhaps I'm just taking a long train ride to clear my mind, and think things over.'

He considered the idea, and then nodded. 'Yes. Yes, I can see that someone in your position would have much to think about.'

'Why do you say that?' she faltered, after a moment.

He raised both hands in the air. 'After such a part as Lucy Entwistle – where do you go from her?'

Their plates were cleared away, and they were brought strawberries and cream in silver dishes. 'Are they really fresh?' she breathed. She tasted them, found they were. 'This is the most wonderful meal,' she sighed.

Julio smiled ironically. 'It is quite exceptional for this train.' He leaned towards her and murmured, 'I think we may be eating from the chef's private supplies.'

They heard a subdued buzz of conversation from the far end of the car.

'What's going on?' Susan wondered.

The head waiter came to their table and spoke a few words to Julio. Julio nodded, and then as the waiter went away, he smiled at Susan. 'They want to show you something,' he said.

She looked up. A procession of cooks and waiters was advancing down the aisle. Those at its head had their hands cupped, they were carrying something. She guessed they were bringing some further delicacy to their table, 'Oh, I couldn't eat another thing,' she protested.

The men gathered round the table. One of those in front unfurled his fingers. In his cupped hands lay a tiny kitten, stirring feebly. The others too showed their furry burdens. The men smiled at Susan's surprise and delight.

'How beautiful! Where did they come from?'

'There is a cat that belongs to this train,' Julio told her. 'And she has given birth. See, their eyes have just opened.'

Susan took the nearest kitten in her hand. She stroked its fragile head with her forefinger. The creature tilted its little chin and licked her finger. It opened and closed its milky blue eyes. Susan laughed delightedly. 'Oh, what a wonder!' she sighed. She tried to give the kitten back then. But the man shook his head and spoke softly to her. She glanced across the table at Julio. He shrugged.

'They want you to keep it. A gift.'

'Oh, I . . .' She shook her head. 'I couldn't. Where would I keep it? And it's far too young to leave its mother – '

'They will wait a few weeks and send it to you. It's no problem for them. The railwaymen will carry it all the way across Europe.'

'It's very sweet of them, but – ' She looked up at Julio in desperation. 'I just don't think I've got room for a kitten in my life. Will you say I'm very, very grateful, but I just can't – '

Julio nodded, and looked up at the man and spoke to him. The man demurred for a moment, but then with a shrug he took the kitten back. Susan looked up at him earnestly. 'It's so nice of you . . . muy bueno . . . but – '

The man seemed unable to meet her gaze. He nodded, and backed away to the rear of the group. 'I hope he's not too upset,' Susan said anxiously.

'I think he is overwhelmed,' Julio said, 'just to be spoken to by you.'

The crowd of waiters and cooks was now backing away up the aisle. Susan waved to them as they went. 'Goodbye!' she called. 'Thank you. Gracias . . . And for the meal . . . adios. How sweet of them,' she said to Julio when she had done.

When coffee came, Susan was suddenly smitten with guilt. 'You know, I hope we're not holding up dinner for everybody else.'

Julio glanced at his watch. 'Perhaps half an hour.'

'Oh, Christ. How embarrassing.'

He smiled at her. 'You're not to worry. They will understand.'

'Well, I wish I could think they were going to get as good a meal as we had.'

Julio pursed his lips. 'I'm afraid your wish will be disappointed.'

'Oh dear,' Susan sighed.

'Cheer up. As I said before: it is enjoyable to be treated as a celebrity, is it not?'

They looked at each other, and then in the same moment burst out laughing at their good fortune. The train began to brake hard. They looked towards the window. There were street lights shining from the blackness, and then, rushing past, the lights of apartment buildings.

'Burgos!' Julio cried. 'I must get out here.' He brushed crumbs of food from the front of his suit and started to rise. Susan looked up at him, startled by this imminent departure.

'Oh,' she said. 'Oh . . .' She looked around her. 'I suppose I'd better wait here for the bill.'

He smiled down at her, and shook his head. 'There will be no bill.' He reached out a hand to her then. 'Come. I should like to see you safely back to your compartment.'

She got to her feet, and picked up her carry-all bag from where it hung on the chair – no mistakes this time – and looked around again for a sight of the head waiter, so that she could thank him for the meal. But he was not be seen. The train had slowed nearly to a stop. 'Come,' said Julio again urgently.

Señor Gomez was at his post in the corridor, and at the sight of the two of them hurrying towards him, he got up from his seat and went to unlock the door to her compartment. Susan turned to the reporter. She felt breathless at the speed of events. 'Well . . .' she said, holding out her hand. He took it, bowed over it slightly. 'That was fun,' she said.

'It was fun,' he repeated. He smiled then, a most beautiful smile. 'It was more than fun for me.' He hesitated for a moment. Then, quietly, 'I could not have imagined that I would meet the real woman who is Lucy Entwistle and not be disappointed. But I was completely wrong, you see.'

She did not know what to say. She pressed his hand. He bowed again, then stepped backwards. They looked at each other. Up and down the train the doors were slamming.

'Will you just tell me one thing before I go?' Julio asked.

'Of course. What is it?'

'We are only up to episode nine here, you understand. Tell me – I promise not to reveal it – does Lucy die in the end?'

She looked into his dark eyes. They seemed to be entreating her to give him the answer he hoped for, to spare him from the worst. But –

'Yes,' she said sadly. 'She does die.'

He lowered his head for a moment. Then he sighed and looked up and nodded. 'Of course,' he murmured. 'It was necessary. I see that.' He was silent again, as if still struggling to deal with the news. Then he nodded towards her compartment. 'Now you must go inside, Susan,' he said, 'and lock your door.' He left her then, without saying another word.

17

While she had been at dinner, the couch in her compartment had been opened out into a bed and made up with sheets and blankets and pillow. There was not much floor space left now. She looked round for somewhere to stow away her carry-all. The only place she could see was at the bottom of the narrow closet situated beside the wash-stand. Straightening up, her glance fell upon the shelf above the wash-stand. The plastic glass had been half-filled with water and there was a spray of flowers arranged inside it. She was touched by Señor Gomez's gesture, but not much surprised by it. She would have probably been more surprised to find no mark in her compartment of the special favour that by now she understood was due to her.

She sat down on the bed, as the train stirred again into life, and watched the lights of the station go gliding by. The window was open a few inches at the top and she felt the breeze on her forehead as they picked up speed. She thought of Julio somewhere out there, perhaps already sitting at a café table, working on his notes. She had done a good job, she told herself. It had taken her totally by surprise, but she had come up with the goods. And she could take pride in that, for she was certainly out of practice at this sort of thing. She hadn't done an interview for so long, hadn't done one in fact, she remembered, since Raymond. Raymond and his tape recorder.

She swallowed, tasting again the coffee she had drunk not long ago. Raymond. No, she decided, that was not a thought she wished to entertain just now. Raymond had no place in the present scheme of things. He belonged to – he epitomised – a condition of obscurity, meanness, hopelessness, whereas now . . . I could step out into the corridor right now, she thought, smiling, and walk down to the restaurant car and cause a riot. I really could. Me!

How about that? she thought exultantly.

The city lights had gone now. The window showed her only blackness, broken by an occasional star of light. She looked around her tiny cubicle, then glanced at her watch. It was ten minutes to nine. She felt suddenly as if she was a child again and had been sent to bed early. She remembered that ages ago – in another life it seemed, almost – she had thought about getting off the train at San Sebastian or Vittoria to find something to read. Too late for that now. She had nothing to pass the time with. And couldn't go in search of entertainment and company on the train. For fear of riot. The lives of the rich and famous, she thought wryly. She stared at the spray of flowers in the tooth mug. They were not well chosen, she decided. Too much yellow.

She rubbed her eyes. She felt suddenly clammy and grubby all over. Well, she had been travelling all day, it was no wonder . . . If Raymond had had his way, she would have been two nights in a row without the chance of a bath. Instead of just this one. She eyed the wash-stand. OK, she thought, cheering up, we'll do what we can. She got to her feet and moved across the yard or so that separated the bed from the basin. She undressed completely, laying the clothes carefully on the bed as she took them off. It was pleasant to feel the cool air from the open window on her skin. She wet her hand under the tap, used the little square of soap to work up a lather and soaped herself down, rinsed and dried, and then squatted naked on the floor to rummage through her carry-all. She picked out her nightdress and put it on. Then she brushed her teeth thoroughly. When she was done, she picked up her watch from the shelf above the sink. It was three minutes to nine.

I had better consider my situation, she thought. I've got plenty of time to do that. She sat down on the bed and tried to compose herself. But nothing useful came to her, her mind was a blank, pierced only occasionally by sudden glimpses of what had happened to her in the past few hours. The joyful crowd at Irun station. And how she had wept in the café there and the people had watched her in such consternation, not knowing how to comfort her, not daring to try. And how Señor Gomez had bowed her on to the train as if she had been royalty. And then Julio – so kind, so flattering, so enchanted to be in the company of a famous person.

A famous person. Famous. She closed her eyes and breathed in the wonder of the thought.

But at last, bit by bit, harder thoughts crept in. One thing was now apparent – she had known it, she realised, from the first moments almost, since the customs shed at Irun – this affair was off, this business she had engaged to do. Over. *Finito*. The invisible speck on the map of Europe? – forget it. She might as well be accompanied by brass bands, she was so far now from any possibility of passing unnoticed. There was no point even trying to think of a solution to this. There wasn't one. All she could do when she reached the end of the journey was get on a plane straight home. She wondered how much the plane would cost. If she couldn't sell the train ticket, she might not be able to afford it. On the other hand, she mused, the airline might be very accommodating – to Lucy Entwistle – and give her credit. Maybe even a free trip. She mustn't be shy about asking. Fame had its penalties, but also its little rewards. Yes, indeed.

She shivered suddenly, and got up and pushed the window shut. Yet still when she sat back on the bed, she felt the chill upon her. She wrapped one of the blankets around her. But she was still cold, very cold. Cold thoughts. In ones and twos they came, and then like a flood, so overwhelming and freezing that she gasped out loud and put her hands up and held her head. Yes, yes, yes. Was it true? Was it possible? Yes. She stood up. She stared across the terrible small room. In the mirror her eyes stared back at her. She fell to her knees. She crawled across to the carry-all and opened it and reached inside. She pulled out the heavy plastic case – which just now she had so calmly pushed aside to get at her nightdress – and crawled back with it to the bed. She remembered suddenly that a few hours ago she had thought to herself that she was facing reality at last when she had decided to call this thing no longer a 'radio' or 'it', but what it was. And had congratulated herself on doing that. She stared at the case lying there on the crumpled blanket.

She would walk up a path, she would ring on a doorbell. A man would answer the door. She would raise the gun and fire it directly into his face. This she had contracted to do. Reality.

She reached out to the case and opened the flap. She removed the layer of tissue paper on top. Then she took hold of the piece of curved black metal and drew it out of the case. She laid it carefully on the blanket. She looked at it for a time. Then she reached into the case again and pulled out more tissue paper. She picked up the plastic case and turned it over. Three blunt-headed bullets fell on to the blanket. She took up one of the bullets and, as she had been shown, inserted it into the chamber of the gun.

I am mad, she thought dreamily, and might as well turn this on myself.

She weighed the revolver in her hand. It was heavy, but so small she had little trouble handling it. So small, she thought, but such a weight of history behind it. No ordinary gun, indeed.

'You've heard of von Ribbentrop, of course?'

'Well . . .'

'Hitler's Foreign Minister. He was over in England a lot before the war. One time he met my dad. And gave him this. As a mark of esteem, you know? For services rendered. Ribbentrop gave my father this gun at a ceremony in the German Embassy.'

How interesting. And it had seemed so perfect, so right, to use a gift from a brute to put down another brute. She had asked Raymond how he had got hold of it. He told her he had been determined, after the news about the inheritance, to claim something of his father's, 'As a memory, you understand. A souvenir.' So he had gone over to the house and looked around and in the end . . .

'You chose this?'

'Yes.'

Wasn't that lucky? He had showed her patiently over and over how to load it, for of course she could not travel a thousand miles across Europe with a loaded revolver. No, the idea was to pause – somewhere between where she got off the bus and Phillip's house – and squeeze the bullets into the chamber. 'Just go behind a bush or something, and do it.' Like having a pee – but why not? She was game for anything. Being completely mad . . . but one thing she was perfectly cool and sane about. She would have to test this thing out. Oh yes, she could not allow that her first attempt at firing this thing should be into the face, the shocked and terrified face of Raymond's older brother. Raymond had argued – when had he not argued? – against this new demand.

'I've only got five bullets.'

'How many do you think I'm going to need?'

Thus spoke One-take Strang, perfectly confident as long as she could have a single serious rehearsal.

'You'll need three,' he had said promptly.

'Three? What are the other two for?'

'They're for luck,' Raymond had said after a moment. He tried to smile, failed. She stared at him, wondering why he seemed so uneasy suddenly. Then she shrugged.

'All right. Three from five – that means we've still got two to play with.'

So at length he had given way, and one morning, early, he had come to her apartment, and they had set out together along the Esplanade, Raymond carrying the Rainbow shopping bag, with the gun inside. They had gone all the way along the Esplanade and then down the concrete steps on to the sea wall. The tide was out, they walked above mud flats. Where the sea wall curved out to its furthest extent, and they were out of sight of the Esplanade, hidden by the cliffs, they had stopped. Susan had loaded the gun with practised efficiency. She had handed it to Raymond.

'I'm not going to be doing it. Why me?'

'The first time,' she had insisted. 'I'd like to be sure it won't blow up in my hand.'

He had shrugged and taken the revolver, and had pointed it loosely out to sea.

'All right . . . well . . . you just – '

'I just pull the trigger, I know. Get on with it.'

The gun had cracked like the snap of a wet towel. 'That's it,' said Raymond casually, turning back to her. She was staring out to sea. 'You're not going to be able to see where it lands!' Raymond chuckled sarcastically. He had pushed the revolver at her. 'Go on. It's got a bit of a kick, but not much.'

She had pushed the second bullet into the chamber. Then held the gun at arm's length, pointing at the idling waters. Then she had turned suddenly, and aimed high up at the cliff. Raymond gave a startled shout and went towards her, but he was too late. She fired and, watching, saw a cloud of chalk spurt off the cliff face.

'Bloody hell,' said Raymond. 'That could have come back at us.'

'Nonsense. I was aiming much too high.' She nursed the little weapon in her hand. In her forearm she still felt the solid little punch it had given her when she'd pulled the trigger. It was a strangely pleasant feeling.

'You satisfied now?' Raymond grumbled.

'Perfectly.' But she did not hand back the gun straight away. She was still looking at it closely. 'Well, there is just one thing . . .' she murmured.

'Yes?'

'What does this mean?'

She pointed at the side of the revolver's stubby barrel. He came up to her shoulder and peered at where her finger lay.

'Can't read it,' he grunted.

'I can.' She narrowed her eyes to read off the tiny raised metal letters. '"Cobra .38 Special". And here – ', she moved her finger to the stock, 'it says "Colt" and "Hartford, Connecticut".'

'What of it?' said Raymond after a moment.

'I thought that the Nazis gave your father this gun.'

'They did.'

'You would think they'd have given him a German gun, wouldn't you?'

Raymond stood thinking. 'Maybe,' he suggested at last, 'they got a good deal on these things. Just for giving them away.'

'Yes,' said Susan thoughtfully. 'That's possible.'

There was a long silence.

'Or maybe . . .' Raymond bowed his head, 'maybe my dad was telling whoppers all the time.'

The gun felt suddenly heavy and clumsy in her hand. She looked out over the flat, dispiriting water. This ends it, she thought in sudden panic. Another word and the whole bubble bursts for ever. She looked back at Raymond. He was still staring glumly at the concrete beneath their feet.

'Of course he wasn't lying,' she said firmly. 'What you said was right. The Nazis bought these from the States. For presentation purposes.' She moved the gun from side to side, delighting in its sudden new lightness. 'No,' she said, handing it back to him then. 'I don't see any problems now.'

They had started back the way they had come, walking side by side, never speaking. Amazing. How should one entitle such a picture? *Lunatics at Swayncliff Taking the Sea Air*? She had plodded onwards, well satisfied with the morning's work, thinking it all seemed pretty straightforward now. Very pleased that after thirty-seven years of life she had finally fired a real gun, an accomplishment much suited to her day and age, and one she had left undone for far too long. She would like some breakfast now. She asked Raymond to join her, hoping on the whole that he would say no. She was in luck. He'd said he had things to do. She had watched him slouching off, the shopping bag trailing from his hand. Then had gone home and made herself scrambled eggs and bacon and a nice pot of Earl Grey tea . . .

Enough, Susan thought wearily now. She had been holding the gun negligently in her hand as she crouched on the bed, its barrel pointing more or less at her head, so that if she had pulled the trigger she would have had a reasonably good chance of putting a hole in herself . . . but she was not going to do that. She was not going to do it when anybody else was in the line of fire either. Not Phillip, certainly. Not Raymond – though she acknowledged a certain temptation there. Enough play-acting. For had it ever been anything other than that? Poor Raymond, she thought suddenly. He hadn't known at all what he was dealing with in her. She could have told him almost straight away that there was not a chance, never a hope that she would go through with it. After the very first evening, the excitement, the thrill of that moment – 'Oh, Raymond, I could do it!' But all she had meant was: yes, I could carry off this role, I could crack this bit of business, this is within my range.

But not as a real person, of course.

She tried to remember – had she ever given Raymond the chance to understand that he could not rely on her? Or had she been so obsessed with her wonderful cleverness that she had led him on all the while, without offering a clue that some time or other, of course, she would bring the action to a halt and confess it was only a bit of make-believe, just an exercise, an evening out, we hope you have enjoyed yourselves, ladies and gentlemen . . . Poor Raymond, poor punter.

Sucker.

I was given a gun. I was shown a photograph – wouldn't do to shoot the wrong man, would it? The face in the photo didn't look much like you. (The large head pointing aggressively forward, thinning hair, smiling eyes, slight cast in one of them, the left, I think. An attractive face, she had thought, as she had studied it, tried to memorise it, a strong face.) But as he's only your half-brother that might explain it. I was given an address – 'Villa Atè Breve, Monte Rosado, Algarve' – given a ticket, money for my expenses. All real – and only I knew, as I had always known deep down, that I would never, ever, under any circumstances do what I had told you I would do. That it was always – *always* – just a horrible, stupid, bad, bad joke.

An actor's sort of joke.

She found herself thinking of last night. She had come into her hotel room, feeling tired, and had lain down straightway on the bed. She could hear her neighbour's TV through the wall perfectly clearly and she had leaned forward and, defensively, switched on her own set. There was a man on the screen, a man whose haunted eyes contrasted strangely with the facetious smile he was wearing. He was speaking very fast and she could not understand what he was saying. When he paused for breath, the studio audience broke into prolonged applause. The man bowed gracefully in response, though his eyes, while not losing their haunted quality, now also cast a defiant, almost angry look around him, as if the performer was thinking, while the people beat their hands together: well, and so what? It's no more than I deserve . . . She had felt suddenly disgusted at the sight of the man, and had got up abruptly from the bed and switched him off.

The loathing she had felt last night had been, she saw now, as much for herself as for the comedian on the screen. For herself, for all her profession. Tricksters, con men, actors. Oh, they tried to pass for normal and, cunningly, did all sort of normal things, they held mortgages, and had parents and children, and gave simpering interviews in which they pretended to be just ordinary boys and girls like everyone else – but they were monsters really, they were not of the human race at all, and they ought to be shunned by those who were. Instead of, for God's sake, *applauded*. Monsters . . . in the hearts of each of them was a cruel cold conviction that anything was permitted them in the great search for an effect. They were users of people. The truth was not in them. And when they had done with their trickery, what they felt for those they had waylaid and deceived was not contrition, not at all, but contempt and defiance. And hatred, yes, because the applause they had gained could never go on for ever, but would have to stop sometime so that the monsters were forced to get up and to do their tricks all over again – and again and again, until the time when they could do them no longer, and the applause would die away for ever.

Defiance, hatred, total contempt – all this she had seen on the face of the wretch who had flourished on the TV screen last night. And all this she felt in herself. It was Raymond she had tricked unmercifully, and would have gone on tricking and deceiving to the very last moment. He was her pitiful audience, pitifully small, but he was enough. Let there be one pair of hands available to applaud her and she was ready, present, to do her tricks, to go the limit, no matter what the cost – to somebody else.

The train sped on through the night, running much less smoothly than the French one had done. It made her sway back and forth as she sat on the bed. Several times she felt sudden qualms in her stomach. It would really round things off nicely, she thought, if she were sick in here. Señor Gomez could be counted on to clear up the mess, but could the secret be kept just between the two of them with his tendency to sell her to the newspapers? 'Famous Star Throws up in Sleeping Car,' she saw the headline. That made her smile – but not at the joke. No, really she was smiling, purring like a cat with the cream, at the thought that the description could actually be applied to herself, and the world – the world outside her door anyway – wouldn't fall about laughing. Famous star! Yes, she could walk out and vomit in the middle of the restaurant car and the poor fools would love her for it. For what could be more touching than a little hint of human frailty in a mega-being like herself?

But I *did* try, she thought then, as the gleeful smile faded from her lips. I did try to pull back from this daft orgy of showing off.

Tried to spare Raymond from the disappointment that was going to be his. She remembered a night when, gently, she had explained to him that it was not on, that they had only been kidding themselves . . . and that night – she frowned trying to remember – yes, it was the night of the day Tom Scott had come down to see her. They had talked all day, and they'd had lunch, and much later she'd seen him off on the train and she had felt . . . much steadier. Steadier than she had felt for ages. And Raymond had appeared and, feeling steadier, she had been able to explain things to him and – and he had seemed to accept it, so everything was all right, should have been all right, and then some days, some weeks had passed . . . And then, what? Something had happened. Something hadn't happened. It had all gone wrong, but what?

She stared blankly at the window. The train had slowed down, they were moving through what looked like a medium-sized town. There were apartment buildings standing just a few feet back from the track. It must be a hell of a noise, she thought, when a train goes through. Perhaps that's why we're going so slowly. The train was creeping along now. She was able to look right in the apartment windows. In one apartment she saw a man standing up and stretching and then reaching behind him to scratch his back. In another she saw a woman in a kitchen drying a dish. In a third she saw herself on horseback hitting Mike Whiting across the face with a riding whip. She blinked and the image was gone. She scuttled across the bed then and pressed her face to the window. Another apartment building crept across her line of vision. The train shuddered to a halt. She was staring right into a darkened living room. In the back of it, a television set was glimmering and . . . yes! There she was. Having punished Jason Groves, she had turned her steed towards the horizon and was galloping across the moors. She remembered that mare. Her name was Poppy and she had a habit of farting loudly whenever she was on camera. She was as good as gold otherwise, sweet tempered and so easy to handle. Susan had even thought of buying her when the series was done. She couldn't remember why she hadn't now. Probably Mark had disapproved, something like that . . . Now the shot changed to a close up. Oh, damn, she looked good. She couldn't really wish for a kinder shot than that. She had to hand it to Banham. And to Johnny Hazel behind the camera, of course. She had always made it her business to be nice to cameramen – and see how it had paid off. She wished she could hear the music. As she remembered, this sequence had a wonderful swelling score beneath it, faintly reminiscent – well, really very reminiscent – of

Debussy. It was magnificent altogether, this sequence. And for a moment she felt a serene contentment as she watched it, and as she thought of all the talents that had been enlisted to produce this fine moment of film. Dick's talent, and Johnny's, Bob Kunzel wrote the music, the scriptwriter – what was her name? pale, shy woman – Janey! Jane Miller. Nice moment, Janey. And the make up and the costumes and the sound and the grips . . . and herself. Her too. Her especially even. But not alone. Though she had got most of the glory, she had only been a part of it all. She thought with fondness, with love really, of all the others. In that moment, the shot changed again. She saw herself – Poppy going like the wind (company joke) – receding towards the sunset. The credits began to roll. The train jerked into life again. The buildings began to move quicker and quicker across her window.

Tom. It went back to Tom Scott. He had been supposed to have her up to stay with him. He had pressed her to come up to London to stay with him and Louise. And she had wanted to so much. Yet when it came to it . . . he wouldn't even talk to her on the phone. She remembered a terrible night – she had rung Tom's house, and some stupid woman who sounded drunk had answered the phone. And had gone away to fetch Tom. And had come back with a message, with three messages from Tom. Which she had then repeated in a scared, little girl's voice.

Tom says it's not convenient to talk to you now. Tom says he'll be in touch with you, maybe tomorrow.

Tom sends his love.

Ah, thank you. Thank you and good night. And thank Tom for sending me his love, will you?

And she had felt so angry then, so very angry. The days had passed and Tom didn't call, of course. Which made her angrier and angrier . . . And Raymond had always been around. Who also the world had treated so wickedly. She talked to Raymond, and Raymond understood. They didn't talk about Tom, for even to Raymond she could not reveal how low she had sunk, so low that her oldest friends would not speak to her, accounting her so little that they would send her insulting dismissals through the mouths of stupid, drunken women. They didn't talk about anyone in particular at first, but about how unfair life was, how pitiless some people were, how much cruelty and wickedness roamed the world unpunished – it was a shame. Raymond understood. Raymond had suffered too. And in a while they found themselves talking about Phillip again. Phillip the cruel, the thief, the bully . . . But then, Phillip, Tom, it didn't matter, it was just the same beast under different names, and in a little while more somehow it happened, somehow they were back where they had been before, as if Tom had never come down to see her, and she had never been made steady again, so that she could see the difference between reality and a silly, self-pitying charade.

Tom raised me up, she thought. And then Tom let me down again. And I am sitting here, she thought then in wonder, in the middle of Spain, with a gun in my hand, because Tom Scott would not talk to me on the phone.

She stared at it – the thing, the radio, the gun – one last time. Then she scrambled down to the end of the bed and opened the window a few inches, planning to drop the thing out. But at the last moment it occurred to her that it would be irresponsible to go chucking a deadly weapon where some other lunatic – or a child – might pick it up. So she sat back down on the bed and emptied the chamber and then packed the gun and the bullets back in its case. Was it, she wondered, this moment of responsibility, a hopeful sign that her climb back from insanity had at last begun? She prayed that it was.

The last place she saw in Spain was a great city, mile upon mile of lighted streets and houses and factories. She did not know for sure but she guessed it must be Madrid. It was about midnight and she had woken to find herself in the middle of town. She lay under the covers, very warm and drowsy, watching the lights go by.

After all, she thought, nothing bad was going to happen. It had always been just a matter of time before she came to her senses. And, she thought, if I had not waited so long I would not have had this marvellous awakening from my dream. To come out here and be revealed to herself as a star . . . Ah, that was some awakening! She wiggled her toes happily. Out there, a nation of adoring fans. In here, the famous one relaxes and watches the world go by. She had been silly, she had dabbled in foolish and ugly things, and had associated with those who were not worthy of her. But as royalty always may, at the end she could rise above it, above all the dirt and confusion, some of which – it could not be denied – she had created for herself. She could just walk away, without a backward glance, untainted. And nobody dare stop her. At this height, she was entirely safe. Easy lies the head that wears the crown.

Little by little the city slipped away. At last she could see no other light out of her window than that shed by the stars. The clear and beautiful stars. It is a lovely world, she thought serenely, at the edge of sleep. And a cruel one too, and pitiless, yes, all that, she knew that well . . . but lovely none the less. She was so glad she had been able to see it whole. She had thought that she was one of fate's unfortunate ones. But true bad fortune, she thought, would be to spend one's life in the ordinary middle of things, never thrown down too low, never raised up very high. Well, she had been spared that. She had lived in the valley so long. Now she was on the mountain top. She had seen it all, high and low. And on the whole, she giggled to herself, the mountain top is better.

Now how, she wondered just before she slept, am I going to get off this train tomorrow? It'll take a police escort, at least. Oh God, the price of fame! She fell asleep at last, a smile of innocent happiness on her lips.

18

There was noise all around her, but not the noise of the train. The train was not moving. The rattle and sway that had rocked her all night was no more. She had been woken by a strange, toneless booming that had seeped into her sleeping mind. It was still going on. After a time, as she lay there half asleep, she recognised it as the sound of a human voice much magnified. It sounded, she thought idly, just like a . . . a station announcer. Her eyes popped open. She sat up in bed. Through the window, a few feet away, she saw people going by. Some of them glanced in at her as they passed. One man smiled and waved at her casually and mouthed something, a humorous greeting it looked like. Beyond these, she saw more people walking about on other platforms. On one of those far platforms she saw a giant sign: LISBOA – STA APPOLONIA. She was here then. Journey's end.

But not quite, she realised in sudden alarm, as she dragged down the window blind. She still had to find a way of getting out of this station without causing a major disturbance. The people who had looked in at her window just then had not seemed much moved by their privileged view of La Entwistle rising from her bed. But almost certainly they hadn't been able to make out who she was through the filthy glass. To them she must have looked like any other woman in a crumpled nightie, bedraggled and dopey after a night's broken sleep.

She got down from the bed then and went to the basin. She splashed water on her face. God, I look a wreck, she thought, staring into the mirror above the basin. It would never do. She had some responsibility to the people out there, couldn't betray their adoration for Lucy Entwistle by showing up looking a total mess. She dragged a comb through her hair and put on some make up. Eventually she was looking at least presentable. She began to dress. Now she wanted to get out of this compartment quickly. She needed to talk to Gomez, and then probably to some of his superiors on the railway so that a master plan could be worked out for getting her away from the station. And then into a limousine and directly to the airport. It occurred to her then – she stopped buttoning her blouse and stared at herself anxiously in the mirror – that there might be a lot of pressure on her to give some interviews here, a news conference even. She couldn't face it. Yet the pressure might be intense. She worried over the problem while she finished dressing. In the end she decided that she would insist that any interviews would have to be conducted at the airport. She was sure that the facilities would be better there. And safer, that was the main thing. She dreaded the thought of struggling along the platform out there, pressed up against the train by a screaming mob, perhaps forced on to the line . . . or somebody else forced on to the line, scores of people injured. She zipped shut the carry-all bag. She resolved that she would not set foot off the train until she had been assured that all precautions had been taken. Crush barriers, mounted police, water cannon, riot shields, whatever it took.

Whoa, she thought then, easy now . . . this is just panic. There is no need for this. I have been shown all along, ever since Irun so long ago, nothing but kindness and courtesy. Nobody wants to hurt me. They only want to be allowed to watch me pass by. Just a glimpse. And as long as I don't go through any extraordinary contortions trying to avoid them, they will be perfectly happy just to watch and wave and perhaps offer some flowers or other little gifts, just as they did on the platform at Irun.

Yet she remembered then the noise and press of that crowd at Irun, the feeling of a frenzy only just held in check. And how glad she had been for the presence of the customs official steering her through the eager, swaying mob towards a safe harbour. There had only been him, one man, but he had proved a rock in the midst of the tempest. As long as she could have that, she decided, she would be all right. Strike out the crush barriers and the water cannon. Just give her a couple of uniformed policemen and she would face her public gladly. But she did need those two big policemen.

Cautiously she unlocked her door and peered out into the corridor. It was empty. The little seat where Señor Gomez had used to sit was unoccupied. She turned back and picked up her coat and her carry-all. Then she stepped out into the corridor.

'Señor Gomez,' she called in a low voice.

There was no response. No sound of hurrying feet in answer to her call. She tried again, louder.

'Señor Gomez. Where are you?'

She had an idea that Gomez had a sleeping berth for his own use at the end of the corridor, near the exit. She went to it and knocked on his door. No answer. She was beginning to feel frightened. Damn, she thought, he must be somewhere else on the train, perhaps having his breakfast. She would have to go and find him. She didn't want to go walking unaccompanied through the train, but it was a marginally better prospect than stepping out all alone on to the platform.

At that moment, through the window of the exit door, she caught sight of a man in a peaked cap, a uniform, some kind of railway official. Relieved, she went to that door and banged on the window to attract his attention. He was not her old ally Gomez, but still through him she could get the necessary processes under way. Three policemen, she decided, would make a better escort for her.

The railway official looked up as she banged on the window. He stared her for a moment in surprise. And then stepped forward and opened the door. The noise of the station – shunting trains, voices, tramping feet – poured in at her.

'Oh, hello,' she said breathlessly. 'Look, I'll just wait here, all right? If you could go and get a policeman I could talk to.'

The man continued to gaze at her for a few moments, and then he smiled and shook his head apologetically. She thought at first he was refusing her request, then she understood that he had no idea what she was saying. But then, she thought, irritated, he hardly needed to. It was obvious what was wanted surely. She began to ask him (hopeless, of course, she knew even less Portuguese than she did Spanish) if he could bring her somebody who could speak English – 'English, comprendez? . . . or savvy? . . . or . . .' – when he smiled at her again and indicated that she should get down from the train.

She stared at him helplessly. It was just her luck to get a complete dolt to deal with. She looked anxiously out on to the platform. Some of the people going by glanced at her indifferently, but they had not truly seen her yet, she realised. Standing at the exit door, she was still in a fashion protected by the train. The official was no longer smiling. He jerked his head in a manner that decidedly told her she should step off the train. She stared at him for a moment longer. And then she shrugged. Oh well, she thought fatalistically, on your own head be it. Too bad if you lose your job. Too bad if people are hurt in the riot that's about to break out. At least I tried.

She stepped down on to the platform. The official closed the door firmly.

'Obrigado,' he smiled at her, and touched the peak of his cap, and then turned away and walked off up the platform.

She stared after him. He didn't look back at her, not once. After a while she tore her gaze away from his retreating back, and looked fearfully round at the people hurrying by.

Nobody stopped.

Nobody stared.

Nobody screamed or fainted or pushed towards her calling on the name of La Entwistle or pressed flowers in her hand.

Nobody even so much as noticed her.

She stood on the platform as the heedless crowds surged around her. At one point she started laughing, and people glanced at her curiously as they went by. She cut off her laughter then abruptly, and began to walk towards the head of her train, towards the pair of giant glass doors that gave exit from the station. She kept bumping into people. Some of them were kind and smiled at her and even murmured an apology; others snapped at her crossly before pressing on. She gave no attention to any of them. She was thinking how lucky it was that she had not thrown the gun from the train the night before. She was very glad she had not let it go, for she knew now she was going to need it before the day was through. She kept her eyes fixed on the great glowing doors, the sunlight beyond.

By late afternoon she was two hundred miles further south. She was standing beside an orange-painted shelter, watching the local bus move away. Where it was heading, the white buildings of a little town shimmered through the trees. She looked around her. A circle of low green hills. Grass meadows, purple and yellow flowers thick among the grass. A thorn hedge, a fallen oak tree. In the distance she could see a man ploughing a field behind a horse. A rough stone track led off the tarmac of the main road. A small signpost, leaning at an angle, pointed the way up the track. She walked towards the sign. Weather-beaten wood, the letters on it very faint, but she could read them. MONTE ROSADO – 5km. She stared at it, and then at the track to which it was pointing. It ran for about five hundred yards up a bare hill, and then disappeared round a bend. Beyond the hill, she could see the thick, clustered shapes of woodland.

Villa 'Atè Breve', Monte Rosado, Algarve. 5km. Five kilometres! Raymond had never said anything about five kilometres. 'Coach from Lisbon to Lagos. You pick up a local bus there, takes you over to the Atlantic side. It'll put you down right where you want to be.' What the hell was five kilometres? She struggled to make the conversion, was shocked when her first calculation came out at eight miles. She tried again. More like three miles, she decided. Not so bad, but even so – three miles on a hot day? On a rough track? Thanks a lot, Raymond. What is this, one last joke? Or did you think a walk of three miles at the end would put me off, if you told me about it? You shouldn't have worried. You should have known who you were dealing with. Someone who was prepared to go a thousand miles for you at the drop of a few lies.

She hoisted her carry-all on to her shoulder, folded the fur coat over her arm. All right Raymond, your last little joke. Three miles. No problem. She set off walking up the track. She could feel the stones through the soles of her shoes. But it was all right. One foot in front of the other. Keep doing that for long enough, she would get there. She walked along beside the meadow. Butterflies rose and fell among the flowers. The sun shone full on her face, the air was still. After a hundred yards she felt damp on her forehead, on her back. The track rose upwards, but not smoothly. It would run for a little while on the flat and then make a sudden jump to the next level. Those steep bits were hard. She found she was panting for breath and she looked back to see how far she had come. The main road still looked very close, she could almost make out the lettering on the signpost. She turned back to look uphill again. Never mind. One foot and then the other. She would get there. To do the last thing she had left to do. And then it would be over.

She followed the track around the bend. When she looked back now, she couldn't see the man ploughing the distant field any more, or the main road and the occasional speeding car. A hundred yards more, and the track became easier. It no longer proceeded in steep jumps, but settled into an easy upward drift. And the rocks underfoot gave way to sand and dirt. She was surrounded by heathland, brown grass unbroken by a single shrub. The sun streamed almost flatly across the plain. There was no shade at all. But up ahead, perhaps half a mile away, the pine woods began. It gave her a goal that was in sight, within reason. To get out of the sun, to disappear within the forest's cool depth. She quickened her pace.

After twenty minutes, she was passing under the first of the trees. The air was sweet with their scent. At first they stood many yards apart from each other. But soon they were clustering more thickly. The forest floor was bare. Sunlight reached it irregularly through the dark canopy, a sudden sparkling, then the gloom again. Darker and darker as she pressed into the heart of the wood. At last the trees were so high and close together that hardly a gleam of light reached her as she walked. And where she had been sweating a few minutes before, now she found herself shivering with cold.

She had almost decided to unfold her mother's coat and put it on, when the path turned another corner and a few hundred yards up ahead she could see a wall of light. Another five minutes at the steady pace she had fallen into and she broke suddenly out of the forest. Sunlight was streaming directly at her, making her screw up her eyes, and she cupped her hand over them as she peered forward. She was in heathland again. Grass and gorse stretching ahead, a plateau that rose gently before her for about two miles, when it stopped abruptly in a sharp line against the sky. A shimmer of bright reflected light out on the plain caught her gaze. Puzzled, she began walking, away from the forest, towards the distant line, watching the spot where she had seen the light flash. Again the shimmer and sparkle, about half a mile away. And then, across the heath, brought to her on a gentle, salt-smelling breeze, came the sound of a car engine bursting into life. A few moments and then the sparkling began to travel towards her. In a little while she could make out the shape of a small car being driven in reverse. The car was tan coloured, perfectly camouflaged against the heath, except for the light she had seen gleaming upon the windows and the metal bumpers. It was wandering a little to either side of the track.

When it was about twenty yards from her, it came to a stop. In the same moment, she stopped walking. The seconds passed. She was not afraid. As if in a dream, she watched the car door open. A man climbed slowly out of the car, and turned towards her. She stared across the space that lay between them. The sun shining behind him was burning his hair red-gold. His features lay in shadow, yet it seemed she could see him clearly. For a moment she felt no particular surprise at finding him here, a thousand miles from where he ought to be. After all, in her imagination, she had been seeing him on and off, in one location or another, for much of the day. He had ridden beside her on the coach down from Lisbon, and had stood swaying with her in the aisle of the little bus that had brought her from Lagos. Even in the woods he had walked beside her. She had needed to conjure him up so often. There was a lot she had to say to him. There was a lot of abuse and contempt and fury she had wished to hurl at his head. A lot of apologising too she had felt bound to do.

So it was no surprise to see him again now. But she was startled to see how she had dressed him up for this appearance. For instead of the dowdy garments he always wore – and in which he had been clothed on all his other visits today – he was wearing now crisp blue slacks and a pale-yellow sports shirt under a stylish stone-grey lightweight jacket. She noted too other surprising changes as she stared across at him. She had left behind her in Swayncliff a pale, morose-looking fellow, her follower. Humble follower. But this Raymond's eyes were watching her coolly and steadily, without a trace of servility. His mouth was curved in a faint sardonic smile. And the chalky pallor had disappeared, his skin was glowing, sun-warmed . . .

Why, what a Raymond I have dreamed up, she thought, bemused, watching him. A new star in the galaxy – Raymond the Carefree Tourist. She giggled, for a moment unable to stop herself admiring the fertility of her imagination. She had even managed to throw in a brand-new car for him this time!

Then a wave of disgust hit her. Truly, you are insane, she told herself, gazing bleakly now at this fresh apparition. Beyond insane.

'Oh, go to hell!' she snapped. 'I've had enough of you. We've got nothing more to say to each other.'

'Is that so?' the apparition scoffed. 'You sure about that?'

He crossed the few yards that lay between them, and with a quick movement took the carry-all bag from her shoulder. She could do nothing but stand, staring at him, as he searched inside it.

'Is it really you?' she murmured.

He didn't answer but, with a sigh of a relief, removed the plastic case from the bag. He undid the flap and took the gun out. Hefted it in his hand, then slipped it into the pocket of his jacket. He removed the three tissue-wrapped bullets from the case then, and put them too into his pocket. Then he replaced the case in the carry-all and handed the bag back to her with a mock bow. She was gazing at him, this astonishing new Raymond. It was him. It was impossible. It *was* him. Look at this marvel, she thought giddily, this transformation, this Raymond. My God, we both must have needed a holiday so much. She felt an involuntary stir of pleasure. She was so glad to see him looking like this. Anyway, she was glad to see him – an old friend in a strange land . . .

Insane.

'What are you doing here?'

He studied her thoughtfully for a moment. Then he shrugged. 'Thought you might need a lift.' He nodded towards the car. 'You've still got a way to go.'

He turned away from her and began to walk towards the car. She found herself following him. He went to the passenger door and held it open for her. She came to a stop, stared at the car, back at him.

Of all the questions she had to put to him she could think only of asking, 'Whose car is it?'

'Hertz's,' said Raymond.

She found herself settling into the passenger seat. He closed the door and went round to the other side and climbed in beside her. The engine was still running, and he put the car in gear. They moved slowly forward. She was turned in her seat, watching him.

'How did you get here, Raymond?'

'Flew down to Lisbon yesterday,' he answered promptly. 'Saw you off on the ferry, then up to Gatwick. I was at the station this morning, saw you on to the bus. Then I drove straight here. I've been up on the cliffs since noon,' he nodded. 'Gorgeous day!'

'You were at the station this morning?' she said after a moment.

'Sure. Had to check you hadn't got off somewhere.'

'You *saw* me there?'

'I already told you.' He glanced at her. 'Here, what were you doing? You were standing around there for ages. Looked like a zombie. I thought I'd lost you there for sure.'

He turned back to stare at the track ahead. She too gazed forward through the glass. The line against the horizon seemed to have come no closer. They were bumping interminably across this waste of brown grass. The breeze in her face was strong through the open window, and pungent with salt. And Raymond beside her. Raymond!

'Raymond,' she said, 'I want you to give me the gun back.' And when he did not respond, 'I kept it to show to Phillip. I was going to turn back at the station. But I knew I couldn't leave things like that. I had to come down here. And I needed the gun – otherwise I thought Phillip wouldn't believe me when I told him.'

'Told him!'

He sounded quite shocked. She couldn't tell if he was mocking her.

'But now you're here,' she went on, 'and we can tell him together. Or if you'd rather,' she added, when he didn't speak, 'I'll stay away. Let you speak to him alone. If you think that would be best.' She turned away from him. 'And if he even exists.'

'What do you mean – if he exists? Think I'd make him up?'

'I don't know. You've made up a lot of other things.' She looked towards him again. 'Haven't you?'

Raymond whistled a few random notes. ''Course Phil exists,' he said then. 'And he's right here. I've been watching him all afternoon.' He sighed and tapped the steering wheel lightly with one finger. 'So you were going to tell him? And that's all you were going to do,' he chided her, 'after what you promised!'

She started to speak, but he cut her off.

'What were you going to tell him?'

'That you need help. That you're probably sick. That you've been thinking crazy things.'

'All by myself, have I?'

She shook her head. 'No. I wasn't going to try and excuse myself. I'm probably worse than you.'

'What you are,' Raymond said, 'is one half of a conspiracy to commit murder.'

She looked away from him then, stared down at the carry-all bag on her lap. 'Yes,' she murmured. 'Except we never really meant it. Ever.'

'Didn't we?'

At last the line against the sky that she had been watching for so long seemed to be moving nearer. Beyond was clear, pale blue, except where a few small ragged clouds glowed gold and red against the falling sun. She felt so tired. More than tired, bone weary. But the approaching boundary gave her hope. A little while and they would have no place further to go. She would have come to an end at last.

'You're right though,' Raymond nodded then. 'I did make a few things up. Actually,' he chuckled, 'I made up a hell of a lot.'

A pleased smile hovered about his lips, his eyes were clear and bright and full of fun. She thought she had never seen him looking so attractive – not even that first time when he had come to interview her. Come to listen to her, with his tape recorder. To take notice of her. Such a turn on.

You silly bitch.

'There wasn't any inheritance, was there?'

'Well, there *was*,' Raymond said judiciously. 'Dad left a bit when he died. That was five years ago. Phil and me split up what there was. Which wasn't a million quid, that's for sure. Poor sap didn't even own his house. Couple of thousand each, that's all. I don't know what Phil did with his share. Probably something boring. Me, I spent it on getting as high as I could for as long as I could!'

He smacked his lips, and turned to her, grinning merrily.

'Your father wasn't John Blackstone?'

'The Viper?' Raymond chuckled. 'There's no such person. He was a Thorne. Like me. And Phil.'

'And he wasn't a Nazi.'

'Ah, now there you're wrong. In fact, he did hang around with the Mosleyites for a while. And he did contribute to their papers, as it happens.' Raymond held back his secret for a moment, enjoying it. Then, 'He used to make up the crossword for one of them. You know – on the back page. Ten across, six letters starting with A. "What Queen Victoria was not." He showed 'em to us one Christmas when we were kids. We all had a good laugh.' Raymond had a laugh now. When he'd finished, he added rather coldly, 'He wasn't put in jail in the war either. He was in the RAF. Warrant-officer. Had a very good war, according to him. But he was a bit of a story-teller, my dad. Like me. And I never saw any medals or anything. But you see – ' he explained, narrowing his eyes as he stared towards the sun, 'there *was* just a little bit of a basis in fact for that Nazi thing. Which is the foundation of all good stories, so I've read.'

'There was an article,' she said suddenly. 'An article about the auction. You showed it to me. It was in the paper – it *was* in the paper.'

'So it was. Oh, it was real, OK. I mean a real article. I got 'em to put it in at the last moment, breaking news, you know? I just thought you needed a bit of encouragement about that time. Keep you on track.' Raymond chuckled. 'Hell of a row at the office next day when they tried to follow it up. Worth getting fired for though. Cause it did the trick, didn't it?'

He glanced sideways at her, as if looking for some acknowledgment of his cleverness. When it didn't come, his mouth drooped petulantly. 'You don't seem all that surprised,' he complained.

She didn't bother to look at him. 'I'm surprised you're here, Raymond,' she said dully.

'I mean – surprised at what I'm telling you.'

After a moment, she shook her head. 'No,' she said, in the same dull tone, 'I knew you'd been lying to me.'

'Yeah?' Raymond chuckled proudly as if he'd just been complimented. 'When did the penny drop?'

'Oh . . .' She shook her head again, slowly, tiredly. 'I've known all along, I think.'

He turned to stare at her. 'Bullshit.'

'It's the truth,' she said sadly.

'I don't believe you.'

She shrugged, didn't bother to speak.

'Because,' said Raymond triumphantly, 'if you knew I was lying all along – then what are you doing here now?'

She was still silent, and he started to chuckle again. But she cut him off. 'It doesn't matter. But I knew you were lying.' She thought for a moment. 'Except the part about Australia. I thought there might be some truth in that.' She looked at him. 'Was I right?'

'Summer days at Baccara Bay? Poor little Raymond and that big brute Phil?' He waited for a few seconds, enjoying himself. Then shook his head. 'Nah. My brother was never like that. And I've never been in Australia in my life. Want to know where I got all that from?' He was silent for a moment, enjoying himself. Then, '*The Sons of Ricky Defiance!*'

She stared at him. He grinned back at her and nodded. 'It's on at lunchtime, three times a week. It's garbage but I usually try and get home for it. Greg Defiance is the bad brother. He's a real swine to everyone, particularly to his younger brother Ross. Who's sort of dithery, weak, too nice for his own good. A wimp. He takes some terrible beatings from Greg. He gets chased all over Baccara Bay . . . You've never seen it, have you? I kept thinking you would one day. I almost shat a brick when I heard you watched Australian soaps, but – '

'Not that one,' she said faintly. 'I watch the other one – '

'*Love Cures All*,' Raymond nodded. 'I couldn't understand it. That's not just garbage, it's totally boring. Whereas old *Ricky Defiance* always has a few surprises . . . I'd been watching it just before I came to see you that first time,' he explained. 'And I was trying out the Aussie accent. I do that quite often. Take off people I've heard. Movie stars, TV. I should have let you hear my Jack Nicholson, it's pretty good . . . So maybe I ought to have been an actor after all,' Raymond mused.

'Will you give me the gun back, please?'

'Or a novelist. Because even there I added a bit of my own. Creatively. Details, bit of colour. Wasn't hard. Cause I've been bashed up myself in my time. Bullied. You know – in the old school playground. But then,' he nodded, 'what kid hasn't?'

'Give me the gun, Raymond.'

'Not just now,' Raymond said.

19

The car ran forward another couple of hundred yards towards the rim of earth, and then, when it seemed they were about to plunge over it and soar into the milky-blue sky, he pulled the wheel over sharply. The path ahead now ran downhill for a couple of hundred yards, then it turned once more towards the sky. The car slowed almost to a stop. They crept forward round another bend. Then Raymond braked.

The track turned sharply away at this point. Where they were parked, directly in front of the car, a grassy hill sloped down for ten or fifteen yards to the edge of the cliff. The ocean lay beyond and far below. Green, grey-green, then patches of violet and red, reflections of the hovering sun-touched clouds. Then darkening through all the tones of grey and slate into a misty, limitless distance. A half-mile out from the shore unbroken lines of waves began their surge towards the beach. The waves were huge, moving onwards with such force that they would have hit the shore with terrific violence, if they'd been allowed to run all the way uninterrupted. But a few hundred yards from the beach a chain of tall black rocks reared up from the ocean bed. The charging waves pounded into them, throwing up great showers of spray when they hit. Only when they had spent their main force against the rocks did they move on again towards the shoreline, but no longer advancing like killing waves of infantry, now moving in short rushes and retreats, then scrambling onward again until at last they arrived, to tumble harmlessly on to the beach. Susan stared down at the great waves, the rocks, the showers of spray, and beyond them the eternal swell and heave. She felt within her a corresponding swell of relief. As if she had come home, as if sense had been given at last to this endless senseless journey. Why this is what I meant, she thought, this is what I meant all along . . .

She turned to him then, wanting to tell him she was grateful that, even in these bizarre circumstances, he had brought her to see this. He had opened the glove compartment, was reaching inside. He brought out a pair of binoculars, and put them to his eyes. She looked where the binoculars were pointing. They were halted at the very top of a corniche that cut diagonally across the cliff face to end in a valley far below. The top of the cliff wall, hundreds of feet above sea level, was carpeted with grass and flowers. All the rest showed a face of naked earth to the sky. Against the falling sun the cliff now glowed in deep tones of crimson and purple. Monte Rosado, she thought, the rosy mountain. In the valley far below, and climbing up the side of the cliff opposite, was a little settlement, about a score of villas, their red roofs and painted walls – pinks and greens and whites and yellows – making a cheerful splash against the sombre hues of the cliff face.

Raymond nodded and lowered the glasses. The jittery merriment of his manner on the ride here had gone, he seemed intent, preoccupied. He was about to put the binoculars back in the glove compartment – without thinking of offering them to her, she noted, annoyed, almost as if she wasn't there. Before he could replace them, she held out her hand. He stared at the hand for a moment, then shrugged and gave her the glasses.

'Use that to focus,' he said, pointing to the little wheel between the lenses. 'Last house before the beach.'

She saw at first only a blur of pinks and whites. She turned the little wheel until the images became sharp. Neat little villas, side by side. On the marbled patios in front of each stood clay urns filled with spring flowers. She could read the name plates fixed to the doors: 'Bom dia sol!', 'O pescador'. The windows were almost all shuttered. She moved on slowly towards the ocean. Cobbled lanes wandered all over the little settlement. She could see no people anywhere. At last she came to a villa larger than the rest, built some way up the cliff. She read the nameplate on the gate that faced the lane: 'Atè Breve'. From this villa a white wooden porch extended, balanced on stilts against the rock face. On the porch a man and a woman were lounging in deckchairs. The chairs were turned towards the ocean, the falling sun. Between them was a table piled with newspapers and magazines. Two tall glasses were stood side by side on the table. She could even see that they were empty now, except for the twists of lemon at the bottom of each.

'Nice, isn't it?' Raymond commented. 'You get a bit of fog down here sometimes, but mostly it's like this. Course you'd expect Phil to do himself well. All the mugs and Brits go down to the Mediterranean. The Portuguese keep places like this to themselves. These are summer houses mostly,' he went on in detached, almost chatty tones. 'People come down from Lisbon on their holidays.

Most of the year there's nobody here. Except for Phil when he takes a few days off. And whichever tart he fancies bringing with him.'

'Is that Phillip down there?' she asked, still watching through the binoculars.

'Obviously.'

He looked older than in the photographs she had seen. Older, nearly bald, whereas the photo had shown a head of thinning hair. She wondered for a moment, studying him, if she would have recognised this man if she had really stepped up to his door, gun in hand, intent on killing. As she had promised she would. Or would she have at least hesitated for a moment? A moment which would have been fatal. Or rather – for her intended victim – not. For as she had said, a million years, million miles away, in her apartment, in one of their planning sessions, she had told Raymond it had to be done all in an instant, giving herself no time for any thoughts except those of doing the job.

Now Phillip leaned towards the other chair and listened to what the woman was saying. Then he put his head back and laughed. She found she was staring into the back of his throat.

'What's happening?' Raymond asked.

'He's laughing.'

Phillip was wearing a striped T-shirt, a pair of blue latex swim trunks. A vigorous bush of grey hair sprouted from the top of his shirt. The woman – Susan moved on to gaze at her – had on a pair of khaki shorts, and nothing on top. She stared at the sleek, tanned breasts, the brown nipples. She moved up to look at the face. The woman was smiling, still speaking, turning slightly to her left, so that she presented herself in three-quarters profile to Susan's gaze. Dark, almost black hair, swept back. In her thirties, Susan guessed, a year or two younger than herself. A small, strong, square face, as brown as the rest of her. She wore lipstick, and her mouth was a vivid scarlet against her tan. She was beautiful, Susan thought.

The woman had stopped talking, and seemed now to be looking over her shoulder. Susan moved the glasses back to look at Phillip. But his chair was empty now. She caught sight of him then, disappearing into the house. She went back to the woman, who now seemed to be gazing straight up at the car. She had large, light eyes, hazel in colour. For a moment Susan thought she must have seen their car, though it was so far away from her, and hidden almost entirely behind the bend in the path. But then the woman looked down again, and with no indication of any suspicion that she might be being watched, she took up the paperback book that lay in her lap and began reading it.

She took the glasses away from her eyes. 'Who is she?'

'That's Kate,' Raymond said.

She turned to look at him. 'Your *wife*?'

Raymond was sitting bent forward in his seat, staring intently at the valley below, as if he could see with naked eyes who and what was down there. He was silent for a few moments after she had spoken, and then he shook his head slowly. 'What are they doing now?' he asked quietly.

She put the binoculars to her eyes again. 'He's brought her a cardigan from the house . . . Now she's putting it on . . . Now he's kissing her.'

From the villa came distant music. Phillip must have turned on the stereo when he'd gone indoors. Strings behind a wandering flute, the note very sweet, almost syrupy. A familiar tune. But she couldn't place it. From a musical? TV series? Horribly sweet. She lowered the glasses, turned back to Raymond. His eyes were closed, his mouth curved in a dreamy smile.

'Listen to that shit,' he murmured. 'He's on his way to his first million quid. Maybe he's there all ready. And that's the kind of shit he likes to listen to.' He laughed suddenly. 'Why, when I was seven – '

'I know. You passed your grade six piano exam.'

'When I was seven,' Raymond continued as if she'd never spoken, 'I could *compose* better shit than that!'

'Is she your wife, Raymond?'

He opened his eyes, but did not look at her. 'She might as well have been,' he said.

She still stared at him, wanting him to turn to her so she could try to read his expression. But he would not, and after a moment she looked away from him, away from the valley, out at the ocean.

'What are we doing here, Raymond?' she asked at last. She turned back to him. Still he would not look at her.

'Raymond, talk to me,' she said urgently.

'What for?' he said in a tone of mild surprise. He drew his hand across his mouth, then reached into his jacket pocket. He took out the gun and laid it in his lap, then dipped into his pocket again and brought out the tissue-wrapped bullets. He began to unwrap them. 'It'll be getting dark pretty soon,' he nodded as he worked. 'They'll go inside. Have a meal. Probably he'll cook for her. He fancies himself as a cook, Phil does . . .'

In the distance, the flute drifted stickily into another familiar tune. Beatles now. Early stuff. One of the slower ones . . . He slipped the bullets in the chamber, then settled the gun back on his lap. 'Phil's living on site right now,' Raymond went on, in the same mild, conversational tone. 'He's got plans for that place down there, going to knock most of it down, turn it into a leisure complex. He owns half those houses already, going after the rest of them. Some of the owners are putting up a fight – but he'll get them.' Raymond nodded, sounded almost proud. 'He'll get his way. He always does.' He grinned suddenly. 'At least, he would have got his way. Except this time he won't have a chance.'

She stared at him. He was gazing patiently down at the valley. 'Oh for Christ's sake, Raymond,' she sighed. 'What do you think you're going to do? Go down there where they've gone inside, use that thing on them?'

She gestured contemptuously at the gun. He moved it a little further out of her reach. She felt very weary. She had had to take herself all through this process, and now it looked as if she would have to do the same for him. It might be an uphill struggle. In her case it had been that sudden, spectacular – and so brief – dose of fame yesterday that had served to break up the log jam in her mind. Grotesque that she had had to be treated like a living idol before she could start to see straight – still, it had worked for her. But she could think of no equivalent experience to offer Raymond, not fame certainly.

'Raymond,' she said grimly, 'it's a *game*, it always was. We've been playing a stupid game, and now it's time to stop.' When he did not answer, she glanced again towards the ocean, as if seeking strength from it. He was right. It would soon be dark. The sun was a huge orange disc, its rim already starting to dip into the water. She looked back at him. 'Put the gun away, Raymond. Let's get out of here. We'll go somewhere and talk. We'll talk about anything you want,' she promised. 'We'll talk about . . . about Kate, if you like. And what's happened. And if your brother's taken her from you – well, that's – that's wrong. I can see why you'd be angry. I really do . . .'

His gaze had never strayed for a moment from the darkening valley. No sign that he had even heard her.

'Why didn't you tell me about this, Raymond?' she murmured. 'Kate . . . and your brother . . . Why didn't we *ever* talk?'

'Talk?' Raymond chuckled. 'We never did anything but talk. In fact, you're all talk as far as I can see.'

'I don't mean that. Lies. Foolishness. We could have helped each other perhaps, we could have been friends.'

'Friends?' He seemed to taste the word.

'Why not?' she asked sadly. 'We had something in common. I'd lost somebody too.'

The Beatles tune ended on a swirl of violins. She waited tiredly to hear the next.

'Whatever you wanted,' he said, 'it wasn't a friend. You didn't want *me* as a friend anyway. You just wanted to hear stories.'

'Yes,' she said after a long time. 'Perhaps you're right. I'm very sorry, Raymond. But now – ' she said, her voice strengthening, becoming hopeful. 'We can change that, can't we? We can be honest with each other. Can't we start now?' There was no response, not a look, or a sound. 'I'm not what you think at all,' she said in a low voice. 'You think I'm famous, successful. The truth . . . I had a moment. A few silly weeks of dazzle – when I was a queen. But it's gone now. Gone for ever. And it seems I can't bear it.' She wrenched the words out. 'My husband kept me going for a while. He told me lovely stories, that I was going to be a great actress. But of course I couldn't be that. And he couldn't bear that he had failed me. So he ran away . . . Now I have no one. My friends won't come near me . . . What else? I don't think I even have a career any more. I threw it away . . . I'm broke. I – I've got nothing, you see. Nothing at all.'

'You think any of this is news to me?' Raymond sneered.

'I suppose not,' she whispered after a moment.

'You think I want to *hear* any of that?' he said. 'The truth? The truth is shit. Course I know you're all washed up. What the hell would you be doing around me if you weren't?'

She opened her mouth, wanting to argue.

'Ah, why don't you just shut up?' Raymond sighed.

Sod him, she thought at last. She didn't have to put up with this. In spite of all the new clothes, the new looks, he was only Raymond after all. Her follower, practically her plaything. And if he couldn't see she was holding out to him the only lifeline he could possibly hope for . . . And couldn't see that she had been debasing herself deliberately to give him that chance, that she had made that sacrifice . . . then sod him, that was all. She put her hand out, gripped the door handle.

'Right,' she said. 'If you don't want to talk to me . . .'

'What are you doing?'

'I'm going to walk down there.' She nodded towards the valley. 'Perhaps I'll get some sense out of those people.' She pulled down on the handle.

'No.'

He said it quietly, without emotion, but moved the gun away from his lap, so it was pointing at her stomach. She stared down at it, then looked up at him.

'What's this?' she said blankly.

He chuckled at that. 'What's this?' he repeated. He kept the gun aiming steady at her stomach.

'How dare you!' Gladly, she was feeling her momentary panic turning into rage. 'Do you think I'd believe you'd use that on me?' she demanded. 'A liar like you?'

'What else do you think it's for?' Raymond asked.

After a moment, she let go of the handle. She sank back into her seat, staring at him. He nodded and lowered the gun into his lap again. Then he reached once more into the glove compartment and took out the binoculars. He peered through them down at the villa. 'They've gone inside,' he murmured to himself. 'Twenty minutes . . .' He put the glasses back into the glove compartment.

She shook her head. 'What does that mean?' she whispered. '"What else is it for . . ." What do you mean?'

Raymond ignored her. A minute passed in total silence, then another. He was gazing fixedly all the time at the distant villa. She had turned again to stare at the ocean. The sun was half-sunk now in the water. Out there the sky was still bright and clear, but nearer to land it was shading rapidly into night.

'Why am I here, Raymond?' she said quietly, curiously. 'Why did you want me here?' She turned back and looked down at the gun in his lap. She shook her head. 'Not to bring you that. You could have done that. You could have done what I did, caught the train . . .'

'Bit less dangerous for me,' he murmured, 'having you do it.'

She shook her head again. 'But not dangerous enough . . . Not worth risking – bringing me here. Why I'm a witness,' she said. 'I'm the last thing you should want.'

He was watching her now, as she groped forward through the maze. There was a half-smile on his lips, as if he was a master watching the efforts of an apt pupil.

Three bullets. She had brought him three bullets. *Three*. One for Him. One for Her. And one for luck.

For me.

'Why? Why me? What have I done to you?'

'You've done nothing to me,' Raymond said casually, 'except bore me to death with your bullshit for the last few months.' He looked away. She followed his gaze. Now in the valley a single light shone from the villa perched on the cliff. 'Don't you see it yet?' he sighed. 'The maid's off for the night. I told you that. Every Sunday she goes to see her family in Sagres. Tomorrow morning she'll be back. She'll find them down there. And she'll find you . . .'

Raymond smiled and nodded then. 'Something I didn't tell you: when you left Swayncliff yesterday morning, I went up to your flat. Used the key you gave me. I left something there. A photograph of Phillip. Framed. I put it on the table by your bed. Then I had a better idea. I threw it into a corner, against the wall. The glass smashed. Like somebody had thrown it there. Because she was so angry . . .' He turned to look at her. 'I figure when the cops break in to your place they're going to find that photo and put two and two together. Hell hath no fury like a woman scorned, right? You came down here to get your revenge on Phil and on the tart he's been cheating on you with. And then you turned the gun on yourself. That's what I figure they'll think.'

In the dim light his eyes seemed to be burning into hers, demanding her approval. Christ, he is mad, she thought. Not just a liar like me. She opened her lips to speak, but nothing came out. Her mouth was dry, something was gripping her throat, strangling her. In the silence Raymond's gaze became disappointed, ugly. She had to speak, she had to keep him talking. She opened her mouth again, hoping the act of doing it would bring forth the words she needed.

'Yes, it's a – ' She gasped for air. 'It's a good plan, Raymond, it – Much better than I could have thought up. I underestimated you . . . Is this what you always meant? From the beginning? When we first met?'

He shook his head. 'Not in the beginning. I didn't think of anything much in the beginning. Just wanted to see what would happen, you know? Just drift along. All this . . .' he patted the gun on his lap, 'it just kind of . . . kind of *evolved*. That's what I'd call it.'

He checked his watch again. She was driving herself to find something more to say to him. Anything to keep him talking. But there was nothing. It was all garbled. She could make no sense of anything her brain was telling her. Raymond glanced at her once more. There was a hint of reluctance in his manner now. He gripped the gun more firmly, lifted it off his lap. 'Well . . .'

'Raymond, stop this. Just stop it now.' She was fighting to keep her voice steady. 'This isn't what you want.'

'Isn't it?'

'You can't do it. Whatever's happened – this is your *brother*.'

Raymond was silent.

'And her . . . if she meant a lot to you once – '

'She doesn't mean a damn thing to me now,' he said sadly.

'*Raymond* . . .' She fought back a scream. 'You *can't* do it.'

He seemed to think that over. 'Why can't I?'

'Because – '

He shook his head. 'I can't see any reason why not. No reason at all.'

You can't because. Because. Christ. *What?*

'Because you've made a mistake.'

He stared at her. She was gulping for air. Seconds passed. She was getting control again.

'It's not a bad plan, Raymond,' she sighed, her voice becoming at last truly steady. 'To give them the victims and the killer too. No, not bad at all . . . Only you've forgotten something. So it won't work, you see.'

'I've forgotten nothing,' he said crossly. For the first time though she heard the faintest note of uncertainty in his voice.

'Yes. Yes, you have . . .'

Thank God. She should have counted on it. In the end, Raymond was still Raymond. His talent for planning went only so far. Without her, he was bound to make a mistake.

'They're going to know you've been here. The police will know. And how's that going to look? With your brother dead? Your ex-girl friend dead? And knowing you've been here . . .' He was still staring at her. She felt a familiar stir of irritation at his denseness. From across the bay the flute trilled sweetly into a new tune. God, she thought, that old Kathleen Ferrier song . . . 'Your *passport*, Raymond,' she sighed. 'And even if – even if they didn't take a record of that, there's your driving licence. You hired this car, didn't you? They've got you, Raymond. On paper. In black and white. Surely you can see that – '

He waved aside her words as if he was brushing off flies. He reached into the inside pocket of his jacket and brought out a couple of documents bound together with a thick elastic band. He showed them to her. She saw a familiar black booklet, and a plastic-encased green form. Helpfully he switched on the overhead light so she could see them better. 'UK passport in the name of James Alan

White,' he reported. 'Driving licence in the same name. I bought 'em off a Paki in Camden Town. And I didn't give *him* my real name, that's for sure. They're not all that good,' he added. 'Not for two hundred quid anyway. Look – ' He showed her the place. 'Only one "n" in "Britannic". The licence isn't much better. Still, they were good enough to hire the car.' He turned the page. For a moment, she was looking at a miniature photo of Raymond. Head and shoulders against an orange background. Then he closed the passport with snap. Put the elastic band round the two documents and replaced them in his pocket. He stared through the glass again down into the valley. A second light had appeared in the villa.

The sun had slid at last entirely into the sea, leaving only a broad band of red light across the horizon. Red sky at night, she thought, shepherd's delight. It would be a fine day again tomorrow. The flute chirped away in the distance. What is life?/ Life without thee?/ What is left if thou art gone . . .? Susan could never remember the words exactly. Only Ferrier's strange wavering lovely voice.

'Is that where you got the gun too?'

'The gun?' He chuckled. 'You don't buy guns off Pakis. Nah . . . I got this three, four years ago. Up in Nottingham. Bloke was a junky, off his head. He sold it for the price of a fix. He won't remember me. Anyway, it'll be at the bottom of the sea pretty soon.'

'Why did you buy it?'

'No reason. Just thought it might come in handy one day.'

She found she had nothing further to say. She could almost feel him beside her keying himself up to act. She supposed she ought at this moment to be reaching the limit of panic, hysteria, she ought to be begging him to think again. But she had no desire for any of that. She just felt blank. Blank and empty, and quite tired. Since he had shown her the passport and the driving licence, it had been this way for her. She had asked about the gun because it had been on her mind where he had got it from. Now he had told her, she had no more curiosity. She did feel resentment, she noticed, examining herself as if from some way off. It seemed such a damned shame that it should be Raymond that was doing this to her. When she had such contempt for him. And just when she had started to see – after all these months, years of wasted time – a glimpse of the light.

'Well . . .' said Raymond again.

'About that time, is it?' she asked snappily. She was holding on close to her resentment. It seemed the only thing she had going for her.

In the vague grey light he stared at her, surprised by her tone. Then he shrugged.

'Want you to get out now,' he said.

'What for?'

'Because . . . this isn't the place.'

'There'd be a mess, wouldn't there?' she nodded. 'All that nasty blood. Difficult to explain to Hertz, that.'

He peered at her. 'You still think I'm kidding?' he demanded.

'Oh, no, Raymond. Not you. But are you *sure* you've thought it through? I don't see you lugging me all the way down to the villa. So if you're going to put me back in here to take me down, there's still going to be a mess, isn't there?'

He shifted in his seat. He seemed mildly embarrassed when he spoke.

'I've got a sheet of polythene in the boot.'

'*Have* you?' The note of admiration in her voice was not entirely insincere. 'You really have gone into this! Is it a big enough sheet though? I'm quite a big girl. But then,' she nodded again, 'you won't have to cover all of me, will you? What – just the head?'

'Get out of the car!' he snapped.

He reached across her suddenly and pushed down on the handle. Her door swung open. She glanced at it, then faced front again.

'No, I don't think so,' she said.

'I'm telling you. Get out, or – '

'Or you'll what? Shoot me?'

She laughed at him. Contempt. Fierce contempt. All she had left.

'Don't think that's going to work for you now, Raymond. What else can you do? Fight me? Force me out? You can try it.' She looked him over. 'I'm quite strong, you know. I don't know about you. You really didn't do a lot back in the Leisure Centre, did you? You only came to meet me there, nothing else. Not much muscle there, I would think – '

'You fucking bitch!'

With a wild motion he raised the gun and pressed the muzzle against her ear. Oh, Jesus Christ, she thought. And this is it. Over the edge. Into the light. She felt incredibly excited, she felt so alive. She closed her eyes. Is this really how it is? At the very end, this joy? She tried to remember all that she should be thinking of in such a moment. Her parents? But they were dead. Her friends? – might as well be dead for all the use they had been to her. Her life? – oh, not that old thing.

Five seconds, ten seconds. The cold steel against her ear. Her eyes still closed. She sat in darkness. She waited for the light . . . Raymond cried out once. In rage? It sounded more like fear. Well, serve him right. He had brought himself to this point, and now he had to do something. Real. His fault. He could have stayed playing games with her, harmlessly . . .

Raymond cried out again. '*I have to!*' The gun shivered against her skull.

'Go ahead, Raymond. Now or never!'

Had she shouted that? Her ears were ringing.

'You see,' he cried. 'You see . . .'

Shut up, Raymond, she thought. What does it matter? Your problem. Not mine. I am thinking. Wha-at i-is li-ife?/Li-ife wi-ithout thee . . .? She clutched the fur coat to her breast. I am a very little girl, listening to that on the radio. In the kitchen. *Housewives' Choice. Two-Way Family Favourites.* Almost every week they would play that. Fit it in among the Dicky Valentines and the Johnny Rays. And now to Sergeant Terry Midgely at BAOR-19 in Mönchengladbach from wife Glad and children Cliff and Dawn and everyone in Leicester: lots of love, Terry, darling, and see you at Christmas, and here for you is Kathleen Ferrier singing . . .

Wha-at i-is li-ife?/Li-ife wi-ithout thee?/ Wha-at i-is li-ife wi-ithout my-y lo-ove . . .?

And I get up on the kitchen table, and put my head back and throw my arms out, and open and close my mouth as wide as I can, pretending to be Kathleen Ferrier. Wha-at i-is li-ife i-if thou a-art de-ad? And my mother watches and laughs and claps. Her clever little girl, Mummy's little show off. And I am frantic for the applause. Wetting myself for the applause. Just like now.

My first triumph. Aged three. And now my last disaster. Full circle really.

Silly bitch.

Felt then through her skin, bones, the movement of his finger on the trigger. Christ, he's done it. He's broken through at last. At least one of us can. Out of lying, into . . . Good for you, Raym –

The explosion.

Christ!

Mummy.

Can't hear. That's

torn it

Summer

20

In the third week of May, *The Entwistles* began its first showing on Portuguese television. The reaction to episode one from critics and viewing public alike made it clear that the series was going to repeat the success it had enjoyed, not just in neighbouring Spain or in Britain, but in a total of thirty-eight countries around the world so far.

Back in England very few people either knew or cared much about this latest triumph for *The Entwistles*. At this time the main topic of interest in the media world was the acrimonious departure of the director Tom Scott from BeeHive's multi-million-pound *Genghis Khan* project less than a fortnight before the cameras were due to turn. There was a spate of rumour and counter-rumour. Some said that Scott had been fired, others that he had walked out of his own accord. The only certainty was that he had gone. The BeeHive press release that announced his departure explained it as a result of 'creative differences'. Richard Banham, the statement concluded, had agreed to take over the direction of *Genghis*. 'If this project is going to fulfil its gigantic potential, it needs a true professional at the helm,' Mrs Bee was quoted as saying, 'and now, at long last, we've got one.'

Tom Scott passed several very bitter and unhappy weeks following his separation from *Genghis Khan*. At first he was simply bewildered at the turn of events. 'I just don't understand it,' he would complain to his agent, to his loyal friends, Louise, the cleaning woman, anyone who would listen. 'I mean, she was always a bit difficult to work with, we had our little differences from the start – but it wasn't too bad, no worse than anything else I've worked on. We were getting along OK basically, things were looking good. And then . . .' Tom would stop at this point and shake his head distractedly. Or hold it in his hands and groan. 'And then – all of a sudden she just seemed to turn on me. Like a wild animal. As if I was her dearest enemy instead of the bloody director. And I never *did* anything to her!' he would cry out, his voice rising and breaking.

Mrs Bee had cut his budget, not once or twice during the run up to the shoot, but several times a week. She had gone behind his back and hired people to work on the project without consulting him. She had refused to allow any further changes to be made to the script. She would not let him approach the actors he had wanted for the lead parts. He would hire people in the morning and find by the afternoon that Mrs Bee had already fired them. Her manner towards him deteriorated day by day. Finally she refused to talk to him. She would not take his calls, she would not admit him into her presence. The only contact between them was the messages and instructions, issued like Tsarist ukases from the BeeHive offices. The last of these bulletins before he left informed him that there would be no filming on foreign locations after all.

'She promised me Hungary,' Tom would report bleakly as he remembered it, 'and I ended up with Salisbury Plain.'

He couldn't understand it – not just the things she had done to him, but the malign way in which she had done them. All he was able to do, as he recollected events in miserable idleness later, was to date the beginning of the great change in her attitude towards him. That had followed the dinner party when he had welcomed Mrs Bee to his home for the first and, as it proved, certainly the last time. Along with that treacherous rat Banham and his empty-headed bimbo wife. Often Tom went back through the incidents of that night, seeking for clues but never finding them. He even wondered if that unusual mauve concoction that Louise had served for dessert was at the bottom of the mystery. Was my kingdom lost on account of an ice cream? he would wonder pitifully. But even if, he reasoned, Mrs Bee had been bothered by a stomach upset after that night, from the ice cream or the duck, whatever had done it, even if she had been racked afterwards by vomiting and diarrhoea, he could not believe that it would have caused hostility and destructiveness on the scale that she had handed out to him from that time onwards. He could not understand it.

Tom's anger and despair in the immediate aftermath of the débâcle were much increased by his sense of betrayal at the part Dick Banham had played. Banham had moved in so fast to replace him – the interval between the one exiting from the production office and the other arriving was less than an hour – that there could be no doubt that he and Mrs Bee had been in contact and discussing terms for some long time before; in other words during the days and weeks when Tom was still struggling to make a success of the job. Tom did not bother to hide his feelings of outrage at Dick's behaviour, and for a time opposing factions appeared among their mutual friends, one lot claiming that Tom had been cruelly betrayed, another that all was fair in love and war and film making, and that Dick had a perfect right to show interest in a job whose current incumbent was manifestly failing to give satisfaction. But there was a third party, whose numbers increased as time went by, who said that it was all a storm in a teacup after all, that the directing job on *Genghis Khan* represented no kind of artistic summit. Whoever was called the director, it was perfectly clear that it was going to be Mrs Bee's creation in the end. What did it matter who directed it? It was only a handyman's job, and to argue over who should be doing it was like squabbling over who had the right to change a fuse.

In a week or two the fuss died away. People lost interest and got excited about other things. In the hush that followed, Tom was left alone to remember and mourn. This time was the hardest of all for him. He no longer felt energised by his initial brilliant anger. He just felt flat and vacant and sorrowful. Despair settled over him, of a kind that seemed almost terminal in its intensity. For he felt that he had spoiled his great chance. He knew – had always known really – that, given the script, given the BeeHive parentage, whatever he could have managed to do with *Genghis*, the result would not have been up to much: a few scenes of spirited action, and the rest probably fairly mindless. But it would have been a step he was sure – a giant step – in the right direction. He had wanted to move out of the realm of sensitive small-scale creation – where he was known, where he was proficient, where he was so deeply bored – and to prove himself at a new and grander level. In all the accounts of the great careers he had heard or read of there had come this moment of decision to break free from the known and familiar, to reach out for something beyond what had gone before. Even if it meant courting almost certain failure. His moment for reaching out had come. He was sure of it. He had built up the solid base over the years, all those years, and the time had been ripe at last to make the great move forward. And so he had reached out – and it had been snatched away from him before his fingers could begin to close on the prize.

In those bleak weeks, he became aware of how much he had become dependent on a golden and hopeful view of his future. He had been riding on this hope, he saw, for so many years, the promise he had made to himself long ago that one day victory, final victory over all his rivals, would be his. And this triumph he had aimed for, he painfully recognised, had not been wholly a wish for artistic excellence. Of course, he wanted that. Once he had thought it was all he had ever wanted. But often now he feared that these aspirations had not been his true goal. Even more than the aim of directing great films, he had wanted to be seen as a Great Director. To stand acknowledged in the national, then the international pantheon of those who counted in his world. To be showered with the rewards that such a position inevitably brought, the trinkets and prizes, big and small, that the world had to offer its very best. Money, of course, any amount of that – but far more, he wanted the signs of submission from every side. The flattering profiles in the papers, the retrospectives, the seat on the committees, the medals, the knighthood, the Life in the Day, the Room of my Own – a sort of universal, respectful hush when he entered any gathering. At his own level, he too had shared the ambitions of the Khan. Conquest, dominion, the world at his feet, at any price.

(Italian co-producers lurked in the offices of BeeHive, American distributors, East European directors, star actors from everywhere: Mrs Bee had talked casually of the festivals they would be taking *Genghis* to: Naples, Berlin, Venice – Tom would come home sometimes after a day in those offices faint with excitement, seeing so clearly the shape of his future . . .)

And it was all behind him now. His future lay in ruins. The arc of hope that had always risen before him, pointing always towards his ultimate triumph, had snapped off at age thirty-four. He was fated to be known for ever as a nearly man. He was fated never to be known at all.

Louise tried to argue him out of this black gloom.

'For God's sake, Tom. Genghis Khan! What could you ever have done with something like that?'

'You don't understand,' Tom said hollowly. 'It was about scale, epic, magnificence. Kurosawa, Griffiths . . . And then,' he added, for he was still at this time hopelessly involved with the project that had been taken from him, 'he was in fact a most interesting man, Genghis. Not just a bloodthirsty thug. I studied him. He was a wise administrator, a fond parent, he took a distant but real interest in the arts and in scholarship, he – '

'But none of that was in the script,' Louise interrupted, 'and Mrs Bee wouldn't let you change a word.'

'You don't understand,' Tom repeated in the same hollow voice.

He did not know what to do with himself. He saw no way out. He recognised that his ambitions, as revealed to him, had been largely hollow and vulgar, and he was sorry for that. Had he seen them earlier for what they were he might have struggled to change them. But it hardly seemed to matter now; they were wrecked anyway. And they *had* been his ambitions, they had kept him company all his career, and he could not pretend in a moment that they had no more meaning for him. What could he do? At any rate, he felt he could not go back to what he had been doing before, the small and the sensitive, and the eternally obscure. A couple of television offers of this type had appeared almost as soon as the news broke that he had parted company with Mrs Bee. Louise urged him to see this immediate demand for his services as a flattering tribute. He could only see that they could hardly wait to tie him up again in the familiar harness. Like an old carthorse.

He delayed responding to these offers. He mooned about the house. He could not go back, was not allowed to go forward. He talked about doing other things entirely with his life. He might write a novel, or a filmscript. Or go hill farming in Wales. He had wanted to do that very much when he'd been about twenty. Perhaps now was the time for it. One day he remembered dimly, as if it had happened several lifetimes ago, that at Cambridge he had read for a law degree. He became enthusiastic about a new career as a barrister, and sent off to the Law Society for information. When the pamphlets arrived, he took them into his study and pored over them for hours. Louise looked in at last to tell him she was going to bed. He looked up with a scared smile.

'It looks very promising,' he told her. 'What with the exams and then getting established in a chambers, I should be earning real money within at least seven years. We can do it,' he urged her. 'We've been poor before, and it wasn't so bad.'

Louise sank into a chair near his desk and stared at him.

'No,' she said.

'No, what?'

'No, you are not going to waste any more of your time thinking like this. No, you are not going to throw away everything you worked for. Oh, Tom,' she begged him, 'you're used to earning quite a lot of money now. We're used to living on quite a lot of money. We can't go back to what we were. We're not the same people.'

'But I can't go back to what I was doing,' Tom said miserably. 'I've done all that. It's finished for me. I just can't turn back.'

'Yes,' said Louise. 'You must.'

'Without believing in it? Without caring about it? Just going through the motions?'

'Millions of people work at something they don't believe in every moment they're doing it. And they don't get paid a quarter of what you do.'

'But then I'd be nothing more than a hack.' He looked away from her. Of all things, he had never wanted to have to apply that word to himself.

'No,' said Louise again, leaning forward and placing her hands on his knees. 'Look at me, Tom . . . You are not that. Never that. You are a hard-working man who always does a good job. Who never gives less than his best and is respected for it. You're a man near the middle of his career who has commitments, and is going to have more of them soon. You won't walk away from them. You won't walk away from everything you've built up. It's not that I won't let you, or that I won't stick by you, whatever you choose. It's that you *can't* walk away. I know you can't.'

Tom stared at her. Her eyes were calm and steady and confident. It had been a long time since he had heard her talk like this. He felt suddenly very glad that he was married to her. He admired her so much, and respected what she had just said. At the same time, he wished he hadn't heard it. He had been happier with his dreams. And of course he knew that in making her arguments, she was not in full possession of the facts. She did not know that she had been addressing them to a cut-rate Genghis Khan. The conqueror. Would-be. Spoiled. Failed.

He looked down at the Law Society pamphlets on his desk, and shook his head.

'But I can't go back,' he said. 'I physically can't do it.'

When the crisis point had been reached, when they were two months behind on the mortgage payments, when it was not certain whether there would be food in the house next week unless he said yes to one of the despised offers, rescue arrived from an unexpected quarter. Mark Gould, Sue Strang's husband, rang one evening. He was back in town, he told Tom, and he had a script that he wanted to show him. Neither piece of news much excited Tom – in fact, he had groaned aloud when Mark first mentioned the script. What was startling was that Mark claimed to have the money, from Canadian and Hong Kong backers, to get the film made. Sceptically, Tom agreed to read the script. When the messenger brought it round, he took it to the study and, sweeping the legal pamphlets aside, settled down to read it. Half an hour later a frantic yell from the study brought Louise hurrying to investigate. She found Tom pacing up and down, his eyes flashing excitedly, his face wreathed in smiles.

'It's small,' he cried out to her, brandishing the script triumphantly above his head, 'but by Christ it's not sensitive!'

It was a screenplay such as he had only ever dreamed of before. The work of a first-time writer, and – whether because of beginner's luck, or because Mark had indeed discovered a major new talent – the hundred or so pages of dialogue and action were a joy to read. It was fast and funny and honest and, above all, original. And though small indeed in some respects – Tom saw how inexpensively it could be done and how quickly – in its entirety it was by no means small, it had a largeness of spirit. He saw so many opportunities in it for himself to do good work, so many opportunities for actors too – three or four terrific ideas for who should play the leads immediately occurred to him. He was almost certain that what he held in his hands was the key to at least a modest popular success. Fuck that, he frowned impatiently, this could be *huge*. (The springboard, a voice whispered inside him then, to the profiles in the papers, the retrospectives, the medals, the prizes, the Life in the Day, dinner at Number 10 . . .) Stop that! he told himself furiously as soon as he heard the voice. That didn't matter at all. All that mattered was that it was a wonderful piece of screenwriting and he would get down on his hands and knees for the chance to direct it.

With Mark Gould producing.

'Oh, Jesus . . .' Tom's face crumpled. He sat down heavily at his desk.

'What is it?' Louise stared at him anxiously. She was almost as excited as him, though she hadn't read a word of the script yet.

'Who am I kidding?' Tom sighed. 'Mark hasn't got the money. Mark hasn't got a chance of getting the money.'

'But he said he'd got Canadian – '

'Fantasy. Pure fantasy. I know it.'

'Find out,' Louise said firmly. 'Don't give up until you've seen him. What can you lose?'

So, mostly to please her, Tom agreed to a meeting with Mark. He went to it with a sinking heart. He hated to think that his chance to direct this script, this brave, brilliant script, rested on nothing more substantial than Mark Gould's ability to raise money. What ability? Tom thought glumly as he took his seat on the Underground. He's been bunged out of Hollywood, and now he's crawled back here to annoy all of us and waste our time.

Only once before had he been careless enough to get professionally involved with Sue Strang's wayward husband – had Mark even met her at that time? Tom wondered. Anyway it was years and years ago, a period when Tom was still searching desperately for someone to give him the chance to direct his first film. Mark had come to him with a script he'd written. Tom had started to read without much hope – but to his surprise the script wasn't altogether bad. There were some amusing lines of dialogue, whole scenes that stood up well. The central theme of the sexual initiation of a young south London lad by an older woman of German background (Mark gave him to understand that 'in a sense' it was semi-autobiographical) was quite strong. In all it was by no means the worst script Tom had ever read. In a junior capacity he had worked on films based on much lousier material than this. He told Mark that he would be willing certainly to have his name entered in as the potential director for this project.

Neither then nor later did Tom blame Mark for the fact that the film never got made. Though Mark hustled bravely for a few months, there were just too many obstacles in its path. It was a bad time to go looking for finance for a British feature, there seemed to be no money anywhere, even the most experienced producers and directors were having difficulty finding backing. And the project was too expensive to be taken on by television. But the main problem was that they were both too young, too inexperienced, with such short track records. It was a familiar predicament. They couldn't raise the finance because neither had ever made a film before. They couldn't make a film because nobody would give them the money. No, Tom didn't blame his collaborator for the probably inevitable failure of their hopes. What he blamed him for, what he still burned with anger and humiliation over whenever he remembered it, was that awful morning when Mark had taken him to see a candidate for the role of the German woman.

'Ingrid Bergman!'

'The same.'

'But she'd never in a million years – '

'She's very interested,' Mark told him. 'Loved the script. Of course she wants to meet the director before she makes up her mind.'

'I can't believe – '

'And if we can get *her*,' Mark had told him unnecessarily, 'the film's as good as made. So – eleven o'clock tomorrow morning. Can you make it?'

The great star was staying temporarily at a friend's house in St John's Wood. The two film makers met outside the tube station. Mark was wearing high-waisted puce flares, a goatskin bomber jacket, tangerine-tinted aviator glasses, and two-toned platform shoes. Tom had on the dark-grey suit that he'd last worn at his admission interview at Cambridge. Mark had looked him over disparagingly. 'Christ, Tom,' he'd sighed, 'you look like the head prefect.' They had walked in silence through the pleasant lanes of St John's Wood. Tom's stomach was twisting and turning painfully at the thought of the interview ahead. Bergman! To think of the great roles she had played, the great directors she had worked with, her whole glorious legend made him feel faint. And now they were trying to obtain her extraordinary services. It was daring for them to contemplate even meeting her, face to face, as if she was just another mortal. How was it happening? he wondered, hardly able to contain his rising panic. What – he glanced again at his vividly decked-out companion – what fibs and name-droppings and exaggerations had Mark used to get them this interview? Tom didn't like to guess. He supposed that at the very least Mark had assured her that the money for the film was already in place. Well, he could be forgiven for that, Tom reasoned, that was a standard ploy. And it was fair enough. As Mark had said, if Bergman was truly ready to come in with them the finance problem would almost certainly disappear with her signature.

Ingrid Bergman!

After only a minute inside that beautiful little house in St John's Wood, Tom realised that Mark had not just lied a bit to get them into the presence of Miss Bergman, he had actually lied to her about the whole purpose of the interview. It was not altogether clear – but it seemed that the actress was expecting a reporter and a photographer from one of the Sunday supplements. The only words she addressed directly to Tom were 'Where is your camera?' Mark quickly led the conversation in the direction of the script. As soon as she realised what was up, Miss Bergman had risen from her chair and asked them to leave. Her voice was gentle, but the tone brooked no argument.

'Right,' said Mark. 'Shall I just leave the script with you, then?'

'No, please don't do that,' Miss Bergman said graciously.

'Sure,' Mark said, 'Sure. I'll have it taxied round to you then, shall I?'

The door closed on them before he'd finished his sentence. Tom, who had happened to glance at his watch just before they'd entered the house, now automatically looked at it again. They had lasted four and a quarter minutes in Ingrid Bergman's presence.

'Well, that wasn't too bad,' Mark said, 'for a preliminary discussion.'

For a couple of hundred yards, before he finally broke away from him, Tom screamed abuse at Mark. For the humiliation, the shame, the whole horrible experience. Mark affected to be amazed by Tom's anger. Also to be thoroughly disappointed in his performance. 'You stood there like a dummy,' Mark snapped in a rare break in Tom's diatribe. 'Why didn't you talk to her about the film?'

'She thought I was a fucking Fleet Street photographer!'

'Well, there was your chance to tell her she was wrong.'

'She wasn't wrong! She'd been lied to! By you!'

The last words Tom heard from Mark that day, or for many months after, were called plaintively after him as he ran, almost in tears, narrowly dodging traffic, across Maida Vale.

'At least,' Mark cried, 'at least you got to meet Ingrid Bergman!'

With such searing memories, Tom – on this day, so many years later – slowly climbed the stairs to the fifth floor of a run-down building on Brewer Street where Mark had opened an office. What the hell am I doing here? he asked himself angrily, as he tapped on the door. Why, he thought, as he saw through the dingy frosted glass the unmistakable shape of Mark's shadow approaching, the dead beat hasn't even got a secretary to answer the door for him.

Mark threw open the door. He was deeply tanned, his hair cut immaculately close and shaped to the curve of his skull. There were elegant silver highlights at the temple. He cocked his finger at Tom like a pistol and in a mellow California accent drawled, 'Tommy! You old sonofabitch! You've put on weight.'

As he stared at the exotic, newly invented figure before him, Tom bit by bit was able to piece together the elements of the old familiar Mark, the cocky, cunning, alien street boy he had known for so long. And he saw something else as he watched Mark. Bravery, he thought, that's what was always there too. And I never could see it before. Bravery always, and in spite of everything.

Braver than I ever was, thought Tom then, without anger. A hero really. And so he had won Susie – for life if he'd wanted. Whereas I . . . only warmed her bed for a few lucky nights. And for this I've hated him ever since.

He felt a sudden, unanticipated rush of affection. After all, he thought, it's true: I did get to meet Ingrid Bergman.

Mark put his arm round Tom and hugged him. 'Wotcha, cock!' he said in pure post-war south London. 'I've missed yer a lot.'

They went into the office, Mark's arm around Tom's shoulders. They sat on the two second-hand upright chairs which, with a desk and a filing cabinet, comprised Mark's office furnishings. They talked for a while about this and that. And then Mark took Tom carefully through his accounts. He showed him the cheques, showed him the bonds and the promissory notes and the contracts and the guarantees. At the end, Tom had to admit the startling truth. Mark had the money. Just enough money. And he had a script. He, Tom, was about to be recalled to life. Two months pre-production, then, end of July, principal photography would begin.

A week before the shoot, Tom and Louise gave a dinner party at their house. At the last moment Mark Gould was unable to attend, having flown off to Brazil on the rumour that there was money floating around there looking for a film to invest in. Hugh Perkins, who had a part in the movie, and was an old friend anyway, was invited with his wife, as was John Knights, another old friend, presently down on his luck and in need of cheering up. And the cameraman Harry Carver and his wife were asked along too. After a long discussion, it was decided to include Dick Banham and Jeannie Ricketts among the guests. There had been something of a reconciliation between the two directors – they had run into each other in a club one afternoon and had talked quite amicably for ten minutes – and it seemed a good idea to cement the revived relationship by having the Banhams back to the house. Two factors played a part in Tom's willingness to forgive and try to forget the harm Dick had done to him. In his present state of euphoria and in his gratitude for the new opportunity that had come his way he was able to look with greater honesty on the near past and to acknowledge the truth of what Louise had said all along: he had no business to be working on *Genghis Khan*. He had been completely wrong for it.

'I was terrified,' he told Louise one night, as they lay in bed. 'All those horses, all those shaggy costumes – that script like huge lumps of concrete. All that money . . . even after she'd cut it. I didn't know what I was doing. I was scared to death. And she saw it – Mrs Bee could tell.'

'Then she was right to replace you,' Louise said gently.

'Maybe. I guess so.' For a moment, a faint, sad whisper of regret started in the back of Tom's mind. But he dismissed it quickly. 'Yes,' he said, 'she was right . . . But I still don't know why she had to do it in such a way. As if she was paying me back for something. Something I never did!' He shook his head in hurt and bewilderment.

'And Dick did you no harm in taking over,' Louise persisted.

'I suppose not . . . the creep . . . no, I guess not. He always thought it was rightfully his. So I suppose I can't blame him.'

'Then let's have them over.'

The other factor that inclined Tom to think more generously of

Dick Banham was the constant flow of bad news about the *Genghis* shoot. So far three different actors had been employed in the title role, and the present one spent all his time between takes in consultation with his lawyers and his agent. There had been half a dozen different cameramen. The thing was at least ten weeks behind schedule, and millions over budget. The word from the cutting rooms was that there was no hope of salvaging most of what had been shot so far. 'Incoherent' was the kindest word used to describe it. In the trade press the title *Genghis Khan* never appeared now without the adjective 'ill-fated' before it. It seemed that for the first time Mrs Bee and the BeeHive empire had stumbled. On the other hand, the news about her other blockbuster, *Vivien Leigh – Her Life and Loves*, was consistently good, so Mrs Bee's reputation remained virtually undimmed. Dick's reputation, however, was firmly in the mud, and Tom could hardly stay angry with someone in such deep trouble.

'Poor old chap,' he said to Louise cheerfully on the day before the dinner party. 'The latest is that his health is breaking down. Suspected ulcer, they say. We must make sure to have some nice bland food for him tomorrow, just in case. Plenty of milk.'

'Yes, we'll do that,' Louise nodded. She hesitated for a moment, then faced her husband squarely. 'Tom – now that Mark's not coming, I'd like to ask Susie Strang instead.'

The happy smile, which he almost always wore these days, faded from Tom's lips. 'I don't know much about that,' he muttered.

'Come on, Tom. She's been back in London for weeks and weeks and we haven't got in touch.'

She watched him. He had turned away from her, he was shaking his head slowly.

'If you're worried she'll be a wet blanket or something, I don't think you need to. Everybody who's seen her says she's in great shape. And she's doing very well – she's got that part in *Vivien Leigh*.'

'I know . . .'

'Well then, let's have her over. I'd like to. I feel bad about her, Tom.' Louise looked away from him. 'I can't help remembering that night and what we did to her . . . what we didn't do.'

'I remember too.' Tom stared at his feet. 'She hasn't got in touch with us though. What makes you think she'd want to come tomorrow?'

'People forgive, people forget. We can only ask her.'

Louise got Susan's new number from Tina Perkins and nervously telephoned her that evening. To her relief Susan sounded delighted to hear from her and accepted the invitation.

'Dammit,' said Tom, when Louise told him the news, 'I'm going to have to apologise to her.'

'Well, dammit, so you should.'

In spite of his now heavy work commitments, Tom made all the preparations for the party himself. Since the terrible morning following the first, and till now only, dinner party they'd held in this house, he'd done his best to ensure that Louise would not have to exert herself in the least for the remainder of her pregnancy. In fact, he took this aim to extremes; he would have preferred that she never rose from a prone position unless it was absolutely necessary. For he could not get out of his mind the memory of those few hours when he was certain they had lost the baby, when the bleeding had gone on and on and wouldn't stop, and the ambulance came, and then he was following the flashing blue light through the early-morning streets to the hospital and the emergency room.

'For God's sake, Tom,' Louise protested, as he prowled around her, wanting to help her lift teaspoons or turn the pages of a magazine for her. 'It was only a cyst. There's nothing to worry about. The baby's doing fine.'

He could not tell her, nor very easily face it himself, that his deepest anxiety stemmed from his certainty on that morning, as he saw her being carried into the ambulance, that it was not only the baby he was going to lose. Still, as the months passed without mishap, and as Louise continued to look and feel so well, his panic lessened, and an arrangement grew up that satisfied them both, though in fact Tom was not really aware of its existence. As long as he was in the house, Louise stayed in bed upstairs or lay on the couch in the living room, letting him wait on her. As soon as he had gone, she got up and did whatever she liked for the rest of the day. Evening found her reclining languorously again, and welcoming him back home with a brave smile. She was now in her ninth month, and for the first time needed all the help she could get.

The food for the party was ordered already cooked from a local firm of caterers who were quite willing to include some extra-bland items. On the night, when the entrée was served, Tom thoughtfully placed these dishes – a flan, a whole cooked cauliflower, a dish of pulses – as close as possible to Dick's place at the table. However, Dick ignored them and instead held out his plate for the roast beef without any apparent apprehension. He held it out for two more helpings before he had finished, and seemed to be in exceptionally good spirits, eating and drinking with gusto, and cracking jokes. Knowing how badly things were going for him, Tom could only be impressed by his plucky attitude.

He guessed that the others too were relieved to find Dick bearing up so bravely. The atmosphere from the start was relaxed and cheerful. Everyone knew each other pretty well, most had worked together at some time in the past, there was a sense of easy-going comradeship in the air. Tom took some pleasure in contrasting the present occasion with that other and difficult evening when the great panjandrum Gwendoline Bee had been the guest of honour. How stifled, edgy, full of rivalry and doom that evening had been; how pleasant and friendly this one was. And among the ingredients that was making the evening such a success was the presence of Sue Strang. She was quieter than the others. She listened to and enjoyed the jokes and banter and anecdotes that went around the table rather than producing many of them herself. But, as Tom remembered, when Susie listened it was no mere passive act. As the evening went by, he took to watching her stealthily and he saw that she was doing a great deal to make the party go well. She was sitting next to Harry Carver, who had a reputation for taciturnity. Yet from the beginning of the meal Susan had concentrated on him – though not in any way that would trouble his wife – and had drawn him out so skilfully that in a while Harry was chatting away, surprising everyone with his mordant wit, including probably himself. Having set Harry free in this way, she turned her attention to the rest of the table. She was always there with a question, or an apt comment, or just an encouraging nod if the conversation threatened to flag. She was, Tom realised at last, the centre of the party. It was for her in essence that the talk flowed and the jokes were told. Around her the others played and scrapped and flirted, turning to her from time to time to make sure that she was still watching.

Sitting at the other end of the table from Susan, Tom had no chance to talk to her for most of the evening. But towards its end, when some of the guests were still talking at the table, and others had moved away to sprawl in the easy chairs around the fireplace, he went down to the kitchen to fetch more spoons for the coffee, and found Susan in there, at the sink, wearing a pair of rubber gloves and washing the dinner plates. He protested strongly but, without turning round, she told him that she wanted to help Louise. He explained that he would be taking care of everything, Louise wasn't going to have to lift a finger.

'Then I'll do it for you,' she said, and carried on washing up.

And it was there, in the kitchen, after several minutes of nervously creeping up to the subject, that Tom at last got out what he had to say. Most of the time, while he was talking, Susan carried on with the washing up, but towards the end she had turned from the sink and was watching him in a thoughtful way. She let him go on until there was nothing left but the last trailing apologies.

'There's nothing to forgive,' she said at last.

'Yes. Yes, there is. I was a rat to you.'

'And I was behaving like a pest. You probably did the right thing.'

'I meant to phone you. I really did. The very next day. But then the thing with Louise, the hospital, the baby . . . it just went out of my mind.'

'Well, good God, Tom, how can I be angry with you when something like that was happening? Of course you couldn't come to the phone.'

'No,' he said, after a moment. 'That won't do. The thing with Louise didn't happen till after you'd called. Called us three times,' he added sadly.

'Then,' she nodded, 'you were a rat to me.'

'I can't explain it. I was showing off – but still it makes no sense.' He bowed his head. 'One of my oldest friends . . .'

'Fellow artist,' he heard her say. 'Confidante. Sometime lover . . .'

He looked up in surprise to find her smiling at him. He swallowed. He was taken aback to have heard her mention *that*. And Louise just a floor above them.

'No. Don't let me off,' he begged. 'I deserve . . . well, everything.'

'Oh, don't be silly, Tom.' She came to him and gave him a brisk hug. 'It happened. At the time I was fed up. I was very fed up,' she added thoughtfully. 'But never mind,' she went on. 'The world didn't come to an end, and here we are again – '

'Right as rain?'

'At least.' She looked at him soberly for a moment. 'Tom, I don't forget you came down to see me that day in Swayncliff. That was good of you. Nobody else would have done that. In fact,' she said, 'nobody else did. So you're entitled to behave like a rat, for once.'

He put out his hands, rested them on her shoulders. 'You don't know how good this makes me feel,' he sighed. 'I've been carrying it around for so long.'

They were a little awkward together then. Now the moment of

reconciliation had come and passed by, neither of them knew quite what to say next. Just then, they heard a burst of laughter from upstairs, and then Dick's voice, clear and strident, followed by another roar of laughter. Tom made a comical face and Susan chuckled.

'Everyone feels good tonight,' she smiled, backing away from his grasp, turning towards the sink. She picked up another dirty plate.

'Not half as good as me,' Tom glowed.

'Dick seems to be running you close. He's in very good form.'

'Yes,' Tom acknowledged, 'but you can see the pain in his eyes, can't you?'

'No,' she said, surprised. 'I can't. He seems to be having a lot of fun. Cracking jokes . . .'

'It's gallows humour,' Tom assured her.

She turned to stare at him.

'Why do you say that?'

Tom shook his head, but did not speak.

'Because of all the bad news about *Genghis*?'

'Well,' Tom sighed, 'I'm afraid there's not much hope.'

'Don't be too sure,' Susan said, balancing a plate on the pile already on the draining board. 'I was talking to him at dinner. He said everyone's being too quick to make up their minds about *Genghis*. He said he's still got a few tricks up his sleeve.'

'He did? He said that?' Tom frowned. 'What else did he say?'

She glanced at him and grinned mischievously. 'Nothing else.'

Tom hunched over, staring at the floor, thinking hard. 'He's whistling in the dark,' he said edgily. 'I know he is.' When he looked up he saw that Susan was still grinning at him. All at once his features relaxed and he laughed and spread out his hands wide.

'All right,' he said, 'if he can pull it off, good luck to him. Nobody else could. I certainly couldn't. Deep down, I wish him well. You know that, don't you?'

'I know you do,' she laughed and turned again to the sink.

21

She had almost finished. In a little while they would go upstairs to rejoin the others, and soon after that the guests would go home. Tom had been very glad to have them in the house; he would be glad to see them go too. He felt pleasantly tired, ready for bed, to lie beside Louise. Beside the baby that lay within her too. The three of them safe and warm under the same roof – as they were now, as they would be for years and years to come. With a bit of luck. See the guests off and then – he did not even have the washing up to worry about tonight. Susie had done almost all of it. What a gem she was! He was so glad to have her with him again. Contentedly, he watched the long elegant line of her back as she worked away.

'You know,' he said idly, 'I do still think about that day I came down to see you.'

Susan was silent for so long that he thought she hadn't heard him. He wasn't planning to repeat what he'd said, it didn't seem particularly important. He was about to ask her something else, about the job she was doing now, when she spoke.

'It must have been very boring for you.'

'Not at all.' He shook his head firmly. 'I liked it. By the time I left I was beginning to see why you were so attached to the place. In fact, I never thought you would leave.'

'Well, it was time,' she said, not looking round. 'It got a bit gloomy in my house. One of the old ladies died, you see.'

'Ah. The nice one?' He was surprised how sorry he felt to hear the news.

'No. The nasty one. Mrs Baklova.'

'How did it happen?'

'Heart attack. It was sort of funny.'

'Funny?'

'No, it was sad, of course. They found her in the street. About a hundred yards from the supermarket. It seems she thought she was going shopping, she had her bag, her purse . . .' She turned and gave Tom a lopsided smile. 'They worked out she must have died around three in the morning. Not even the Rainbow opens that early.'

'Were you there when it happened?'

'No,' she said, after a moment. 'I was away.' She turned back to the sink. 'I was on a sort of a holiday. I was back for the funeral though . . . Anyway I thought it was as good a time as any to leave. It was just lucky Sam and Sally had a room free. It's only for six months, but I had a drink with Mark the other day – '

'You did?' said Tom, surprised.

'Yes. And I think he's going to give me some money to put down on somewhere of my own. Being as he feels guilty about me.'

'So he should,' Tom said stoutly. He watched her put the last of the dessert spoons in the draining holder. He was still thinking of the day they had spent together. He had an image then, a memory: darkness, and the two of them face to face, and the red glow of the electric fire, a single bar, and her voice carrying on and on, so low and intense. A sense of danger hovering, a threat . . .

'Talking of Swayncliff,' he said, 'whatever happened to that guy you knew down there?'

She had emptied the water from the plastic basin, now she was running the hot tap to rinse out the sink. He raised his voice so as to make sure he could be heard.

'Don't you remember?' He was trying hard to remember himself. 'The one with all the stories. He'd been disinherited, right? He'd lost half a million quid. He had a dad who was a Nazi. He – ' He was running out of breath. Had he dreamed all this? he started to wonder, as he listened to himself. 'Come on, Sue,' he added quite anxiously. 'Surely you remember him?'

She peeled off her gloves and laid them neatly over the side of the sink. She turned round, and looked at him thoughtfully.

'You must be thinking of Raymond Thorne.'

'That's it,' Tom nodded, pleased. 'Thorne. That's the name.' He waited for her to say more. But she kept silent. He shrugged at last. 'So – whatever happened to him?'

'Well, we lost touch,' she said. She thought for a moment. 'We were quite friendly for a while. But then I went on this holiday. And I didn't see him after that.'

She pushed away from the sink, and came to sit next to him on the edge of the table. Tom was frowning, concentrating. Something else, something else about this Thorne fellow . . . His face cleared suddenly.

'Why he was a liar! I remember now. I worked it out on the train going home. It was all bullshit. There was an article!' he cried out triumphantly. 'An article in the paper he worked on. About an auction. And that's all he had. And I bet it was a phony!'

Susan was swinging her long legs casually back and forth under the table.

'I worked out how he could have done that. I know something about this, Susie,' Tom insisted, rather loudly for she didn't seem to be paying much attention. 'Remember I did that play once? *Tabloid*? Well, probably you don't,' he grumbled. 'They put it on at a ludicrous time of night . . . Anyway, I did a lot of research for that one. And for instance – '

He explained his theory. It had to do with advanced computer techniques, desktop publishing, reams of misinformation fed into electronic circuits. She listened to him patiently, and when he was finished she nodded.

'Yes, perhaps that's how he did it.'

'Bound to be,' Tom said. He was puzzled by her apparent lack of interest in his discoveries. 'Well – ' he went on somewhat uncertainly, 'well, I knew it wasn't kosher somehow, what he was saying. I worked that out in the train. And back in town, in the taxi . . .' He strained to remember more. 'And I worked out – I thought he was trying to wind you up, Susie. He was trying to get you angry at somebody.'

'Phillip.'

'Who?'

'His brother,' she said in the same detached tone.

'That's right! I was going to call you when I got home, tell you you should watch out for him, something was wrong. I didn't call you,' he added after a moment. 'I don't know why. I'm sorry.'

She turned to him, and gave him a friendly smile.

'It's all right, Tom.'

'And anyway,' Tom said rather awkwardly then, 'I may have been wrong. I shouldn't be talking this way about a friend of yours, I guess.'

'No, you were right. He was lying to me.'

'All of it?'

She hesitated. 'More or less.'

'When did you find him out?'

She was silent for a moment. Then she shook her head. 'I think I always knew it. From the beginning almost.'

'So you knew when you were telling me all that stuff,' he grunted. 'Thanks a lot.'

She turned to him swiftly. 'I'm sorry, Tom. I didn't mean to deceive you . . . I didn't really know I was doing it. I can't explain.'

They were silent then. Copying her, Tom too began to swing his legs back and forth. It was very pleasant, he thought – even though he was still irritated to find she had been deceiving him, knowingly or not – to be doing this, side by side with his old friend. Upstairs several other old friends waited for their return. They ought to make a move soon, Tom thought. Rejoin the party, couldn't leave Louise to carry the burden of it on her own for too long. But in the meantime – he watched his legs appear and disappear before him – yes, this was very nice.

'What was the point?' he said suddenly. 'I don't get it.'

'Of telling me lies?' She shook her head. 'In a way I don't think they were lies to him.'

'What were they?'

'Stories. Stories he told himself. To make his life bearable. It was true he hated his brother,' Susan said slowly. 'Some of the time.' She shook her head again. 'Not because of all that stuff he told me . . . You see, Phillip's very successful. And Raymond – well, Raymond isn't.'

'How's that his brother's fault?'

'Of course, it isn't. But it was all supposed to be different. When they were children, Raymond had been the bright one. Most likely to succeed, passing all the exams with flying colours, all that. Phillip was the stupid one, they thought. I don't think he was stupid at all, just biding his time . . . He joined the RAF when he left school. They taught him to fly, and then he worked for an airline, made pots of money, invested it. Now he's a property developer, and he's rolling in it. Huge success. Whereas Raymond – he grew up with an idea he was some sort of a genius. He's tried a lot of things to prove it, but he never gets very far in anything –'

'Oh God,' Tom sighed in gloomy recognition. 'A man of promise.'

'So – there he is. Forty-three years old and he's got nothing, can't hold a job, can't understand what's happened to him . . .' She shrugged. 'That's all it was really. A lot of envy and disappointment. And Phillip's really behaved pretty well to Raymond over the years. Gives him money and so on. Gets him out of trouble. When he can find the time, when it's convenient – you know, between deals – '

'What kind of trouble?' Tom asked.

Susan looked away. 'Raymond had a drug problem for a long

time,' she said. 'I think he may still have one, though he told me he hadn't.'

'Christ,' Tom sighed. 'What a winner!'

'Yes. A winner . . . Anyway I think that made it worse for Raymond, his brother helping him out. Rubbed it in somehow.'

'He told you all this?'

'In the end. We had a long talk.'

She was silent for a moment. Then in a still quieter voice, 'And then there was some trouble about a woman. Which brought things to a head.'

'A woman?'

'Raymond met someone. And he thought his luck had changed at last. He was so pleased that he invited his brother out to dinner to meet her. To show her off. To show Phillip he could do pretty well for himself too, if he wanted. So they all met. And then . . .'

'In a little while they'd gone behind his back and it was goodbye Raymond.'

She turned to him in surprise. He shrugged and after a moment she nodded sadly.

'Old story, isn't it? Poor Raymond . . . Well, it happened,' she sighed. 'And then he met me – and it was on his mind.'

Comfortable, mildly intrigued by what she was saying, Tom watched their feet swinging to and fro.

'But that was pretty lousy of his brother.'

She nodded. 'Oh yes. Phillip behaved like a bastard, definitely. I think that's probably how he is. Sees what he wants and goes straight for it. I should think he's quite a ruthless person. Whereas Raymond . . .' She smiled sadly.

'I certainly could see why that would make him angry,' Tom said fairly.

'Yes,' she said, still with a sad smile. 'Except I started to think in the end there probably wasn't all that much between Raymond and this woman in the first place. I think he only knew her a couple of weeks before he lost her. But she was going to change his life, of course . . .'

Tom shook his head. Glanced at her. 'And you – just lost touch with him?' he asked. 'After this holiday?'

'I got a letter from him a few weeks ago. Miss Chalmers sent it on. He's gone up to Nottingham. He knows people up there and he thought they could help him get a job.'

'Did you write back?'

'I didn't see the point. We were never exactly friends.' She thought for a moment. 'He told me once I was only interested in him for his stories. And I think he must have been right, cause when he stopped telling them I didn't find him interesting at all. Mind you, I think he felt the same way about me.' She looked across the room for a moment at the large old wooden clock that hung ticking loudly on the wall. 'Anyway, Tom – you know how it is. When the production ends, so do the friendships usually, don't they?'

Tom puzzled over this remark for a moment. Then gave up. 'Well, I think he's got a hell of a nerve,' he grunted. 'All those lies. I hope you told him off.'

'I didn't really feel like doing that,' she said gravely. 'Because it wasn't all his fault. In fact, I was to blame just as much as him.'

'*How* were you to blame?' he scoffed.

But she didn't answer. He watched her still, sad profile for a few moments. 'Strange business,' he said suddenly. She glanced at him. 'Him carrying on like that,' he said. 'Pretty strange, isn't it?'

She looked away. 'I don't think so. I think it's probably quite ordinary.'

'Ordinary?'

'Yes . . . I think the world is probably full of people like Raymond. With bad thoughts in their heads. Looking for somebody to blame for their lives. Full of silly stories and terrible things they'd do, if only . . . And most of the time it's harmless. It just buzzes around inside them and never gets out. As long as they don't find anybody to listen to them. That's what I blame myself for,' she said seriously. 'I listened to him. And encouraged him. I gave him an audience. Which was a crazy thing to do. Nothing would have happened, if I hadn't listened to him.'

'What happened?' asked Tom, puzzled.

'Nothing happened,' she said after a moment. 'Except I behaved so badly.'

To Tom this sounded like a regrettable throwback on Susie's part. It took him back to that day at Swayncliff when she had been so intently churning away at all the problems and sorrows of her life and blaming herself quite unreasonably for all of them. Really, he thought, there was not much of a mystery here. Susie had let herself be kidded along for a while by this fellow. So what? He'd met a few of these small-time, small-town bullshitters himself in his time, and they could be pretty convincing. In fact, he'd been taken in himself on occasion. But again – so what? As long as Susie hadn't come to any harm and, looking at her – at least, reviewing her performance this evening – he could see that she certainly hadn't.

But there she was, still looking so guilty and so sad. About *nothing*, he thought, torn between concern for her, and irritation. He decided it was time to change the subject. And to throw in a positive word or two to get her out of this mood.

'So where did you go on your holiday, Sue? It seems to have done you a lot of good.'

He saw her relax then and knew he had said the right thing. She turned to him smiling. 'Oh, nowhere special,' she said. 'Here and there. I was on the move.'

'You seem so much happier with yourself,' Tom encouraged her.

'I don't know about that.' Her smile turned somewhat crooked. 'I'm trying to get there. I'm not sure I have yet.'

'You're doing a lot better than me, anyway,' he sighed.

'Why, Tom, you seem calm, you seem very happy.'

'I'm happy because I've just had the most fantastic luck. I'm happy because I've been given a terrific script and just enough money to make it. But take all that away, and there's not much. I've got no philosophy, Sue. If I'm not on top of the world, I'm nowhere.'

Susan looked at him thoughtfully, but did not speak.

'I mean,' Tom said idly, 'when I think you could quite cheerfully sit down and have a drink with Mark – after all that's happened . . .'

'I wasn't all that cheerful, actually.'

'Well . . . but still you did it. And you didn't make a great drama out of it. I admire that.'

She glanced at him for a moment, then looked away. 'Listen, Tom,' she said in a rather hurried way. 'I want to tell you something. Maybe it'll make sense to you.'

She was silent then. Half a minute went by.

'Yes?' Tom prompted her gently.

'Sorry,' she said. 'I was thinking.' She drew in a breath. 'Tom – do you remember how I used to be? In the old days?'

'Course I do.'

'Didn't you think I was pretty – well – *solid*, back then? Pretty stable?'

'Absolutely. You were –'

'Hard-working actress. Good pal. Always there to be leaned on. Never forgot anybody's birthday. All that sort of thing?'

'A rock, Susie. You were like a rock.'

'I was, wasn't I?' she nodded. 'I was also completely mad, you know.'

Tom stared at her. 'Now, Sue – ' he started anxiously.

'Oh, yes, I was. Barking mad. That was a part of me too . . . I don't mean,' she said quickly when he tried to interrupt, 'any more mad than anyone else. Though I may have been. But I kept it hidden more then anyone else. I hid it completely. Till Lucy let it out.'

'Who?'

'Lucy,' she said bitterly. 'Lucy bloody Entwistle.'

At length, Tom stirred. 'She's just a character, Sue,' he said gently.

'I know what she is,' Susan muttered. 'And I know what she did. She let out the monster.'

'What kind of a monster?'

'I don't know – a three-year-old monster, I think . . . A terrible child. Out of control. Sure the world revolves around her, crazy with rage when she finds out it doesn't . . . As a matter of fact, it was no fun at all seeing Mark the other day,' she said then, confusing him with her sudden change of direction. 'Not at first, anyway. He was very pleasant,' she said. 'Very kind. Pleased to see me. As if I was an old friend, you know? From ages ago. There he was,' she smiled shakily, 'the great tragedy of my life. And to him I was just an old friend. Perhaps not even that . . .' Her voice had started to struggle and fade. 'An episode. An actress he'd worked with once and it hadn't come off really. Bit of a disappointment . . .'

'No, Susie. It's not true. Mark loved you. Certainly he did – '

'Oh, come on, Tom! He can't stay with any woman. He's always got to have a new one. He's got one now. Tippy – or Bippy – I forget. He found her in California. Nineteen years old. She's an actress too. Or will be when she gets her first job. He spoke very warmly of her. She's a child of light, this one – a sunbeam – her funny little ways . . . Oh, let's face it,' she smiled angrily, 'I'm just one in a long procession.'

'He didn't marry any of the others,' Tom reminded her, 'because he didn't love any of the others.'

She stared at him. Tom nodded to show that he meant what he had said. After a moment, she looked away and sighed. 'Yes. All right, I think he did love me, in his way. For three years. Which is pretty amazing for him.' She was silent for a time. 'I'm sorry,' she said then, 'I got off on the wrong track. What I meant to say was . . . Well, there we were, having drinks, chatting away. At least, he's chatting, and I'm looking at him, this man I've been grieving over for God knows how long . . . And I suddenly saw – well, I saw *Mark* again. All that he is. Perfectly nice man. Brighter than average. Who I find very sexy. Who I'd been married to once. Shame it didn't work out. And – ' for a moment her eyes were suddenly bright with rage, 'it was utterly stupid of me to let him damage my career.' Then as quickly the light died, calm returned. 'But that's *all* it was. A shame. Sad. Very ordinary. Not a world-shattering event after all. And, oh, Tom,' she sighed, 'it was such a relief. To be seeing him that way. So good. It felt like . . . like the genie was back in the bottle. No more great dramas and tragedies. No more pain. I'd been hugging the pain for so long. I suppose I thought as long as I kept hold of it, then I was keeping hold of Mark too, even after he'd gone.'

'But how does Lucy Entwistle fit into this?'

'Oh, Lucy . . . Lucy showed me the way.' She rolled her eyes at him, and opened her mouth in a grimace of despair, like a silent movie star. 'Love without end. Stupendous suffering. Incredible pain.' She thought for a moment. 'The problem was, this was real life. And the pain was hurting me. I'd grown sick with it.'

'But it had gone? When you saw Mark again?'

'Yes. Mostly. Enough so I wasn't hurting, anyway. And I could enjoy him again for what he was. A nice man really, I'm very fond of him . . . And I could even feel sorry for him a bit. Poor guy, all he'd been looking for with me was his usual three months' fling. But I had to drop on him like a ton of bricks. *Make* him marry me. The worst idea in the world!'

He thought she was still smiling, but at that moment he saw her raise her hand to her face and brush the back of it against her eyes. He wanted to put his arm round her, at least to speak to her, comfort her – but, as if frightened of not being able to finish, she took a deep breath and hurried on.

'All right. What I'm trying to get at. What I meant to say to you – what I've thought ever since then: this is what I must do now. Stop seeing everything as a great drama – and myself at the centre of it. Just grow up. And hold the monster back – not hide it this time, only let it out bit by bit like everybody else does.' She was staring at him now, her words were urgent, tumbling one after the other across the space between them. 'And if I could do all this, then I could start to see things how they really are again. If I can sweep all the *shit* away that's blocking the view, then I can get on with other things. I can get on with what really matters.'

'And what's that?'

Tom waited eagerly for her to speak. He really wanted to know the answer to this. And it must have shown comically on his face for she began to laugh. She put up her hand then and touched his arm.

'I'm sorry, Tom.'

'No problem,' he said stiffly.

'No, it's just . . . what matters? How should *I* know? I've only just got the monster under control again.' She thought for a moment, then hesitantly and almost shyly, 'I've been thinking probably it's nothing very important. Just little things. At first anyway. You know – getting up in the morning, and doing a decent job. And stroking Sam and Sally's cat. And evenings like this, with my friends. Just being alive . . . Does this sound like crap to you?' she asked then abruptly.

'Oh, no,' Tom said politely, 'not at all.'

'Well, it does to me a bit.' She sat frowning, her head lowered. 'And yet . . . it must be there somewhere, Tom. Something about . . . not being so greedy, not wanting so much, yes – ' She nodded firmly. 'It's there – in the little things, seeing their value, I'm sure of it.' A moment, then she grinned at him awkwardly. 'Only I ought to add – I've also realised that the little things cost money too. Mark didn't agree to pay for my mortgage just out of the goodness of his heart. I had a lawyer send him a letter first. And I told him when I saw him that if he didn't pay up, well, I still knew a couple of reporters, and some people still remembered Lucy Entwistle, and he could see if he liked how he'd look in the papers. Him and me and little Bippy . . .' She checked Tom's expression, nodded, looked away again. 'Not so nice of me, was it?'

'I'm sure you – '

'What I've figured out, Tom,' she interrupted him soberly, 'is that I'm too old to be a bloody fool any more. I can't spend any more time being crazy. I'm a working actress. Or I'm not anything. I've *got* to work. And – ' She looked at him directly, 'I don't want anyone ever to say again, "I hear she's still trouble." '

'Nobody ever will,' Tom said firmly. 'Nobody could now. And if they do, I'll tell 'em it's nonsense.'

'I know you will, Tom,' she said softly, 'if it's convenient.'

He looked up in surprise, and for a moment he thought he saw a wariness, even an edge of dislike in her gaze. It confused him greatly – but then she laughed, and jumped down from the table. 'Come on,' she said, standing before him, 'you're neglecting your other guests.'

He put out his hands and held her shoulders and smiled happily at her. 'We've come through, Susie,' he said contentedly. (She was smiling back at him. He had been mistaken. Of course there had been no dislike in her eyes, not even for a moment.) 'We've both come through, and we're doing OK.' He was silent for a time then, not looking at her, thinking. When he looked up, he tried again to smile. She was watching him gravely.

'I'll tell you what though,' he began very quietly. 'I really love this script I'm going to do. It's so funny and clever and . . .' He stopped, and sighed. 'But if you want to know the truth – I'd have given anything to have made *Genghis* work. And I think sometimes: I'm never ever going to film a cavalry charge – or a sacked city with the sun going down behind it – or a million barbarians moving across the steppe and . . . and I just can't bear it. I don't exactly know why that's what I want, but it is. And it breaks my heart to think I can't have it. So it had better be the little things that matter,' he concluded glumly, ''cause it looks like I can't have the biggest things, what I want the most.'

'But maybe those are the things that aren't good for you, Tom,' she said quietly. 'Perhaps that's so for all of us.' She hesitated, then, 'What Raymond Thorne wanted . . .' She stopped again, frowning intently, as if she was trying to grope her way into the heart of a dark maze. But at last she sighed and gave up. 'No, I don't know what he wanted. Except to wipe out everything that had ever happened to him. And for once to do something on his own, to have a success. I think he'd have preferred to do something good,' she said slowly, as if still thinking aloud, 'if there had been a choice. But good or bad – just to do something for once. Only Raymond can't do anything . . .' She smiled slightly then. 'Except smash up photographs. He can do that. And put holes in rental car roofs. That's about the best he can do. Which was lucky for me.'

Tom had hardly heard the last part of her statement. He was considerably irritated to think that even for a moment Susie had mixed up his own serious dreams and longings and disappointments with the ravings of that provincial cuckoo she'd known once. He was so annoyed that for a moment he decided he would say nothing more to help her. But almost immediately he relented. There was one important item that had been on his mind for several minutes, something that he felt needed badly to be said, and he would not let mere pique stand in the way.

'Susie,' he told her gently, 'please don't ever say to me again that you were mad. Or crazy. Don't think it even. Because it's not true. And never was. And if you're thinking,' he added when she tried to speak, 'of when you were with that lying bastard in Swayncliff, then forget it. The only crazy one was *him*.'

'No, Tom,' she said soberly as they turned towards the door, 'I think I was as bad as him. For a while anyway.'

'How can you *say* that?'

'Why else would we have found each other? I can't think of another reason. It wasn't anything as sensible as sex, for instance.'

There was a shout of welcome when they came back into the room, and several pointed jokes from Banham about what they'd been doing away for so long. The jokes fell entirely flat, which didn't seem to ruffle Dick at all.

'Ah, it reminds me of the old days,' he sighed, 'when people were always sneaking off together at parties. Didn't Tom and Susie sneak away a few times back then too? I seem to remember they did.'

'Behave yourself!' Jeannie hissed.

Louise felt she couldn't stay up any longer. She moved slowly and awkwardly round the room to hug each of her guests good night. 'You're an old stirrer, you are,' she told Dick affectionately. She and Susan hugged each other especially close.

Jeannie said as Louise came to her, 'Just think, next time we see you, you'll be a mother.'

'Touch wood!' almost everybody cried out.

'Why . . .' Jeannie looked round, flustered, at the others. 'Nothing else can go wrong, can it?'

Tom followed his wife from the room to help her upstairs and to see that she had everything she needed. When he came back he found everyone ready to say good night. He was genuinely sorry to see this.

'Stay a bit longer,' he urged. 'One more brandy before you go.'

The guests agreed, and everyone settled round the table again. Tom went along it, pouring a measure into each glass.

'We should have a toast,' Tina Perkins said.

'What should it be?' said Jeannie.

'Tom's film, of course,' Dick Banham said. He looked across to where Tom was sitting in Louise's old seat, and smiled warmly. 'It's going to be terrific, Tommy. Here's to success.'

Tom checked his old rival's expression carefully, but could see nothing but sincerity there. He nodded his appreciation, but then held up his hand to stop the others before they could drink to him. 'No, I've got a better toast.' He looked across the table to where

Susan sat. 'I want to drink to my old friend,' he said, smiling at her, 'who's come back to us at last.'

'She's been back nearly three months,' Jeannie pointed out.

'Well, she's just come back to me,' Tom said. 'And I'm going to drink to her.' He raised his glass. 'Our Susie – welcome back!' And the others echoed his toast.

Susan shook her head, embarrassed, but she looked around the table at her friends, smiling gratefully at their tribute.

'She's not just back,' Tina said, 'she's back in triumph.'

'That's right!' said Rosie Carver, who was also an actress. '*Vivien Leigh!* How's it going, Sue?'

'One hears nothing but good things about it,' Dick said, much to Tom's admiration for he could detect not a shred of envy in his colleague's voice.

'I think it's going quite well,' Susan nodded. 'Of course, it's not great art or anything – '

The two directors smiled indulgently at this, and then glanced at each other.

' – but I think it's going to be fun. Minna's awfully good.'

'Minna Kelley is a brilliant idea for Vivien,' Hugh Perkins declared.

'Yes. It's so nice for her too,' Susan said. 'She's never had a real chance at something big before.'

'But isn't she too old?' Jeannie asked.

'They've got this other girl to play the very young Vivien,' Susan explained. 'Very pretty. Minna takes over at about twenty-five, and it's a really good match.'

'How's your part, Sue?' Tina asked.

'Not bad. I'm Mrs Grace Beaufort, a high-society lady who's a sort of companion and confidante to Vivien in her later years. It's not a real person actually. It's a combination of two or three real people. I have a couple of good scenes, but mostly I'm just standing around listening to Minna.' Susan grinned. 'I have to say, "Tell me all about it, Vivien, darling," about fifteen times every episode. Still I was very happy to be asked to do it.'

'Doesn't sound like another Lucy Entwistle,' John Knights observed.

'God, no!' Susan sighed. 'And I'm glad of it. She wore me out that lady.'

The other guests were watching her curiously. Tom stepped in to help out.

'Susie found playing that part a bit of a strain,' he explained. 'Very glad to put it all behind you, aren't you, Sue?'

'Oh, more than that, Tom,' she breathed. 'You know, sometimes I've had a feeling Lucy took me over for a while. I mean,' she went on in the same low voice, 'even after the series ended. I've been – bit over the top. As if her hand was still on me . . .'

Her voice trailed away into silence. The other guests continued to stare at her. Tom, seeing a certain smile appear at the edges of Dick's mouth, stepped in again.

'Oh, well, that's not a bad thing, surely? As I recall, she was quite a lively, positive person, wasn't she?'

'Oh, Tom, she was *nuts*!' Her surprised blue eyes met his across the table. 'Why, once she let a man make love to her just so she could get him into position to stab him in the back with a pair of scissors!'

'Ah, yes,' Dick beamed. 'The fabled exit of Jason Groves. He came and went in practically the same moment, didn't he? I think we did that awfully well,' he added complacently.

Tom attempted to ignore him. He leaned across the table to Susie.

'Well, you haven't done anything like that,' he chuckled reassuringly.

'Me?' she said. 'Oh, I've done nothing at all . . . Anyway – ' she took a deep breath, smiled round the table. 'I'm very glad to have somebody nice and calm like Mrs Beaufort to do for a change. And – ' she looked across the table again at Tom. 'I believe I've got you to thank for it in a way.'

'Me?' said Tom in surprise.

'Yes. I gather Mrs Bee was at your house once when my name came up. And she's an old friend of mine. We hadn't seen each other for ages, but she recognised my name. So she got in touch with my agent. And when I came back from holiday there were all these telegrams waiting for me.'

There was a long silence. Dick Banham stirred at last.

'You're an old friend of *Mrs Bee*?'

'Well . . .' Susan smiled, 'when I knew her she was called Wendy Strong. We were in rep together up in Yorkshire years ago.'

'You were in rep with Mrs Bee?' Hugh Perkins breathed.

'That's right. Then apparently she went out to the States and got herself a rich husband – '

'But Mrs Bee's an American.'

'No, she's not,' Susan chuckled. 'I don't know how anybody could be fooled by that act of hers. Of course she was always putting on some sort of an act. Back when I knew her she was playing at being a Home Counties deb. Actually I believe she comes from up north somewhere. Salford . . . or Stockport,' Susan said vaguely. 'Somewhere like that. Anyway, she hasn't changed a bit . . . well, she has, of course – but not deep down. We talked for ages. And then she asked me to look at this Mrs Beaufort part, and I jumped at it naturally. It's funny,' she mused, 'she always used to look after me in the old days – and here she was, still doing it. She's terribly loyal, you see.' She smiled then across the table at Tom. 'And it all happened because she heard my name again. In this very house.'

A buzz of conversation followed this speech. Dick, in particular, was flabbergasted to learn that Mrs Bee was originally from the north country. 'But she's our All-American presence in London,' he protested at one point. 'She's our Super-Yank. This is serious, Susie. You've blown her cover.'

'Oh, it's all right,' Susan laughed. 'Wendy told me she'd had about enough of the American angle. She felt she'd used it as far as it would go, and it was getting a bit exhausting for her. Anyway she's decided that it's us Europeans who are the up-to-date people nowadays, and the Americans who are old-fashioned. So she wants to switch teams. Or get back on to her old one. I think she's trying now to find a way to gently spread the word about where she really comes from . . . And look, you see!' Susan smiled delightedly. 'She's found a way. She's using me!'

The guests had gone on to explore further these revelations when they were interrupted by a sudden harsh laugh from their host. They all looked curiously towards him.

'What's up, Tommy?' Tina enquired.

'Nothing,' said Tom. 'I was just thinking of a funny story I heard once.'

Dick held up his hands and called for silence. 'Historic moment. Tom Scott tells a joke!'

Tom stared at the crumpled tablecloth before him. It had all come back to him as Susan had been speaking. The weeks of humiliation and bewilderment with Mrs Bee, the shame of being let go, then months of despair when he could see no way forward in his life. He had thought that he had got rid of all that, but it was there, all of it, deep down, still churning around, curdling his soul.

'It's about this Roman centurion,' he began slowly, 'the one who crucified Christ. He's down in Hell now. And they ask him if he's learned anything from his experiences . . .'

He came to a stop. The guests waited and watched him, most of them wearing hopeful smiles. Tom brooded for a moment. Then shook his head, proceeded.

'"Yes," says the centurion, "I have learned one thing . . . Be very careful who you crucify. He might turn out to be the son of God."'

After a somewhat baffled silence, most of the guests laughed politely and then went back to what they'd been discussing before Tom broke in on them. But Susan still sat in silence, still watching Tom. At last she leaned towards him and said gently, 'What made you think of that story?'

He felt a great bitterness in his heart, and wanted to say cruel things to her. But as he looked up, the urge died away in him. He thought of all the years of their friendship and of how it had survived so many hard patches, even this last, worst one, even estrangement and betrayal. The expression in her eyes was concerned and loving. A little while ago, he had seen dislike and anger in those eyes. And fair enough, for he had wronged her. But she was still his friend. True friends – he thought, he hoped against hope – could forgive even the failure of friendship.

To have Susie back again, in his house, at his table, his friend still; to think of all the other old friends – even that shit and charlatan Dick Banham – that in spite of everything he had managed to hold on to; to know that Louise was upstairs now, safe and well, and that they still loved each other; to know that, touch wood, he would be a father very soon. All these were more important than anything else in his life. He knew this with utter certainty. Next to them the other things were not worth considering, they just didn't count.

He thought at last that he did truly understand what Susie had been saying to him in the kitchen. That it was only the apparently modest things of life that mattered; the huge sweeping dramas that captured attention were only the froth on the sea of life after all. He knew that her words were true – even if they did sound like crap. Perhaps, Tom thought suddenly, we have to make the truth sound like that to help us wriggle away from it. Yet it remained the truth, the everlasting light, and to depart from it was to live in darkness, as he had done for too long. As he watched Susie, as he thought of these things, Tom felt at last the pain and mortification of the last months ease away from him for ever. He was so glad to have had his eyes opened to the truth, and so grateful to her for opening them. Tomorrow he might forget the lesson she had taught him. Tomorrow, he thought sadly, he probably would forget. But at this moment he understood – and it showed that there was hope for him.

Make me modest and humble as Susie is, Tom prayed. Give up this awful hunger for glory, success, the world at my feet at any price. Genghis Khan. Let me be only . . . loyal husband, good father, faithful friend. And let me only desire to do well the work I have been given, for its own sake . . .

Oh, and please God let it be, a familiar spirit started whispering inside him then, my great leap forward, my passport to success, glory, the world at my feet . . . Tom fought back honourably against this voice as soon as he was aware of it. Tomorrow perhaps he would have to return to the old bad thoughts, but tonight, in Susie's presence, he felt only clean and good. He felt as he had used to feel so many years ago when he would wake up in her bed under the martyred eyes of Ché Guevara. He felt almost holy.

He reached across the table to her. 'I don't know why I thought of it,' he smiled, as their hands touched. 'It was just a silly joke. It didn't mean anything really.'

A NOTE ON THE AUTHOR

Peter Prince lives and works in London. His novels include *Play Things* (which won the Somerset Maugham Award) and *The Good Father*. He has also written several screenplays, including those for the award-winning BBC TV series, *Oppenheimer*, and a feature film *The Hit*.